GATEWAY: PIOCHE

JEFF DAWSON   LARRY WELCH

GATEWAY: PIOCHE

JEFF DAWSON

LARRY WELCH

JEFF DAWSON   LARRY WELCH

GATEWAY: PIOCHE

Copyright © 2013 by: LDDJ Enterprises Publishing

Second Edition

ISBN 978-0-9839740-3-1

This book is a work of fiction. Any resemblance to actual people, living or dead is entirely coincidental.

Acknowledgments

As with any works there are a host of people to thank. Editor, Bev Harrison for her endless patience with my stubbornness. Debbie Welch (Larry's wife) for inviting me into their home and helping us mold the story. To Bobbi Lee Hunt-Healey for another wonderful cover. and last but not least, my co-author Larry Welch, who, without the idea, this work would not exist.

TABLE OF CONTENTS

CHAPTER 1

SUCCESS!

WEDNESDAY, MARCH 6ᵀᴴ 10:00AM, 2015

"General!" yelled a jubilant Professor Skorzenzy into the 400" LG overhead wide screen. "The machine works! Captain Christopher has returned of sound mind and body. He holds in his hands the treasures of Egypt once thought lost, and his renderings of the happenings are astonishing, to say the least. It is time we put the machine to the task we set out on. The correction of all..." General McCulloch's hard facial features remained passive as the good doctor danced around like a madman, or a child who had received a treasured Christmas present. "...the mistakes of the past! We have the tool to control our destiny!" The word destiny did not escape the general's attention. He would allow the doctor a few more minutes of elation before he broke the news.

Doctor Leonoid Rostov Skorzenzy was a man beyond reproach. His paper on the integration of Quantum Physics and Extrapolated Thermodynamics with Applied Electronics was leading the scientific community in time travel research. He published the paper two years after the cancellation of the "Superconducting Super Collider Project" in Waxahachie, Texas. It was his first taste of governmental waste, meddling, and foolishness. He and his colleagues continually warned Washington of the mismanagement of funds and the colossal waste occurring daily. They knew that if the current trend of unchecked, irresponsible spending continued, it would result in the promising project meeting an ignominious end. Because of the rampant spending, he notified his team to keep secret diaries of all the experiments and the results in case the facility was shut down without warning. So the surprise of the program being discontinued in 1993 came as no real shock.

The government led the people to believe the main purpose of the "supercollider" was the generation of a more environmentally friendly energy source, and soon, the production of Middle Eastern Oil would be a thing of the past. That was partly true. The main purpose of the project was advancing time travel. Skorzenzy and his team were   led by the government-appointed scientist, Dr. Richard Alexi Chavez (he was a competent scientist, but his loyalties were to the members of the US House Budget Committee) knew if they could reduce the emissions of the enormous heat generated during the initial inertia of time travel, they would be successful. This was the lynch pin that kept delaying further experiments. The inception of fiber optics assisted in the heat conductivity issue, but it still wasn't enough to thwart the enormous amount of energy required to power the machine. Many times the fibers became overloaded and melted, resulting in an immediate shut down. Dr. Skorzenzy believed he knew why the problem kept cropping up and destroying otherwise very promising experiments. The Intel and Texas Instruments processors of the day couldn't handle all of the information streaming through the lines required to efficiently run the electromagnetic inverse particle separator, or in short—EIPS. Skorzenzy discussed the issue with the engineers of both Intel and TI. They agreed to work on the problem together. Of course, when the collider was shut down so was their research, but the technology was resurrected in 2005 with the new project, code name TS – *Time Slip*.

The paper and its contents were brought to General McCulloch in 2005 by Doctor Loerke of the Department of Energy. Doctor Loerke briefed him on the exact contents and theories Doctor Skorzenzy proposed. Based on the briefing, the general made contact with Skorzenzy and proposed he be placed in charge of the new project with no meddling or budget constraints from Washington. Skorzenzy balked at first, but the lure of finishing the work he began in Texas was too enticing to turn down. He agreed; always knowing in the back of his mind that this venture too could come to a sudden and abrupt end.

"Doctor, I too have some interesting news." replied McCulloch.

General McCulloch had been a true stalwart to the project. He agreed with the philosophy of going back in time and possibly altering a few events in history for the better, such as Vietnam. It was his belief the war could have been won with the proper guidance, execution, and political backing. If Richard Nixon had been supplied the correct intelligence concerning the effects the B-52 "arc bombings" were having on Ho Chi Minh and the populace, he (Nixon) would not have called off the air campaign in the hopes the Paris Peace Talks would yield results.

His illustrious career spanned four decades. He learned the ways of the military and politicians. The latter he cared not for, but being the leader of the Joint Chiefs of Staff, he learned how the game was played no matter how it affected the men under his command, or the consequences of canceling programs. He had become what he feared the most as his career moved forward—a military political pawn. Just the thought forced bile from his stomach to the back of his throat. It had to be done no matter how many billions of dollars had been spent on the current project.

"Doctor, effective last night at 00:01 hours, the project is canceled. All funding has ceased. The complex will be completely shut down by the end of the week. All personnel will receive new assignments."

The words hung heavy in the air. The professor was stupefied. His work over the past decade was now producing fruit, and just like that, he would have to abandon his life's work, again? This was absurd.

"General, did you not hear what I said? It works. We have proof. We can proceed with the plan we envisioned so many years ago. It works, General—it works."

His words were frantic and pleading. He knew how easily the winds of Washington moved from day to day. All they wanted were results. They cared not how they were achieved or obtained, as long as the taxpayers' (he always cringed when he was reminded they were spending the hard-earned money of the American people) money was properly spent. What bullshit! They print as much money as they choose to further their own agendas. If the American people only knew how much was being wasted, they would revolt.

This time the money wasn't being wasted. This time it was achieving a technology that would spare the world of the most traumatic events in history. They could make the planet a better and safer place. The Duke of Austria would live, and the millions of French and British men would be allowed to live full lives instead of fertilizing the fields of Argonne, Verdun, and Flanders with their youthful blood. The ovens at Dachau and Auschwitz would never see the light of day, for Adolf Hitler wouldn't live long enough to reap his wrath on the world. Lincoln and Kennedy would live.

The atomic bomb would still be in its infancy. Roosevelt would never approve the Manhattan Project. The Cold War would not fill any history books, for without the infamous destruction of Germany, no wall would separate Berlin. The soils and fertile lands of the Delta and Highlands in Southeast Asia would be the rice center of the world, instead of the soil where over 58,000 young men and women would shed their blood in a war the politicians refused to fully support and win. The fools in Washington care nothing of their fellow Americans or mankind in general. They strive only to pursue their own greed and political agendas.

"General, surely there is a mistake?" The question came out as a plea more than a question.

"I'm sorry, Professor. The project is canceled. There is nothing I can do." The screen went blank with no other explanation.

This isn't over, General. No, this isn't over by a long shot. I cannot stop them from cutting off funds, but I shall remain behind in my hidden quarters, and reap revenge when the opportunity arises. My work and that of my colleagues will only temporarily be placed on hold.

A slight gleam sparked in the old man's eyes.

Yes, I shall bide my time.

* * *

SUNDAY 10:00 HOURS

"Has anyone seen or heard from Skorzenzy?" queried General McCulloch.

"No sir, not since the day you informed him of the shutdown," replied Captain Wilson.

"No matter," commented the general as his eyes scanned the vast room. "Congress refused to listen. This is the first time we achieved the desired results and are immediately terminated. The folly of Washington. Captain, I've been in this man's army for over forty years and still don't understand how it operates."

"Yes sir."

"Captain, shut it down and lock it down."

Captain Wilson turned off the control console, walked over to the large bank of light breakers and pulled down the switches. The men were shrouded in darkness except for the emergency lights leading into the hallway. The only sounds were the echoing of their highly polished shoes tapping the cold pavement as they exited.

* * *

Two weary eyes peered at the monitor as they walked away.

"We shall meet again."

CHAPTER 2

GRADUATION

JUNE 2016 STANFORD, CALIFORNIA

Six long years of cramming for exams, drinking endless cups of coffee, Red Bull, and any other caffeinated sugar-packed drink; the endless study groups and all-nighters were finally coming to an end. Muki, Larry, Judith, and Abdul were reaching the promised land—G R A D U A T I O N!

* * *

The four accidentally met during a concert their freshmen year in L.A. back in 2010. They, like one hundred thousand other kids and adults (wanting to relive their past teen years once more) packed the Coliseum for the "Final Rites Tour" of The Who, Stones, Steppenwolf and Pink Floyd. There would be special guest appearances during the concert, but those groups were kept under wraps. The media billed it as the largest concert ever to hit the Pacific shores. Tickets started at $100 and went as high as $20,000. The event would start at 6:00pm and stop when the applause and encores died down. They were crammed in like sardines and even though the music was great, it was their parent's music (all but Muki). They just wanted to say, "they were there." It would make a terrific story for the kids when they decided to start families. But that was the furthest thought from their minds right now; their bodies were surrounded by music, while their brains were deep in studies.

After talking with each other for a few hours, they were fascinated at the striking similarities they shared. Their dreams and ambitions were mirrors of each other. The bond they formed that night would take them through the gates of education and into the world of commerce. They agreed that until all obtained an advanced degree, the first graduation was only for the kids who promised mom and dad they'd get a degree, then a job. They knew this was a lie. Most of the kids would wind up working for mom or dad and continue living at home while they decided what they really wanted to accomplish with their lives. Not this bunch. They would pursue master's degrees. Until that time, the only celebrating would be the occasional night out for a few drinks and recreation. Otherwise, they would ramrod their studies to the finish line. Oh, one other important item, they would have to have double master's majors. Obtaining just a bachelor's degree was considered child's play. Muki chose Electronics and History. Larry—Computer Science/Civil Engineering. Judith decided on Math/Thermodynamics, and Abdul took Physics/Chemistry. On that night, Muki, Larry, Judith and Abdul forged an academic alliance.

Muki Nguyen came from a very humble family. Her mother stayed home taking care of the children, while her father supplied the American-backed government with a daily supply of fish. As the fledgling army of South Vietnam rapidly deteriorated, her father knew what would happen if his family fell into the hands of the Communist aggressors—death. He would be found guilty of helping the Americans, and thus labeled a traitor and assigned for re-education. The rest of the family would either be assigned to re-education camps, sent to brothels in the north, or the final indignity—a bullet to the head.

Her family became unwitting celebrities when their picture was placed on the cover of Time Magazine during the mass exodus from Vietnam. The fall of Saigon forced many to either flee the country, or hope the Communist government of Ho Chi Minh would show leniency. That was unlikely. Her parents brought all the possessions they could carry to the docks, hoping to find a junk that would allow them passage to the United States and away from war-torn Vietnam.

The captain of the boat took everything they owned, but the price wasn't enough. He demanded that Muki's mother satisfy him on the long, treacherous journey. The family had no choice—

rape by submission, or death by Ho Chi Minh. Her father convinced his wife she would be saving them from certain death; her acts would not bring shame upon the family. When they reached the Promised Land, they would find the nearest priest, and she would be cleansed of her sins.

After thirty days of tempest seas and multiple sexual violations from the captain, they arrived in San Francisco along with thousands of other refugees. They were processed, and wound up settling around Fisherman's Wharf. Being that her father was an accomplished sushi chef, he was able to restore honor to his family's heritage and provide a semblance of self-sufficiency. The family was never rich, just comfortable. The one lesson her parents constantly ingrained in her was, "Knowledge is power; never take your studies for granted. You, not the teachers, must always push yourself to be better. Knowledge is power. Complacency and guilt accomplish nothing." She took the words to heart and excelled in her school work. She expected her parents to be proud when she scored a 1400 on the SAT as a sophomore.

"No!" her father snapped. "Do better. Knowledge is power."

She didn't despair. During her senior year, she achieved two accomplishments—1600 on the SAT and a full-ride scholarship to Stanford.

Her father only said, "Muki, knowledge is power. You have traveled well with the first phase; now for the second."

She didn't receive a car or vacation to an exotic location like many of her peers did for accomplishing much less—only her father's words. If her parents wouldn't give her an appropriate present now, she would do it on her own when she graduated from Stanford. It's not that she disliked her parents, for she loved them dearly, yet she tired of the stories they constantly told of the "old land" and the Communists. She felt they should let it go, but then again, she hadn't witnessed the horrors of war and the killing of civilians. That wasn't her life, it was theirs, and she would do her best to break the chains of the past and start her own history.

Larry Kowalski Jr. was a freak of nature. His father was an All-American linebacker with The Texas Longhorns and played a few years with the Baltimore Ravens, until a knee injury ended a very promising career. Unlike many of his teammates, he didn't blow the signing bonus money; he invested it wisely in several start-up companies like Yahoo and Microsoft at the suggestion of his wife, Sandy. The dividends kept his family afloat while he finished up his "real" business degree at the University of Texas at Arlington where he met his bride-to-be, Sandy Williams. With her urgings and support, he accepted a full-ride scholarship to North Texas University to pursue a master's in Business. To the surprise of his parents, he completed the program in less than ten months.

His mother, Sandy, received a degree in Home Interior Renovations from the University of Texas and opened a small, home-based business that allowed her the flexibility of working with her high-end clients of University and Highland Park, while at the same time being a supportive wife to Senior and being a mom to Junior.

Larry was the spitting image of his father at six feet four and two twenty-five pounds—with one flaw. The athletic gene passed him by. His physique was the product of his father's lineage, except for the flaw. All the Kowalski men were physically large, naturally imposing, and sports-minded. Junior loved hearing the stories of his great-grandfather, Sergei Kowalski, who faced down first the Germans in 1939, and then the Russians in 1944, at gunpoint. He never succumbed to their wills, while at the same time, he didn't infuriate them to the point of being sent to a camp or being conscripted. His voice carried an authority that matched the weapons of his enemies.

The outstanding quality Larry possessed was an analytical brain. At an early age, problems that stumped his playmates when it came to puzzles or math problems were no challenge to him. He solved them with great ease. At the age of five, he mastered the Rubik's cube in under thirty seconds much to the dismay of his parents. They had tried for over a decade and could only get one side completed. He breezed through junior high and high school with no problems. The only real issues he encountered were with jocks and girls. Junior was an easy target for he was shy and awkward. No matter how many times his father told him it was okay that he couldn't excel in sports, the kids at school would take pot shots at him, until one day during his senior year, the captain of the football team tried to embarrass him in front of a girl he was really enamored with.

"Hey, Junior. I need someone to carry my books. Since you can't run a straight line, I choose you to be my servant." Larry ignored the comment as he had so many times before, but Jimmy just wouldn't relent.

"Kowalski, I'm talking to you! Now come over and pick up my books."

The little girl he was sweet on, Jenny Allen, pleaded with Jimmy to leave him alone.

"Hey, bitch, don't tell me what to do."

That was it. Larry's father raised him to respect women and treat them with kindness. It was time Jimmy learned that lesson firsthand. Junior turned on his heels, and before anyone could react, Jimmy was pinned to the wall a good six inches off the ground. His eyes were filled with terror as he hung suspended in the air. Larry didn't care for violence, but he had reached his limit. While everyone waited for Larry to decapitate Jimmy, he only stared deep into Jimmy's eyes. He uttered one word, "Apologize."

In a hoarse tone, Jimmy forced out the words, "Jenny, I'm sorry."

"Sorry for what?" demanded Larry. His hands constricted Jimmy's throat tighter.

The words came out in a strained voice, "Sorry...for calling you...a bitch." Jimmy feared if he spoke poorly, Larry might permanently end his football career. He looked at Jenny with pleading eyes.

"Jimmy, I accept." She smiled at Junior as he loosened his death grip and unceremoniously dropped him on the floor. Not a word was spoken. Junior picked up his books and made his way to class as if nothing happened. Jenny called out for him to wait up; she wanted to walk with him. It was the first time he genuinely smiled walking to class.

It was no surprise Larry was the Valedictorian of his class. After all, he scored a 36 on the ACT and 1600 on the SAT and was receiving a full-ride academic scholarship to Stanford. He was nervous having to give the address to a class of twenty-five hundred. His mother told him to speak from the heart, and all would be well.

"To all of my classmates, our journey has only begun. We drilled for the last three years in science, history, mathematics and literature. Has our toil gone unnoticed? No. For those of us who took our studies seriously, the horizon is now just now dawning. For those who didn't, hope is not lost; it's misplaced. I wish all of you much success in wherever you venture in your endeavors."

In that many of his fellow classmates, along with faculty, rarely heard Larry utter more than a few words at any one time, they sat in stunned silence and reverence as he delivered the most eloquent and stately graduation address any of them had ever heard. And even more amazing? He wasn't using notes. However, there were a few students who knew Larry was a master at subterfuge, and sooner or later he wouldn't be able to maintain this straight-man attitude. He was too big of a Star Trek fan to let such an auspicious occasion pass without a bit of levity. They were right.

"Class of 2010, I would like to end this wonderful exercise with a quote from one of the great literary minds of our generation. "Mr. Scott, beam me UP!" Larry promptly took the mortar board off his head and flung it high into the air. The class exploded in a chorus of cheers.

Judith Anderson traveled a treacherous path through life. The actions of her ancestors were always tugging at her. The stories and books she read concerning her late great-grandfather disgusted her. How could a country as educated and sophisticated as Germany, allow these men of questionable motives to come in to power? Her great-grandfather Martin Bormann, Hitler's personal secretary, was in the middle of the greatest travesty ever bestowed upon mankind.

Her parents told her, "It was their duty to warn and watch the world to make sure no more men like her great-grandfather and others like him, ever came to power again. The Third Reich destroyed Europe and killed over sixty million men, women and children. War did not discriminate against sex, race or religion. It killed all who stood in its way or were inadvertently placed in its cruel path."

Judith realized the only way she would ever accomplish the family mission was to receive the best education available. She would spend all her idle hours poring over books and literature in the local public library and on the internet. Her time was limited, for she was an All-American softball player in high school. Her parents, Charlie and Rose, were excellent athletes in college. They were good enough to make the All-American teams in football and softball, but by their sophomore years in college at Harvard, they chose to concentrate on their studies. Sport was a good avenue to release pent-up energy, but would it honestly make the world a safer place? No, but knowledge would. Her parents both graduated at the top of the class, number one and two respectively, with degrees in Law. With these degrees, they would be able to help those who would be oppressed by representing them in the courtroom or by entering the distasteful arena of politics.

Judith followed in their footsteps until her senior year. The family took a trip to Florida for Spring Break to visit her mom's parents in Gainesville. Going to Disney World didn't interest her at all. It was fun and all, but it wasn't teaching her anything. Her grandfather, Ralph Cahill, suggested that since she didn't want to go to the beach or have fun like the other kids her own age, how about going to the drag races? Judith had watched some of the boys back home work on their cars and talk about their exploits of speed and torque. They always said racing was fun, but building the car was the test of knowledge. Any idiot could depress an accelerator. The challenge was building a machine designed to mix energy, torque and power to the wheels. That is what separated the men from the boys.

She accepted his offer and was never the same. The sound of purring engines, the smell of high-octane fuel, and the feel of raw power being transferred to asphalt or concrete hooked her. She convinced him to spend most of the day around the pits. Her analytical mind was jotting and noting every move the crew made. She admired how the Crew Chief barked out orders and joined in to assist with the monstrous machines. They worked like an orchestra in perfect rhythm. Every tool was properly laid out within easy reach. The men and one woman on the crew never stumbled. They worked at a feverishly frantic, yet balanced, pace. No one cussed (as some of her classmates would regale) or yelled at each other as they performed their tasks with perfect precision.

The Crew Chief for Jerry Smith's car noticed how the girl of, say seventeen, was watching the activities with the eyes of a preying hawk. He approached her and invited her to help. Judith was in shock until she felt the strong hands of her grandfather pushing her under the yellow barrier rope. From that day forward, her thirst for driving and working on cars was set. She was hooked.

Upon returning to her grandparents' home, she announced to her parents she was dropping out of softball and wanted to start racing cars. As her parents sat in a stunned silence, Ralph informed them that little Judith was an official honorary member of four-time champion Jerry Smith's dragster team, "Revenge."

Once back home, her dad bought an old Alpha Romeo, pledging, "He would help her if she maintained her grades. If the grades slid, so would the car, straight back to the junk pile where it was acquired."

She worked like the devil on both. Her senior year she qualified for a few of the local races with limited success. What was it the boys said? "Understanding how to harness power was the real success." She graduated with honors, not to mention a full ride to Stanford, yet it was the racing circuit she needed to master. When she wasn't studying for school, she spent her free time reading and researching auto mechanics.

It wasn't until she read *Exhausts and Manifolds* that all the pieces fell together. One could build an engine with all the horsepower known to man. It was the transfer of the waste gases and their ratio to dispensation that would turn her average car into the machine she envisioned. She learned the craft by failing and crashing more times than she could count, but as the summer came to a close and her honorary pit member, Jimmy Smith, could give her a helping hand, she won the last race of the season at Charlotte, North Carolina. Next stop—Stanford.

Abdul Farad was born into an honorable family of means. His father and mother served as Professor's Emeritus at Delphi University. They embraced teaching as others embraced a remote or a six-pack. In 1995, they were invited to teach at SMU in University Park, Texas. They often wondered about the teaching techniques and the ways of American scholars. They exchanged many messages over the years inquiring on how the American system worked and the challenges they might face if ever chosen to teach in America. The messages they received were full of praise and guidance if the day should ever occur. And that day did arrive. The family of eight packed their belongings and jetted to the hot plains of Texas.

The surroundings of the university were immaculate. They loved being able to walk to class and enjoy the interaction with the students. The environment was much more conducive to teaching and raising a family versus the hustle and bustle of everyday life in Delphi. They were at home, as were their children.

The most prodigious of the children was Abdul. His mind was a thing of wonder. No matter what the topic, he conquered it with ease. At times, he would sit in on lectures his parents would recite. He loved showing up the so-called "undergraduates" with his grasp of economics and business. Many of the students came to despise him, and complained loudly to the department heads that the "boy" was a serious distraction to their studies. They and their parents weren't paying $15,000 a semester to be upstaged by a child. In order to keep calm in the classrooms, Abdul was informed by his father he would no longer be allowed to attend lectures, thus leaving him free to explore his own devices, and vices, depending which one he chose.

Academically, he was brilliant; no subject could keep his attention. It didn't matter what AP classes the high school offered; he would consume a semester's worth of knowledge in a week. The principal at University High School begged the parents to withdraw him from the school and find an institution more suited to their child's "special needs." They would have none of it.

Instead, they hired a young man from the campus to tutor Abdul on the days he wasn't required to attend classes (by request of the principal), and to be individually instructed in advanced courses of mathematics and chemistry. It was a good match.

Abdul consumed the knowledge as fast as an SUV gulps down gasoline. The only problem, the tutor, Jason Dudley, was a notorious prankster. He was an ardent follower of the movie *Animal House,* and with Abdul's willingness to learn all that was new and exciting, they banded together and pulled off as many pranks on students, staff and faculty as possible without being thrown into irons. Their escapades were all too well known, yet no evidence was ever identified at the scene of the crime implicating them. Even Mark Harmon or David Caruso would have a difficult time solving the crimes.

One prank of particular mention was when a guest speaker was invited to the social affair of the year for the literary students and faculty. Barbara Reagan was invited to host the gathering. Jason and Abdul volunteered to be ushers for the highly coveted event. When Barbara took the stage, each knew she had a habit of adjusting the podium's microphone. She was a very tall woman, and Sony had not manufactured a suitable microphone for her stature. On cue, she lightly grabbed the flexible cable to move it up and forward. The movement triggered a motion detector which activated the small explosive pouch of blue, powdered ink at the base of the mike-head, saturating the poor woman's face and pearly white dress. She looked like a Smurf! There were many suspicions, but unfortunately, those responsible with security were never able to identify or capture the culprits, even though everyone knew who was guilty.

When graduation day arrived, everyone, including his parents, were elated. Abdul graduated at the top of his class with a scholarship to Stanford. The relief that swelled across the campus was meritorious enough that the bright purple (another prank) bells of 1st Presbyterian rang all day announcing the accomplishments for the Class of 2010, and the departure of one Abdul Farad. Even his parents were allowed to pull the strings of the colorful bells. Would California be ready for such a brilliant student? At least University Park would receive a reprieve.

* * *

The four (realizing the journey was ending) sat around

Judith's beat up coffee table four hours before the commencement ceremonies, feeling dejected. As agreed, none accepted any of the multiple job offers piling up on the floor. They weren't quite ready to end the alliance they'd forged six years ago.

The lowest offer came from the Scripts Institute in San Diego for Abdul. Entry level position: *Scientific Expedition Division cordially makes an offer of $100,000 for the first year, with ample raises available after an established work history is properly documented. Adjustments in pay would incrementally increase fifteen percent for the first three years of service.* Abdul threw it on top of the offers Judith received—one from MIT as an associate professor in Advanced Applied Mathematics—starting pay, $125,000. The group joked amongst each other at the offers. Yes, all of their parents were as proud as peacocks, but is this what they toiled over for the last six years, to become stuck in research facilities, or worse, a classroom full of minds which wouldn't be able to grasp the concepts they so desperately sought? No. There must be more. Larry turned on the TV and found one of his favorite movies, *Rounders*, starring Matt Damon. He loved the movie and the way Matt's character took on the mob and attempted to save his childhood friend from an inglorious end. Muki joined him.

"Larry, have you ever watched the movie *21*?" He didn't stir or even acknowledge her presence. He was completely wrapped up in the scene where Damon acquired a seat with the local police force to try his luck. "Larry? Larry!"

"What? Can't you see Damon is about to get the crap beat out of him? Don't ever go to a gunfight with a deck of cards." He laughed at his own joke.

"Larry," cooed Muki, "I have a movie I think we should all watch." Muki's suggestion struck Abdul and Judith as odd. She never talked about any movies, old or current, so why would this one hold meaning for "little" Muki.

"What's it about?" asked Judith.

"These four kids, with help from their math professor, go to Las Vegas and wind up beating the house until they were exposed by the security team. The movie never really says how much the group won, but it had to be in the hundreds of thousands before they were caught. It's really kinda cool. I think we should go to Vegas and try our luck just once. What do we have to lose?" The others answered her with blank stares.

"Come on, guys. We spent the last six years of our lives immersed in books. How many football games and school activities did we pass on to keep our grades up? I, for one, am ready to have some fun. I'm not ready to go to work for IBM or Google. I want to live a little, and I also suggest, based on the money we win, to take a summer trip across the States. It's time we put the books down and enjoy the fruits of our labors." The idea was more than tempting. Judith was the first to chip in.

"I'm in. It would be good to get some fresh, clean air back in the lungs and explore the world beyond academia. I'm all for it. I believe if we agree to this venture, we leave all electronic devices behind us. We can each take a cell phone only for calls. No FB, no games, no shit; only the wind and air flying through our hair under a clear blue sky."

Abdul pondered the idea for a moment and realized he would be going where 'no man had gone before'; well at least he hadn't ventured or traveled far. "Aye, Captain, (in his best James Doohan impersonation). I'll make sure the crystals are properly charged, and the transporter is in excellent operating condition."

"Will you please shut up," barked Judith. "One more reference to that retarded series and I'll show you warp drive right through the door."

"Aye, Captain."

Judith rolled her eyes and threw an empty can of Pringles at the Scotty wannabe.

Muki excused herself from the room and returned a few minutes later. "Guys, I think we really need to watch this movie. Larry, can I please put this in the blue-ray so we can all watch?"

The scene Larry was transfixed on was Damon and his buddy getting the crap beat out of them for cheating the cops. "Stupid boys," quipped Larry.

"Larry? Larry!"

"Huh? What is it, Muki?"

"Can I put his movie in? I think you'll like it."

"Yeah, go ahead. I know this much, if I ever gamble, I'm

taking a gun to a gun fight."

The others looked questioningly at Larry with his last comment. Abdul couldn't pass on the opportunity.

"My dear Larry, I think you should rethink that process, for I fear you would forget to load the weapon of choice. And once you realize the error of your ways, I shall not be the one to clean your drawers. BEAM ME UP SCOTTY!"

Larry glared at Abdul as he rose from the worn leather couch heading to the kitchen for another Red Coke. "Mr. Scott, one more remark like that, and I'll see to it the transporter scatters your atoms across the universe." He winked as he passed by Abdul.

"Aye, Captain. That would cause me much discomfort, for I fear—"

"Enough, you morons. Shut the fuck up or I'll splatter both of your warped minds into the closest wall," yelled Judith.

Muki laughed at both the boys' remarks and the tongue-lashing Judith was bestowing upon them.

For the next hour and a half, the four were glued to the twenty-inch forty-two inch flat screen. They listened, learned and watched as they attempted to understand the intricacies of playing Twenty-One. Before the credits even started, all four proclaimed, "Let's do it!"

CHAPTER 3

ROAD TRIP

The ceremonies had been boring, to say the least. The foursome attended the event more for their parents' sake than their own. Unlike many of the other graduates, they used the scholarship money as intended. It wasn't used for lavish parties or road trips "just 'cause they could." It was used wisely for educational purposes. Now it was time to spread their wings and venture out into the world. Of course, each parent stood with pride as their child walked across the stage and accepted the sheepskin that would propel them into the working world. While some hooted and hollered or mooned the group of attendees, our four solemnly received the paper and waved at the audience with no unwanted fanfare. They exited stage right, and immediately disbanded from the remaining students. The act of throwing a mortar board in the air was childish to say the least; they had bigger fish to fry, and couldn't wait to pack the car and head east into the sunset and try their luck just once.

Each parent greeted and congratulated their child for a "job well done" and wished them well. As a whole, they were extremely disappointed upon hearing that their children were not going directly to work, but rather on some ridiculous vacation across the United States. Muki's parents were the most distraught. They never took a vacation. They worked seven days a week and felt vacations were only for the selfish. Muki hoped someday they would understand that the flag of Ho Chi Minh and his Communist Party was ten thousand miles away. It was time they too enjoyed the fruits of their labor, but she doubted if they would enjoy such lavishness. Spending money on themselves would probably never occur, but Muki was an American and was going to enjoy her Americanization. She would start a family someday, and they would honor the past of her parents while also forging out and learning everything grand about being an American citizen, without the weight of an oppressive government bearing upon her or her family. It would take time.

Larry's folks understood the trip without blinking an eye. Larry Senior knew how cruel life could be at times. He clearly remembered the day when Larry Davis of the New York Jets cut his knees out while executing an illegal block for Terrance Williams in the 2000 Divisional Play-off game. Once in the trainer's room, x-rays indicated a compound fracture of the femur, and a dislodged kneecap. The doctor pumped Larry full of morphine to ease the pain. The MRI the next day revealed an even more gruesome result. All of the ligaments and tendons holding the kneecap in place would have to be completely reconstructed. His days of playing football were over. He would be lucky if he could walk without some type of assistance for the rest of his life.

So, when his son told him and Sandy that he and three other classmates were holding off until August to take up permanent employment, they wholeheartedly agreed with the venture. "Son, you have the rest of your life to work. Have fun and be safe." Excellent words from a father.

Mom, on the other hand, took a different approach. "Junior," she said with a stern voice ,"I want you to have fun and be safe like your father suggested; however, I'm not ready to be a grandmother any time soon. Make sure you carry an ample supply of Trojans, for if I receive a call in the fall declaring a child is on the way, I assure you, it will not have a father. Understood?"

What else could Junior say as his father laughed, knowing his mom's words were not idle threats. "Yes, Mother. No Larry III's in the near future."

She kissed her son and stepped back as Dad shook his hand one more time.

"Congratulations Junior. I love you."

Abdul's parents were elated with the news of the pending trip (as was the City of University Park). It meant he wasn't coming home, to possibly pick up where he left off. Many of the faculty inquired as to when Abdul would be coming home. The parents informed the residents that he was going on a summer vacation with his classmates. You could almost see the tension and nervousness leave their eyes with the wonderful news.

Professor Wilburn, Dean of Economics, was the most relieved. He didn't know how many more potatoes in the exhaust he could handle. He tipped his hat and gladly provided an envelope with $1,000 to further Abdul's pursuits. It was much cheaper than replacing the exhaust system on his 2014 Mercedes 3000I. "Tell Abdul I wish him all the best in his pursuits."

Judith's parents were excited, yet apprehensive of the cross-county road trip. How many times had they seen her explode at the drop of a hat when order wasn't maintained, and a tightly planned schedule fell apart because of outside incalculable circumstances. The most recent disaster occurred two years ago when she was home for the summer. She had qualified for the final race of the season. Jimmy Smith agreed to be in the pits and provide any assistance she required. The car, a rebuilt 1976 GTO, was ready. Jimmy and his crew checked every possible mechanical item one could think of that might fail—or, so they thought.

With five laps to go, and Judith in a commanding lead, the front tire started feeling loose. She called Jimmy on the com and informed him how the car was handling. He suggested she pull in so they could check it out. She declined and decided to continue the race. Her lead was ten seconds. A pit stop would require a minimum of eleven seconds and the lead. She would push the car forward, and it would yield to her will. With only two laps to go and the championship in her grasp, the front right wheel vibration was increasing with each revolution. It felt as if the ball joints or tie-rods were coming apart. She slowed down entering turn four when disaster struck. The wheel collapsed, sending the car skidding into the wall. Everyone was extremely anxious as the emergency crews descended on the scene. Judith was physically okay—the car was totaled.

That night, as she anguished over losing the race and nursing her newly won bruises, Jimmy told her the cause of the accident. Three of the lug nuts sheared off. She erupted.

"What did you say?! Lug nuts? Lug nuts? What incompetent

idiot allowed such a minor defect to cost me the championship? Well? Who the hell inspected the car?" Jimmy tried to get in a word, but she wasn't finished.

"This is shit, you hear me? SHIT! I lost the race because a bunch of grease monkeys' heads were so far up their ass, they couldn't tell the lug nuts needed to be replaced? SHIT! That's what it is. One hundred percent SHIT!"

No one would ever have guessed the problem because everything on the car was new, even the lug nuts. It would be a few years before they were informed by the manufacturer that they had mistakenly received an improperly labeled shipment of high-performance products from their supplier. The parts house knew the quality was okay for normal everyday driving, but not racing vehicles. The parts shipped would never endure the stress and demands a race car required.

Her parents hoped the kids joining Judith knew what they were getting into.

They quietly hugged Judith as they handed over the envelope. "Thanks Mom and Dad."

* * *

The four reconvened at Judith's apartment. They gathered around the worn coffee table, and threw down the envelopes that their parents had given them. Judith sat in the middle of the old sleep bed couch. Muki sat directly across from her on her prized bean bag chair. Larry and Abdul grabbed two wooden chairs from the kitchenette and stared like vultures at the white envelopes.

"Well Captain, shall we examine the booty or just stare?" quipped Abdul.

"Abdul, only you could ruin a moment like this with your not only weak impersonation of James Doohan, but also your juvenile female references. And you wonder why you can't get laid. Hell, you can't even find a hooker on Hollywood Boulevard to put up with your bullshit for two minutes. I wonder why?"

Abdul looked at Larry, ignoring Judith's flattering compliment. "Captain, I suggest the next time you review Star Fleet's Manual on Female Crew mates, make sure you read up on their behavioral tendencies. This one seems to have a screw or two loose. Abdul flashed a smile at Larry. "Aye, Captain, I believe her pending threat would truly upset the time continuum."

The boys attempted to enjoy the laugh among themselves, until Judith threatened them with a six-inch by one-foot thermodynamics book.

Judith returned Abdul's smile. "The only thing being interrupted are the few synapse that seem to operate in your pea brain!"

Muki knew this conversation could end in disaster, for Abdul never missed a choice opportunity to jibe Judith. "Come on guys, let's see what we have. Save the bodily injuries for another day. I don't think our parents included major medical with the presents." They both relaxed and moved their eyes to the envelopes. Each graduate chose one and opened it.

When the counting of cash and checks was completed, there was over $20,000 on the table. They were hoping for more, but it was an adequate amount for Vegas. It would allow them to use the additional $10,000 they collectively saved over the last six years for the traveling and sightseeing.

"Okay, when do we leave?" smiled Larry.

"Tomorrow morning. I have a few items to check out with the car. Be back at the apartment at 7:00am sharp. If you're late, don't bother showing up."

6:00AM

The morning sun shone brilliantly as it crested the distant tops of the Sierra's. The air was fresh and cool as the prevailing westerly winds pushed the Pacific Ocean's crisp, clean scent towards the interior of Southern California. She loved the smell of the salty air as she sat in peace on the balcony savoring her one real vice—freshly ground Colombian coffee beans. Her friends didn't understand why she was so against Starbucks or any of the other fine coffee houses. She literally turned up her nose and informed them that they wouldn't know a decent cup of coffee if it were poured down their throat. She couldn't understand why people drowned the real flavor of coffee with whipped cream,

French vanilla, hazelnut, or any other supposedly exotic flavors. Coffee, like a good car, should never be tinkered with. It was a crime to bastardize one of God's greatest gifts to mankind.

She cringed when she first saw decaffeinated beans, and almost confronted the store manager for such a travesty, until she recalled that one of her dad's good friends (who had introduced her to the fine beverage) was forced to drop the full-leaded brand for the lesser, based on his doctor's recommendations. Samuel Goodwin had been struck with a minor heart attack. His doctor told him no more liquor, nicotine or caffeine. Sam could handle the first two, but cutting out caffeine? Not happening. It took a few years for him to enjoy and appreciate the taste of decaf, but he succeeded. He still missed the full flavor, yet he also enjoyed not being in the hospital. It was a small price to pay. She relished the memory of them sitting on her parents' spacious redwood deck in the morning hours discussing school, politics and cars. And yes, even though she would chide him about his weak coffee, she agreed the trade-off was worth it.

As she smiled and reminisced, the doorbell buzzer blared, breaking the serene morning calm and her few pleasant thoughts. She shuddered at the sound, and thought to herself, *I should have disconnected the fucking alarm a long time ago.* She stood up and pushed the talk button.

"Who is it?"

"Good morning, Judith. May I enter?"

She glanced at the twelve-inch plastic Stanford clock hanging behind her prized fern. 6:15am. Forty-five minutes to launch. *Wish she could have waited another fifteen minutes,* she thought.

She hit the *unlock* button allowing Muki to enter the apartment. *I still have a quarter of a pot of coffee to savor before our big adventure starts,* she contemplated to herself.

Muki heard the lock unlatch and proceeded to the living room. She threw her worn travel bag onto the couch and directed herself to the kitchen. She knew Judith well enough that she wouldn't receive a proper salutation. Judith proved one too many times that she cared not for the so-called "niceties" or "proper etiquette." She was the most beautiful, reclusive woman she knew. Judith's hard body and flowing brunette hair was all the rage on campus. Many of the boys in her classes severely struggled to maintain their concentration during lectures. She was stunning. How many times did Muki see boys trip and stumble as Judith commandingly walked across campus in an old pair of very short cut-off jeans and a braless T-shirt?

She paid them no mind, and if one was foolish enough to approach her and ask if it were cold outside, they wound up on the pavement with cuts and bruises. Judith was, as some of the boys openly stated between themselves, "That is one bad-ass bitch." Judith never looked back at her would-be pursuers. She raised her right hand and flipped them off. She could have any boy she wanted, but there was something under her surface demeanor that reflected a violent storm brewing in that beautiful body. Muki asked her once why she was so angry and refused any and all advances. The smile from Judith's face vanished. Her deep green, beautiful eyes flashed red with anger, and she would never forget the words she spoke.

"Look me in the eyes, Muki, and listen very carefully. "NONE—OF—YOUR—FUCKING—BUSINESS."

It wasn't the words that shook her up; it was the look of utter hate which boiled in her green orbs that scared the hell out of her. She never again broached the topic.

Muki entered the kitchen, picked up a partially-washed cup and poured herself some of Judith's "black gold." She added a few tablespoons of sugar and a dash of milk. Stirring it together, she took a sip and savored the taste. Satisfied it was the correct combination, Judith moved out to the balcony, and took a seat in the cheap plastic patio chair.

"Morning, Judith."

No response as Judith stared at her cup, taking another deep drink. Her body stirred as the caffeine coursed through her veins, recharging her system while increasing her senses.

"Are you drinking it black or did you pussy out again with sugar and milk? You know, if you're going to bastardize my coffee, why not go to Starbucks or Quick Trip and quit wasting my perfect brew."

Muki was used to the accusations, "Because I can't get this type of superb customer service any other place."

Judith nodded in agreement, revealing a seldom seen smile.

6:50AM

"I bet those juveniles think I'm kidding. They have exactly ten minutes, and we're gone. I really hope—"

The door buzzer screamed, interrupting the morning serenity once again. Before she hit the talk button, two voices were booming into the speaker. "Ensign, let us in! Let us in! The Klingons and Romulans are at it again. They've knocked out the main engines and shields are only 50 percent."

Judith fiercely pressed the talk button down.

"Shut the fuck up you juveniles, or I swear I'll leave your asses here." Nothing but laughter came through the speaker.

"Muki, why did I ever agree to let them join us? I swear, a full month with them? Someone will die before we return."

Muki could only laugh quietly as she shrugged her shoulders. "Hey, at least the trip won't be dull."

Judith spun around and headed to the door. Muki wondered why she didn't major in psychology and psychiatry. Judith would make the perfect subject for study. It was odd that after all these years, the boys' humor stayed on the same path, even though Judith would leash her tirades on them. It never fazed them. But if they irritated her as much as she proclaimed, why did she allow them to hang around? Wonder what Freud would think of this peculiarity?

She could hear Judith yelling at the boys as they noisily entered the living room.

"Hey, Judith," called Larry. "Have any more of that cheap coffee? Abdul was running late and wouldn't stop so I could buy a 'good' cup at Quick Trip."

The glare she heaped on Larry could have melted an iceberg. She said not a word and pointed to the kitchen.

Larry picked up a dirty cup, snatched a dish towel off the counter and did his best to clean it up. "Don't want to get any cooties," came the low words from his mouth. "Abdul, you want some of Judith's specialty or would it better serve as propulsion fuel for the thermonuclear reactors?"

Before Abdul could respond, Judith picked up a calculus book and threw it into the kitchen. Larry ducked down as it crashed into the refrigerator, knocking off half of the magnets as it fell to the floor.

"Now I know why you gave up softball. Hard to play the game making such shoddy throws." Larry prepared to duck again for fear Judith would pick up something bigger. Instead, she sat down on the couch and threw him a smile with a one-finger salute.

"Okay, enough of this bullshit," she commanded. "We have a lot of miles to cover today, so let's get the car loaded and stop wasting time. I'm ready to try our luck."

The four finished their coffee, packed the Camaro, and pulled onto I-5. The trip would require roughly ten hours of good, hard driving and schooling in Twenty-One. Plenty of time for Larry to teach the other three the nuances of the game. They weren't going to deliberately beat the house as the kids in the movie *"21"* did. Of course, they hoped they'd be lucky and win some money. He convinced them that of the extra twenty thousand, they would hold back five. Judith balked at the idea, but relented that a little caution was warranted. She didn't want the vacation to be shortened due to a lack of foresight or funds. She was looking forward to seeing Washington D.C. And digging up all the information she could on a certain infamous family member.

Begrudgingly, Judith agreed to let Larry dictate the schedule for the trip. They would drive four hours, then stop for food; repeat the process again, and then spend the last forty-five minutes or so jamming to tunes. This would allow them a chance to relax and recharge. Once they arrived at Caesars, they'd grab five hours of sleep and hit the Twenty-One tables by 2:00am. They would play for six hours and leave whether they were up or down as the winnings dictated.

During the drive, they would attempt to memorize the seven decks of cards he'd prepared. Each knew there were eighty-four face cards, twenty-eight aces and two hundred and fifty-two *small* cards. Since they couldn't bring laptops, he used a piece of sturdy cardboard as a table. He would deal out three hands and a phantom dealer. He would then call out the cards being flipped over. Each player would place a bet, and attempt to keep track of the cards being dealt while calculating the odds of obtaining a winning hand.

The first two hours were frustrating to say the least. No one but the house was winning, and winning big. Larry calculated the "house" was up $15,000. In two short hours, his understudies were broke! Larry sternly instructed them that they were trying too hard to win.

"The key to the game was staying calm and relaxed. Stop playing poker and start thinking," were his words of wisdom. "Judith, why in the world would you agree to a hit when you're holding seventeen?" She was prepared to defend her position until Larry continued his train of thought.

"The dealer was dealt a three. So far, only two face cards have appeared. Muki drew a five and Abdul drew an eight. You were holding seventeen. The odds of the dealer going bust were 80 percent. The small cards have played through. Instead of being smart, you got greedy and went bust. The next four cards were face cards. The dealer would have gone bust, and you would have collected $10,000. Instead, you lost. Stop gambling and start thinking." All three of them listened to the teacher as he instructed them on how to stay calm and play the game. "Don't let the game play you."

The next two hours went much better. The group broke even with small gains here and there. The lure of winning big was still in the back of their minds. Abdul was the next one to feel greedy. Instead of remembering the cards played, he only looked at the ones on the table. His winning hand would have yielded $10,000—instead he was busted.

"Okay, it's been four hours. Time for a break and something to eat."

Muki couldn't believe the time passed by so quickly. "What? It's been four hours already? Let's keep driving. I think I'm starting to figure the game out." Judith and Abdul nodded in agreement.

"No!" demanded Larry. "We stick to the schedule. Judith, find a place to pull off. We all need a break."

For once Judith asked a question. "Why?" She'd become

fixated with the game. Her brain was starting to recognize combinations and the averages of beating the house.

"Because I said so. You see, my small minds, you are developing the gambling bug. Do this at the table and it will be a very short vacation. Now Judith, find a place where we can all decompress and regroup."

She reluctantly agreed with Larry's logic and started looking for the blue highway signs on the outskirts of Bakersfield indicating dining establishments.

"Wendy's okay everyone? It's the next exit. Speak now or I keep driving." Wendy's it was.

They exited the car, only realizing then how tired and exhausted their bodies were. They were all physically and mentally drained from the exercise. Larry was right; they needed the break. They would rest for an hour, not thinking about cards at all. They would only discuss the sights and sounds for each city they'd chosen: Denver, Kansas City, St. Louis, Nashville, and D.C. Any other cities would be a bonus.

For two weeks, they'd poured over the maps deciding where to travel. It would be their only vacation before they entered the real world of the working class, and settled down to what they hoped would be enriched lives. In a methodical method, they picked Denver for the Rockies. Sure, they could see the Sierras which were only a short distance by car, but they didn't have Pikes Peak, and Mt. Rainier in Washington State was too far off the beaten path, plus Denver was home to the Colorado Rockies and baseball.

During their junior year, the four discovered they all loved baseball. It started with the most unlikely of individuals. Abdul was raving about the errant throw the pitcher Johnson executed, allowing the winning run to score. "What was he thinking? Any little leaguer knows not to make that throw. It cost the Giants the game and a shot at winning the series. Stupid, stupid, stupid."

His comments sparked a debate which put studies on hold for the next three hours, with all agreeing with his assessment except Judith.

"Welch should have held the ball and took his chances with the bases loaded and one out. The defense had been spectacular all night, and could easily have turned two and gone into the bottom of the ninth hoping to break the tie and win the game."

For Judith, it was her second passion—racing was first and foremost. However, racing didn't have the strategy baseball lent. Racing is "balls to the wall, fuel consumption, and drafting." Baseball is a whole different ball game. How many games were watched where a passed ball, an errant throw, or a muffed routine fly ball changed the tempo and the outcome between victor and loser. She loved the thrill of not being able to calculate or foresee the possible outcome. Her partners in crime were also drawn to the game, also for its intricacies and unknowns.

So, Denver was an obvious choice. They would visit Pikes Peak, then catch a Rockies game. Candlestick or Three-Com Park was nice, but the balls didn't fly as freely due to the atmospheric conditions caused by the cold air blowing in from the bay. Coors Field was known, along with the Ballpark in Arlington, to be a "pitcher's nightmare" and a "hitter's paradise."

Kansas City and St. Louis didn't offer a lot of sightseeing (with the exception of Gateway Arch) based on the search engines they called upon. What they did offer was more baseball—Royals and Cardinals. Nashville was Muki's choice. She loved Elvis Presley songs (much to the other's chagrin) and the history of country music. She convinced the group they needed to broaden their horizons on the music stage and spend at least a full day touring the town and people. Sold!

D.C. It goes without saying that D.C. would become a hub as they ventured up and down the coast in a fifty-mile radius garnering, exploring, and learning all the history they could about these United States.

"Okay, ready for lesson number two?" asked Larry.

With a definitive 'yes', trays were picked up, trash emptied and potty breaks commenced.

Judith asked if anyone else cared to drive. She wanted to sit in the back with Larry and watch him deal the cards. She wanted to be able to visualize each and every combination as they appeared. *What?* They all thought. *Judith was relinquishing control of her prized Camaro?* No one jumped at the opportunity. She asked again in a more pleading tone. Larry was the designated dealer and teacher. Obviously, he wouldn't be driving, so that left Muki or Abdul. Abdul was competent enough if one didn't examine all the tickets and minor fender benders he escaped from in the confines of University Park. That left petite little Muki.

"Okay, I'll drive, but I don't want to hear any comments on my driving skills. We won't set any speed records. Okay?" The three agreed as Judith handed her the keys and jumped into the back seat. There was another reason she wanted to sit in the back, but that would have to wait.

The next four hours were more intense than the first. Larry only allowed each player a maximum of three seconds to decide if they wanted to raise the bet, take a card, or hold. The pace became maddening as each player called out their moves. Larry kept pushing the game faster and faster. The responses were becoming mechanical. They were playing without emotion or anxiety. The group never second-guessed. He was teaching them how to count cards without knowing what they were doing. He knew if they got on a hot streak, the house might get wise and call their own hand. This he didn't want to occur. . He decided it would be best to split up into two teams. After two or three hours, if one of the players decided to try a different table, that would be acceptable. But, it couldn't be at a table another pair was playing at. He hoped this provided a low profile in the event one or two of them starting winning big.

Hours seemed like minutes as each decided to hold, pass, fold, or bet. Minutes turned into microseconds with the split decisions Larry was demanding.

"Time!" proclaimed Larry. "Final results for round two – Muki $7,500, Abdul $10,000, and last but not least, yet most irritating, Judith a cool $25,000 – for a collective pocket of $42,500. Well done Ensign, well done. Muki, find a place to pull over. It's time to recharge for the final push.

"Next stop, according to the sign—Jean, Nevada. Sure hope they have a store. If not, next stop—Vegas."

They pulled in to what many would consider "a spit in the bucket" of a town. The interstate was hailed when it was first built in 1963. Many of the bordering towns, such as Mesquite and

Bunkerville, watched sales plummet as US 90 became obsolete to Californians headed to the lure of vast riches and wealth in the "Oasis of the Desert." By chance, Jean was dead in the path of the surveyors. The highway department could cut off miles running the new Interstate Highway from Bakersville to Las Vegas by way of Jean. When the plan was proposed, the town council agreed to keep their small, home-town look, and leave the developments and commercialization to "Big Sister." They would welcome travelers and provide eateries and accommodation for those who were leaving town broke, or needing to gain their misplaced confidence before hitting it big.

Much to their surprise, Jean might look like a hiccup on the map; in reality, it was a town of ten thousand. Muki eyed a truck stop and suggested they eat at the "Trucker's Diner." "If truckers eat here, it's got to be good."

The three were a bit shocked at the suggestion, yet the parking lot appeared to be full of trucks and the all-hated "four wheelers." The three would-be patrons voted a unanimous 'yes'.

Muki nosed the Camaro between a 1995 Porsche and 1960 "tricked-out" Impala. They slowly forced their way out of the car. Muki and Abdul lay down on the cherry-red hood. They were utterly exhausted, while Larry and Judith pulled themselves from the back seat with a renewed vigor. Instead of the training session draining them, it had the reverse effect. Judith wished her treasured Colombian coffee, at nine dollars a pound, could give her the same boost.

Judith took a long healthy stretch (exposing every fine curve of her body), oblivious to the patrons staring out the window at the spectacle. Her full, round breasts and hard nipples were straining to burst through the tight, white T-shirt. Many of the diners stopped to admire the show in place. A spoonful of corn missed the intended mouth, winding up in the owner's lap. Another spilled tea down his designer shirt, while another voiced all of the other men's thoughts, "Damn."

Without an idea of the show she was providing the weary 'concrete cowboys,' she declared, "I'm starved. Let's eat."

The waitress, a woman well into her fifties and a veteran of the antics of truckers, herded the four to a booth close to her station. She knew how the regulars might react to a bunch of college kids, especially the one who was probably "Miss July 2014."

"Kids, My name is Katie, and I'll be your waitress tonight. If you need anything, don't hesitate to call. And honey," her eyes fell on Judith's, "if I were you, I'd put those puppies on low beam or cover them up."

Judith glanced down at her chest and blushed just a bit. The last four hours apparently triggered every erogenous zone she possessed. Sure, she engaged in the random sexual act to blow off steam, but nothing ever energized or excited her like the last four hours. Her senses were on high alert, including the eyes she now felt bearing down on her. Her comrades knew exactly what Katie was talking about. Every eye was trained on Judith as they walked to the booth. Judith appreciated Katie's concern.

"Miss Katie, we'll be alright, but if we need you, I'll call." Without a second thought, Judith stood up eying each man who couldn't stop staring. The timid ones went back to eating. The married ones asked for their checks and left, yet there were always those who couldn't get enough.

She addressed the gawkers."What's wrong? Never seen a pair like this before?" Before anyone could answer she continued. "From what I'm seeing, the answer is no. And for those who are still having second thoughts, your best dreams will remain that, dreams. So eat your dinner and fuc—"

Larry knew what was coming next. He also knew they were on enemy turf, which Judith was inflaming. *Just once, just once, I wish she would think before speaking.*

"Honey, that's enough. Let these nice people enjoy their meal. Please sit down. I'll go get a sweater from the car." The words were loud enough for the disenchanted men to hear. He hoped he had calmed the savage beasts. In a voice only Judith could hear as he pulled her back into her seat, he said, "Do you have a death wish? I don't, so shut the fuck up, okay?"

No one ever talked to her like that, at least not face to face. The sternness of his words and the seriousness in his eyes calmed her enough to sit down and relax. She realized that if she didn't gain control of her deep-seated anger for the lineage she couldn't control, she and she alone, would be her own destruction and enemy. It was time to rethink attitudes and actions.

Larry returned in a few minutes with a worn-out Stanford hoodie which Judith quickly put on. He was relieved to see none of the customers had acted on their inclinations or desires. Katie took each order and guaranteed "it will be out in a jiffy." She motioned for Larry to follow her. He told the others he needed to wash-up before dinner. As he walked towards the restroom (passing by Katie's station), a hand pulled him to the side.

"Sir."

"Yes ma'am."

"I was serious about having the food prepared quickly. The only reason a ruckus didn't break out is that I promised two of the regulars a much-desired date. It calmed them for the moment, but let's be honest, my body isn't quite as alluring as your young friend's. So please, eat your dinner and don't dawdle. They might regain their confidence, and I don't think either one us wants an unpleasant confrontation."

"Thank you…umm…Katie. I'll make sure we don't cause a scene."

Katie winked at him as he continued to the restroom.

Dinner was served in record time.

"Captain," stated Abdul. "I don't think the synthesizer is this fast. They must have a warp drive converter in the kitchen." Larry would usually have enjoyed the joke, but not this time.

"Abdul, shut up and eat." Larry's words were threatening.

"And if I don't follow your orders? Will the safety of the universe be at stake?" Abdul laughed out loud, even Muki and Judith joined in.

"Abdul, just eat," came the words through clenched teeth. The abruptness of Larry's demeanor caught them all off guard, and like small obedient children, they lowered their heads and ate.

"Here's your check, kids. You can either pay me here or at the counter. Whichever is easier." She winked at Larry.

"Thank you. We'll pay at the counter." Larry noticed that even though the crowd changed every five minutes, two men sitting close to the entrance by the window were spending way too much time nursing their coffees.

"Who needs a pit stop before we start the last leg?" The girls chimed in, 'yes', and like girls, went together. Larry watched the men as their eyes were none too pleasantly scanning the pair.

"Abdul, let's go."

"What? No words of wisdom? No great insight of the universe?"

Larry knew Abdul could go on for much too long with his line of questioning.

He roughly interrupted. "See those two men by the window?"

"The rejects with the plaid shirts and worn-out caps?"

"Yes, them."

"You afraid the virtue of our women is in jeopardy? I will take my phaser—"

"Shut up, you idiot. I'm serious." His abrupt response was being scrutinized. Abdul leaned a little closer to Larry.

"Our waitress bribed those two men to leave us alone. Apparently, they didn't take kindly to some upstart Playmate mocking them in front of their brethren. We need to leave here as soon as the girls return. Understood?"

Abdul looked at the men again and noticed their eyes were penetrating into Muki and Judith as they re-entered the dining area.

"Agreed. Let's go now."

The boys slowly rose from the booth without causing concern.

"Okay guys, what's next? Muki and I aren't ready to climb back in the car. Since we weren't allowed to enjoy our meal, we need to get some coffee and diffuse some more."

"No, Judith. We have to go," fired off Larry.

What's wrong with Larry? He is never this demanding, thought Judith.

"No? No? Who the hell are you, to tell me no? You're not my mother or father. Where do you get off telling me what to do, anyhow?"

Her voice was getting louder as she started berating Larry. "Let me tell you something, you juvenile delinquent, that is my car..."

Larry couldn't help but feel the eyes (especially the two pairs in question) staring at the four. Katie hurried to the table and offered the regulars a free refill. They declined her request, got up from the booth and started approaching the students.

"...and if you don't want me to leave your ass in this shit-hole of a town, you'll show me some respect or I'll kick your ass all the way back to Stanford." The men were now three feet from the four.

The largest man, probably in his mid-forties, with a beer belly that would make Miller proud and a physique to match, chimed in. "What's wrong, sonny? Having a little trouble with your wild filly? My buddy Ray and I got just the cure for breaking her. I think we'll take her outside and teach her some manners."

Ray joined in. "Yep, Billy boy and I got just what she be needing to learn her elders some respect."

"Look guys, we don't want any trouble. We're passing through and need to get back on the road." Larry tried to push by the men, but they set up a formidable barricade.

"Not so fast. We'll let you go just as soon as we had our dessert." They stared straight at Judith's chest.

"By looks of it Ray, I'd say she's got plenty for each of us. You take the right, and I'll take the left."

For the first time in her life, Judith felt true fear. Nothing like crashing in a race car. That came with the sport. This was different. The men were directly threatening to rape her.

"Tell ya what Billy, I don't mind sloppy seconds, so while you're knocking her front out, I'll be in the back getting some of that split end while you bronc and tame them melons. We can test out that new full-sized bed I installed last month in my Peterbilt."

"Sounds good to me, Ray. We gonna split her real good and maybe teach her a thing or two."

Katie was attentively listening to the men. She knew they were capable of pulling it off. No one ever stood up to them, and when a police report was filed, no one dared to show up and verify the charges.

"Come on boys, sit down and have some more coffee, let these nice folks go about their business. We don't want any trouble and Katie can't wait to be a sandwich with you two." She hoped her offer was enough to allow the kids to be on their way—unharmed.

Ray glared at Katie. "When we're finished with her, you're next."

Judith's gut tightened at the thought of being manhandled by them. She was infuriated, yet refrained from inflaming the situation.

The next words spoken were quiet and specific. "Gentlemen,"

"Well lookie here Ray, we've got us a little egg roll. Tell ya what, when we've finished polishing our rods with 'Miss July', I think we need us a slant-eye as an encore."

"Hell yeah, Billy. I always heard it was horizontal."

Muki stood her ground." Will you please let us pass? We have a pressing engagement and would hate to be late."

"Billy, I'd hate for them to be late so let's split the egg roll first. Be a good tune-up for the little princess. I bet this one's so tight, she'll be screaming for a month." The men let out a deep, evil laugh as they rubbed their crotches.

Larry attempted to pull Muki back; she held her ground.

Ray attempted to push Larry out of the way. As his hand grabbed Larry's, a slender brown arm redirected Ray's hand and arm and spun him 180 degrees. The next few seconds were a blur to the untrained eye. Muki spun Ray around, planting her left hand in his lower back. His size was perfect for the moves the neighborhood kids had shown her. Using Ray as a workbench, she planted her right foot just above Billy's tibia and shattered the patella. He went down in a moaning heap.

She turned 90 degrees to her left, and let out a small cry as her right elbow crashed into the soft joint between Ray's radius and humerus. She quickly moved her right foot onto Ray's right patella and dropped it three inches. She held on to his left arm as his massive weight pulled him to the ground. With one good jerk, the sound of tendons and ligaments snapping was loud and gruesome (it would take more than Tommy John surgery to repair the injury).

Billy turned over, whimpering in pain. "You little Asian bitch; when I get up—"He never finished his sentence as she thrust her foot squarely into the area he had so recently described to her.

Judith, Larry, Abdul and Katie stared in awe; first at Muki, and then at the two not so imposing figures on the floor. Muki took stock of the situation and smiled as if she'd just aced a history exam. "Okay, I think we can go now," and moved towards the counter.

Larry agreed. "Oh yeah, that's a good idea. Come on guys, let's go."

Katie (in shock at the current events) gladly rang the ticket up and took the money from Larry. She couldn't help but ask Muki a question.

"Little girl, I've seen a lot of strange things in my life, but I'm here to tell ya, that beats all I've seen in these parts. Where did you learn to do that?"

"Yeah," said Judith. "I'd like to know the same thing."

She looked at her friends then turned to Katie. "Never enjoy the cookie, until the fortune is read."

"What the hell? Excuse me. What does she mean by that?" asked Katie.

Larry and Judith had a good idea what she meant. In a hushed tone, Larry bent over an inch or two as he handed Katie at ten-dollar tip, "Don't fuck with an egg roll you didn't order."

"Amen to that, Mister. Amen to that."

Katie turned and picked up the phone and dialed the sheriff's office.

"Dale, you and Jimmy need to come down here. You won't believe what just happened. Billy and Ray are messing up my mopped floor and are bleeding all over the place." A noticeable smiled surrounded her mouth.

* * *

"Where the hell did you learn to fight like that?" queried Judith.

"Yeah," asked Abdul. "How'd you do that?"

"The streets. Remember, I grew up around the docks, and some of the boys thought I needed to know how to defend myself.

Nothing special." Her modesty was amazing. She single-handedly took down two of the most despicable men in these parts with ease.

"Captain, forget the photon torpedoes, we have Muki power on board."

The tension was broken, and they shared a good, hearty laugh. At least, Larry appeared to be laughing. All he could think of was how ineptly he'd behaved. He was larger than the assailants, yet he possessed neither the instinct nor the athletic ability to intervene. Hopefully, Judith wouldn't think any less of him.

"Okay guys, back in the car. In thirty minutes we'll reach our first destination, and we have one more quiz to complete before testing our new talents. Who's driving?"

"I am. It's my car and I need to burn up all the adrenaline pumping through my system. Damn Muki, If I'd known you were such a badass, I might have been nicer when you doctored your coffee." Muki just smiled.

Judith stopped to fill up the tank then turned her flaming red Camaro on I-15 and pushed the speedometer to eighty. "Okay Larry, what's the final quiz?"

Expecting some revelation or major final exam that would ensure their success at the tables, Larry pulled out a Marlboro Light (he seldom smoked, but he needed to calm his nerves after the recent encounter) lit it up, took in a deep drag, and slowly exhaled the blue smoke as his body slowed down, "The final quiz..." More of a question than a statement. "Nothing. Turn up the tunes and let it roll, baby."

The sounds of Bob Seger's Silver Bullet Band jamming out "Night Moves" filled the car as they thundered north and the sun slowly set behind the Sierras.

CHAPTER 4

VEGAS

The four spoke few words as they sped towards the lights, excitement, and the lure Vegas offered so many people. Larry made sure the music never stopped so his compadres stayed loose and kept their minds clear. Clear minds would be their secret weapon at the tables, plus they were all revisiting the events at the diner. It pained him that he was incapable of thwarting the truckers. Someday he was going to have to will his body to obey the commands of the mind. Many had suggested through the years, "his body was willing, now to connect it to his mind." He always rebuked the offers. He knew his athletic abilities paled in comparison to other boys his age. Tonight, it was glaringly apparent—a change must occur. Unlike him, his father and uncle would have easily disposed of the "rednecks."

He knew Judith elicited a lot of unwanted attention on campus, but those were mere boys, *these* were real men who threatened her. Someday soon, she needed to learn how to harness her anger. If not, she could pay a heavy price with her abrasive attitude—rape, or worse.

Larry couldn't help but occasionally glance at Judith. The only observation the "rednecks" at the diner were dead on about was her looks. She possessed the appearance and body of a Playmate. It was difficult for him to focus on the road as the lowering rays of sunlight reflected off the outside rearview mirror, exposing her perfectly shaped chest. It heaved in perfect rhythm with each breath she inhaled. At times, he felt they beckoned to be fondled and suckled. Yes, the thought crossed his mind more than once, but he knew how harshly she rejected all would-be admirers—a deathly stare followed by a short volley of unflattering comments to her suitors.

The thirty-minute drive seemed to take much longer than the

first nine hours. Time appeared to be suspended as the mile markers slowly counted down to their final destination.

Only once was the quiet broken. "Are we there yet, Captain?"

In unison, Muki, Larry and Judith obliged a response to the Star Trek wannabe, "NO!"

Although they had all seen Las Vegas in movies or postcards, nothing would prepare them for what awaited. Five miles out of town, the glow of lights from the city overpowered the shroud of the jet-black night sky.

"Look at that, guys. How would you like to pay that light bill?" asked Larry.

The other three stared ahead and took in the scene. They felt a small bit of dread grip them. Subconsciously, they were getting a glimpse of the city that had dashed so many high hopes and turned many potential millionaires to peasants, who then had to justify why they were now the proud owners of two home mortgages, or explain why the money for college was gone.

"Don't let the lights overwhelm you, guys. The original owners of this town knew exactly what they were doing. The city was built for one reason and one reason only."

"What was that?" inquired Judith.

"Money, money, and more money. If you follow your history, Vegas was a perfect haven for the East Coast mob bosses. Gambling is legal in Nevada; not so in New York, Chicago or Kansas City. Sure they drew a lot of top headliners like the "rat pack" and Elvis, but that was only to convince the "jet set" to come and visit. They were served the best food, given the best tickets, but it was a lure. The bosses knew if they treated common people with respect and dignity, they would legally haul in millions. One of the best marketing tools they built into the casinos was no clocks and no windows."

"Why?" asked Abdul.

"Money, my friend, money. Time doesn't exist when you start playing. Take away a person's concept of time and they'll keep spending their money until they have none. They won't realize they just spent eight hours leaning over the craps table or playing Twenty-One. Time will only reappear when they retire to their rooms or walk outside and realize the sun is bearing down from a clear blue sky. So, take it in for what it is—the entire town is one monstrous gambling house!"

Ten minutes later, Judith pulled her *baby* under the Romanesque stone entrance of Caesar's. Larry was hoping like hell the glamour and opulence of this replica building of Old Rome didn't overwhelm his friends' senses and cause them to forget why they'd come. He could tell by the oohs and aahs emitting from their constricted throats that a reminder was necessary.

"Okay, you guys get us checked-in and I'll park the car. Do not go in to any of the gaming rooms. Stay in the main concourse. Understood?" All three nodded as they exited the car and retrieved their luggage.

Larry pulled away hoping they heeded his warning.

Judith walked up to the perfectly polished, granite top check-in desk. "Room for Kowalski/Anderson."

The young female desk clerk checked her reservation board."Yes, Judith and Larry?"

"Yes."

"May I have your credit card and ID, please?" How could this employee be so nice knowing how many of the guests left with empty wallets? What did Larry say, *"it was built to take your money?"*

"Not this time," she softly said.

"Excuse me, ma'am?" The overpowering pleasantness of the clerk was becoming unbearable. She wanted to reach over and grab the bleached-blond bimbo and tell her to quit being so damned nice. She and her friends weren't the typical gamblers, and would see to it they wiped the smiles off the employees as they scooped up their earnings and left town with their pockets full of cash.

"Oh, nothing, nothing at all. Are the rooms ready and where are the elevators?"

"Go down the hall to your left. Pass by the VIP entrance. The elevators will be on your left. Have a wonderful stay at Caesars and if you need anything, my name is Natalie."

Judith restrained from speaking her mind. "Thank you,

Natalie."

She then picked up the key cards and turned around. "Muki, where's Abdul?"

"I tried to stop him, but you know how he is. He said he only wanted to take a peek. Something about the sound of phaser fire was drawing him like a magnet to steel."

"If that little shit is in the casino, I'm going to kick his ass since I can't very well do it to Natalie."

Sure enough, they found him in the middle of the Palace Casino. His eyes were bulging out of their sockets. Never had he witnessed so many sights and sounds. The mass of humanity was overpowering as they were frantically pushing buttons on the electronic slot machines or taking another hit from the dealer. More than one waitress asked if he'd like a drink with the lure of providing a phone number for a nice tip. He was losing his senses. *This is what Larry warned us of*, she thought. *It is built to take your money.*

Judith's eyes were bearing in on him with little compassion. "Abdul. What the hell are you doing?"

"I just wanted to try this machine one time. What could be the harm in trying just one? "

"You know what Larry told us, and I now see why he was trying to prepare us. I can feel the electricity in the air, and if the desk clerk's niceties were an indication of things to come, we could easily spend too much money too fast."

"Excuse me, would you like something to drink?" asked one of the patrolling hostesses. Abdul's' mouth dropped to the ground. This girl—no, woman—was a perfect match to Megan Fox. The outfit she wore was tailored to catch every tantalizing curve her body offered. Her penetrating blue eyes (must have been contacts) were staring into his soul, or worse, his wallet.

"I...I...aahh...aahh..."

A deep voice answered the question Abdul was struggling with. "Thank you, but no. My friend needs to get some rest." The three were shocked into reality as Larry rescued Abdul.

"Okay, well if there is anything I can do (a seductive smile spread across pearly white teeth), please don't hesitate to let me know."

Larry glanced at her name tag without taking her full beauty in his sights. "Thank you, Cheryl, we'll let you know."

Larry (like a mother bear rounding up her cubs) guided the three to the elevators. Without calling out anyone in particular, he reiterated his previous thought and warning. "There is a reason I told you three to stay out of the casino. The lure of relinquishing 'our' money is too great a temptation just to frivolously throw it away. We came to play Twenty-One, and that is what we're going to do, and with some good luck and planning, we'll walk out of here with deeper pockets than when we entered."

He led them to the elevators and escorted them to room 1010. As they made their way to the room, Judith kept wondering how Larry knew so much about Las Vegas. *Had he ever been*? In all the years she knew him, the only trips he took were back home to visit his parents on holiday or a brief summer vacation. *How does he know so much?*

The four entered the room and were taken aback by the opulence. All but one. The planners knew how to welcome guests! Any dignitary would find the accommodation more than adequate. Two perfectly made queen-size beds. An ample supply of fresh towels with all the toiletries anyone could want. An oversized wall dresser housed a fifty-inch plasma flat screen and a small, well-stocked liquor cabinet. Everyone but Larry was impressed.

Judith jumped onto the first bed and claimed it for the girls. Muki and Abdul followed suit. Larry was standing in front of the huge bay window staring over Las Vegas Boulevard in deep thought.

Judith couldn't help but examine his broad shoulders and well-sculpted backside. Why hadn't she ever noticed this before? Irrelevant, or was it? "Larry, how do you know so much about this city? Have you been here before?"

He continued gazing at the night life of the streets. Cars clogging the main boulevard, taxis darting in and out for a new fare, the kids on the corners handing out (actually dropping more than being passed) cards promoting every strip club or sex line in town, and of course, the few prostitutes not good enough to work for the many escort services in town.

"Larry, did you hear me?" came an emphatic reminder. "Larry!"

He stood silent as a statue remembering the night his father took him, along with a former teammate, to Atlantic City after the Ravens thrashed the Jets. It was a memory he'd like to forget.

"Dammit, Larry. Am I talking to myself? I asked a simple question and believe I deserve a simple answer." She got up off the bed and thought about approaching his wide, muscular back in order to receive an answer.

Abdul jokingly warned her. "Be careful, young one. He could be discovering all the secrets of the universe, or even better, he could be pondering all the positions he and Cheryl might share." The thought of Larry being with Cheryl disgusted her. She took two steps towards him.

"I heard you," came the quiet words. "Dad and I were invited to catch a Ravens/Jets game by one of Dad's old teammates, Leroy. After the game, Dad told Leroy "we" would take him to Atlantic City.

"The Ravens kicked the shit out of the Jets. General Custer had a better chance than New York. The final score was 35-7. The victory gained home-field advantage for the Ravens and sent the Jets, a lowly 2-14, back to the drawing board." Larry slowly turned around, continuing the story. "We went to Harrah's. Dad liked it because it was on the northernmost side of the boardwalk. It drew a fair crowd but nothing like the one farther south. He liked the idea of being able to go outside and enjoy the calm of the sea and the waves coming in off the Atlantic. To him, it was a two-for-one; he could have fun and relax at the same time, without being buffeted for autographs and tourists saying, 'Hey, I know you' while he was concentrating on a hand." He stopped for a moment reflecting on the night. Judith, Muki and Abdul dared not interrupt. The fierceness in Larry's eyes indicated the night did not end well."

He turned around, facing his friends, staring at nothing.

"I was watching Dad and Leroy hammer away at the Twenty-One table. They were both up $5,000 apiece. Not too bad seeing how Leroy received a $10,000 bonus that day for making the play-offs. So why not spend a little of their winnings and add to

the New Jersey coffers so the Jets could afford a good draft pick."
He paused again rethinking how the evening unfolded.

"Two other men joined the table Dad and Leroy were playing at. They played very conservatively, throwing out comments about how cold the cards were. Dad told him they just needed patience and eventually their luck would turn. The men nodded in agreement and kept playing. After five hours and $10,000 up each, Dad decided it was time to call it a day. Leroy agreed.

"Before Dad got up he looked me in the eye and said, 'Son, remember one thing about gambling. It's a business. Treat it as a job and you'll always walk out with money in your pocket. If not, you'll wind up like our friends here who think gambling is a game.'

"They picked up their winnings, both tossing a $500 chip to the dealer, thanking him for such an entertaining evening. The dealer quickly deposited the chips in his pants pocket and continued dealing.

"Dad said, 'Come on son, let's get some air, then go back to the hotel. Leroy, want to join us?'

'Sure man. I could use a good stretch and maybe get something to eat.'

"Dad looked down at his gold Rolex as we walked outside. 'Leroy, it's 3:00am. Knowing your appetite, everything you eat will go straight to that enormous ass you carry around, and coach will blame me for you breaking weight again.'

"Leroy and I both laughed. Dad was right. Every time Leroy went over his optimum weight, the linebacker coach blamed Dad for the problem. 'Kowalski. How many times do I have to tell you to keep Brown at the correct weight? Are you deaf or just stupid?' Dad took it in stride and told the coach he'd handle it."

He walked past Judith to the mini bar removing a water.

"The night was brilliant. We walked outside and were immediately met with a brisk easterly wind full of the Atlantic salt air. We walked up to the boardwalk and rested on the rail. We didn't notice anyone else near us. Dad knew something didn't feel right, but let the thought slide—for the moment.

'You guys were pretty lucky tonight. What's your secret?' came the words. It was one of the men who'd been playing at the same table. He appeared to be Italian by his accent. He was all of five feet eight and maybe 175lbs. Dad turned his head innocently enough. 'Patience my friend, patience.'

"What should have been a leisurely encounter rapidly turned ugly.

'Patience huh?' The man looked back at his accomplice. 'Manny, why the fuck didn't we think of that? If we had patience, we too could have screwed the house and walked out with our pockets full.' He then looked straight at Dad. 'Look you motherfucker, if we wanted a history lesson, we'd still be in school, but I think Manny and I are little too old for that.'

'Yeah Carlos, we too smart for school. We got our own way,' replied Manny.

'Look guys,' Dad was trying to be nice, 'it's been a long day, and we don't want any trouble, okay?'

'Trouble? Manny, this cracker and his "boy" don't want any trouble. Manny, you want any trouble?'

'He moved his head side to side. 'No trouble, Carlos.'

'Tell ya what cracker, why don't you and Uncle Tom there just hand over the money and there won't be any trouble. Capisce?' The word "boy" disturbed Leroy, but the reference to Uncle Tom was too much.'

Larry walked back over to the window, crushing the plastic bottle in his hand.

"'Hey, you little Italian whop!' The words boomed over the wooden boardwalk, bouncing off any structure which attempted to stop them. 'If you and your scrawny friend don't beat a fast path to the nearest pizza house, you're gonna become a flying pepperoni. Capisce?'

'Hey nigger, I wasn't talking to—" Dad hated the word nigger. Each time the word was uttered on the field in rage, Dad would single the offender out and make sure he never used it again. He was fined and ejected from a few games for "unsportsmanlike conduct". He didn't care because the next time he faced the player, those words never came across his opponent's lips, or at least not loud enough for Dad to hear them.

"He grabbed Manny by the throat and pulled him close. 'Apologize to my friend or he's right. You will become a flying fucking whop.'

"Manny tried to force a few obscenities out of his constricted windpipe. The only sound was a frantic plea.

'Hey man. Let him go, or you gonna be swimming with the fish before the night is over.'

"I looked over at Carlos. He was wielding a nasty-looking, highly-polished/sharpened six-inch knife Dad and Leroy were strong and fully capable of handling most situations which arose. This was different. These guys meant business. Without thinking, I took off looking for a cop. I could hear Leroy yelling with his booming voice, 'YOU MOTHERFUCKERS...' "

"All three were sitting on the edge of the bed taking in the terrifying tale, daring not to interrupt.

"I couldn't have been gone more than five minutes when I returned with a couple of local cops. The sight that greeted us was gruesome. All four men were lying on the ground. Manny and Carlos weren't moving. Upon a quick examination, Dad had a nasty cut just above his left kneecap, and Leroy was holding a severe laceration on his right arm. The knife Carlos produced was buried deep in his back while blood leaked out of Manny's gut. It was a gruesome sight." The three gasped in shock as Larry described the macabre scene.

He turned staring at them; fire emanating from his eyes

"Does that answer your question, Judith? Yes, I've been here, and I learned. Any other questions?" His eyes were boring into her. She could see beads of perspiration pooling on her forehead. This wasn't the 'geek' from Stanford. Before her stood a man, a real man.

"No," came her meek reply.

"Okay, back to business. Abdul, what the hell were you doing in the casino? Were my instructions not clear?" Abdul shook his head in resignation.

"Alright, everyone is allowed one mistake. I guess it's for the best. You three got a taste of how fast the environment can flood your senses and become overwhelming. Lesson learned?"

They nodded in agreement.

"Good, let's get some food, grab some sleep and prepare to *rip this place!* Everyone in?"

All three stood up, formed an impromptu circle around Larry, raised their dominant hand, slapped high-fives and called out in unison, "This place is ours!"

* * *

The 2:00am wake-up call came right on time. Larry knew the clerk would be punctual. Sleeping guests might be getting some much-needed rest, but it also meant they weren't spending money. Judith was closest to the phone. Her first reaction was to send it screaming into a wall. She hated being awoken by anything other than her prized stereo with the Blues Brothers tune "Rawhide" to get her going. She jerked the receiver off the bracket. "Who the hell is this?"

"Good morning. This is your hostess Natalie." Natalie? Natalie! The words conjured up a scene best portrayed in a *Halloween* movie or even better, *Freddie versus Jason.* Judith's blood started boiling as she pictured *sweet* Natalie's demise.

"Listen you little—" Larry vaulted out of bed and wrenched the phone from her hands.

"Thank you for being so prompt, Natalie."

"I hope you are enjoying your stay, and if you need anything, don't hesitate to call."

"Thank you, Natalie. I believe everything is in order. Again, thank you for being so prompt and (he deliberately and concisely spoke the next word) c.o.u.r.t.e.o.u.s."

Judith could only stare at Larry with contempt and longing in her eyes. In all the years she'd spent around him, she never remembered seeing him with his shirt off and only sporting boxers. She was amazed at how perfectly sculpted his chest and upper-body muscles were. He never went to the gym or anything. He was always studying and would make snide remarks about the guys who would spend hours trying to build up the perfect body in hopes of luring some unlucky co-ed to their beds.

She pulled the pillow over her head to hide her disgust with Natalie interrupting a perfectly good dream, but also to hide the red tinge covering her face.

"Okay sleepyheads, ready to make some money?"

"Aye, Captain, but why must we battle so early? Surely the reactors need more charging before we venture off into the universe?" Muki agreed with Abdul's analysis.

"Because, Mr. Scott, the Romulans will never expect an assault at such an hour. Now, get moving!"

"Aye, Captain," came the groggy reply from Abdul. "Oh Captain, I don't think the Romulans will be impressed with your physique. Might think about finding a new tunic for battle."

Larry had forgotten, in his haste to save the room phone (and Natalie) from perfect destruction at the hands of Judith, what he was wearing. Despite his physical stature and well-developed body, he seldom went about advertising it.

"Good point, Scott." Larry moved to his overnight bag and pulled out a shirt he prized. It was a black T-shirt with a wicked-looking vampire on it. The vampire on the shirt appeared to be one particularly seductive and nasty female. Her mouth was wide open brandishing her fangs with blood streaming down them. He believed it would be his good-luck charm. It might even distract the dealers just enough so they wouldn't be able to concentrate completely on *beating the guests*. It would be his own secret weapon. Intimidation was the key. The house had its weapons; Larry had his.

"Come on guys, let's get moving."

One by one, the group made for the bathroom in shifts and prepared for the upcoming battle. Abdul suggested they get something to eat.

Larry flat out said "No! The casino wants you to eat before playing. The food they serve is packed with calories and sugar—another ploy. Eat too much and the house gains another edge," said Larry "No. We eat when we're done."

"What about coffee, surely they don't doctor that?" quizzed Judith.

"Coffee, juice, or milk is fine. But no food." The other three reluctantly agreed. "Judith, do us one thing."

"What's that, Larry?"

"Don't make a scene, please. We all know how pernickety you are when it comes to coffee."

"Aye, Captain. Two-to-one she throws the cup on the floor

when she realizes it isn't one-hundred percent Colombian blend."

"I think the odds are more than three-to-one she loses it," quipped Muki.

Judith shot out a stare that would kill and stormed into the bathroom. The words coming from behind the door were far from flattering as she described her accompanying trio.

Larry's words were quiet but audible from the other side of the door. "Best get it out of your system now, Judith. We don't want to see you escorted out." She heard them laughing behind the door.

"You all think you're so damned funny, don't you? Just wait until I break the house and wave my winnings (her voice started softening) in your face. You won't be laughing... (an image of Larry standing before her reflected onto the steamy mirror filling her with fire and desire) ...at me." She felt her blood heating up as she admired the image and pictured his muscular body pressing against hers. *You won't be laughing,* she quietly whispered to herself.

* * *

Larry led the three into the heart of the casino's nerve center—roulette wheels, electronic slots, and crap tables. However, those weren't the ones being sought out. They were all high-risk with the odds stacked against the most seasoned players. Hoots and hollers occasionally spiraled above the sounds of the other players and luring electronic voices emanated from the machines guaranteeing everyone was a winner. Every place you looked, the persuasion of becoming the next millionaire pulsed through the room like a gigantic magnet.

Larry let the group gain their bearings before moving them to their appointed destination—Twenty-One.

"How's your coffee, Judith?" he asked.

She glumly looked at Larry. "Motor oil tastes better than this shit."

"Good, glad you like it. Abdul, looks like you owe Muki some money already. It's been five minutes, and she's still holding the cup." A small smile crept across his lips with the words.

"Aye, Captain. It looks like she's pulled a hundred and eighty on me. Don't think I'll ever figure out women of this universe."

Judith saw an opening and took it. "How about any universe, you twit."

"Abdul, you can pay me after we've tried our luck. It would be bad luck to admit defeat before the battle has even begun." Muki's words were wise and true.

"Aye, my little Asian lotus blossom. You are wise beyond your years."

"This way, guys." Larry had pinpointed two tables. Each one only had two other players, who were looking weary from a night of having the house allow them to win on occasion, but in the end, they would leave the table with less than when they started.

"Remember! We aren't gambling. We're playing."

Larry pointed to Judith and Abdul. "You guys take the table to the right. Muki and I will take this one." Judith found herself feeling a little disappointed. She was hoping to sit with Larry if for no other reason than to be close to him. She was noticing he carried a hidden aura of confidence. "Good luck, guys. See you in five hours," he quipped as he and Muki headed to the table he'd chosen.

As Larry anticipated, the first few hours moved by quickly. He and Muki were holding their own. The cards started out cold and were continuing the trend. The odds were moving in their favor. There had been over eight different players over the hours. They were the typical "get rich quick" folks. They would win a few hands and get greedy only to watch the house, with one swipe of the hand, relinquish the would-be winners to grumbling losers. Each player would leave the table complaining how they'd been cheated or even better, "should have quit while I was ahead." They were right on one point; they should have quit while they were ahead instead of placing outrageous bets on hands that were doomed from the start. They were gamblers, not thinkers.

He wondered how Judith and Abdul were doing. He would occasionally hear Abdul rattle off some reference to Romulans or Klingons, a sure sign the cards weren't being kind. But nothing from Judith yet. He took that as a good sign. This wasn't the appropriate atmosphere for her violent temper to come boiling out. He looked back to make sure all was going well.

The only movement he detected was Judith's body slowly moving in and out. It was the calmest he'd ever seen her. Good, it appeared she was playing the game and not gambling. Something else caught his eye, her perfectly shaped butt. This wasn't the time for distractions. He turned around, displaying a grin to Muki, and prepared for the cards he knew were coming.

As he calculated, the cards were turning to the players' advantage, at least his and Muki's. The chips slowly started piling up in the next hour. Patience was paying off. Each player started with $5,000 each. It was agreed that if they dropped to one thousand dollars, they would walk away and wait for the others. They were not, under any circumstance, to try their luck at other games or machines or, a real no no, sit at the table with their friends and start chatting. This could cause unwanted attention. They were instructed to get something to eat and then immediately retire to the room and wait.

Abdul was out first. No big surprise. He showed promise in the car, but he was too easily distracted. "Aye, Lieutenant, you've gotten the best of me this round. I look forward to our next millennium meeting." He tossed a fifty-dollar chip to the dealer and made his way to the waiting buffet.

Judith hadn't heard or noticed he'd left. She was eyeing the cards and calculating bets. Another couple at the table were amazed how fearlessly she made her bets and awaited the next card. They could easily have mistaken her for a computer if it weren't for those firm nipples struggling to be freed and unencumbered. The male of the couple couldn't resist striking up a harmless conversation,

"Nice stack. Feeling lucky tonight?"

Judith was thinking if she should hold or hit. The dealer was showing fifteen without the down card. She was showing fifteen. Her bet was $4,000. She'd seen this hand in the car. She knew the odds were in her favor. She upped the bet to $5,000 and held. The small cards were becoming thinner with each turn. She held. The dealer held and flipped the down card. Ten of hearts. Bust!

"Damn honey," came the words from the Southern

gentleman. "I think I'd trade your stack for hers any day." His female companion let out a nervous laugh while Judith slowly raised her head, turned to the right and bore her eyes deep into his soul. She took a drink of her lukewarm motor oil, placed it back in the cup holder (without looking) and slowly lowered all but one finger on her right hand, then smiled.

"No need to be rude, darling. I was just joshing. Come on baby, let's find greener pastures." Judith smiled as the bothersome couple departed.

The tension and excitement she felt in the car during the test runs were nothing like the live sport. She was enjoying the game, and she was winning. It was more exhilarating than driving her car in competition. Each hand she won triggered another minor orgasm. Racing would get her adrenaline moving, but never had it ignited her engine. She knew she was winning. She knew the cards were falling in her favor. One thing she didn't notice was how much she was winning. Someone else did. He took a seat at the end of the table and watched.

The pendulum was swinging for Muki and Larry as well. The cards were coming fast and furious. They were on the third and last shoe of the shift. The shirt appeared to be working its magic. Larry kept a close eye on the dealer's hands as each card slid out of the shoe. The customer who complained about being cheated was right. The dealer knew what he was doing, and with a sleight of the hand, easily delt cards that guaranteed failure for the untrained eye. The dealer made no such move with Larry's. He'd done it to Muki twice, but not Larry. He played him head to head. Maybe the dealer feared that the caricature on his shirt would come to life if he attempted to cheat its owner.

Muki was still holding her own. She'd win a few and lose a few creating a good balance and low profile for her and Larry, as his stack started growing. His initial stack of $5,000 had grown to $55,000. He knew the next hour would be his last. The shift would change as would the cards. Starting over wasn't an option nor what they agreed on. Five hours and they were out no matter what the outcome. Larry decided it was time to shift into high gear and make the dealer earn his keep or actually congratulate a player for having a good night. He looked back one more time to check on Judith. Her breathing appeared to be deeper than before. She was definitely into the game. His eyes also fell onto the player at the end of the table. His gut tightened just a bit.

"Twenty-one to the young graduate," exclaimed the dealer, Jerry. Larry was beaming. He was up $50,000 with ten minutes to go, and by his count, there were only thirty cards left in the shoe—he decided to go for broke.

"Thank you, sir."

The dealer wasn't the only one congratulating the graduate; another pair of eyes also noted the winnings.

"Jerry, let's play one more." suggested Larry.

"Very good sir," replied Jerry.

The cards were true. Larry was looking at the ten of spades and king of diamonds. Jerry showed king of hearts. Muki was silently contemplating her hand—six of diamonds and ten of hearts. She held her bet at $500. If she won, her winnings would top $4,000. She held. The two other players at the table had folded. Larry took a deep breath, picked up five $1,000 chips and called. He took another deep breath in as the odds of the dealer flipping over the last remaining ace was not in the house's favor. Jerry smiled as his left index finger tapped the next card in the slot. Larry saw everything in slow motion as the card effortlessly crossed the green table and started to turn up. His heart sank heavily as he identified the ace of diamonds. Twenty-one to the house came the slow words tumbling out of Jerry's mouth. Larry was dejected. Had Jerry made a switch? Had he forgotten to "play the game" instead of gambling, or was it just bad luck? Larry congratulated Jerry and flipped him a $500 chip. "Thank you Jerry for a very entertaining evening. It has been a pleasure."

"Thank you, sir. We hope to see you again, sir." Yeah, Larry knew the dealer was sincere, as even though he lost $5,000 on the last hand, he was still walking away with an extra $40,000 of spending cash. No, it would be some time before he would give Caesars a chance to win back their money.

"How'd you do?" Judith's words were soft and even.

"Not too bad. I think we have enough for maybe an extra week or two on the road. How'd you make out?" Larry turned around and looked at her. Her hair and body was covered in sweat. Her chest was moving up and down unusually heavily. He couldn't help but notice her perfectly shaped nipples, (held in check by a sheer, red, Victoria's secret bra), protruding from her saturated white T-shirt.

"Not too bad if you consider $70,000 not bad." What did she say? $70,000? No way. No way. Judith could see the unbelievable look in his eyes. "Just look down and see." She was holding a wooden box (courtesy of the house) containing her winnings for the night.

Larry couldn't have been prouder of his star student. Muki stood in amazement at the winnings. She felt dwarfed by her friends' take. "I should have stayed home. Between you two, we could spend the whole summer on the road while Abdul and I provide the money for tolls."

"Let's go to the cashier and cash out. We don't want it all in cash. We'll take $10,000 in cash, $20,000 in travelers checks, and the rest we'll put in a joint account. Muki, go get Abdul while Judith and I take care of the money. It's time we enjoyed some of our winnings." Muki departed from the two "big winners" and went to retrieve Abdul.

"Judith, I think we should stay one more day and take in a show or two. What do you think?"

"That would be great. I think we've all earned it. One more day won't upset our vacation timetable, and we've all earned a night of fun and pleasure."

* * *

Nathan Francisco also admired the winnings of the kids, but he lived by a code, "Money that comes to Vegas, stays in Vegas." He would let the kids enjoy the winnings for a short time before making sure the money was returned to its rightful owners. He looked at his right-hand man.

"Arturo, looks as if they'll be spending another day here. Call some of the guys. We need to set up a watch. We don't want our friends leaving without saying goodbye."

Arturo pulled out his phone and punched the speed dial. "Louie, Nate wants you and Michael to get the guys together and meet us at Caesars. We've got some bird watching to do."

* * *

With the banking done, they all enjoyed a well-deserved five-star dinner, then bought tickets for Cirque du Soleil and Tom Jones. With the work done, they retired back to their room, pulled the shades and quickly passed out. They were exhausted.

* * *

"Louie, watch the elevators. Call if there are any changes."
"Yes boss."

* * *

The shows were everything they were billed as—outstanding and brilliant. Tom Jones wasn't the group's first choice of entertainer, but they couldn't help enjoying how the women (mostly in their 50s and 60s) were still throwing different pieces of underwear on the stage at the aging singer. He might have lost a step or two on the stage, but his personality showed through his years of performing. He was a true entertainer in every sense of the word.
    "What now 'O' great leader? What lands shall we conquer?" Larry knew exactly what "lands" Abdul was referring to. "Ladies, want to see how the girls in Vegas dance?"
    Judith jumped in. "Sure. I've been itching to see Abdul in action. This will be worth the price of admission." Muki would have preferred to go back to the room and watch TV. She didn't say a word and went along with her friends.

* * *

"Nate, they're going to Spearmint Rhino."
"Follow them," came the short response.

* * *

Abdul was the first to break the silence as they walked to the limo, "That was a waste of time. I don't understand why no one thought my comment was funny."

"What did you expect? A kiss or something? Asking a girl to check out your warp drive was lame to say the least." Judith's remark was filled with sarcasm and humor. "Anyway, they weren't that good looking. You were better off being rejected."

Abdul couldn't argue the fact. The girl he targeted, Cherry, was a beauty at first sight. Her curves were soft and hard. Her breasts appeared to be a product of silicon valley as they swayed awkwardly with her moves, not like Judith's. Cherry offered Abdul a table dance for fifty bucks and no touching.

Judith laughed at the proposal. "Abdul, if you pay her five dollars that would be too much. Look how she moves. All she wants to do is rub against you a little and steal fifty bucks."

Cherry wasn't amused with Judith's remark. "Think you can dance better than me, Bambi?" That was Cherry's first mistake, yet she continued. "I'm a highly trained professional and know what I'm doing."

That was her second mistake. Unbeknown to her friends, Judith was a very promising dancer in high school, until she suffered a terrible accident during a performance and ripped the tendons and ligaments to shreds in her ankle. The doctors wished she'd broken it. As it was, her dream of pursuing a professional career in dancing ended. She could still perform as long as the moves weren't overly strenuous or taxing.

"Cherry, I have no doubt you are a highly trained professional, just not in dance, and yes, I will dance rings around your skinny ass."

Cherry took great offense to the remark. "Tell ya what, Bambi," as she moved the gum around in her mouth, "we'll have a contest to determine who can dance. If I win, not only will Apu owe me fifty bucks, you will owe me a hundred since I'll be entertaining two guests at once."

"And if I win?" inquired Judith, with a hint of seduction in her voice. Cherry hadn't thought that far. The idea of losing never entered her mind. Realizing Miss Cherry was attempting to formulate a thought, Judith continued. "I'll make it easy. When I win, you will pay my friend here $100 and give him a free dance if he so chooses. Deal?"

Cherry thought it would be a cakewalk and accepted the terms. That was her third mistake. Three minutes later, Cherry was pulling a crisp $100 bill out of her white, lacy garter and handing it over to Abdul, who was starstruck. But it wasn't just him who was in shock. Muki, Larry, Cherry and a host of others were stunned with the performance Judith let loose. She was magnificent! Her body moved through the air with consummate ease and wile. She displayed every aspect of her hardened body.

The house lights danced and played on her firm body with each move she performed. No one, even the seasoned regulars, had ever seen a woman so wrapped up and confident in her own movements. Even Cherry stopped to take in the show. Judith became lost to the world as she let her hands move up and down over her taut figure. Her fingers flowed around her breasts and between her thighs as if she wore silk gloves. It was the most erotic show any of them would ever see in their lives. Before the song stopped, a thunderous applause burst forth from the tables surrounding the group. A stream of five-dollar bills rained down on their table. Cherry meekly handed over the money, deliberately brushing against Judith's breasts, quietly whispering, "You can dance for me anytime."

"Judith, where did you learn to dance like that anyway?" queried Larry.

"High school."

"Well I must admit, that was quite a performance. This must be the first time any man or woman walked out of a strip club with more money than when they entered." All agreed to that point.

"Guys, it's been a very wonderful and exciting evening. I suggest we get a bite to eat and call it a day. We need our sleep, and Judith wants to leave town as the sun starts setting. Tomorrow we leave on our next adventure."

"Aye, Captain, it's time to recharge the crystals and prepare for a new battle. The Klingons will not win two in a row. I'll be ready next time."

"Abdul," interjected Muki, "is it possible for you to speak in English, or must you always speak in a tongue none of us care to listen to?" Larry and Judith nodded in agreement.

"Oh yes, my small Asian ninja, badass, martial arts master. I speak so others may follow and learn."

"The only thing we learn from your so-called intelligence is that it's severely lacking." The tone she used was patronizing at best. It was the first any of them were seeing this side of Muki. First the demise of the rednecks at the diner, and now hard, straight sarcasm?

There was a reason she'd hesitated to enter the strip club. She never elaborated about her parents' lives in Vietnam. None of them knew that one of her aunts was captured when Saigon fell, and was forced into a house of pleasure for the victors from the north. None of them knew the degradation which fell upon her namesake, so she kept it to herself. That's why she would rather have stayed in the room watching TV than thinking about her aunt performing for the venomous North Vietnamese Communist bastards!

Larry hustled his group into the waiting limo and instructed the driver to take them to the Shibuya. As Larry proceeded to slide into the car, he felt a mild twitch in his stomach, the same one he'd felt at the casino. His eyes caught a glimpse of a man on a cell phone wearing sunglasses.

"They're moving again."

"Keep them in sight, Louie. Fail now and—"

"I will not fail, Nathan."

"Good." The line went dead.

* * *

The phone rang at exactly 5:30pm awakening the conquerors of Vegas. Judith wasn't as abrupt this time with the interruption of her sleep. In a half-awake voice, she answered the call. "Hello."

"Good evening, this is Natalie your hostess for the evening."

"Hello, Natalie."

"Is there anything I can get you and your friends? The

manager has instructed me to comp your party with anything you wish." Judith pondered the thought for a moment. Should they go downstairs and eat or would it be better to dine in the room? "Natalie, can we still get breakfast at this hour?"

"Yes, anything you want."

"Okay, send up four plates of sausage, bacon, scrambled eggs, toast with jelly, blueberry muffins, a pitcher of whole milk, orange juice and good, hot coffee. We also need four fried eggs, sunny-side up and six hard-boiled eggs."

"Will there be anything else, Miss Anderson?"

"Get some cinnamon rolls," called out Larry. "Got to have cinnamon rolls."

"Yes, six cinnamon rolls."

"Yes, ma'am. We will have the order delivered in twenty minutes. Is there anything else?"

"No Natalie, that will be all, and thank you for being such a wonderful hostess." It was easy to be humble when you realized you not only beat the house, but the house was offering free food in the hopes you might stay one more night. Not this time. This group was leaving with their pockets full.

"Breakfast will be here in twenty minutes. I'm taking a shower and getting ready for the midnight drive."

The group finished breakfast, took a shower and gathered up their belongings. Larry smiled as the words of Julius Caesar moved through his mind, *vini, vidi, vici.* Yes, we did and closed the door.

"You guys wait here. I'll go and get the car. Be back in five."

* * *

"Boss, they're moving again. Looks like they're leaving town."

"Keep an eye on them. Make sure you identify what type of car they're driving. We'll be there in ten minutes."

* * *

Larry pulled Judith's Camaro gently under the entrance,

extremely careful not to park too close to any of the other guests' cars, cabs, or limos waiting for their patrons. He didn't want to have to explain to her why there was a new ding or scratch on her baby. The three appeared from the perfectly polished glass doors. If you didn't look and notice the gold frame, it would be easy to walk right into the glass panes, creating a moment of amusement and embarrassment, all in one. And if a guest happened to be holding their new Apple iPhone or Android, you would become a YouTube sensation in seconds.

"Let's go, guys," called out Judith. "The sun is setting, and I want to catch a few rays in the rearview mirror before the real drive starts. I love starting on the road at twilight. It energizes me." Muki and Abdul followed in her footsteps. The bags were placed in the trunk with precision. They didn't notice the Gray 2010 Cadillac that pulled in behind them.

"Everyone packed? Sure we didn't forget anything? Cause if you did, it's too late now. The road is mine!"

Judith sat down in her plush red seats and turned her baby over. The sound and feeling of the power under the hood reverberated through every sense. She could feel through the steering wheel if all cylinders were firing. She loved the feeling of power. Muki and Abdul climbed into the back seat as they were the smallest. Larry smiled at them as they crammed into the not-too-spacious rear seat. His eyes couldn't help but notice the dark-skinned man motioning to the men in the Cadillac. His finger pointed slightly at the Camaro.

CHAPTER 5

PIOCHE, NEVADA

"Let's blow this town!" resounded Judith. She engaged the selector to *drive*, and pulled her baby onto the crowded Las Vegas Boulevard, making sure no tourists or foreigners were gawking at the female patrons strutting their stuff, thus accidentally hitting her car. "Keep your distance you morons, if you know what's good for you," she yelled out the window.

Larry was watching the traffic as she tepidly maneuvered *her baby* into the teeming road. "Is there a problem?" he asked.

"No. Just want to make sure these foreigners are bona fide American drivers and don't pull any right lane driving shit."

"Okay."

"Captain, is there a problem? Point out the alien offender and I will—"

All three responded to Abdul's ill-timed comments.

"SHUT UP!"

"Captain, if you need me, the phaser banks are charged and…"

"SHUT UP!" they yelled again.

She nudged the car through the packed street, making her way west onto Sahara Boulevard and hopefully freedom. The signs for I-15 loomed ahead as the last rays of sunlight glistened off the Sierra Nevada mountains to the west. The rays of light danced off the snow-covered peaks creating deep dazzling purple and orange hues.

"Larry, take a picture before the sun sets. Isn't it beautiful?"

Larry pulled his Apple 400 iPhone out and snapped a few quick pictures. He really liked this phone. Unlike its predecessors, it contained an anti-vibration device. It was almost as good as Nikon's new 5000 RX. "I'll forward them to your email."

Judith's eyes never wavered from the peaks as her whole

body absorbed the scene. "Okay."

The car pulled up to the stop light at the intersection of Sahara and the service road and the wide expanses of the interstate. She punched her ten-selection CD player and chose her favorite all time album, Bob Seger's *Night Moves*. As far as she was concerned it was the greatest album produced of all time, and that included the Beatles' *White Album* and Michael Jackson's *Thriller*. No one could describe the life of a band the way Bob did. His words and melodies were exquisitely written. She'd hoped he would have been at the Mega concert in Los Angeles, but according to the press release, he was recovering from a bad bout of laryngitis.

The light turned green. She turned to the right and the expanses of I-15 and US 93. Her right thumb depressed the volume increase button until the sounds were booming out of the open windows. She could feel the vibration from the song "Night Moves" pulsating through the speakers in time with the rhythm of the concrete rumbling through the Michelin tires. She was becoming one with the road.

"Buckle up, boys and girls. Mama's gonna take you for a ride." The speedometer quickly approached eighty mph in a flash. It felt as if the car were riding on a mill-pond ocean.

Judith was lost in the words of the song as the Camaro stretched its legs and went into cruising mode. The song also had Larry thinking back to the night at The Spearmint Rhino. He could see Judith moving to the music of AC/DC's "Thunderstruck." Yes, she had brought the thunder down that night. There wasn't a loose pair of male jeans in the house. He flashed his brilliant white teeth, laughing to himself at the sight his memory re-created. The smile slowly disappeared as he looked into the side-view mirror and adjusted the knob for a better view. Yes, it was the same car with the same men fifty yards behind them. The twitch he felt at the casino and when they were loading the car was starting to gnaw at him again. This wasn't a coincidence. They were being followed.

* * *

"Boss, I got 'em. They ain't going nowhere."

"Louie, if you lose them, remember, there is plenty of desert out here, and we have plenty of shovels in the trunk."

"Boss, don't worry. I'm on this."

The words were short and harsh coming from Nathan, "You better not, or you'll be joining Archie and his boys."

How could Louie forget what happened to Archie? He and his boys came in one night to Caesars to celebrate their good fortune at the track. It must have been their lucky day. Not only did they pocket a cool $20,000 at the track (of course they were given some real good paid tips); they were cleaning up at the blackjack and craps' tables. The group was up $100,000 in winnings. They thought the night would never end. It didn't. It was okay for people to win at Caesars, but when people from out of town started winning big, that was unacceptable. Nathan changed the commercialized slogan of "What happens in Vegas, stays in Vegas," to "Money comes to Vegas and stays in Vegas."

He was proud of the coined slogan. Archie and his friends were never allowed the time to enjoy the earnings. Nathan and his boys followed Archie and his men for one hundred miles. They pulled up alongside Archie's car and shot out the front tire. The accident was deadly enough. Most of the occupants inside the car died after it tumbled a three-sixty for the third time.

Nathan and his boys relieved the dearly departed of the day's hard-won earnings, packed them into the trunk of his car and disposed of the bodies deep in the desert. It would be months, or better, years before the bodies were discovered, if ever.

Louie knew the target tonight was kids. He didn't have a problem with killing adults, but kids? They were the same age as his own son and daughter. But they had been way too lucky, and it was as Nathan said, "Money comes to Vegas and stays in Vegas." His only regret was that Nathan was very specific about the brunette.

"No one touches her. We are only after the money. If anyone has any ideas of breeding her, you'll be joining her. Capisce?"

Each member acknowledged the mention loud and clear, "Yes sir."

* * *

The road sign stated they were coming up to the split for I-15 and US 93 in five miles. Muki and Abdul were nodding in and out of sleep. Judith's eyes were transfixed on the white stripes passing by in a blinding flash under her halogen high beams.

Larry reached over and turned down the song "Main Street."

"What the fuck are you doing, Larry? When you drive, you can choose the music. For right now, I'm driving, and if you don't want your fingers broken, you'll take them off that volume button right now."

"Judith, we're being followed." The words took her by surprise.

"What do you mean?"

"Yes Larry, what do you mean?" Muki quietly asked.

"I think we're being followed."

Judith looked at Muki in the rearview mirror and rolled her eyes. Muki wasn't quite so sure this was a joke.

"Okay, Sherlock," retorted Judith as her sarcasm spewed out, "what makes you think the bad guys are after us?"

"When we were playing, there was a guy sitting at the end of your table, Judith. He was more interested in watching you play than playing his own hand. I got the same feeling I had back in Atlantic City."

"You're being paranoid, Sherlock. No one's after our goodies or virtue," Judith laughed at her wit.

Larry continued.

"There was also a guy who congratulated me on the night's winnings. His smile was anything but flattering. There was something sinister in his words and looks." Larry was now getting the attention of the girls.

"I noticed the same guy at the strip club and also in the lobby when we were checking out. I didn't say anything because, like you, I thought I was being paranoid. However, I took note of the car he got into as we were leaving Caesars. It's the same Cadillac."

Judith depressed the volume button to mute.

"Do you think we're in danger?" The question from Judith

was full of angst. She was remembering the two truckers back in Jean. The thought sent a shiver up her spine.

"I don't know, but I'm betting they aren't out taking in the sights. Like my father and Leroy, I believe they feel they deserve our winnings more than us."

Abdul stirred a bit noticing the music was no longer blaring at warp speed. "What's going on?"

Muki leaned over. "Larry thinks we're being followed, and he's serious. This isn't the time for any Star Trek or Star Wars bullshit. He's dead serious."

"What do you suggest we do?" Judith was serious with the question.

"We need to make sure they're not following us. I don't want to make a wrong assumption. US 93—The Great Basin Highway exit is coming up. Let's exit and head north. If they are following us, I'll try and see if I can map out an escape route.

"Wouldn't it be better if we stayed on the interstate?" asked Muki.

"I don't think so. If these men are after the money, they'll stop at nothing to relieve us of the winnings. They could do it at a rest stop or a diner along the way when we stop. They might even go so far as following us to Denver. No, we need to be sure and lose them if at all possible. There's the exit, Judith. Turn on your blinker and stay calm."

She eased the car off the interstate.

* * *

"Boss?"
"I see it. Follow them."

* * *

"Which way, Larry?" Judith forced the words through her parched lips.

"Left. We're going north. If they continue following, we'll take Kane Spring Road and head towards Caliente and Pioche." Judith obeyed and turned the car north onto 93.

"Judith, one other thing. I don't want them to think we know they're following us, so keep it around seventy. Let them make the first move. Two-lane highways don't allow as much maneuvering room as the interstate. When the time comes, I'm sure you and your baby will perform adequately." She nodded in agreement.

* * *

"Boss?"

"Take a right. We'll use the service road for about a mile and then double back. We don't want to frighten our friends." Nathan's thin smile covered his rough face.

* * *

"Are they following us?" Judith was more scared than curious.

"No. They turned right." They all released a deep sigh of relief.

"Captain, it appears you got a bit spooked."

"Abdul, a good Star Fleet commander never underestimates his prey. Too bad you haven't installed a cloaking device. We could certainly use it."

"Aye, Captain. Blame Star Fleet command. They felt it beneath themselves to use stolen property for our own ventures." Larry and Abdul (even the girls) enjoyed the small sparring. They all became much more relaxed.

"Okay Larry," questioned Judith. "What now?" The question wasn't as innocent as it came across.

"Let her ride, Judith. I don't think there'll be many cops patrolling tonight. Let's see what you and your baby can do."

Without a second thought, she turned mute off and floored the accelerator pedal to a surging ninety-five mph. Her three passengers were amazed at how effortlessly she navigated the curves. At no time was anyone worried about their young lives being extinguished. Judith knew exactly how to anticipate each curve and dip in the road. They were sailing on glass and jamming to tunes.

* * *

"Louie, turn around. We don't want to lose them now, do we?" Nate's order was precise.

No, Louie didn't want to lose them. He couldn't help but notice the barren landscape as the moonlight reflected off the sagebrush and sand. Losing them wasn't an option.

* * *

Larry pulled out a Marlboro Light (much to the displeasure of Judith), flipped open his Zippo lighter and ignited the end. He always enjoyed the first drag filling his lungs with the sweet taste of nicotine. He only lit up when he'd averted a particularly strenuous moment, or was facing one.

"Drop one ash on my seat, and you'll be smoking it through your ass." She didn't care if people smoked; she just never understood the habit and wasn't about to let him damage her baby.

"Don't worry, Judith. I have it well in hand."

She turned the volume down enough to talk without yelling. "Do you really think they were after us?"

"I don't know, maybe I was being paranoid. It felt as if I were back in Atlantic City the night Dad and Leroy killed those two guys and walked away with relatively minor injuries. Maybe I overreacted."

"Aye, Captain, it was a good drill to keep the troops in line. Next time let us know if it's only a drill. I wasn't properly—"

Muki led the charge. "SHUT UP!"

Larry finished his partly-smoked cigarette, flicking it into the dark Nevada night. He pulled the GPS locator up on his phone.

"We should be arriving at the junction of 375, 318 and 93. We can take 93 straight into Cedar City and hook back on I-15, or if you feel adventurous, you can keep going north to Wendover and catch I-80. The second would definitely be the scenic drive. Dealer's choice."

Judith smiled at having options. She also knew that her baby's engine could have a voracious appetite for fuel.

"Which route has more fuel and rest stations?"

Larry glanced once as he magnified the four-inch screen and panned the easterly path. "Cedar City would be the best option."

"Then Cedar City it is."

* * *

"Arturo, you see anything yet?" Nate was getting impatient, and Louie was feeling desperate. Arturo was standing up in the back seat. The special sunroof was open so he could use the AN/PVS-24 night scope.

"I think so, boss. Yes, I see them. They're about two miles ahead." Louie let out a sigh of relief.

"They're turning left at the junction."

"Good. Louie, keep this current distance. Don't want to scare them. We'll intercept them at the 93 N/E junction."

* * *

The night air was rushing through the open windows; exactly what the doctor ordered after a few grueling days in Vegas. The air was hot and dry, but with the sun down, it also provided a crisp, clean coolness to the plants and animals that were baked daily. *How does anything survive out here during the day?* thought Judith. It amazed her how teeming the desert was with life. She thought about the brave men and women who tested fate back in the early nineteenth century crossing this barren wasteland with only the provisions a Conestoga wagon could hold. *Those were true pioneers. Everything else we do pales in comparison.* Judith had slowed her baby down to a respectable seventy mph. She sure didn't want to run out of gas in the middle of nowhere.

Larry dozed off as the whine of rubber on asphalt vibrated him in and out of consciousness. He thought he saw a pair of headlights flicker in the side-view mirror as his eye lids danced up and down.

* * *

"Louie, we're ten miles from the junction. We'll play this the same as Archie. I want you to speed up, and I'll shoot out the front tire. When the car stops rolling, Michael and Arturo will get the bodies and stash them in the trunk. We'll go through all of the luggage and make sure we collect everything that belongs back home. Any questions?" No one answered. They all knew their jobs.

* * *

Judith saw the junction signs approaching. She could continue straight and make for Cedar City or turn north for Wendover. The gas gauge was sitting at half full. It would be fun to travel north and keep testing the Nevada asphalt, but it was a long way to Denver and from what Larry said, it would add at least two hours to the drive to Denver. She decided on Cedar City. They could catch I-80 on the way back. She looked up in the rearview mirror as she chose another fine selection of music, *Blue's Brothers Live*. There was a pair of headlights closing in.

* * *

"Now, Louie. Go!" The 4.6 liter dual overhead camshaft Northstar V-8 roared to life. Nat checked his custom-made Desert Eagle knowing it would only take one round to turn the tire on the Camaro to burnt rubber.

* * *

Judith watched the headlights approaching at a screaming speed. "Larry. Larry. Wake up. They're back!"

Larry quickly brought himself to consciousness. He looked into the side mirror. It was the same pair of headlights from earlier. He was correct in his first assumption. These men wanted what they'd taken from Vegas and obviously would go to any lengths to obtain it.

"Judith, have we passed the junction for 93 E and 93 N?"

"No, it's coming up in about one-thousand feet."

"Good, keep your current speed. The road going east is straight and wide open according to the GPS. I want you to let them close within fifty feet. They aren't going to try and ram us or push us off the road. I believe they're going to try and pull up alongside and either force us off the road or shoot out the tires. You need to let them get almost side by side and slam on the brakes. They'll shoot by us like a rocket at this speed. Take 93 North and gun it. I'll check the map for our next move."

Judith said nothing. She kept the approaching lights in full view. She was preparing for an exceedingly dangerous, yet vital, move. Her driving skills were about to be severely tested.

"Muki, Abdul, wake up—we're being followed." They both rubbed their eyes attempting to focus in on Larry. "Guys, we're being followed, and I don't think they want to congratulate us on our good luck at the tables. I believe they want to collect what we won and dispose of the evidence. Judith and I have worked out a tentative escape route. Be ready to brace yourselves and make sure you're buckled up."

Muki and Abdul stared at each other in disbelief, but followed Larry's instructions. They knew by the tone in his voice this wasn't a prank.

"Can you see any of the passengers, Judith?"

"Yes. I can see one man. From what I can see, he's giving the driver directions, and I think he has a gun in his right hand."

"Okay, keep your eye on the passenger. If he lifts his hand into a firing position, let me know. We might have to change our plan." Judith kept one eye on the road and one on the passenger. For most, this would be a real challenge, but then most aren't race car drivers. She had learned the art of concentrating on the road and the gauges simultaneously.

"Here comes the junction, one hundred feet and closing. Keep your speed."

Without moving her eyes from the passenger who was starting to raise his right hand, she informed Larry, "I know exactly what I'm doing. You make sure you're strapped in tight.

This is gonna get hairy."

The intersection was now only fifty feet and closing fast. She could see at least two gold teeth in the passenger's mouth as the Cadillac was coming alongside. The men in the car were all dressed in very dark suits. Facial recognition was impossible— what wasn't though was the gun being pointed at the front tire. The face of the passenger was taking on a menacing smile as it appeared he was lining up for the shot.

"Hang on!" She slammed her foot on the brake. Smoke billowed out from the screaming tires. Normal street tires would have immediately blown out from the intense friction between rubber and asphalt. When she bought the car, Dean Smith suggested they put some real tires on it—Michelin 5000XL's at $1,000 each. Couldn't have her sliding into a ditch doing eighty around a curve. She thought she heard a loud pop as the Cadillac rocketed by her at seventy mph. Before the car came to a complete stop, she was romping on the accelerator again, spinning the car one-eighty degrees and shooting back to 93 N. The race for time had begun.

* * *

"Dammit," yelled Nate. "The bitch braked just as I took the shot. Louie, turn us around. She wants to play games, does she? We too shall play games with her."

"Yes boss." It took over four hundred feet to bring the Cadillac to a stop. Louie frantically turned the car around and took up the pursuit.

* * *

"Now what?" demanded Judith.

"I'm looking. The next town is Pioche, about twenty-two miles up the road. There are also a lot of dirt roads in the area."

Muki and Abdul were regaining their breath and senses from the radical moves Judith had just put the car through. In a trembling tone, Muki threw out a suggestion. "Shouldn't we try to find a police or highway patrol station in the next town?"

"Yeah," chimed in Abdul. "Let's go to the cops."

Larry thought about it for a minute looking at the small town approaching on the GPS. Population: two-thousand. The chances of the town having a full-time police force were remote at best. "No, we have to lose these guys. If they follow us to the police station, and it's open, they won't hesitate to kill all of us. No, we have to lose them. Judith, keep your foot on the accelerator. On the south side of town, there's a branch road, Business 321."

"Got it," came her calm reply. "With some good luck, I'll drive circles around them." She hoped.

* * *

"Do you see them, Arturo?" The words were harsh and hateful. Nathan never anticipated the female driver would attempt such a dangerous move. He wouldn't make that mistake twice.

"No boss. No sign of them."

"Keep looking dammit! Louie, if you lose them..." Nothing else needed to be spoken.

Louie pushed the accelerator farther down.

* * *

Judith swung the car onto 321, cautiously moving the car into the sleepy little town. There were a few buildings dotting the business district, showing very little, if any, life. The only signs of activity were the flashing lights from the Overland Hotel and Saloon. She was surprised the residents hadn't rolled up the sidewalks.

"Okay genius, now what? Do we stay on 321 or take 322 into downtown (she laughed) Pioche?"

Larry glanced at his GPS satellite map. As he feared, there was nothing in town to offer a really good hiding place. He needed to find a location where they could catch their breath and plan the next move. "Stay on 321. The elementary school is just up the road. I doubt they have any parking lot lights. It'll be a good spot to regroup."

"And if it does have lights?"

"We'll take our chances."

* * *

"Arturo, see anything?"

"Not yet, boss."

"Boss," added Louie, "You want me to take the split or pull into the police station?"

It had been a while since Nate had paid a visit to his second cousin Alonzo. It'd been five years since the family reunion in Vegas for Alonzo's daughter's wedding. He doubted Alonzo would be up, but hey, they were in town. "Good thinking, Louie. Let's see if the Chief of Police is in."

* * *

Judith pulled the car into the dark parking lot. Larry suggested she turn off the lights, but leave the engine running. The four got out and stretched their nervous twitching legs. The full moon cast an eerie glimmer off the asphalt and surrounding buildings, as the cool breeze blowing in off the foothills of the Sierra's revived their dampened spirits—a little.

"Now what?"

Larry studied the layout of the town. "I don't know. We can't go backwards."

"Why is that, Captain? They wouldn't expect us to backtrack."

"True, but if they have more friends, they would certainly have a car south of town waiting on us. That would be the smart move. No, we have to keep going north."

"North to where, genius?" demanded Judith. "Wendover? We'll never make it."

Larry knew Judith was right. Those guys wanted the money and weren't worried about how they obtained it. "There's a police/fire station not more than a quarter mile up the road. I doubt our pursuers would take up position there. I think it's our best bet. We might be able to hold up there and wait for the sun to rise."

"And if that doesn't work?" snapped Judith.

Larry's mind was racing a thousand miles a minute trying to

plan out an escape, and the last thing he needed was Judith's sarcasm."I don't know. Okay? I don't fucking know. It's not every day you get chased by the mob, but if you have a better idea, then it's time to share it. Okay?"

Judith quickly backed down. She didn't appreciate being reprimanded by anyone, yet she was willing to take a small lashing from Larry. "Okay," she sheepishly replied.

* * *

"How ya doing, Alonzo? What's it been, five years since I kicked your ass?"

"Nathan, it's been over ten years, and as I recall, it was you lying on the ground, not me." Both men embraced each other with honest laughter, applying a kiss to each cheek.

At first glance, one would have thought they were brothers. Each man was six feet two, a hefty two fifty pounds, large arms, and jet-black hair. The only difference was the full, black mustache on Nathan and his two golden teeth.

"What are you and your friends doing in town?"

"Well, we got a problem with some college kids. They took something that doesn't belong to them, and we think they're holding up here."

"Do you need some help with the problem?" queried Alonzo.

"That's not such a bad idea. I don't think they'll go south; I'm betting they're going to make a break to the north in hopes of escaping. The boys and I will go north and cover the 321/93 junction. You stay here and herd them towards us if they backtrack. How's that sound?"

Alonzo flashed his pearly whites. "Like herding the steer to the slaughterhouse. Let me get a few coffees to go before we head out."

Nathan was all for a good shot of caffeine. Alonzo was a master with espresso, and his special blend would provide an added burst of energy and alertness his crew would need, for the upcoming encounter. "Sounds good to me."

* * *

"There it is on the left, Judith. Looks like somebody's there. The garage door is open, and the lights are on. This could be our lucky night." Larry took a deep breath of relief as she slowly pulled the car into the parking lot.

"OH SHIT! IT'S THEM!" Without a second thought, Judith slammed on the accelerator leaving a choking cloud of blue smoke in the parking lot.

"WHICH WAY DAMMIT. WHICH WAY?' Came the panicked words from her mouth.

"WHICH WAY?"

"NORTH. GET ON THE HIGHWAY AND GO NORTH!" yelled Larry.

* * *

"Shit. It's those kids!" Nathan forced the words out as he choked on the hot coffee, and tasted the burning rubber in his nose and mouth.

"Louie, quit standing around and get the car started. Alonzo, you take the lead. They'll be more inclined to pull over for a cop." Alonzo agreed.

He jumped into the 2005 Chevy Blazer, turned on the lights and took up the chase.

* * *

"Shit, now the cops are following us." Judith could see the cherries spinning brightly on top of the cop car. "What the hell are we going to do now?"

The words from Muki were succinct and calm. It was the first time she had offered a suggestion. "Stay calm and he'll find us an off road. It's obvious the cops and the men chasing us are acquainted. Just stay calm, Judith. Larry, find us an escape route." Larry glanced down at the GPS and found something odd, but a potential hiding spot.

"Judith, I need you to push yourself and your baby as fast and as hard as you can. In three miles, we'll be taking a hard right, but you can't leave any skid marks on the pavement. Understood?" Judith nodded.

"What did you find?" asked Muki.

"I don't know. It appears to be some kind of government complex or something. Most of the area is blacked-out with these large green circles. I can make out one road and maybe an outbuilding. I think it's our best bet." He handed his phone to Muki, who agreed with his deduction.

Abdul leaned over looking at the screen. "Captain, think we'll find any Klingons?"

Larry reached back for the phone and sent Abdul a decidedly unfriendly glare.

Judith pushed the car to one-hundred mph. Larry started counting down the distance to the turnoff, glancing back and forth to make sure he couldn't see the flashing lights of the cops. He started counting down for Judith. "Four hundred, three hundred, two hundred." The engine was easing up. "One hundred, fifty—NOW!" Judith was already anticipating the turn. From the description he'd provided she could take the turn at thirty with no problems.

It didn't appear the road Larry chose was in use. The yellow center stripe and the white ones for the edge of the road were well-worn and faded. It didn't matter. The surface was solid, and she was pushing the speedometer back to eighty.

* * *

"I don't know, boss. They could have turned off anywhere. I can call some people in Salt Lake and Wendover to keep an eye out, but other than that, we could spend the next two days driving up and down these roads looking for them."

Nathan pulled out a cigar, clipped the end and lit it up. "I think you're right, Lonzo, I think you're right." He drew in a deep draw from it. "Lonzo, if you wanted to hide something and didn't want it found for say six months or a few years, what would you suggest?"

"About a mile back there's a road that goes east for about two miles and dead-ends. The four-wheelers and bikers usually don't go out there. They prefer doing their thing about a mile off the road."

Nathan thought about it for a few minutes as he pulled out his Desert Eagle.

"I warned you, Louie." The gunshot was soaked up in the desert sands.

CHAPTER 6

THE COMPLEX

Judith never applied the brake as she sped down the old abandoned road. Larry kept a vigil with his eyes glued to the side mirror, hoping against hope he didn't see any headlights. He knew the road he'd decided on in the heat of the moment provided no exit route. The complex (whatever it was) appeared to cover ten square miles as indicated by the massive green circles on the screen. Even with its vast expanse, there weren't a lot of roads to choose from. The one they were on was the main drag with a few feeders connecting to it. The headlights started to reflect off something metallic in the distance.

"Larry, looks like a fence."

"Sure does. Keep going."

She didn't need to be told twice, and eased the car down to a calm seventy-five mph as they flashed by what appeared to be an old guard shack. They didn't stop to investigate. She plunged the car deeper and deeper into the dark. If they'd stopped, they would have noticed the weathered sign on the guard shack's door. In large black letters on a white background—UNITED STATES ARMY PROPERTY: TRESPASSERS WILL BE SHOT."

* * *

A small icon appeared on the monitor with a warning message scrolling across the bottom, *intruder alert.* It wasn't the first time something had triggered the motion sensor at the entrance. He pulled up the surveillance camera feed, and saw dust slowly settling back on the pitch-black road. *Damned high school kids.*

* * *

"Okay Judith, ease up. I don't think they're following us anymore. Muki, Abdul, you guys doing okay?"

"Aye, Captain, but I fear if you don't find a place to pull over, we could have a cataclysmic accident in engineering."

"Abdul, you so much as put a wet spot on my seat, and you'll spend the rest of your life sitting down to pee. Understood?"

"Aye, then pull over. I would still like to bear some children for the academy." Muki nodded in agreement.

"Okay, I guess anywhere will do." She pulled the car over, turned off the lights, but left the motor running. The adrenaline rush was starting to wear off. She felt complete exhaustion as she stepped out to regroup and reconsider the last few hours. The diner was distressing enough, but this was different. Those men wanted to kill them and leave no witnesses.

Larry walked around to her side of the car as she stretched her hard, weary body. *My God, she's beautiful.* As she attempted to relax from the long stretch, her legs gave out. He arrived at her side just in time. She felt Larry's strong hands catch her to avoid the impending fall.

"Thanks."

His hands were feeling her warm, perspiring skin. The sense of her racing heart ran through his arms, igniting his hidden feelings of want and desire. A strange, tight knot pulled at his stomach as his mouth went dry. It was the first time he'd embraced her, and he wasn't disappointed.

Instead of being outraged and lashing out at him, she hesitantly replied, "Thank you."

"No problem. Can't have our number-one driver getting injured now, can we?"

She tossed him a sweet little smile as he nervously held her quivering body.

"Don't mean to break up the lovefest, Captain," blurted out Abdul, "but what are we going to do now?"

Judith wriggled out of Larry's grasp. "Look, you little shit, one more comment like that and—"

Muki had heard enough. In a soft, forceful voice, "Judith, shut up."

The only sounds heard for a minute or two were the crickets hidden deep in the surroundings.

Once the uncomfortable silence passed, Larry continued his thought.

"Good question Abdul. I think we should see if we can find a building with a little shelter and hold up here for the night. I don't want to tempt our good fortune." The other three agreed with Larry.

"Okay Einstein, where to?" queried Judith.

"According to the GPS, there's some type of building three miles ahead of us. We'll try that one first."

"You sure about that, Captain?"

"Why, Abdul?"

"Muki, you want to tell him or should I?"

"Go ahead, you saw it first."

"While we were answering the call of mother nature, we noticed a huge building about fifty feet away. When I say huge, I mean Enterprise huge. I thought my eyes were playing tricks in the dark, but the longer I stared, the larger it became. It was blacker than the night. You know the vision, right?"

"Yes, kind of. What's your point?"

"What is something that large doing in the middle of nowhere?" Larry pulled up the GPS and saw what Abdul described was underneath one of the large green circles.

"I don't know, and I'm too tired to think about it, okay?" The answer didn't satisfy Abdul or Muki. They were all tired and hoped the building Larry was directing them to would have a place they could sleep and relax. They would visit the topic when everyone was rested and thinking a little straighter.

"There it is, home sweet home," commented Judith.

Abdul peered through the small back window. "Doesn't appear anyone's home."

"Well, there's only one way to find out. Judith, pull the car to the north side of the building. Looks like there's an old parking lot which might provide a little cover."

Judith concurred, and pulled her purring baby to the side of the whitewashed, drab-looking structure. She was pleased to see there was an old carport to pull under. The weather on the west slope of the range could change with the drop of a hat and result in large hail stones pummeling her baby, which wasn't a pleasant thought. "You did good, baby." She put the selector in *park* and turned off the engine.

Larry slowly approached the front door with trepidation. It appeared that whatever the complex was, it hadn't seen any life in years. The military is known for a spick and span ideology; this place didn't show any of those time-honored practices. The white paint was cracked and peeling. The screen door was tattered from the vicious foothill winds that roared down the west slopes and battered anything in its path. The hinges creaked loudly from lack of proper lubrication. The tarnished brass doorknob shifted up and down as he turned it—the locking screws were loose.

"Hello? Hello?" Nothing but silence greeted his welcome. He found a light switch which he flicked up and down a few times with no results. "Judith, is there a flashlight in the car?" Without answering, she disappeared and returned with an emergency Streamlight Strion LED flashlight.

"Will this work?" She flipped the light on, illuminating a scene straight out of Halloween. The place could have doubled for Michael Myer's abandoned house.

The first room, twenty by twenty feet, consisted of a desk and file cabinets. The dust was a good quarter-inch thick and blew around with the breeze coming through the open door. There were no phones or computers on the desk. To the left, was an empty gun rack designed to hold at least six rifles or semi-automatic weapons. Muki peeked into the metal file drawers out of curiosity.

To the right of the desk was another door. Judith led the way. She turned the knob. The door didn't budge. She tried it again with the same result. "Dammit, it's jammed."

"Here, let me try." Larry approached the door, with the same result.

"Larry," quipped Muki, "look to the left of the jamb. Looks

like it's a security card reader."

Larry hadn't noticed it. It blended in perfectly with the frame and the worn, white paint. "Okay, that could be a problem."

"Aye, Captain. Remember when the automatic doors didn't respond to motion commands?"

Larry thought about that for a minute.

"Yes, I do. When technology isn't cooperative, nothing can replace a good swift kick."

He moved back about two feet, raised his right leg and sent it crashing into the wood door. BAM!

The door exploded open with the impact of his foot, showering the dark room behind with wood splinters. The sound of wood shrapnel echoed across the walls.

"Thanks for the reminder Abdul. You might be of use yet." Muki and Judith quietly laughed at the comment.

Judith led the way with the light, revealing a room sixty by fifty feet. She moved the light to the left revealing stainless steel equipment and a sink. Upon closer examination, it appeared to be a large kitchen.

"Looks like this is where they ate," she mumbled.

She panned the light around the rest of the room. It was barren with the exception of half-a-dozen wire-framed military beds.

"Looks like WWII surplus. Good to see they spared no expense for creature comforts or unexpected guests," she observed.

Abdul, like the others, wasn't impressed with the accommodation, but he didn't care. "I don't know about you guys; I know it's not the Ritz, but it beats sleeping in the car. I'm taking the one under the window. You three can fight over the other fine furnishings. Oh, and I would like to make a request." His comment was directed towards no one in particular. "I'd like a 6:00am wake-up call. I will also need a small glass of orange juice with some scrambled eggs and not too overly cooked ba—"

"Shut up Abdul."

* * *

It wasn't exactly room service that came knocking at the door for the morning wake-up call. Rather, it was a group of squirrels looking for scraps of food, or perhaps just taking time out to play in a previously uninspected building. They quickly scampered through the swinging screen door and bolted right into the large cafeteria. They stood on both haunches sniffing the air cautiously. They detected two distinct smells, one unwelcome (people) and the other, meat of some type.

They slowly made their way towards one of the sleeping bodies. The smell intensified. Instincts told them to find a different food source, but the pull of the morning brunch on meat was stronger than the thought of safety. They silently jumped on the bed and frantically began searching for the treasure. Abdul's sleep was rudely disturbed with the feel of teeth gnawing on his front pocket. At first, he thought it was part of his dream until he felt sharp teeth and claws burrowing into his lower right front pocket. "WHAT THE HELL?" The squirrels froze in their tracks. It was hard to say who was more scared. Abdul's eyes locked with the scavengers.

Judith looked over and started laughing. "Abdul, don't turn down a good thing. That might be the closest you ever get to the real thing."

Abdul wasn't laughing. Larry and Muki were both looking at the spectacle, quietly laughing under their breath.

"If I had a phaser, I'd blast you two little shits into atom dust." The pair looked at each other and made a hasty retreat out of the damaged door, dejected and hungry.

"What's wrong Abdul, not your type? Wonder if they were both males?"

"Judith, you are such a bitch." She took the comment as a compliment and smiled.

Larry looked around the room slowly focusing his eyes on their new surroundings. "What time is it?"

Muki looked down at her silver digital Seiko. "6:00am. A very early 6:00am." She slowly sat up stretching her small arms and wriggling the sleep from her body.

"I don't know about you guys," said Larry as he looked around the room, "but I could sure eat something. Judith, what else is in the trunk of the car?"

"I have a few goodies for just such an occasion." Judith got herself out of bed, stood up and performed a full-body stretch. The sunlight pouring into the room marked every one of her curves. The sight of the sun penetrating and exposing her body beneath her tight-fitting T-shirt definitely removed any morning fog Larry might have been experiencing. *God she's beautiful.* Judith finished the morning stretch and shook her sparkling brunette hair. "Muki, want to join me?"

She knew exactly what she meant. "Sure, let's go."

Abdul looked at Larry. "Why is it that they always go in pairs?" Larry shrugged his shoulders. The question crossed his mind as one of the great mysteries of the world.

"Scotty, I have no idea. I doubt if even Freud would be able to shed light on that timeless question."

The girls came in a few minutes later, carrying two backpacks, looking very refreshed. "Next?"

Larry and Abdul made their way towards the door. Judith didn't look back as the boys exited, but she couldn't resist another jab at Abdul. "Larry, I'd be careful. Abdul might still be a little frisky from the morning activities."

"Judith!" yelled Abdul.

"It's okay, stud. You take the left tree, and I'll take the right."

The girls set the backpacks on the stainless steel counter and sorted the bounty – Fruit Loops, Honeycomb, bottled water, beef jerky and Judith's coffee.

"What are you gonna do with that, Judith? I'm sure the gas isn't on. How you gonna heat the water?"

Judith never left home unprepared. She always remembered the race her father took her to out in the boondocks of North Carolina. When she woke up the morning of the race, she was greeted with the words from Jimmy Smith, 'out of coffee.' It was the worst race of her life. She swore it would never happen again. "Don't worry, the other backpack has a portable gas stove in it. I never leave home without it."

"Ah," is all Muki could say.

The boys came back and found the girls munching on the

prepackaged five-star breakfast. "What? No eggs or bacon, Captain? I will report this to Star Fleet as soon as communications have been restored."

Judith glared at Abdul. What's new. "Look you little shit, you don't have to eat anything, and you sure aren't getting any of 'my' coffee. Got it?"

"Come on, guys. Can't we drop this bullshit interaction for at least one day?" the disgust in Larry's voice was abundantly evident.

"Sure. As soon as he acts like a real man and not some Trekkie nerd from the '70s."

The slight to his favorite show was too much. "Look, you frigid bitch. Star Trek was the most ground-breaking show of its time. But you wouldn't know that would you? Of course not. Your head is so far up your ass most of the time, you have yet to enjoy life." Abdul's outburst was, to say the least, unexpected. "How many dates did you turn down over the last six years? Well? Oh I know, about one hundred. Why?"

Judith attempted to defend herself with a quick retort.

"I'm not finished yet. We are so tired of you strutting around with your Playmate body and acting as if no one notices. Well, guess what Judith, you might be one hot piece of ass, but I would prefer the squirrels over you anytime." Judith almost dropped her precious styrofoam cup. She could feel her hands trembling with fear instead of anger. Her mouth was slightly opened as if she were going to speak, but more in shock. He wasn't finished.

Larry pulled out a Marlboro and lit up.

"Just like back at that diner. If it weren't for Muki, I really believe those two rednecks would have given you a serious attitude adjustment. It's time to drop the charade and quit acting all big and bad. You aren't impressing anyone." Sweat was seeping through his shirt as the tirade diminished.

Larry took another long drag and exhaled the blue smoke. It clung heavily in the air. None of them spoke. Never since they had known Abdul, had they seen this side. No one knew what to say.

"Excuse me, I'm getting some coffee and jerky." Abdul pushed by Judith and picked up a cup.

Larry took one more drag, dropped the burning butt on the floor and then crushed the spent Marlboro. "Well, now that's out of the way, think I'll get some coffee and Fruit Loops. Muki?" She moved with him to the counter. Judith stood in the barren room by herself.

"Larry."

"Yes?"

"Can I bum one?" *Can she what? She doesn't smoke. She doesn't drink and she never uses drugs.* Larry's eyes questioned her request.

"Larry, can I bum one or not?" Instead of attempting to talk her out of it, he pulled one from the pack and handed it to her.

"May I also have a light?"

"Yes." Larry pulled out the silver Zippo, flipped it open and spun the roller, igniting the flame. He gingerly moved his hand out of the way.

She leaned over, sucked deep on the one-hundred. Her virgin lungs seized as the harsh smoke invaded the pristine organs. Her first exhale was more of a violent cough as her body resisted the invader. She took in another deep drag. Her lungs were a little more accommodating—her brain wasn't. The sudden rush of nicotine reduced the oxygen-rich air in the veins. She felt a little dizzy but retained her balance. She took a swig of her liquid gold then stared at Abdul. "You little shit. I didn't know you cared." Muki and Larry's eyes moved to Abdul.

"Well dammit, I do. If you took a chill pill instead of biting everyone's head off, you could be a seriously cool chick." Judith thanked him for the compliment.

Larry bit down on some more jerky, washing it down with Judith's blend. "Okay guys. Is the Jerry Springer Show over?" They both turned and smiled at Larry.

"Aye, Captain."

"Yes, Larry, we're cool."

"Good. I've been thinking about our current predicament. The Rockies won't be in town for two more days. I think it would be wise to stay here at least one more day. I don't want to allow our friends another opportunity to fleece our money. I believe we should do a little exploring. Everyone game?"

"Aye Captain."

"Why not. Beats standing around in this empty room." Judith dropped the cigarette on the floor and ground it out.

"Sure Larry. Which way shall we go?" asked Muki.

"Well, I've been thinking about that. It's obvious this room was built to feed and house about thirty men. There has to be another door somewhere in this room. It doesn't make sense based on the outside layout, that there are only two rooms. Let's fan out and start tapping on the walls. If there's a hidden door or entrance of some type in the wall, the sound should be hollow."

* * *

"Smart kids indeed." The old eyes studied the four as they slowly felt the northern wall for any sign of a hidden door. "They might be able to help me with my plans. Seems I'll need to give them a little help." A slender finger slid the cursor over the icon, *unlock.*

* * *

Muki turned one of the dials on the large industrial stove to the right and heard a click. She felt the stove move out from the wall about half an inch. "Larry, I think I found something." What she didn't know was the latch also unlocked the refrigerator from its resting place.

"What did you find?"

"Come here. The stove moved out from the wall when I turned the dial."

Larry approached her and examined the floor. "Look guys, she's right. It has moved."

"How can you be sure, Captain? It could be an illusion."

"No. Look at the refrigerator to the right. There's a noticeable gap between the wall and the unit. See the track mark?" Judith brought her flashlight over and poured the beam into the crevice. Sure enough, something had moved.

Muki glanced up at Larry, "Now what?"

"Let's see what else might move."

The four of them poured over the stove moving all of the dials and opening the oven doors. Nothing. They stood back perplexed. Larry was getting frustrated "We're missing something, I just don't know what?"

"Captain, I don't know. Maybe something is hidden in the refrigerator? Maybe we shall find some well-aged steaks or milk. It is times like these a synthesizer would come in handy." He grabbed the large stainless steel handle and commanded as he pulled the latch open, "Computer, I would like...." As the door opened the sound of old gears engaging crept out from behind the wall.

"Ah, Captain?"

"Keep pulling, Abdul. There's something back there."

Abdul continued. The farther he opened the door the more the space between the wall grew.

"Keep going." How the unit was moving away from the wall was unexplainable. There were no tracks or obvious wheels, yet it continued to move.

Judith was the first to offer a theory. "Could it be magnetized? Abdul could have triggered a mechanical magnetic sled lying under the floor. That would explain why there aren't any tracks on the floor."

Larry tossed her idea around. "Judith, there would still be tracks of some type, wouldn't there?"

"Not necessarily. If it's magnetic, there could be a buffer zone of energy created between the floor and the refrigerator allowing it to float instead of slide."

"Sounds reasonable."

"Okay, Captain. That's as far as it goes."

Larry and Judith studied the scene. Even though the unit was now three feet from the wall, revealing a dark void, there was no access to the void. "Judith, shine your light. Let's see what's back there." She shone the light revealing more darkness.

Muki was the first to notice the obvious. "Look guys. It has to move either to the left or right. Look how it's no longer flush with the counter. Let me try something." She went back to something her father told her years ago about Asian philosophy, *'when in doubt, the obvious is hidden before your eyes.'*

She closed the door against the wishes of her friends, moved to the left side of the unit and pushed.

Larry knew she was no match for such a heavy unit. "Muki, it won't wo—" The unit slowly starting hinging to the right, much to everyone's amazement.

"I'll be damned," muttered Larry. "How'd you know?"

"Old Asian proverb." She smiled as she finished pushing the refrigerator until it mysteriously locked to the floor revealing another entrance. "Judith, do you have any more flashlights?"

Judith glanced at Larry and hurried back to the car.

* * *

His eyes remained glued to the monitor. "Clever kids."

* * *

Judith returned with another flashlight. She handed it to Larry and immediately refilled her coffee. The others stared at her as they contemplated the dark void in front of them. "What? Can't let it go to waste." They returned their stares into the abyss.

"Captain. Shall we move forward on impulse engines or shall I prepare the reactor for warp drive?"

Larry was irritated with Abdul's constant Star Trek reference. This time he was right. Should they use caution or plunge directly into the unknown? "For the moment, impulse engines only. However, be prepared to engage the warp drive if it gets dicey.□

"Aye, Captain."

Larry took in a deep breath and cautiously moved forward. He and Judith led the way, methodically moving the small round orbs over the hallway. The walls were heavy with condensation from years of neglect. They did notice a string of embedded lights in the wall that had been unresponsive to the switch they found when they entered. The only discernible sounds were the shuffling of their feet on the damp concrete floor and the occasional drop of water to the floor.

They walked for almost four-hundred and fifty feet. Muki

commented as the beams of light danced off the dark, wet walls, "Well, I guess we can mark off Carlsbad Caverns from our list of things to do."

"You got that right," quipped Larry. "This place has everything but the stalactites, stalagmites, and bats."

In a hushed tone, Judith agreed. "Yeah, but we have squirrels."

They continued descending into the void. "Okay, if this doesn't end soon, I vote for going to Denver." Judith's remark was more of a demand than a question.

Larry continued moving the light from side to side. "Just a few more feet. If we don't come upon anything of interest, we'll turn back. Okay?"

"Okay." They plodded on into the dark.

"Look up there." Larry's light was shining on a metallic door with a control panel to the right. "Looks like an elevator."

"Well, that's just great. What are we supposed to do, generate our own power so it will work?" Judith's disgust was apparent.

"We've come this far. Might as well see if it still works." Larry turned the light on Muki. The beam shone off her deep black eyes. "You brought us here. Take the honors."

Muki appreciated the offer. Intellectually, she was the equal to her partners. Socially, she always stayed in the background until she was called upon. She was surprised, yet pleased, with the offer.

"Thank you, Larry." She approached the panel and pushed the power button on the panel. A few seconds passed after her finger pressed the damp plastic button. Lights flickered on and off revealing a dark black *down* button. The noise they heard reminded them of sounds from an old black-and-white horror film. Loud banging and shrill screams of metal grinding against metal resonated behind the ominous black door. The whirl of motors turning joined the cacophony as they echoed in the hall.

They stood back from the door as if anticipating the appearance of Michael Myers, Jason or worse, Freddie Kruger. Abdul's eyes darted back and forth waiting for the door to open. "I hope this doesn't lead to the boiler room. That's where they killed Freddie." No one said a word.

One minute passed after Muki pushed the button. The tension mounted with each second. The sound of machinery stopped. The air was thick and stale. The *down* button brightened as the doors shuddered open. The overhead lights flickered with a hint of shorting out from all the accumulated moisture in the cover.

"Shall we?" suggested Larry. Timidly, each one entered the small room. Larry reached out and pushed the *down* button.

"I don't want to rain on anyone's adventurous parade, but what happens if we get trapped and can't get back up?" Abdul did pose a valid question.

"We climb back up." Larry's words were dry and unconvincing.

The same thoughts ran through each one's mind. Would the cables support the combined weight? Was there enough lubricant left on the bearings so they didn't seize up? Would the elevator take them to the desired location, or would they become trapped and never found? A logical answer, and sound decision, would have been to turn around and continue with the planned vacation, instead of venturing into the unknown. Yes, those were the thoughts as the door closed, and they began their descent into the unknown.

Muki cautioned herself from speaking her mind. *If this place is abandoned, what was providing the power for the elevator? Would not everything have been turned off? The light switches in the hall didn't work, and there was no power upstairs. Where is the power coming from?*

"Something on your mind, Muki."

She looked up at Larry. "Nothing of concern, just thinking."

* * *

"Good, it still works. Keep coming my children. If the plan I'm formulating works, we shall breathe new life into "MY" machine and those treacherous bastards will pay for their insolence. How dare General McCulloch and Senator Hodges pull the plug on "my" work? They will rue the day they were born. I spent ten years building this masterpiece and with the wave of a pen, they canceled everything!" His voice was trembling with rage as he ranted at the monitor.

"We could have changed so much. We could have spared millions from the injustices of WWI, WWII and Vietnam. We could have built the perfect society and government ever chronicled since man's existence. Instead, the fools chose to be cowards and have temporarily thwarted my plans!" He was frothing at the mouth with hatred as he stood up. "NO! The fools. They canceled the project and turned a blank eye. Justice my friends! Justice will be mine!" He collapsed back into the swivel chair exhausted from the tirade.

* * *

For two minutes, the elevator descended into the depths of something. What, they didn't know. Abdul again broke the uneasy silence encompassing the compartment.

"Scotty, I need more power."

"Captain, I don't think the dilithium crystals can take anymore."

"Dammit Mr. Scott, more power!" His imitation of Kirk and Mr. Scott were a welcome relief even to Judith. The others chimed in with their favorite characters.

The elevator came to an uneasy stop and shuddered. The doors opened more slowly than when they had first done so. They stepped out into a massive black cavern. The lights flashed off a multitude of computer monitors, light fixtures, and an apparent abandoned armory. They could hear a very low hum. "We must have activated some auxiliary generator," commented Muki.

They split up in twos in the hope of finding additional lighting. The first switches did nothing but click. The two groups moved cautiously deeper into the expanse. For some reason, the area to the right was much darker than the area they were in as if there were a massive hidden cavern. So far, nothing of importance. Several desk tables with monitors, and old IBM tower computers. Probably no more than an Intel Pentium 4 processor.

"How ancient," mused Larry, "and to think, they sent men to the moon with less memory than our cell phones. They were true pioneers. I can't imagine life back then. Absolutely primitive," he stated. His comments produced uneasy laughter as they kept exploring.

After a few minutes, Larry made the discovery that the room they were in must have been an admittance area for visitors or workers. No research facility would have an armory in the main sector. There had to be more lurking in the darkness. They agreed to move into the dark unknown, but before going, Larry wanted a picture standing next to the archaic equipment. He believed archaeologists would find much amusement with his antics. The group begrudgingly agreed to take a few quick pics, and then proceeded into the abyss.

They found themselves in another dark, empty corridor. This one was much larger than the entrance. It was twelve feet tall and thirty feet wide. Heavy drops of condensation were slowly migrating down the walls and covering all of the overhead piping. The floor was damp but not wet.

Odd, thought Abdul, *if the facility were indeed empty, depending on how long it had been abandoned, the floors would have an ample covering of water. There was no sign of recent activity.*

Another large steel door greeted them at the end of the two hundred meter—long hall. There was a panel on the right allowing entry, with a key slot and keyboard. Larry punched the apparent *on* button. The panel lit up. *Please enter your password,* commanded an electronic voice. Larry punched in his Social Security number just for fun. *Please enter your password,* commanded the voice again.

Judith was becoming dismayed. "Guys, there's no way to get past the door. There could be a million variables, and we only have four weeks of fun. Let's turn around and leave. It's been interesting, but looking at this door is not my idea of excitement, plus I'm starting to feel claustrophobic."

"Calm yourself," said Muki. "Let me try something. I have an app I downloaded before we left, and if my charger port matches up with the console, it might work. Give me three minutes." Judith reluctantly agreed. Muki hooked the device up and hoped it would work some magic. Muki watched as the numbers lit up on the password screen. It was a twelve-digit code. This was going to take longer than three minutes. Two minutes already, and only two characters matched.

A slender finger moved to a keyboard and entered the correct passcode. The characters appeared instantly on the console. The door hissed and moaned as it slowly opened. The kids were in shock. Muki, more than the others. *How did all the characters appear at once? The app wasn't designed that well, or so she thought.* "Larry, did you see how they all appeared at once?"

"Yep. Kind of weird, but then this is prehistoric equipment. Let's see what you've uncovered."

The four entered the massive cavern. They could feel its size wrap around them. There were a few emergency lights on, revealing a room the size of a football stadium. It rivaled the Death Star stadium in Arlington, Texas.

"Wow!" Was all they could say.

"What the hell is this place?" queried Larry.

"Prehistoric technology," jibed Muki. "Mr. Spock, any ideas?"

"Ensign, until the sensors have properly scoped the area, I refrain from making an illogical conclusion." Abdul couldn't help himself. Even Judith was impressed with the room.

"Okay, now what?" she demanded.

"We shall explore," replied Larry as he moved ahead without the others.

A pair of eyes peered over the top of reading glasses glued to the monitor. *Such curious children. Obviously not sent by the government. They could prove beneficial.*

Larry found a bank of light switches. "Scotty, I need warp speed now!" he exclaimed as his right hand pushed down all four switches.

Stunned silence bathed the room. The lights illuminated the most advanced equipment any of them had ever witnessed. None of the equipment was stock or from the shelf.

"Prehistoric, eh Larry?" added Muki and Abdul.

Words failed to describe what was reflecting off their retinas. They stared in amazement and wonder.

In a hushed tone, Judith whispered, "And we thought Stargate was something. Look at this place." A myriad of switches and console panels covered the walls. There was a main station platform that Larry and Abdul slowly approached.

"Mr. Spock, shall I transport you to—"

"Knock it off, Abdul. It's time to be serious for a change. What do you think it does?" Both of them scanned the panel. It was enormous. Six feet by three feet. "Seriously, what do you think it controls?" All eyes scanned the room and saw nothing that would warrant so many different controls. Judith and Muki were walking fifty feet in front of them scanning the floor for clues.

"Uh guys, come here for a minute. I don't think this is a floor." The boys were confused.

"Judith, if you're walking on it, it has to be a floor," mocked Larry

"Listen as we walk," she said

It was subtle, but it was there. With each footstep, there was a quiet echoing underneath them. They all walked around the floor listening. The verdict was agreed upon. It was a false bottom, but to what? After ten minutes, and a comparison of notes, the cover was thirty yards in diameter. They went back to the control panel and studied all the different controls looking for a clue that would possibly open it. Larry noticed an unlabeled button that showed a little more wear than the others.

"Guys, it would make sense that this button opens and closes the floor. It's more worn than the others. Shall I?"

Judith's patience started to wane. "Either push the button or let's go. I'm bored stiff."

Larry couldn't help but look at her and smile."Why is it math majors are so linear?" They both chuckled while Judith rolled her eyes in exasperation.

"Get your panties out of a wad. We're thinking."

It was times like this she wished she could literally roll her eyes into the back of her head. *Why are boys so immature?*

Proof—a masters doesn't guarantee intelligence.

* * *

"That's right, push the button," came a coarse voice behind the dim light of the IBM monitor screen.

* * *

Larry glanced at Abdul and nodded. "Mr. Sulu, engage." He pushed the button. A few seconds passed with nothing. No motors were heard spinning or gears cranking. Silence. And then a small vibration was felt reverberating through the concrete floor. Five pairs of eyes stared as the false floor slowly folded back into a recess. No appreciable noise was detected. It moved effortlessly and quietly. The signs of any moving machinery didn't escape the wary, logical mind of Abdul. His mind couldn't grasp the concept of an apparent concrete floor (at first thought) moving like a polymeric elastic plate with great strength. Kevlar had proven some of the characteristics, but all the experiments they attempted with making it structurally sound and elastic ended in failure. He was watching theory in action.

The floor opened revealing a dark, massive platform. A few security lights illuminated the platform. It was thirty-six feet deep and one-hundred and twenty feet circular.

"Captain," Abdul spoke to no one in particular, "we have a hole."

Judith knew exactly what Abdul was referring to. "Shut up you juvenile delinquent, because it's the only hole you might ever enter in your lifetime."

Her eyes rolled as he finished her thought.

"God, boys are so immature."

Muki quietly laughed with Judith. She knew Judith's words were wrong, but chose not to make mention of a rendezvous not too long ago.

Larry broke the tension. "Um, guys, I hate to break up this apparent love fest, but seriously, what in the hell have we discovered and what is its purpose?" Larry noticed the tall overhead hoist cranes when they first entered the control center. They couldn't have been for installing material, for if they were, why were they still in place? The cables attached to the hoists were at least four inches in diameter. These were much larger than the ones he worked with at the GE plant in Philadelphia, where they built the generators and turbine engines for the Burlington Northern Santa Fe Railroad Company. No, these were much larger and the straps/slings hanging on the walls were for heavy equipment. They looked large enough to carry a fully-built electric locomotive. But that was only supposition.

"Larry, are you suggesting there is more to this than meets the eyes?"

"Aye Scotty, I am."

"Will you morons drop off the Star Trek references and speak like normal people, or is that asking for too much?" quipped Judith.

Muki chimed in. "It's above their pay grade." That brought the boys back to reality.

"There has to be a manual of some sort concerning the operation of this machine. I suggest we spread out and see if it still exists. What we have uncovered is very intriguing, to say the least, but I would really like to do one of two things." Judith's words were terse and concise. "One, we find the manual and understand what the machine does, or two, if we don't find it in two hours, we leave and continue with our vacation."

Larry was the first to answer, "Dammit Judith! Quit being a killjoy. Just once—just once in your life—would you take a chill pill and let your hair down?" Using her own words, "Is that asking too much? Every time we find something of interest, you get bored and ruin all of the—"

"All right. I'll concede this one time. Instead of two hours, I'll allow four. Remember, I have the keys and won't hesitate to leave your asses." Larry knew she would do it. It wouldn't be the first time she'd left in a huff, and they'd been abandoned to find other transportation.

The other three agreed to the terms and discussed which areas each would search.

* * *

A spindly finger turned off the monitor. The hand moved down to the right and unlocked the desk shelf. The figure arose, moved to his left and quietly dislodged the lock. A thin smile broke across nicotine-stained teeth in much need of a dentist's attention. "Yes, my children, seek and ye shall find."

The specter walked away from the door and disappeared into another room, which would be most difficult to detect even to the trained eye.

CHAPTER 7

DISCOVERY

The four agreed to split into singles this time. They were confident they were the only ones wandering about the complex. If something were going to happen, it should have already shown its ugly face. So far, the only intruders that kept them on their toes were their own inner demons.

Abdul took the area around the control panel. Larry would inspect the cavernous hole in the floor. Judith would inspect the concrete walls to what was agreed was the east side, and Muki would concentrate on the west. If, after four hours the search yielded no results, they'd resume with their vacation plans. It would make for a colorful, yet unbelievable, story when they returned to civilization.

"Abdul," the words thundered out of the dark hole, "find anything?"

"Negative, Captain. It appears the alien race, much more advanced than ours, has left no trace for a primitive society to claim artifacts for further inspection and analysis. I fear Star Fleet command will not be issuing commendations for our efforts. Have you found anything of interest in the giant cavern, Captain?"

"I believe I have. I don't have a clue about how to operate the machine, but come on down and have a look." Abdul obligingly left his post and started descending the vertical iron ladder.

Judith felt a chill invade her spine. "Who is it?" she called out. She turned around to find the space behind her empty. *It must be my nerves. I never liked dark places and this one definitely takes the cake.* A few minutes passed, and the feeling hit her again. "Dammit. Who's there?"

The feeling of someone or something staring at her was overwhelming. It felt as if the past she'd subdued for so long, was trying to burst forth and take control of her soul. The thought sickened her stomach. *How could she be related to such a vile and disgusting man? Why did her mother consider it necessary to inform her of the past? It would have been best if she knew nothing of her disgusting genealogy.* The feeling of dread passed as quickly as it appeared. She kept moving along the smooth walls, sliding her hands palm down along the slick granite surface, hoping to reveal a hidden crack or crevice which wasn't caused by Mother Nature, but rather by man.

"Aye, Captain. What treasures have you found?"

"Quiet. Did you hear that?"

Abdul glanced around the cylindrical walls. "No. What did you—"

"It's Judith. Judith, are you alright?" It was a few seconds before a reply came.

"I'm fine."

"Okay, be careful." Larry turned his gaze back to Abdul.

"Look at this wall. It's not a wall at all. It's a garage door."

"Yes, I believe you're right. Only problem is, what type of vehicle requires a door this large?"

"I don't know. Come over here. This is really interesting." Abdul followed Larry into the center of the floor. "This is either motor oil or hydraulic fluid. Hard to tell by the viscosity, but it is from a mechanical device."

Abdul agreed with the findings as he rubbed the liquid between his fingers. "Aye."

Muki methodically eyed the wall. There was something different. She took a few steps back and retraced her steps forward. *Yes, there is something different here, hidden, but here.* She moved her small, delicate fingers over the oddity in the wall. Her father's words filled her mind, *"The obvious is always hidden before your eyes."*

Where is it? Where is it?

Her left index finger moved across a small indention in the wall. *There you are.* The black cover was hinged at the top. She pushed the cover inward and detected a button. Without calling out to her friends, she wanted to make sure of the discovery. She pushed the button recessed in the hidden compartment. The wall to her left silently opened, revealing a narrow hallway bathed in white florescent lights. At the end of the hall was another door. This one looked out of place. It appeared to be a normal metal door with an accessible handle.

She called out to the trio with her diminutive voice. "Judith, Larry, Abdul. Come here. I think I've found something." It took the three a couple of minutes to locate Muki and her discovery.

"Muki, do you have a sixth sense or are you always this lucky?" asked Judith.

"I'd like to think it is my superior Asian intellect that guides me in the right direction." The other three stared at her with raised eyebrows.

Abdul leaned towards Larry, "Superior Asian intellect? Who's she kidding?"

Muki threw a deceptive smile to the boys. "My ears complement my brain, Abdul." As Abdul regrouped himself, she flashed a quick wink and grin.

Judith bored with current sparring match. "Well, are we just going to stand here all night?" Her hands were firmly locked to her hips in a rather imposing stance. "You three can stand here. I'm going in and see what surprise awaits us."

She moved down the gleaming white hall, approached the door, and expecting another obstacle, she firmly turned the knob. It offered no resistance and obeyed her hand's command. She pushed the door open revealing a small ten by ten foot office. Her first impression was the very stale smell of tobacco. It permeated every sense on her body and enveloped her clothes like a dark shroud. To her left, was a nondescript metal military desk with three side drawers and one middle one. On the top, was a flat screen monitor connected to an IBM 10000 tower. The wireless mouse and keyboard sat idle, flanking the monitor. The roller chair was old and worn. The plastic trashcan to the left of the desk was overflowing with old newspapers, coffee cups and soiled Kleenexes. "God. Someone needs to clean this shithole up."

Larry, followed by Muki and Abdul, entered the small office. "Muki, have you ever seen one of those before?" He was pointing at the IBM tower.

"I've never, ever, seen one, but I did hear a few guys talking about it in the electronics lab one day. They were convinced it was pure science fiction. I think one of the guys referred to it as "Colossus" from a film made back in the '70s. The system was designed to control the United States nuclear arsenal."

Larry thought about that for a minute."Okay Muki, so what's the big deal? I could do that from my laptop with the correct codes."

"Yes, you could, but could you also redirect satellites, direct all military moves, monitor the traffic in New York, Dallas, Los Angeles, and Miami at the same time?" The blank look on his face answered her question.

"Oh, but there's more. It has the ability to override and invade every computer system in the world and not be detected. It has the ability not only to block hackers, but it can send out a pulse to any hacker, no matter how many routers and servers they attempt to use to hide their tracks, and fry the invading units. It's a deadly weapon. According to the guys, the reason they didn't think it would ever be plausible is that there isn't a server or hardwire connection that can handle the massive amount of energy to run the system. The early tests were complete and utter failures."

"Why? They could run the information through fiber optics."

"They tried, but failed. The operating system is so powerful it was drawing more information than the glass lines could carry. It generated so much heat pulling the information, the lines melted without heating up."

"Well, it looks as if someone was successful. Abdul, I believe this could actually power the Enterprise."

Abdul could only nod his head in appreciation of the equipment.

"Okay, thank you for the history lesson. Now, let's see if we can find anything that tells what and how all of this works." Judith sat down and started pulling out the steel drawers.

Larry and Abdul gave the 10000 a thorough examination, hoping it would mysteriously reveal its hidden secrets.

Muki moved around the other three and started examining the bookshelves. Something was bothering her. The smell of tobacco was indeed stale. Yet, depending on how long the complex had been abandoned, the smell wouldn't have been as strong. The odor reminded her of the brand her father smoked. She couldn't remember the name, but she knew it was a form of pipe tobacco. Amphora, that's the brand. Amphora (Orient). Even though his friends and fellow smokers tried to explain this was, at best, a low-end tobacco and there were other much more satisfying and aromatic brands available such as the brown or red patch blends, her father was sticking with the Oriental cut.

She directed her attention back to the task at hand while also trying to understand another more pressing issue; where were the auxiliary generators located and how were they operating? Were they hidden inside the structure she and Abdul stumbled upon last night, or were they hidden deeper underground? Wherever it was coming from was in excellent working order. If they were auxiliary (as she thought), what type of fuel was powering them? But more importantly, if they ran out of fuel, how were the tanks being filled, or even more intriguing, by whom? She let the thoughts recede into the back of her mind as she intently scanned the metal shelves for clues.

"Nothing here. The desk is empty. Only a few blank yellow legal pads and dried-up pens." Judith spun the chair 180 degrees, clipping Larry in the thigh.

"Dammit, Judith. Look where you're driving." Larry reached down and started rubbing his bruised thigh.

"Shouldn't have been standing so close, or were you trying to get a better view?" She raised her left eyebrow, pushed her prominent chest forward and displayed her girlish grin. Larry's face instantly turned scarlet red.

"No. I was examining the computer."

"Sure you were." She deliberately engaged in a seated, complete body stretch filling her lungs to full capacity. As she slowly expelled the air (watching Larry's eyes the whole time for a reaction), she threw out a question. "Muki, anything?"

Her small hand glided over the various books and three-ring binders. "I think so." She grabbed the gold bonded one. Unlike the other material on the shelf, this one showed signs of being handled numerous times. The gold binding was worn on the top and the bottom, indicating hands were grabbing the top to remove it from the shelf and the bottom as it was pushed in place.

"Well, bring it over here so we can all see it."

Muki placed the ten-inch-thick binder on the metal table. Judith opened the gold cover. The handwriting was scrawled and uneven, making it difficult to read.

The following material is my lifelong work.

For years, man has dreamed of the unknown.

The depth of ocean secrets: Jacques Cousteau

The Moon: Conquered in 1969

Space Travel Exploration: Voyager and Neptune

Universe Studies: Hubble Space Station

One frontier has yet to be obtained. It was fantasized

in "The Time Tunnel," "Twilight Zone," and the

"Philadelphia Experiment". But it has never been

conquered. Many theories have arisen to the quest.

They failed miserably.

The first real attempt was performed in Waxahachie, Texas

in 1995 (two years after funding was cut).

We successfully reversed the flow of energy,

buffering the distribution of molecules

to a manageable disintegration rate.

The object we used was a small aluminum can.

The results were marginal.

The can disappeared for exactly five seconds.

When it reappeared, the can was whole with one oddity:

the letters were rearranged spelling KCOE.

This was encouraging yet disappointing.

We could not use it on a live subject until we understood what happened.

Unfortunately, the amount of energy we used, knocked out all the power in the county.

The surge was discovered along with the men who caused the disruption. We were escorted out and barred from further activities. FOOLS!

In 2005, this complex was founded by the US Army in an attempt to perfect time travel. Let me be specific: The machine is for reverse time travel, not future events.

It was agreed that "future" time travel could have dire consequences.

What if World War III erupted, or a meteor crashed into the Earth?

What landscape would the traveler be greeted with? Death?

We agreed to let the future lie in state.

The past however is well documented. We could assign an exact place in history and revisit the past, knowing at least

we would be arriving in somewhat familiar circumstances, and surroundings.

Judith stopped reading for a moment. "Do you think they were successful? Imagine going back in time, and if not altering events, seeing them played out first hand."

"Aye Judith, but think of the damage one could do."

"Or undo" added Larry. "My dad and Leroy could avoid the encounter with those thugs that night, or I could have been quicker and summoned help before they were injured."

"Don't be juvenile," quipped Judith. "They didn't design it for such trivial issues. They were looking at a larger picture." Judith knew exactly what she would change, no matter what the cost.

"Judith, keep reading," suggested Muki.

"Okay."

It was agreed, if the machine worked,

we would travel back to Pearl Harbor on

December 7, 1941 and witness the

surprise attack launching America into WWII.

If the trip was successful, we would then go back two

more days armed with photos and descriptions of the

impending attack.

The envelope would be handed to a local courier for delivery

to Admiral Kimmel and General Short

in the hopes they would be better prepared for the assault.

If the initial experiment became successful, it was agreed

by all parties to correct the mistakes of the past.

We were going to insert a group of men with vehicles

and weapons to kill Ho Chi Minh and General Giap.

The next venture would be saving John Fitzgerald Kennedy.

At first, we were going to travel back to the night John took the

ill-fated PT-109 into the Iron Bottom Sound.

He chose to patrol the straights to disrupt the Tokyo

Express (destroyers and cruisers resupplying Guadalcanal).
We would attempt to warn Captain Kennedy of the
impending danger, but thought better of it.
Being a wounded veteran of WWII played into the
plans his father Joe was brewing.
We would send the same team to Dallas and take positions
at the Grassy Knoll, the Book Depository and
the bridge on I-35, watching the motorcade as it
progressed west on Elm.
Per General McCulloch, if we can't stop the assassination,
at least we might be able to capture some of the
men responsible for the conspiracy and hopefully
put to rest who actually masterminded the act.
We (I) would make them pay for the transgression.
Unfortunately, our efforts were stopped cold.
The FOOLS. HOW DARE THEY INTERFERE!

Washington wanted this machine
and now they have it, but what do they do with it?
They scrap it with the stroke of the pen.

They must have messed themselves when
we showed them the diagrams for the Pyramids.
The insertion team returned with multiple photos
of how and who built the Pyramids. It was fascinating!
Who would ever have considered the scaffolding and pulley

systems used?

No one!

The answer was in front of us all the time, but
as normal, the academians refused to believe it was so
simple. And the transport system they developed to move
the massive stones rivaled our own interstate system.

Brilliant! Absolutely brilliant.

The Civil Engineer on staff, Mr. Roberts, stared
in disbelief at the simplicity of the construction.
He was planning on doing further research to
assist in our modern (?) building techniques.
The bastards in Washington instructed all
records to be destroyed.

Destroyed! Destroy history?

That's why we built the damned machine.
To learn, not suppress!

History was ours to right, but no, they
deemed it too dangerous. They who
spent billions on atomic bombs, planes
and missiles, stop ME? Ludicrous.
We held the ills of the world in our hands.
We could right the wrongs. We could have stopped
Hitler in 1928 and saved millions of lives.
No, instead the operation was halted.

Why? Money? National Security?

No. Bureaucrats who cowered in the corners.

Bureaucrats who control the fate of 300 million people daily.

300 million sheep!

Most of them couldn't pull their shoes out of a pile

of shit with written directions and diagrams.

Sheep. All of them.

Judith was working herself up into a frenzy. The thought of traveling back and killing Adolf Hitler was music to her ears. If Hitler would have been killed, her great-grandfather wouldn't have become the monster history portrayed him as. No, history didn't paint a rosy picture, it was dead-on. Her great-grandfather was an evil, vile human, who deserved to have been caught and hanged like the other conspirators.

Larry didn't care for the darkness pouring out of her mouth or eyes. "Judith, take a breath. They're just notes."

"These aren't just notes. These are the writings of an intelligent scientist who should have been allowed to change history. Think of everything this complex could have accomplished for the good of man instead of the evil."

Larry wasn't quite so sure. "Judith, what would happen—"

Muki took the lead as Larry's words were failing. "If we went back and changed history, how would the future look?"

"I don't care how it would look. Hitler and his henchmen should have all been strung up and killed before 1933 and saved the world from the insanity."

"No, Judith. That's not true. Sure, they could go back and kill Hitler, save Lincoln and Kennedy and even more important, possibly saved Jesus Christ from being crucified. But what would be the ramifications?" Judith was not swayed and kept staring at the words.

Even Abdul was agreeing. "Judith, changing events in history is a very dangerous business."

"Why?" she yelled. "Because you saw it in a Star Trek

episode, or some other bullshit program?" Her words were sharp and hard.

"No, Judith. Because our past is our future. Change the past and you roll the dice for future events. Are you willing to gamble the lives of billions of people in order to kill a few and save millions, or do we accept the past and plot for a better future?" For once, Abdul showed why he'd obtained a perfect 4.0 average his entire life.

"Damn," said Larry, "I didn't know you had that in you, Abdul. What other surprises are hidden?"

Abdul threw his mischievous smile towards Larry, "Captain, the universe is a vast unknown complex."

Muki was ignoring the boys, and laid her hand gently on Judith's right shoulder. "Judith, let me finish the notes. I think you've read enough." She didn't flinch or resist. Instead, she stood up and surrendered the seat to Muki, never taking her eyes off the notes as they swirled through her mind. *Great-grandfather must die.*

Muki glanced over the page looking intently for where Judith left off.

I know what the future holds.

Nothing.

I know they will never attempt to re-open

this place.

I will stay behind and finish what "I" started

with or without their help.

I will figure out how to operate it on my own.

I will avenge the ills of the past.

I will avenge the dead who can no longer speak.

I will rid the world of evil, hate and ignorant

government officials.

Her diminutive voice was rising as the hate spewed through the notes.

I shall save humanity from its failings.

I shall see to it

that those who brought destruction on others,

shall feel the fires of hell licking at their heels.

The damned will be damned, and evil will be suppressed!

I shall see to it!

Professor Leonoid Rostov Sikorsky

September 4, 2015.

"What was the date of the entry again?" Larry looked very confused.

Muki read it again. "September 4, 2015." The words trailed through the air.

Abdul was the second to put two and two together. "If the complex closed in March of 2015, are you telling me that he has been here ever since?" The question was compelling yet eerie at the same time.

Muki was the first to make the connections. It would explain the numbers instantly appearing on the key lock screen. The serviceability of the elevator and the current source of power required to run the equipment. Yes, as he said in his notes, '*I will stay behind and finish what "I" started with or without their help.*' "He's still here," she said.

She stood up, looking at Abdul, "Yes. He's still here. He never left. It explains many things I didn't understand."

"Muki, are you leading us to believe that he's been here for nine months in hopes of making the machine work?" Larry couldn't fathom how a person could survive for that length of time.

"Yes. If there were proper provisions and fuel, I believe from what we've seen so far, it's very feasible."

Larry wasn't convinced at all.

"Come on Muki, no way. I have a vivid imagination, but not this vivid."

Muki stood her ground. "Larry, he's still here."

Judith's thoughts were not engaged with the current debate; she was burning with the thought of her great-grandfather burning in hell. "I don't give a shit if he is alive, dead or hibernating. All I care about is can we get the damned machine to work?" Her outburst caught the other three off guard. "We have the manual, and between the four of us, we should be able to figure out if it works or not." She quickly glanced at the three. "Well?" The words were more of a demand than a question. "We need to figure out if it works because if it does, I have a score t..." She let the words fall off before her secret surfaced. Her friends waited for her to finish without interrupting. Her next words carried none of the recent passion. "I have a matter of interest to satisfy."

They spent the next two hours poring over the manual to digest ten years of work in mere minutes. The task would be insurmountable for the common person, but these kids weren't common. They could read a twelve-hundred page book in under an hour and retain ninety-five percent of the critical information with no problem. Muki had suggested they have a contest one day to see who could read the fastest and retain the most. Judith won hands down. She devoured Rise and Fall of The Third Reich in under two hours. Her three friends grilled her, question after question, for the same length of time. The only question she stumbled on was Herman Goëring's second wife's name. The correct answer was Emmy Sonneman. Asked why she didn't remember, she gave a typical Judith response. "She wasn't important. His first wife Carin von Kantzow was. He named his hunting lodge after her—Carinhall."

"Man," was all Larry could say. Abdul and Muki finished reading within minutes of Larry. Judith had finished thirty minutes ago, running the schematics and power start-up through her memory banks.

"Took you all long enough. I know how to start it up."

"Judith, from what I read, are you sure we should do this?"

"What, losing your balls Larry, like you did at the diner? Damn right we should do this." The thought of traveling back was engulfing her.

His faced turned red, not from embarrassment of his prior performance, but of Judith taunting him over his ineptitude. "No," he declared. "I just don't think it's a wise move. What if we can't turn it off?"

"Larry, now you're being a pussy. I know how to turn it on and power it down. It's absolute genius." Larry wasn't so sure about the genius part. "Muki, Abdul – remember the large structures you saw when we first arrived at night?" They nodded in agreement. "Know what they are?" They glanced at each other and shrugged their shoulders. Judith was pleased Muki's luck failed her this time.

"Those buildings are solar/wind catching buildings. "The environmentalists and Green Groups would drop dead if they knew the US government had perfected the system five years ago. And the battery manufacturers would keel over knowing they'd been chasing the wrong path Uncle Sam was funding to increase battery life. The issue was never how to store the power; the issue was saving the power." Her deduction made no sense to any of them.

"How are they different, Judith? Storing and saving are the same." Muki was stating an observation and fact.

"No, they're not. That's the problem yet the simplicity at the same time. We've been trying to store the energy instead of saving it. We couldn't see the panels or the turbines because they're shielded under a retractable concrete dome. Obviously, on a sunny day the panels are used; windy days, the turbines. When the weather pattern is split, they use both. Follow me?"

The three nodded.

"Now comes the trick. We've been locked in on storing the energy for a rainy day instead of saving it. Professor Skorzenzy solved the puzzle. If the captured energy is stored in batteries, it becomes static. Think of a car battery. It has 12 volts and 600 amps. The amount of amps determines whether there's enough power to start the car. The volts are only for running the electrical components of the vehicle. When driving, what device is running the battery?"

At first, no one spoke, thinking it over. "The alternator." She noticed agreed nods. "The alternator keeps charging the battery while you drive. Without it, the battery would be drained in minutes, rendering your vehicle useless. Well, that's what everyone has been trying to manufacture on a large scale with minimal luck. Electricity, like any product, will go stale if not kept in flux. The professor figured out how to make it work. The batteries which run this complex and machine, were built with internal perpetual motion diaphragms."

"Perpetual what?" queried Abdul.

"Perpetual motion regulating diaphragms. I don't have time to explain the science, but it's rather simple. The batteries for the site are stored in six large buildings. Larry, remember you kept talking about large green dots on the GPS not allowing you to see the ground?"

"Yes. Why?"

"The buildings are underneath the dots."

Larry recalled how large they were.

"Do you know how big those buildings are, Judith?"

"Yes, they're large enough to hold all the batteries required to supply five years of continuous energy once the batteries are fully charged."

"Okay Judith," asked Muki. "How does it work?"

"Can't you guys see it? It's right in front of you." She started laughing as she explained the secret. "It's so obvious it's ludicrous." She was beaming with her newfound knowledge, which wasn't sinking in. *How could I be associated with such simpletons?*

"Let me say it slower. P.e.r.p.e.t.u.a.l—"

"Knock it off Judith, and get to the point." Larry wasn't amused with her theatrics at all.

"Okay, once the energy starts being collected in the cells, the cells start generating hydrochloric gasses and mass. Did you ever hear anyone tell you to be careful around a hot battery?" She wasn't concerned or interested if anyone threw out an agreement or question and continued her explanation. "The reason is, hydrochloric gasses build up inside the case, and if opened when the battery is hot, the introduction of air can cause a nasty explosion. The professor figured out how to harness the gas and force it through the diaphragms, keeping the stored energy fresh. Once the chain starts, it never stops, thus resulting in an unending amount of fresh energy. Thus, perpetual motion!" She was drained yet energized after explaining how the power was created and kept the complex alive. Sweat slid down her face and chest while she slowly calmed down.

"Any questions?"

* * *

The concealed microphone in the 10000 worked perfectly. The entire discussion was piped into a small desk speaker.

"No questions, my dear," replied the raspy voice. "No questions."

CHAPTER 8

POWER UP

Judith instructed Larry and Abdul in the proper sequence for powering up the components.

It was an ingenious design. It rivaled the Air Force's ballistic missile system, requiring two people to initiate the start-up. The sequence was precise and exact. The ingenious part of the system was the built-in *fail-safe*. Each button triggered a timing system displayed on the left and right side of the panel. Upon enacting one button, the timer would start on the next counter. The intervals for depressing or pulling the switches for the power-up were never the same. The 10000 automatically changed the sequence each time the machine was started up. Thus, the sequence was never the same. It was hack-proof.

Yes, if one were able to penetrate the first line of firewalls, suppressors and routers, the console controls would detect an invader if it tried to access the panel. A hacker would be looking for multiple random signals, sequences and paths. That would be the trigger for the 10000's virus system to go into high gear. The end result for the hacker would be a very long-term jail sentence. The 10000 had the ability to pinpoint the location of the attacker in under a minute. Local law enforcement would be notified, and descend upon the intruder like a Chinese finger torture. There would be no escape.

Larry and Abdul attentively took their stations and prepared for the test. "Ready?" called out Judith. She was still poring through the manual and checking her mental notes.

"Ready," they both replied. Their eyes were concentrating on the vast lifeless controls laid out before them.

"Capt...I mean, Larry." He looked up to his left, stunned that Abdul used his real name. "I believe we are really venturing where no man has gone before, and to be honest, starting this machine up is scaring the hell out of me." Larry couldn't agree more.

"I know exactly what you mean." But what if it does work? What if he could go back and help his dad and Leroy that night in Atlantic City? "Don't worry about it, Abdul. If the test works and we validate the initial experiment, maybe we can call it a day and continue with our real journey."

"Are you two morons ready or are you going to continue talking?" Judith's eyes were burning into both of them. They could feel and sense her intensity. Larry took the lead. "We're ready when you are."

"Good." The words were hard and final. She was taking the stance of a Mission Control Director. She would accept no excuses or child's play. The thought of traveling back in time was enveloping her soul.

She never looked up from her notes as she barked out commands. "Muki, is the chair ready for placement?"

"Yes."

"Lower it into the pit." Muki pushed the green button activating power to the overhead crane. She pushed the *up* button and the chair started ascending. As the chair lifted off the floor, she smoothly started walking towards the platform. The crane was designed to move with the operator and respond with her movements.

"Larry, Abdul – are both the sequence counters reading zero?"

A stereo response, "Yes."

"Prepare for sequence activation." She studied the notes once more.

"Boys, move your power levers to the on position on my count. Three, two, one. Now!"

Simultaneously, they moved the levers to the *on* position. A low humming noise filled the room.

"Larry, push the initiate scrambler button on my count. Abdul, keep your eyes on the sequence counter. Once Larry starts, the process must be perfect." She could feel the power of the complex filling her body.

"Larry—three, two, one. Now!"

He pushed the button. The entire console lit up in every color and shade known to man. She looked up from her notes, admiring the faces of the boys bathed in the rainbow of colors. Their eyes were transfixed to the panel while their minds were locked to hers.

"Abdul, scrambler button two, when counter numbers turn green. You will have only one second. Don't fuck it up. Call out done when finished."

Abdul said nothing. He nodded. His eyes were glued to the counter and the button. He was trying to anticipate the light change. Small beads of sweat started appearing on his face. Green!

"Done!" He took a deep breath.

"Larry, scrambler four." His eyes darted around the panel scanning for the button. Green!

"Done." Larry glanced at Abdul. His face was filled with intense concentration.

"Scrambler five."

"Aye, Ensign. Done."

"Knock the shit, Abdul."

A muffled "aye" followed.

"Scrambler six."

"Done." Beads of sweat were forming on Larry's brow, not only from concentrating, but from the heat emanating from the panel.

The sequence counter numbers started moving quicker and quicker with each button depressed. The tempo was that of an orchestra laying in wait for the audience to respond. The first tempo was *lento* and slowly moved towards *allegro*. The audience was in sync with the conductor as she took them on a frenzied ride.

"Scrambler ten."

"Done."

"Scrambler fourteen."

"Done."

"Power feeds two and three."

"Where are they, where are they," muttered Abdul. The buttons weren't close enough for one hand to depress them in a second. He positioned both hands on the panel watching the sequence counter.

Green.

"Done."

"Power feeds four and five." Larry noticed the same problem and placed his fingers appropriately, waiting for the counter to turn green.

"Muki, is the chair in position to be lowered?"

"Yes."

Green. The buttons required more than normal pressure as they locked into position. His fingers were getting sweaty. "DONE!"

"Conductor releases four, six and seven."

Larry was stumped. "Repeat again." His voice was nervous and cracked.

"Conductor releases FOUR, SIX AND SEVEN, MORON!" He didn't hear or detect her sarcasm, only the switches and buttons he needed to worry about. The counter moved quicker. Green. "FOUR, SIX AND SEVEN, DONE." He quickly moved his hands on his shirt to wipe off the accumulating sweat.

"Conductor release one, two and three." Abdul easily found them and prepared for the green light. "Done."

The humming in the building increased in intensity, but the sound remained steady as the sequence counters' tempo increased. The panel lights appeared to be in sync with the humming. The boys' faces were alight with a myriad of colors as if the control panel were a spinning strobe.

"Intake valves, one through four."

"Shit, four operations? Shit!" Green. "ONE, TWO, THREE AND FOUR, ON!"

"Capacitors four through seven."

"Repeat." The light show was interrupting Abdul's concentration. "Repeat dammit, repeat!"

"Capacitors, FOUR THROUGH SEVEN YOU—"

Green.

"Four through seven activated." Droplets of sweat fell to the panel.

"Muki, lower the chair." She pushed the *down* button. The

hoist cables quietly lowered the chair into the cavern. She could feel her hair standing on end as if she were walking into a field of static electricity. The entire platform was glowing with an unseen energy.

"Final phase. Masters one through six and seven through twelve." The boys knew exactly which controls to work.

Green. "Done."

Green. "Done."

The pace was frantic. The orders she barked were drowned by the deafening humming. Somehow, the boys heard each command. Her voice was being magnified with the vibrating air. More commands. More acknowledgments. The boys and Judith were saturated with sweat. Muki was absolved from the three as she watched the chair come to rest on the platform. She hit the quick-release button disengaging it onto the floor. The chair appeared to be absorbing the energy surrounding the void.

"Last command!" screamed Judith. The boys only heard a calm steady voice say *last command.*

"When the sequencer light turns blue, slide the bar marked SLIP to the left." She repeated the command not knowing if the boys could hear her.

"DONE!" Came the words from Larry and Abdul. Silence enveloped the room. Only a low humming was pulsating through the floor and walls.

The control panel was bathed in white light. The flashing stopped. Calm flowed over the four.

"I did it. Son of a bitch. I did it." Judith beamed with the successful power-up.

Larry wiped his face with his soaked shirt. "Don't you mean, we did it?"

She looked up. "Of course. We did it."

Abdul was still transfixed on his half of the panel. His words weren't so sure. "What exactly have we done?"

"We started it up, you Star Trek idiot. Aren't you always talking about other universes, warp drive and space-time continuum? That's what we've done."

"Great, now what?" Again, his words were unsteady.

Judith approached the panel and roughly pushed Larry to the

side. "We select a date and turn the calendar dial to a time and place we choose, you idiot. Muki, is the chair in position?" No response. "Muki, is the chair in position?" Judith's words carried annoyance with them. "Well?"

"I think you all need to come down here and see what's going on."

"Muki, all I need to know is if the chair is in position. That's a simple question. So, is it—"

Muki ignored Judith's impatience. "Larry, Abdul – you need to come down and look at this." The boys wasted no time. They wanted to distance themselves from Judith in hopes she would regain her composure.

"Captain, what the fuck is that?" Larry couldn't believe it either. The chair was suspended six feet off the floor. It was spinning around in a perfect three sixty. It was moving so fast if appeared to be stationary. Nothing any of them learned could provide an answer. It was dumbfounding.

"Larry," asked Muki. "What do you think? Should we continue with the exercise or shut it down?"

"Muki, I'm not sure. The section I read about the molecular conversion can't harm us or the complex. The only danger is something falling into the chamber while it's activated. The danger occurs when the stream is broken or bumped by an object not already acclimated to the artificial magnetic field. If the stream is disrupted, the original object will instantly result in total molecular separation and reanimation in seconds, thus the original object, and the foreign one, will become one and the same with a completely different molecular structure."

Abdul pondered the thought for a moment. "So, a good example would be if a person were being transported, and a foreign object entered halfway through the process, those beings would become one?"

"Correct."

"So this machine could be the great-great-great-grandfather to a real transporter?" His apprehension was dissipating.

"Abdul, you would be correct."

Muki still wasn't convinced though. "Larry, do you still think it's a good idea to test the machine? What if something goes wrong?"

Her skepticism was weighing on Larry. He knew Abdul was changing his thinking; Judith was hell-bent on trying it. Even his own curiosity was challenging the course of caution. "Muki, I think it's safe. Let's go ahead and finish the test run. After that, we'll see what happens."

"Okay Larry, but remember, the only information we will gain, is that the chair comes back whole. We won't know if it actually travels to the specific time frame or not."

* * *

Shut the little Asian girl up. She could ruin everything.

* * *

"Well? Are you three going to gawk at a normal household chair, or are we going to make a little history of our own?" Judith's composure was slowly returning, but her impatience remained high.

"We're on the way up," answered Abdul.

They congregated around the control panel trying to decide where to send the chair. Muki was right. It didn't matter what time frame they chose. There would be no hard evidence if it ever arrived, just that it returned in one piece. They agreed to set the dial to June 10th, 1997. Location 38° 53' 53.5" N Latitude and 77° 02' 09.9" W Longitude: The White House. They hoped that maybe the chair would wind up in the Oval Office and with luck, there might be a stain or two, that upon further examination, might reveal DNA of the sitting president and his young intern. Well, maybe.

"Who read the portion on time propulsion?" Judith asked.

Larry answered. "I understand the molecular structure of items sent and their reanimation."

Abdul was next."I'm familiar with the working of the 10000 and the virus systems."

Judith looked at Muki. "Imagine that. Miss Lucky got the section on how to actually move the objects into the past and bring them back. Muki, show us what you know."

She reluctantly approached the panel as if she were looking into the future. "I don't think we should do this." Her comment shocked Judith.

"What do you mean?" Her voice was threatening. "The boys and I didn't spend ten minutes sweating our balls off to have you decide to wimp out."

"Judith, we don't—"

"We don't what? If you won't do it, I'll read the manual myself and figure out how to do it, you shit." Muki abruptly turned and bore her black eyes into Judith.

"Listen Barbie, I've tolerated all of your fucking shit for the last time. I bailed your ass out at the diner, and how many countless times on campus. No more." Her voice was even-tempered yet serious."I will not listen to your rantings or beratings anymore. Of all of us, you are the most spoiled, ungrateful bitch I've ever known. And if you don't shut your fucking mouth, I'm going to shut it for you. Understood?"

Larry and Abdul took a step back not knowing what to expect. Abdul leaned towards Larry. "I've never seen her like this. I mean, she's one sweet little Asian, but I've never seen this side of her."

Larry tilted his head as Abdul's words sank in. A very small grin appeared as he looked at Abdul.

"Are you saying what I think you said?"

The question woke Abdul up. He needed to backtrack quickly.

"Uh...no...I mean she is...ah..., you know." The words failed him.

"Scotty, I believe I know exactly what you're saying."

"Shit," was all he could say.

"You and Muki?" The thought triggered a small chuckle from Larry.

"Man cannot live on warp speed alone, Captain."

"What the hell are you two laughing about? Muki is threatening to ruin the experiment." Judith turned her anger and embarrassment on the boys. She'd seen what Muki was capable of and wanted no part of it.

"Nothing, Judith." Larry approached Muki. "As I said, it'll be alright. We're safe. Go ahead and let it fly." He placed his right hand on her left shoulder as a father would to a daughter, hoping to convey some reassurance.

"Okay."

The process for initiating the propulsion wasn't difficult. She slowly pulled the black lever attached to the side of the panel straight back. The black monitor in the middle of the panel turned on, revealing the massive doors. They strained to open. The humming sound increased. Next was the red surge protector button. The humming further increased. The panel lights started flickering again in their bizarre dance.

The air was again being filled with a warm electric feeling. The hairs on their arms and heads started to frizz. Next, the SLIP activator button. The humming notched up another tone. Their skin started itching with the energy flowing through the room. Muki took a deep breath in and held it as she pushed the last button, SLIP ENACTOR.

The humming stopped. They could see the chair in the monitor stop. It hung motionless while being bathed in a bright, subdued, white hue. The chair appeared to be a living organism.

Before any of them could blink, it disappeared. The air filled with a heavy silence. The humming stopped. They stood motionless staring at the empty monitor. A strange residual hue hung in the screen. The color didn't register. It was its own creation.

Larry was in awe."Okay, anyone believe what just happened?"

Abdul was still dissecting and cataloging the events. "I believe we actually reached warp speed. Do you think it was transported back in time, or did it vaporize?"

Larry shook his head, "I have no idea." He took a deep breath and finally settled back into his own body. It was the first time since the power-up started he felt normal again except for his heart racing at 140bpm. "Damn," came the quiet words. "Is everyone all right?" He looked at Judith and Muki, noticing a bright sheen surrounding their bodies. "Judith, Muki. You girls okay?" They appeared to be in a deep trance.

"Judith! Judith!" Larry grabbed her by the shoulders. Her eyes were glued to the panel, yet they were looking at nothing. "JUDITH! Snap out of it!" She dragged her right hand across her face pushing the soaked bands of hair from her face. Her eyes were deadpan. No emotion radiated from them.

"What are you doing, Larry? Get your fucking hands off me."

"Hey, I'm checking to make sure you're okay."

Judith took stock of herself without letting the others know that she too was concerned. She noticed her increased heart rate and her drenched clothing. Her eyes started to refocus and take in the strange, warm hue filling the room. "Yeah Larry, I think I'm okay." Her voice returned to normal.

Larry turned his attention towards Muki. "You okay?" She too was transfixed to the monitor. Small beads of sweat hung from her thin, black hair, and then cascaded to the panel. "No Larry, I'm not all right. Physically, nothing is wrong." She turned her wet face towards his. "Mentally, I'm not sure. At the time, I didn't think it mattered, but a section of the manual was missing."

Larry's look was confusing. "What are you talking about, a section is missing? We all read it, or at least everything that was available."

"True Larry, but a section is missing."

Larry scanned Abdul and Judith for a clue. "Did either of you notice any torn pages or an area that was overlooked?" They shook their heads in the negative.

"Muki, what section is missing?" Her eyes did a quick, yet complete, search of her own body. "Larry, does your body feel different? Is your heart racing with no physical activity? Judith, Abdul – the color of your hair has changed." The words took them by surprise. Larry looked at both of them, and again at Muki. It was true. Judith's hair was now a reddish-brunette; Abdul's showed flecks of gray, and Muki's was darker than pitch with an unnatural sheen. Before Larry could address the issue, Muki stepped in.

"Do you realize how many electrons and positrons this machine generates? The number is off the charts. Scientifically, it's impossible. We conducted many experiments in the lab, and could only generate enough power to run a small hydro electric dam. Nothing spectacular to be sure. This machine generated over one-hundred million times one-hundred megawatts in a few seconds. More than enough energy to run every electrical device in the world for years." She let the knowledge sink in.

"The amount of electrons and positrons filling the room during the process would take the most sophisticated measuring devices ever manufactured to record the amount of gamma rays we were just subjected to." The mention of gamma rays got everyone's attention.

"Muki," asked Larry, "if what you say is true, we should all be dead. Right?"

She didn't look up. "Yes. The amount of radiation created should have burned us up in seconds. We wouldn't have felt a thing. We would have internally imploded from the massive heat, and then the magnetic field surrounding us would have crushed our remains to dust. The gravitational force generated is 1one-hundred times greater than the Earth's."

"Then why are we still alive?" asked Abdul. "If what you say is true, we should have died halfway through the sequence?"

"I don't know. Maybe it's the material lining the walls? Maybe the professor developed a buffer filtering out the gamma rays? I don't know. What I do know is we have been exposed—"

The word exposed triggered Larry. "Protective clothing. There is no section on protective clothing. How could I have overlooked that?" His words were true. His words prompted an immediate search by his friends as they checked their skin for unusual burns or blemishes.

"Captain, I'm proud to say my shorts are clean, and everything is in operating order.

"Larry smiled at the comment. "Same here, Abdul."

Judith rolled her eyes as the juvenile in the boys was starting to resurface.

"Well, we're not dead, at least not yet. If the section is missing, where would the clothing be?"

"I'm sure they took it when the facility shut down. No sense in leaving behind expensive equipment when it could be used somewhere else," replied Larry.

"So what are we supposed to do now?" quipped Abdul.

Judith responded first. "Finish the experiment. And Abdul, if you get the idea you might need to die, please do it someplace else. We have work to do."

Her hard words weren't unusual; it was the tone and iciness of them which caused concern. Judith's temper was becoming harder and more difficult to anticipate since reading the manual. Larry hoped it was only temporary, but it didn't appear so. She was becoming completely wrapped up with the surroundings and the machine, almost as if it were possessing her in an unreal manner.

Abdul's patience was growing thin with Judith's continued ranting. He started moving threateningly towards her. Before he could attack, Larry broke the tension.

"Scotty, it appears our executive officer might need a visit to sick bay. I'm sure Dr. McCoy and nurse Chapel could provide the correct remedy."

Abdul stopped and agreed.

"Yeah, she could use about a thousand milligrams of morphine or Dilaudid. That'd knock her ass out."

She paid the comments no mind. Her focus was on the control panel.

"Muki, bring it back. It's been an hour. Let's see if it returns." Muki wasn't going to argue the issue.

* * *

Yes, my children, bring it back.

* * *

"Okay, Judith." She looked down at the button denoting RECOVERY.

Without thinking, Muki depressed the button. A whirling sound resonated from deep in the hole. The lights on the panel went black. The same strange hue seeped out of the launching pad. It bathed the room and surrounded them in a deep blanket of electricity and color. It was the same warm electric charge surrounding them when the chair disappeared. Larry tried to tell Muki to shut it down, but the words wouldn't come out. Lightning bolts danced from the launching pad floor to the overhead crane, adding more confusion and intensity as the machine whirled. The kids were frozen as the energy climaxed. A thunderous *whoosh* filled the massive hall, followed by abject darkness. The monitor on the panel was the only visible light. The chair appeared in the middle of the screen.

Her words were quiet with awe. "It worked," uttered Judith. "It worked."

She was the first to exit the control panel and descend the iron ladder to the floor of the launching pad. The metal was still warm from the reaction. Larry tried to tell her to wait. He knew she wouldn't listen, so he motioned his partners in crime to follow.

Judith ran her hands over the chair making sure it wasn't a mirage. Yes, it was still whole. The wheels worked, the recliner worked, the armrests were complete. The back sliding adjustment was in perfect order. She looked up as the others gathered around.

"It works," she proudly exclaimed. "The fucking thing actually works!"

Larry wasn't as convinced. Sure, the chair returned with no appreciable damage and apparently whole. But what proof was there it actually arrived at its destination?

"How can you be so sure it actually went to the White House, Judith?" She cringed with his lack of confidence.

"Larry, if it didn't work, explain this." She stood up and spun the back of the chair for the others to see. They couldn't believe their eyes. They all knew what the stencil mark represented. They had all seen the symbol behind the press secretary during interviews. It was unmistakable—the seal of the President of the United States was stamped on the back panel.

"And if that doesn't convince you, explain the red lipstick marks on the front of the chair?"

The three peered down. "Lipstick?"

CHAPTER 9

SKORZENZY

The four were staring at the chair as if it contained a mystical brilliance of the past. Yes, the seal of the president was authentic. Yes, the trappings of red paint or lipstick were prominently visible against the highly-polished black leather. Would this be proof enough to vindicate or crucify the sitting president of the time? Would he be reindicted for lying before Congress, or better yet, could the evidence be used by opponents of the Democratic Party and prove their allegations? Maybe the evidence could be used (if verified) to spawn a new trilogy of past presidents and their sexual escapades in the White House. The cast was there. FDR, JFK, LBJ and now WJC. Too bad they weren't all alive. It would make a great reality show for FOX. Hell, they might do it anyway.

Abdul was seriously considering all the above. "Guys, wouldn't it be cool if we could prove what we're looking at? I mean, think of the book deals, films and speeches we could give. We wouldn't have to work for years." For once, Abdul made sense. Of course, everyone was waiting for some type of Star Trek reference, but they were pleasantly disappointed.

"We have the rest of our lives to work. I don't know about you guys, but I would much rather travel the country on someone else's dime and have a blast doing it. We would probably be able to milk this gig for a good year, if not two. And the best part is that I could return to Highland Park, look up my old tutor Jason, and raise some serious hell at SMU." The idea put his mind in overdrive.

Not waiting for responses, he continued mapping out their futures. "Think about all the chicks, Larry. They would be standing in line for us. Everyone would want a piece of fame." That was it. Abdul was doing well, until he decided fame and fortune would allow vast opportunities to have any woman he wanted.

"Abdul," interjected Judith, "even with fame and fortune, your odds of getting laid by a real woman will remain the same; one hundred times ten to the minus 100th power."

"Don't be so sure about that, Judith." Muki flicked her black orbs towards Abdul, remembering a night not so long ago. "It could be his ticket to unknown pleasures."

Judith ignored her thought and redirected her focus. "Okay, the machine works. I think we need to take it to the next level."

Larry's eyes narrowed. His brow became wrinkled as he comprehended the next step. "Judith, are you seriously considering having one of us travel back in time?"

Without a moment's hesitation, the reply was a concise. "Yes."

Larry was afraid she'd say yes. He, like Abdul and Muki, was acutely aware of her personality change in the last few hours. Judith was always overwrought and highly strung, yet since the team started examining and learning the intricacies of the machine, her attitude had turned for the worse. It was much more intense and focused. It was almost as if she were hiding something from her past, which streamed to the surface. Why now? What was driving her? It was time for a meeting of the minds.

* * *

If my plan works, the children will need these.

Skorzenzy removed a key from his pocket and unlocked the locker door. Inside, was one gravitational suit he'd meticulously kept clean and maintained over the years. Next to the actual machine, the suits were his crowning achievement. They weighed no more than five pounds each and easily fit over street clothes. He learned from the experiments in Waxahachie that in order to survive time travel of any type, special clothing must be developed to handle the immense magnetic g-forces the body would be subjected to. The key to survival was in deflecting the magnetic forces away from the body to avoid being crushed. He performed this by reversing the properties of electricity. The suits were charged with negative ions by a small, portable battery which fed thousands of tiny fiber optic branches. The negative energy surrounded the user, protecting them from the crushing magnetic forces.

He gingerly removed two of the pearly-white suits, closed the locker door, and proceeded to the hidden door.

* * *

"Have you lost your mind? Did you not see the chair spinning around in the chamber? There is no way in hell I'm going to be a guinea pig and risk my life."

Judith threw a very mean glare at Abdul. "No one is asking you to do shit. Do you think I would consider yourself for such an important experiment? As I said earlier, you'd have better luck with a blow-up doll than a real woman. This is much too important a mission for the likes of you." Her voice was rising. Larry decided it was time for a cooler mind.

"Judith, lay off Abdul. No one said anything about us actually transporting ourselves back in time. The risks are too high. I agree with Abdul. We have no idea what type of forces the machine emits." He knew she wasn't listening; he knew she was looking at him, but her eyes were somewhere else. A place he needed to find. A place that was filling all of her thoughts.

"We don't know if the molecular structure of the chair went through a transformation. It appears to be whole, but is it?" His question caught a small glimmer in her eyes. "What if one of us is successful in traveling back in time only to reappear in a pile of indiscernible goo, or worse, never come back at all? Abdul and Muki have more experience with these studies than I do. Muki, is it possible to return in one piece or will we be scattered across the universe?"

Abdul took the lead. "I don't know. It's possible we could return whole—"

"Or we could have our atoms rearranged to the point we could be alive and dead at the same time. The physics is very complex. From what I've read, the gravitational forces generated would crush the human form before it was ever transported. A human would need—".

No one heard him enter the room or approach them. The voice was clear, yet worn. "A suit to properly protect the fragile human body."

Four sets of eyes turned to find the voice.

"And you would be?" probed Larry.

"Professor Leonoid Rostov Skorzenzy, at your service."

Larry gave the so-called professor a quick once-over, attempting to decide if this really were the man responsible for the machine. "How do we know that? You could be one of the night caretakers making sure nothing bad happens." Leonoid ignored the comment.

"My dear son, do you think a common caretaker would have designed the power system for this machine?" His comment was sarcastic and flippant. He walked past the other three, moving straight up to Judith. "My dear, since you seem to be the only true believer here, this suit will allow you to travel to a different dimension with no harm to your beautiful young body." Even Skorzenzy was taken aback by her figure. Her eyes immediately transfixed on the suit. She reached out to grab it, but was stopped as Larry grabbed her arm.

"Not so fast, Judith. I have some more questions for the good professor."

"Of course you do, son." His voice recognized Larry. His body language did not. "What would you like to know?" As Larry formulated a question, the professor continued. "Please follow me back to the office. Being of advanced age and the government seeing fit to remove all the sitting furniture, there is only one comfortable chair for a man of my age." He didn't wait for an answer. He placed the suits on one of the empty metal desks and departed to his office. "Coming, children?" Judith followed like a puppy being tempted with a treat. Larry, Muki, and Abdul held back for a few moments.

"I don't like him," commented Abdul.

"He's hiding something," said Muki.

"I know, I know. I don't trust him either, but what choice do we have? We could leave right now, but Judith isn't about to go. I gather you've noticed the strange look in her eyes? She's not leaving until whatever is possessing her is released. So, I suggest we play along, for the moment, and see what happens." The other two agreed and followed Larry towards the office.

When they entered the room, Skorzenzy was sitting in front of the 10000 which was up and running. Judith was perched to his right watching the screen as it flashed through the files the professor was scanning. "See my child, it's perfectly safe, and with help I can—"

"Can what, Professor? You can what?" Leonoid was not pleased with Larry's interruption of his mini lecture. His eyes never left the screen.

"I can..." realizing his almost poor choice of words he recanted. "We can correct the errors of history and save millions of lives. That's what we can do."

"With all due respect, Professor," chided Larry, "I don't believe that's a wise course at all. I'm of the opinion we should leave the past alone, and concentrate on the present."

"Young man, you are correct. Tampering with history is a taboo taught us since the invention of generating electricity. Many felt allowing light and telephone service were the doings of the Devil himself. Granted, there have been a few liberties taken with the technology, but overall, how would our world work without them? Imagine not being able to call anyone you wanted to— instantly. Imagine a world without light. Imagine waiting weeks or even months to hear of a loved one's passing? My son, I'm not suggesting we completely change history, but rather, modify it a bit."

At no time did Skorzenzy look at Larry. His subject was Judith. He could feel her passion for the project. It exuded from her pores. Her eyes never left his as he weaved his pompous, self-serving explanation to Larry and the others.

"Professor, I stick with my original position. I cannot see where anything good could come from such an adventure." Skorzenzy was becoming irritated with Larry's interference.

"My son—"

The words were direct and hard. "Professor, please stop referring to me as your son. I have my own father."

"I apologize for the slight, Larry. I meant no harm. What if we could go back and visit the past in order to unravel unanswered questions. As you can see from the chair, the questions concerning infidelity in the White House are sitting, no pun intended, right in front of you. Does that not interest you in the least?" His tactic was working. Instead of pushing Larry to accept his idea, he was coming around, with curiosity, via the back door.

"Well, yes. That is interesting but still—"

"But nothing. You have the proof to correct the mistakes and misgivings of the event. If handled properly, no real harm would come to the president of the time. It would make a good story and possibly line your pockets with a dollar or two." Abdul was now extremely interested as this was his line of thinking.

"Yes!" shouted Abdul. "We would be sought out for our expert knowledge and firsthand evidence of the dastardly deed. Well, at least his wife thought it was. See Larry, we could take the past and cash in. We wouldn't really have to work for years. Think of it as an extended vacation." He was starting to side with the professor.

"Abdul, I'm still not convinced." Larry looked to Muki for confirmation. She remained silent, as did Judith.

The thought of traveling back and correcting the mistakes of the past was foremost in Judith's mind. She would do anything to eliminate the family's tainted genealogy. Her great-grandfather must die. He was a member of the most vile regime history ever chronicled. Yes, the Romans, the Russians, and the Persians all retained a portion of rape, pillage and death, but nothing on the scale or the efficiency her great-grandfather purported. The deliberate and intentional elimination of humans—based on birthright and sexual preference—was disgusting and repugnant. She knew if she were allowed to travel back and eliminate him, she would not exist. It would be a small price to pay if it meant millions of people were allowed to live their lives in peace.

"Professor, I'm still leery of delving into the past. Abdul might be correct in that we could cash in on the past and avoid permanent employment for a time, but we would still be tempting fate, wouldn't we?

"My so...excuse me, Larr—" His words were drowned out as

Judith broke out of her trance.

"Larry, shut the fuck up. Okay? Just shut the FUCK UP! Are you so ignorant you're unable to grasp what's sitting in front us?" Her eyes bored deep into his. He could feel them probing his soul for an answer.

"Whether you agree with the professor or not is irrelevant. What is relevant is saving millions of lives from being exterminated by the will of a few men. It is our duty to travel back and eliminate those who will stain the records of mankind for centuries. This is not a choice; it is a mission which we must pursue and fulfill. Who gives a fuck what people think? They will think less, once they find out we possess the means to correct the past." Sweat slid down her temples as she ranted.

Her outburst didn't come as a shock to her friends. Since the start-up of the machine, her temper and persona were sharp and unforgiving. What intrigued Larry the most, was the passion in which she ripped his ass. Whatever he detected was about to come bubbling out of her. He needed to find out what it was. Knowing her rant would probably escalate rapidly, he had to know. He needed to know what burned inside of her.

"Judith, those are the remarks of an unstable incoherent woman. Are you," he bit his tongue knowing the comment would unleash a sleeping volcano, "PMSing again?" The look in her eye answered his question. She was going to explode as they'd never seen before.

"PMS? You think I'm on the rag or something?" She walked right up to Larry, toe-to-toe, invading his personal space. He took a few steps backwards attempting to escape. No luck. The room was too small as she cornered him against the wall. She moved in for the kill.

"PMS? You have no idea what you're talking about!" she raged. "Did your family kill millions of innocent people? Did they deliberately slaughter thousands just because they didn't like the way they looked? Well, did they? You sniveling pile of shit! Did they? Answer me, dammit, ANSWER ME!"

Larry did his best to regain his composure in hopes of saying something to calm the situation. "Judith—"

"Shut up, you idiot. Do you know what it's like to carry the burden of a tainted family history? Have you any idea what it's like to wake up every day and realize who your ancestors are? Do you ever wish you hadn't been born, knowing the evil hidden in your genealogy? Do you?" The strength of her voice started fading as her pent-up past poured forth. Tears were pouring from her eyes as she faced the other three. "How would you feel knowing your great-grandfather was part of the largest mass murder in history?" Her eyes fell to the ground.

Muki took a few steps towards Judith, making sure she didn't enter her personal space. She extended her right hand and grabbed Judith's sweat-covered left arm. "Judith, what is it? What are you so ashamed of?"

Judith slowly raised her head, looking into Muki's face. "Martin Bormann. Martin Bormann is my great-grandfather." The shame of the words creased in her face.

"My great-grandfather was the personal secretary to…" Her words trailed off covered in sobs and tears.

"Adolf Hitler," finished Larry. "My God, your great-grandfather was part of the Third Reich. Judith, I didn't—"

She wiped the tears from her face. "No one knew. It wasn't something I wanted to advertise."

Skorzenzy did his best to offer solace. He knew she would help him if he helped her. He also knew it wouldn't be wise to jump right in and send her back to avenge the family name. No, they would take this one step at a time.

"My child, what a burden you have carried in your short years. I too have a somewhat tainted past when it comes to that terrible time in mankind's history." He waited to see if his words were registering. He hoped she would have at least nodded her head; instead she kept close to Muki.

"My father was also in the war."

Muki was the first to make the apparent connection. She inquisitively raised her eyes to hear the professor out.

"History doesn't paint a very favorable opinion of our ancestors who fought for their country and leaders. Instead of studying and detailing the brave men who fought to correct the ills of the Versailles Treaty, it concentrates on the worst the Third Reich conceived—persecution, systematic death and vengeance."

Muki was particularly interested in the history lesson. Larry and Abdul were showing remote interest. Larry couldn't identify the feeling welling up, but he feared the professor was delivering a sales pitch aimed at Judith.

"Professor." Larry's words were short and sarcastic. "Would you have us believe that what Adolf Hitler and his henchmen performed was somehow noble?"

"Dear boy—"

"Professor, I'm not your *dear boy*—"

"My apologies Larry, I meant no harm." Larry was going to be the one he would carefully have to move into his court, or else he might need to somehow isolate him from the group. His judgmental attitude could possibly unravel his plans. "No, I'm not condoning what a few fanatical lunatics were responsible for. I'm merely stating there were great minds of military genius and science produced during the war. Look at the technical advancement of the human race during the sixteen short years of the Third Reich. The world went from simple wooden planes to jet engines. We harnessed the atom. We made space flight possible. Never in the annals of history did the world change so rapidly in such a short time."

Larry studied the facts for a minute, as did Muki. Muki spoke in the hope that Larry would listen a little longer. She needed to quench her curiosity.

"Professor, what you say is true. Nothing can be refuted, but look at the cost. Do you think the victims in London are pleased the V2 resulted in space travel becoming a reality?" Her question was justified without damaging the professor's ego.

"My child, excuse me, Muki, yes, there was much tragedy and death associated with the construction of the weapon. I'm not so naïve as to think only of its initial purpose." Caught up in the moment, or recalling the brilliance of the brilliant German scientists, he failed to heed his next words. "We were the masters—"

"We?" queried Muki. Her question aroused suspicion with her friends. They were all (including Judith) taking a very disturbing interest in his remarks.

"Excuse me, a slip of the tongue. I meant to say *they,* the men under Van Braun were men of great genius. Think of the final months of the war. Were the Allies and Russians truly advancing rapidly to end the reign of the Nazi Germany? Yes and no. The real prize wasn't a land laid to waste by continual bombing; it was the men who devised the weapons. That was the real prize. Jet propulsion, synthetic fuels, rocket technology and stealth planes. That was the prize. Instead of starting to rebuild a decimated country from the ravages of war, the Allies plundered Germany of their most prized possession—knowledge."

Everything Skorzenzy said was true. Muki knew this. It would be years before the British, Canadians, French and Americans would start assessing the damage and pass the Marshall Plan. But before that, they were more concerned with rounding up the most coveted prize—scientists. The Russians were doing the same, along with stripping what would become East Germany of her manufacturing base and sending it back to the "Motherland."

"Professor, I agree with the synopsis. Yet, you also addressed military genius. Could you elaborate a bit more?" She scanned her memory banks and knew the question that could unlock her suspicions. "When you speak of military commanders, are you referring to Guderian, Halder, Rommel or Skorzenzy?"

The last name sparked immense curiosity among her associates, especially Judith. The look in the professor's eyes answered her question, but she needed everyone to hear the answer. She continued probing a little deeper.

"Professor, I'm curious about three events I've studied in depth: the airborne invasion of Crete, the abduction and freeing of Mussolini and finally, the first units to offer organized resistance to Operation Market Garden and the Commando group codenamed 'Operation Grief.'"

Her friends were stunned with the directness of her question. They knew she was moving towards a common goal, but weren't sure how. The professor knew exactly where she was going. Only a student of history would link those major events to one man—his father, Otto Skorzenzy.

"My child," he made no apologies this time. "You are well versed in the annals of history. Someday, I should meet your

instructors and thank them for producing such an astute prodigy."
He did nothing to evade her inquisition. He could have weaved a
deceptive scenario deflecting attention from his past, but that
would accomplish nothing. Rather, it would raise more questions
and suspicions, which would be counterproductive to his agenda.

"You are correct in your connections. I will not address each
question individually as the answer will result with the same
answer. You are referring to my father, Lieutenant-Colonel of the
Waffen-SS, Otto Skorzenzy. I am proud to say his name, but with
caution. He did what any man in his position would do, he—"

Judith was fully alert and not in a good way.

"Your father was part of the Third Reich? If so, then he is
just as responsible as my great-grandfather for perpetuating this
horrible injustice on humanity.☐ The fire faded from her voice.
"What I wouldn't do to go back and rewrite this page of history."

Yes, my dear, what would you give to go back and turn the
clock? With a little more encouragement, she will be an excellent
ally.

"I agree with your assessment one-hundred percent, my
child. Imagine if we could eliminate the politicians of the time,
and spend our energies and resources on science and research
alone. Think of how far the world would have advanced while
saving (not that he cared for the millions of lives snuffed out)
countless lives, and moving mankind forward in a positive and
humanitarian way." His oration was rapidly sinking in on Judith.
Not so with the other three.

"Professor," asked Larry, "If you are so touched by the
evilness of the Third Reich and the crimes committed against
humanity, why do you speak so proudly of your father? Wasn't he
convicted of war crimes and treason for his part in the war?" As
the professor assessed the accusation, he was rescued by an
unexpected soul.

Muki knew Otto Skorzenzy had escaped capture awaiting his
de-nazification trial. He was never officially charged with treason
for wearing stolen American uniforms during "The Battle of The
Bulge."

"That's not true, Larry. Skorzenzy was exonerated of the
charges when it became known that the British were fighting

behind the lines wearing German uniforms. He went on to live out his life, not actually on the run, but keeping a rather low profile with the help of the ODESSA organization. The only crime he really committed during the war was fighting for his country and his beliefs."

Muki wasn't pleased to be supporting his stance, but the facts and history were clear on his part. He fought as any soldier would have for his country. "Professor, you would be correct. The charges against him were never pursued, and yes, he was allowed to live out his life 'under the radar', free from his accusers. But once he escaped the hangman's noose, he dropped out of sight. How did a man of such prominence become a ghost? "

"Wonderful, little girl. I couldn't have stated the facts any more clearly. Thank you for helping an old man out."

"Professor, I'm not attempting to corroborate your story, I'm only stating the historical facts."

His tone was cold and condescending. He needed to keep Judith engaged and keep Muki off balance. She might inadvertently stumble upon some facts she wasn't aware of. "Yes, yes, child. However, let us return our attention to the issues at hand." He stared deep into Judith's soul. She responded by raising up her head and locking onto the professor's gaze. "What if we could travel back to say, 1938, and eliminate Hitler and his henchmen?"

Muki didn't care for the direction Skorzenzy was plotting.

"Professor—" Her words were rapidly cut off as Skorzenzy tired of their debate.

"Are you so naïve not to understand what we can achieve? Are you willing to let millions upon millions of innocent people die because you feel some moral obligation to allow the events of history to remain unchecked? Or maybe you are satisfied with the killings of millions to achieve the goals of fools?" This was an argument Muki would have a hard time winning.

"Professor, I'm only stating that—"

"Enough," interrupted Judith. " Muki, that's enough. You have no family shame to contend with. You have no idea what it means to carry the burden of the past upon your shoulders. The professor and I do. We live it every day we look in the mirror. It surrounds us as would a choking fog. It's always there. It never goes away, no matter how many times you blink your eyes and wish it away. You wake every morning seeing the past."

Skorzenzy had her. She was one-hudnred percent on board with the suggestion, but he wasn't going to interject just yet. Let her continue to speak, and maybe she could convince Muki and Abdul it was a mission worthy to pursue. Larry, hopefully, would fall in line. If not? Well, let's see what happens.

Judith was emphatic and determined. "Professor, I'm in! It's time to cleanse the evils of the Third Reich from the pages of history. It's time!"

"Excellent, my child, excellent. Anyone else feel the same as she?" His question hung in the thick air.

Larry nodded his head in disagreement. Abdul said nothing. Muki liked the idea, yet she still held reservations, but if they could go back, maybe her ancestors who perished in 1945 when the United States firebombed Tokyo, could also be saved. "Professor, I'll agree to the proposal on a few conditions."

Skorzenzy was inwardly ecstatic with her changing views. "Yes, go ahead."

"We need to properly test the machine. One of us needs to go back in time to verify the machine works. I suggest we go back to Dallas, Texas, November 22, 1963."

Skorzenzy wasn't pleased with the suggested date. He knew what happened and why it happened. The conspiracy theorists were correct that Oswald didn't act alone, but the true culprit wasn't the AFL/CIO, or the mob bosses who lost millions when Castro came to power; it was a combination of forces, plus one no one ever imagined. He calculated the risk was worth it. Even if the true conspirators were uncovered, the story would remain as it should be—buried.

"An excellent choice, my dear. I suggest we start the preparations."

CHAPTER 10

SUIT UP!

"Let me explain how it works." Skorzenzy picked up the lightweight unit off the console and passed it around so each of the kids could perform a thorough examination.

"The material is a hybrid of Kevlar. It contains the same properties and resilience, yet as you can tell, it is extremely light and malleable. We discovered some time ago, albeit by accident, that Kevlar could be condensed during the polymerization process. Instead of leaving the liquid in hydrochloric acid, we replaced the mixture with acetone and mineral spirits."

"Professor," spoke up Abdul. "I don't mean to interrupt the lecture, but mixing acetone with mineral spirits isn't going to cause any type of catalytic reaction. Both of the products are bases and inert in their state. The chemicals could never achieve the desired reaction you're describing."

"You would be correct, Abdul. By themselves, they just make a rather undesirable soup. However, when mixed with hydrochloric acid, the results were stunning as you can see."

"Yes, that would answer the catalyst question." Abdul slowly moved his hands over the suit looking for any flaws from the spinning operation. His touch was soft, yet thorough. "Professor, I've noticed something rather odd. Granted, I'm no seamstress, but the suit is void of seams." The others gathered around looking for telltale signs of threads connecting the arms to the torso, along with the legs connecting to the body. There were none.

"Again, you would be correct and very observant. We developed a process where the entire suit could be spun as a single unit for excellent integrity. A good example of the production process would be a grain silo. Have any of you ever seen one built?" They looked at each other with uncertain eyes.

"As you know, grain dust is highly volatile and flammable. It took decades for farmers to understand why the silos were literally "blowing-up" in front of their eyes. The problem—air was seeping in through the joints of the concrete. Understand, they built them in stages. Air is full of moisture, and it would permeate into the grain and start the fermentation process, which would start releasing gases in the confined space. Opening the doors to the storage bin and introducing fresh air to the pent-up gases would result in a most undesirable and deadly result—explosion. When the problem was identified, silos were built in one continuous pour, thus alleviating and minimizing the invasion of outside air and moisture to settle into the grain. Another device added is a blower. It keeps the moisture in the grain to a minimum, thus thwarting a combustible atmosphere."

Larry wasn't as enamored with the agronomy lesson as his compatriots. "Professor, we all appreciate knowing how to build a grain silo. I'm sure with the education we received, it will come in very handy someday. However, it doesn't address the issue why the suit has no seams."

Skorzenzy furrowed his brow, holding back his instant anger with Larry's interruption. *Keep it up Larry. Keep it up. I will surely have a surprise when the time is right, and the other three have taken my side.* He relaxed his facial muscles and let the anger slip away. "I apologize for getting off point. You see, the forces the TIME SLIP generates is immense. The g-forces have been measured at 20 *g*."

"What?" quipped Judith. "Twenty *g*'s? Nothing can survive that type of pressure. A human body would be atomized and crushed before reaching 12 *g*'s for a prolonged period of time."

"You would be quite correct, my dear. The experiments we conducted in Texas showed the same results. The original suits were sewn together with the latest materials available to NASA. They were too large and bulky. Granted, they were a marked improvement over the suits used for the Space Shuttle and Saturn project, but we weren't satisfied. The suits would disintegrate when bombarded with forces of 12 *g* and above for over two minutes. The dummies inside the suits fared no better. They were useless and discarded after each test. It was, as I previously mentioned, a stroke of pure luck we came up with a solution. Our goal was to keep the weight of the suit at five pounds while also providing excellent flexibility and fluid movement capabilities.

Funds were rapidly drying up in Texas. The collider project was spinning out of control, and the budget overruns were becoming too large for Washington to overlook. Thus, any purchase of new raw materials was suspended. We worked with what was available. We had nothing to lose. The results were spectacular. The diluted hydrochloric solution increased the strength of the crystallized solution ten-fold and reduced the dried weight ten-fold. We were elated, to say the least. The next step was figuring out how to spin a suit that would be solid. We enlisted an ex-NASA seamstress to join our team. She worked magic in a matter of weeks. We finally had a prototype that met all the requirements. Unfortunately, it would be fifteen years before the suit would be perfected."

The professor took a breath, studying his students. The science and mechanics behind the manufacturing fascinated them. He could see them all using whatever sciences they studied being put to work as they continued their examination.

"Professor, what is the g-force rating?" queried Judith.

"It has been tested at 25 g's with no noticeable elongation or deformation."

"25 g's? That's incredible." Muki and Abdul nodded in agreement. She then asked the real question. "Okay, the suit can take the pressure, but what of the occupant?"

"Again, my dear, you are correct. If you'll notice, you can just barely discern small threads on the inside of the suit. Yes?"

They had only been examining the exterior of the suit. No one had done a thorough search of the interior. Muki noticed it first. "Yes, it almost feels like fiber optic lines."

"You would be correct. There are two miles of fiber optic cable woven to the inside of the suit." Larry's attention was more concerned with the professor's motives than his explanations.

"Let me guess; we're going to call ET?" Before the professor could answer, Abdul interjected.

"Larry, shut the fuck up and let the man speak." All three stared at Abdul. In all the years of cohabiting and studying, Abdul never raised his voice or showed any sign of an aggressive nature. He always took life in stride and moved along. After all, he was the comic relief the group sorely needed. But this? This was new and unexpected.

"Abdul, I was only pointing out—"

"Shut up, Larry. Hear the man out. This is all making sense a little at a time."

None of them noticed the small gleam in the professor's eyes. *Excellent. One to go.*

"Yes, Larry, may I continue?" inquired the professor. Larry could feel everyone's eyes boring into the back of his head. Before he could answer, the professor continued.

"Before *we* were interrupted, I was describing the fiber optics of the suit. If you notice, there is a small pocket sewn on the inside covering the right breast." Abdul found it.

"A small portable battery pack sits inside the pocket. You will also notice a small lead connection." Abdul confirmed the professor's description.

"The battery supplies the power to the fiber optics." Abdul was confused. Judith was fascinated. Muki was intrigued, and Larry didn't give a shit.

"Why do you need fiber optics?" asked Muki.

"An excellent question. As Judith pointed out earlier, the immense pressure generated by the machine will crush the human body to pulp. The magnetic field the machine generates is tremendous. We needed to come up with a solution to counteract the field and protect the body."

"Like a force field of some sort?"

"Correct, Abdul. A force field."

Muki was grasping the concept. "When power is supplied to the fibers, it creates its own magnetic field. I understand the theory, as we attempted a few minor experiments in the lab, but the results were inconclusive and poor. No matter how strong a battery we used, the experiment failed. Why?"

Skorzenzy knew he almost had number three.

"My child, we too thought it was a matter of power to combat the forces. No, power wasn't the issue—polarity was."

"What?" she asked.

"Reverse polarity with a fresh power source is the answer. Most batteries have a positive and negative energy flow. Right?

Obviously the answer is yes.

"What happens when you reverse the cables on say, a car?"

Judith knew this one as it had happened during a pit stop in California. "You fry the electronics and wind up with three thousand pounds of scrap metal."

"You would be correct, Judith. But what if your battery were reversible? What if you eliminated the negative terminal and only used positive energy? Of course, there is still a ground in case of a failure, but the energy is all positive."

This thinking went against every know principal of electronics Muki had learned and worked with. The idea was absurd, to say the least.

"Professor, excuse me, but that's impossible. You must have a negative reaction for a positive one."

"You would be correct, Muki, but you are also incorrect. With common batteries, there must be a definitive flow. If not, batteries lose their power and die over time. Take the Chevy Volt, for example. It was hailed as the gateway to electrical car power. We know how that worked out. It was too expensive to produce and had a very limited driving range. It was a great idea for those with daily commutes of less than twenty miles, but for the rest of the country, it wasn't a desired option." Larry was chomping at the bit to interrupt and steer the discussion away from the professor, yet based on his last comment, he decided to remain quiet for the moment.

"The same technology that runs this complex is the same that powers the suit. Fresh, pure, endless energy. Eliminate the negative ions and the power is pure and refined."

Muki still wasn't convinced.

"I'm sorry, Professor, it's not possible. There are always negative and positive ions present. You just can't whisk them away."

"What if you could? Let me ask you a question. Are you familiar with the dynamics of electric model trains?" Muki was miffed with this rudimentary question.

"Of course, Professor."

"Are you familiar with the massive train set in Hamburg, Germany?"

Yes, she was. It was the largest model train set in the world. She remembered the first time she saw the website "Miniatur Wunderland" and was amazed at the technology being implemented.

"Good. Did you know that during one of the exhibitions, two trains collided with each other?"

She wasn't aware of this minor event, but based on the size of the system, it was a true possibility.

"No, but I could see where it could happen with so many trains moving at one time."

"True, the accident I'm referring to occurred when two trains collided head on." He let the words sink in.

"That's not possible. The engines are set up where one side receives the positive current, and the other the negative. You can reverse the polarity of the tracks, but you can't change the polarity of the engines. It's impossible for two trains to move in opposite directions on the same track."

"That's what the German engineers concluded. Yet it occurred. The article was published in Modern Electronics ten years ago." She did remember seeing mention of the incident. It was one of the lesser stories that month. "They never pursued the issue and haven't had another occurrence. Bottom line—for a few seconds the tracks were charged with only positive energy."

"Professor, are you suggesting that the freak occurrence of a model train set is the source of the power system for the suit?" Skorzenzy let out a small chuckle.

"In so many words, yes. Obviously, the technology and science are much more elaborate and sophisticated. In principle, the answer is yes. Pure positive virgin energy flows through the fiber optics creating a negative magnetic buffer, thus protecting the user."

Larry still wasn't convinced. "Okay, let's say you're right. Why wasn't the chair pulverized?" For once, he didn't aggravate Skorzenzy with his query.

"A good question. The force from the magnetic field allows the atoms to become one."

"Like a transporter?"

"Exactly like a transporter, Abdul. When the chair was

spinning around, you saw it, didn't you?"

"Yes."

"Or did you? Basic physics would dictate that based on the g-forces, the chair should have been crushed, yet it appeared to maintain its molecular structure, or does it? The eyes see what they want to because the mind is not capable of processing the high speed the object moves at."

"Fascinating. You have built a real-life transporter."

"Well, yes and no. It will send you back in time to a specific setting, but unlike your favorite show, you must wear the suit if you wish to survive. Maybe in ten or twenty years, we shall be able to eliminate the suit, and reduce the magnetic field generated to allow safe unencumbered time travel. Until then, this will be the model for the future."

The kids disseminated the new information. There was one more question that needed to be addressed.

Abdul and Muki were now poring over the suit, looking for any minor flaws or inconsistencies. Muki looked up at the professor and asked the obvious question. "Professor, does it work?" Her words were tainted with curiosity. Abdul and Judith directed their attention back to Skorzenzy, awaiting his reply.

Before he could answer, Larry could restrain himself no more. "Sure it does. Didn't you see that pack of pigs flying yesterday?" His comments were an unwelcomed intrusion to all. In unison, they replied without looking at him. "Shut up Larry!"

Excellent. This is moving along nicely. Now, how shall I remove Larry from the group as his friends willingly assist?

"Of course it works. Let me show you." Skorzenzy moved to the console and depressed the button marked video feed. The massive screen jumped to life. "Children, you are about to witness what few eyes have seen, and the reason this complex is no longer funded. On March 16, 2015, we performed our first and only experiment with a human subject. We sent Army Captain Julian Christopher back to the Egyptian Empire. We were hoping to recover a few artifacts or pictures to prove how the pyramids were constructed."

"Professor, we know how they built the pyramids. It's been well documented through the annals of history," replied Muki.

"You would be correct. The problem with our history books is exactly that. They are ours. They weren't written by the men who actually built them. Watch and learn."

The massive screen came to life revealing the inner sanctums of a room the group hadn't discovered yet. The moderator's voice was unmistakably Skorzenzy's as he addressed the group watching the video.

"Gentlemen, it is with great pleasure and excitement we travel back in time to witness events of the past. Instead of standing here and narrating the entire ten-minute clip, I shall allow Captain Christopher's words to describe the secrets of ancient Egypt as he cataloged them."

The screen was filled with the Great Pyramids at Gaza in ancient Egypt, all in a different phase of construction. The picture displayed reminded many of the movies of the '50s and '60s— *The Ten Commandments* and *Cleopatra*. It was striking. Hollywood almost got it right without knowing it. The scene was filled with thousands of workers moving the massive granite stones to a specific point. The workers/slaves moved in unison. The only sounds were those of the Egyptian superintendents and foremen barking out orders to their lead men to ensure each stone was properly lined up and set.

"If you notice, the workers do not appear to be in poor health." He zoomed the camera in. "They appear to be healthy and alert. You will also notice as I pan the camera, the Egyptians are working hand-in-hand with the labor force. This would suggest that even though many of the workers are slaves, they are working as a cohesive force and not as a rabble. I'm now going to show what appears to be the main construction management site." The camera zoomed onto a tent of one-hundred feet by one-hundred and fifty feet. There were numerous tables filled with charts and maps. The tent was bursting at the seams with management and architectural teams. One could see men coming and going every few minutes with great haste, passing on orders and directions to the men in the field. The events unfolding were no different than a modern construction site. Granted, there was no modern machinery assisting with the tasks—everything was done by manpower.

"As you can see, the ongoing events are similar to a modern construction site. One thing I had noticed before I started filming is the amount of survey crews at work." The camera panned to six different locations. Men were standing by transits and making notes. Large rolls of woven fabric were at each station. A man would grab the end of the fabric and move as directed by the surveyor to a specific point and stop. The surveyor made a notation and sent the man to the next station.

"As you can see, the fabric is the measuring chain. You will also notice that each survey site is in line with the other. I'm assuming this is for perfect alignment of the structure. I'm also assuming there are similar sites on the opposite side of the structure; which unfortunately I cannot see." The men in the room nodded in agreement.

"Now, I want you to direct your attention to the stone placement. This is fascinating. Our books have assumed through the years how the stones were handled and placed. Many said the pyramids were initially built oversized, with ramps to allow the stones to be placed. Look again." The men stared intently as the stone Captain Christopher was focused on was moved and effortlessly slid into place.

You could hear the sound of astonishment from the dignitaries.

"That's impossible," said Larry. "Each one of those stones weighs over two tons. There is no way that happened."

"Really, Larry? Are you suggesting your knowledge of construction procedures is more sophisticated and precise than those of the Egyptians?" Skorzenzy waited for the reply.

Larry fired back. "How do we know this isn't some staged event? Anyone with an ample budget could have produced this."

"Really? Keep watching."

The voice of Captain Christopher came back. "Gentlemen, I'm sure you are as dumbfounded as I am. Instead of seeing the obvious, we overscrutinized the construction procedures. It is time for the historians to rewrite the books concerning pyramid construction." All heads nodded in agreement.

"I'm sure there will be many men and critics who will put no credence or validity to the filming of this event. That is understandable, and I'm sure you gentlemen will all agree with my deduction. So, in order to add credence to this amazing discovery, I will be returning with a few artifacts to authenticate the journey." The camera panned towards two items resting on the hard-baked sand—a papyrus drawing showing the dimensions of the stones and a measuring staff. He turned the camera on himself and concluded the brief documentary. "Gentlemen, I can say without a doubt, the machine works. These items I bring back are proof of our venture. I look forward to returning and discussing the finds. Captain Christopher out."

The lights turned back on. Skorzenzy took his place on the podium. "Gentlemen, it is time to open the champagne and prepare for the arrival of Captain Christopher. General Swanson, I trust you will phone General McCulloch and Senator Hodges with the news?"

Swanson stood up."Professor, I need to use the secure line and report to General McCulloch."

"Yes, of course you do. Use the phone in my private office. It is very secure." The general took his leave to inform Washington of the event.

The screen went blank.

"The rest of the film was inconsequential. When Christopher returned, we were amazed at the artifacts. They were genuine. Unfortunately, the powers in Washington didn't see it as such. They didn't grasp the magnitude of the discoveries or how we could implement the technology to help mankind. They hid behind their veils and stopped the funding."

"Why?" queried Judith.

"They didn't believe mankind was ready for such knowledge. They were pleased that all the money poured into the project had actually produced positive results, but they weren't willing to use it for fear of the unknown." He let the words rest a minute as his students absorbed them. He believed he knew how to completely convince Muki and Abdul this was a good idea. Larry would either join in, or he wouldn't.

"Imagine making a few minor changes in our most recent history. What would the Middle East look like if Hussein, Mubarak, Arafat, Khomeini and Gaddafi were eliminated? Would there have been coordinated world terrorism? Would the Western world have been held hostage over outrageous oil prices? Would blood have been spilled to keep oil at seventy-five dollars a barrel?" His words were true, and his points were sinking in.

"Countless lives would have been saved," replied Muki. "Countless. But even if those leaders were eliminated, what guarantee is there that their successors wouldn't implement the same policies?"

"An excellent question. We would leave a type of calling card to inform those who ascended to the position that if they chose the same path as their predecessors, they would be joining them."

Judith couldn't hold back her thoughts any longer. "Enough of the historical debate. I'm convinced the machine works, and require no more explanations. When do we go?"

CHAPTER 11

PREPARATION

Everyone but Larry was on board, even after Skorzenzy showed them the artifacts Captain Christopher had returned with. No mistake, these were actually from the correct time period, even though there wasn't a carbon machine available to verify exact dates. Muki had handled enough authenticated papyrus scripts of the era to recognize a fake or an authentic artifact. She gazed with amazement at the intricate measurements and details of how the stones were cut at the quarries then moved to the site. The directions were simple and direct in the legend. Even Larry had to appreciate the engineering depicted on the scroll. Albeit skeptical, he couldn't deny the machine actually worked.

The Professor allowed his new pupils to examine the artifacts with no interruptions. They needed to become totally immersed and mesmerized with the treasures of the past. The longer they stared, the more questions they asked, the deeper they would fall under his guidance. He contemplated the next issues as "his" students studied his next move.

The next question would be, who would go first. Judith? Much too ambitious and self-centered. He knew where she wanted to go, but she needed to learn a little temperament. Larry? NO! He's not convinced, and will be the last one before I go, or maybe I shall have him join me. I shall consider this further. The young Star Trek fan? He would be a good choice but still needs a little more convincing. Yes, the young Asian girl, Muki. She would be perfect. Her attitude is correct. She is fascinated with the prospect of studying history firsthand while at the same time keeping her eyes and ears open. She is not easily swayed, and will keep a clear mind in a difficult situation if it should arise. Yes, Muki should go first.

"Children—"

"Excuse me?" Judith's eyes bore into the professor. "Children? You have us mistaken with someone else. We are fully grown adults and do not take kindly to your inference." The intensity and fierceness was resurfacing in her tone.

"Excuse me, Judith. I meant no harm. Students. Is that more pleasing?" The tone was a bit condescending.

"No," replied Larry. "Call us by our names only."

"As you wish. My apologies, but it would be a bit redundant calling each of you by name each time I require to address a topic." He pondered the minor dilemma for a minute, then reached the obvious conclusion. "Graduates. Is anyone opposed to the moniker?" No one spoke up. "Excellent, then 'graduates' it is. After careful consideration I believe, if she isn't frightened by the thought, Muki should be the first to travel back in time. Her success will settle your concerns and eliminate any lingering doubts."

"What?" yelled Judith. "Why should she go first? She's no better than the rest of us. If anyone should go first, it should be me."

"Granted Judith, my decision is not meant to slight any of the graduates. Only, that I believe Muki's grasp of history and thirst for more knowledge would ease all of our fears and doubts, that is, if she is willing to go?" He moved his eyes to Muki, as did the others.

She never flinched or showed the excitement welling up inside. She stared at the stone schematic while formulating her response. She needed to be calm and cool. Too much enthusiasm could jinx the deal; not enough could be viewed as too complacent and unappreciative. She raised her eyes looking for reactions from her friends. Judith's eyes were full of hate and contempt. Abdul's were of bewilderment, and Larry's showed distaste for the whole venture. She could sense he was pleading for her to decline. Choosing her words carefully, she replied. "Professor." Her tone confident and clear. "It would be an honor to represent our group and travel back in time. I have a few questions though before we proceed."

Excellent. She's accepting the challenge.

"Yes. What concerns are you speaking of?"

"The suit. Based on everything we've learned, I'm sure the suits aren't one-size-fits-all.

"Correct."

"And without the suit, the trip would be impossible to undertake."

"Correct."

"Then how is it possible for one of us, especially me, to travel back without a formfitting suit?"

"An excellent point. The suits are custom-fitted for each traveler. Because of the high security of this installation, it was mandatory that the fittings and construction be performed on site. Down the last hallway, is a room where the suit will be spun to your exact requirements and specific needs. Next question." She was too smart to have only one. He would have been highly disappointed if she didn't have at least one more question.

"The next question is twofold. How long will I be gone in real time, and how long will I be suspended in the next dimension?"

"In real time, Muki, that depends on how long you wish to stay in the past. In the case of Captain Christopher, it was agreed we only wanted to observe the events of ancient Egypt. We agreed eight hours would be ample if he were properly placed as dictated by the coordinates we used. Seeing how his clothing and skin color would be difficult to camouflage, he convinced us that he would be able to remain hidden while accomplishing the mission. So, his time was exactly eight hours."

"And if it's eight hours there, then it's eight hours here?" she asked.

"Correct. Time is not altered at all as far as minutes, hours and days are concerned. We aren't accelerating the timeline. It remains the same." She thought about that for a few moments.

"Okay, next question. If the traveler were to get in trouble or find themselves in a compromising situation, is there any way to send a signal to alert the complex of impending danger or a medical issue?"

"Yes, there is. The battery, which powers the fiber optics in the suit, has a small red button on it. If the traveler becomes distressed or compromised, he or she only needs to press the button, and the signal is received back here. We promptly start the return sequence, and the subject will be retrieved within two minutes." She studied his response for a moment, trying to convince herself the trip was worth the risks.

"Okay, one last question. I'm sure the device was extensively tested?" Her tone wasn't as sure.

Abdul was particularly interested in how a radio signal from the past could travel to the future. It was obvious the technology of the past would not be able to accommodate modern technological requirements of the future.

"Professor, excuse me for my ignorance, but how is that possible?"

Skorzenzy wasn't expecting this line of questioning. No, they had no way of receiving or sending messages from the past to the present. Once the traveler was placed, they were on their own. There was no way to open a rift in space and keep it open once the individual was in place. He needed to think fast.

"Since we only used the machine once, which was successful, it was not necessary to test the device. In theory, once an individual arrives at the destination, a magnetic field encompasses the body allowing a small portal to remain open, which produces a small rift for electronic signals to pass through."

"Professor, according to all the quantum physics theories, that would be catastrophic. Creating a rift in the time continuum will drastically alter the electronic and magnetic fields of both universes." Abdul's line of questioning was becoming uncomfortable and discouraging.

"Excuse me, son. You have seen for yourself with the video the machine works. You have seen the authentic artifacts from Egypt." Abdul agreed. "Then why would you question whether the machine is safe or not?" The only argument Abdul could muster was theory, not application.

"Professor, I meant no harm, rather pointing out the theory of—"

Skorzenzy had had enough. "Exactly." The words were hard. "Theory? It's theory you speak of? I speak of fact. Before you is the theory in practice. Are you denying your eyes? Are you questioning the decades of experiments performed to achieve perfection? I have the proof; you have the books. Which one garners more credibility?"

There was nothing he could add. The professor was right. He was looking at the theory in practice.

"I apologize, Professor. I meant no harm. Of course, practicality outweighs theory." Skorzenzy scanned for other questions from the group. None were forthcoming.

"Good, now it is time to decide what era you wish to go back to."

Muki had been fascinated with the JFK assassination in Dallas. "Professor, as I mentioned earlier, I would choose November 22, 1963 in Dallas, Texas."

The date did not escape him. He knew the day well—all too well. His father and uncles spoke about the topic very freely when they vacationed in the Caribbean. At home, the topic was never broached or hinted at. In private, it was the center of discussions.

"My dear, and why would you want to see JFK killed? What could you possibly learn from such a tragic event in American history? Would it not be wise to let the man lie in peace? Surely there is a more desirable area to visit?" He was cautious with his tone. If he couldn't talk her out of the choice, then he would take the chance, hoping the family secret would remain a secret. Even if she did learn the truth, she would have to leave the facility alive to make the knowledge public.

"No, Professor. That is the area I wish to travel to." Without arguing, he agreed.

"And where have you decided to be placed? The Grassy Knoll? The overpass on IH-35 and Commerce, or the Book Depository Building?"

Muki thought about the choices. The professor had left out an important landmark, which could provide her a panoramic view of the motorcade as it turned onto Main Street from Market—The Dallas County Records Building. If placed on the roof, she would have an unobstructed view. "Professor, I believe the best vantage point would be the Records Building."

A hint of panic flashed through his eyes. "Are you sure about your choice?"

"Yes, I believe it would provide an excellent view." The professor was cringing.

"My dear, please rethink your choice. If you are transported to the roof of the Records Building, I fear you would become a guest of the Secret Service before you could hit the panic button."

"Professor, it wasn't until Kennedy was killed did the Secret Service increase the advanced vanguard of men to seal off buildings and rooftops. It will be perfectly safe and provide, as I stated earlier, an excellent view of the motorcade, the Grassy Knoll, and the Book Depository Building." He knew her mind was made up, and if he pressed too hard, she might start asking embarrassing questions.

"Very well, Dallas it is."

It was agreed (although begrudgingly by Judith) that Muki would go first. Skorzenzy led them down the only corridor they hadn't explored when they were earlier searching for secret rooms. He removed a small chain of keys which resembled nothing any of them had ever seen before. Each key was one inch long, no more than a sixteenth of an inch thick, with no discernible keyed grooves. The professor scanned through five of the keys before settling on one. He slowly moved towards the wall and brushed against the gray concrete. A small panel immediately moved back revealing a slot. He placed the key in and waited. A low hum whirred from behind the wall. A section of the wall 4 x 6 feet slid effortlessly to the left. Florescent lights flickered for a moment then held steady, revealing a room no more than 30 x 30 feet. The only visible equipment was a small circular platform in the middle. Above it was a machine resembling the lower body of a spider.

"Wow," remarked Abdul as he entered first. We have truly traveled to another dimension in time."

The professor couldn't agree more. "Yes, you have." He looked at the others and waved them in. "Shall we?"

Muki went first, then Judith, and finally Larry. Skorzenzy followed the group in, waved the key over an unseen sensor, allowing the door to close behind them. There was no sound as it closed.

The professor majestically waved his hand at Muki, "Please

move onto the platform." Nervously, she moved towards the raised circular platform and stepped up. Her eyes were darting around the room, attempting to understand the process she was embarking upon.

"Relax my dear, everything will be fine." She wasn't reassured with his words.

Skorzenzy moved to the left of the platform and ran a different key over another unseen panel. A small part of the smooth wall slid back exposing a compact control panel. "Graduates, please join me. I wouldn't want you to get tangled up in the web."

"Muki, please discard all of your clothes except your undergarments. He preferred to be proper. The word underwear was much too brusque for him.

She stared in shock. "Professor, my clothes?"

"Yes my dear, your clothing. How else do you think we will achieve a skintight fit? We can't have you running around in the past in your present clothing now, can we? Trust me, this is not a perversion of some type. It is a mandatory requirement to protect your body when you travel."

Still not completely convinced, she slowly started unbuttoning her blouse. "My dear, at this rate Mr. Kennedy will be shot three more times. Please, the process is very safe, and your virtue is in no danger." His words calmed her inner nerves, and she proceeded to disrobe.

Skorzenzy noticed the boys were taking maybe too much of an interest in her actions. "Boys, please. Show her some respect."

Larry and Abdul's faces flushed with embarrassment. They turned and stared at the control panel.

"Anyway, we can watch on the monitor," said Skorzenzy as he hit a video feed button and indeed, a crystal clear picture of Muki appeared on the screen.

Judith's attention was directed at the cylindrical object hanging from the ceiling. "And how does this work, Professor?"

"Watch, my dear. Muki, are you ready?"

She stood shivering slightly in the cool room. "Yes, I believe so."

"Good. Now relax and stand still. The probe will start with a laser beam encompassing your body. The measurements will be fed into the mainframe and digested. The machine will then start your custom suit. Do not panic when it starts. The material will feel as if it's squeezing you as the weaving process starts covering your body. That is natural. In a few seconds, the pressure will disappear as the fabric adjusts to your measurements. Ready?"

Her voice emitted a bit of hesitation. "Yes, let's proceed."

"Very good," replied Skorzenzy as he depressed the button marked *engage*. The lights in the room went black. For a few seconds, the only illumination in the room was from the display monitor and the control panel buttons. The darkness was broken by a bright-colored purple beam coming out of the cylinder. It encompassed Muki's body with a deep warmth. The boys' eyes were transfixed on the monitor. Muki appeared to be in a deep trance. After ten seconds, the room went black again. A loud hum was emanating from the cylinder as a small sphere appeared from the tube. A white light bathed over Muki. A small wand emerged from the sphere and moved down to Muki's feet. The professor had left out one important detail. Once the machine started the weaving process, in order for the lower part of her body to be encased, a magnetic field would slowly lift her off the floor.

The spindle started spinning around her body until it reached a speed so fast the wand appeared to be suspended in air. They watched in disbelief and amazement as a thin stringy substance started coating her feet, ankles and legs. The monitor detected Muki's heart rate and blood pressure were increasing as the material form-fitted on her small body. Her eyes opened in shock as the material squeezed her skin. But as suddenly as she resisted the material, she relaxed and closed her eyes. In a minute, the process was completed. Skorzenzy shut down the machine, and Muki floated back to the platform as the residual magnetic field slowly dissipated.

"How do you feel?" he asked.

She moved her hands over the new suit. "I feel fine, and the suit appears to fit perfectly." She unzipped the front and found the pocket and the connector for the battery. "This is amazing," was all she could say.

He walked up and gave the suit a thorough examination.

"You are quite right, my dear. The fit is perfect. Now, are you ready for the next step?"

"Yes."

"Then let's go send you back in time and see what mysteries we can solve."

CHAPTER 12

NOVEMBER 22, 1963

Skorzenzy led Muki and the others back to the main control room.

"Muki, I need to go over a few things before we begin. When the machine starts working, according to Captain Christopher you'll feel a little nauseous at first. This is a result of the magnetic forces pushing on the suit. Within a few seconds, the power pack will detect the pressure and start compensating the effects. The second thing you'll notice is an electric field of static electricity dancing around you. According to the captain, it is some type of illusionary field. None of the instruments or video feeds have picked it up. Since the project was shut down, I haven't had the resources for further investigation of this phenomena, but I assure you, it is also harmless. Thirdly, and most importantly, is don't move for any reason. Once the field has detected your presence and measurements, the field is set. Any movements will disrupt it and send you into the vortex of magnetism. The results will be most detrimental.

"What do you mean detrimental?" questioned Larry. His protective nature was on high alert as his suspicions appeared to be correct.

"Larry, the first experiment was performed with a dummy. One of the technicians didn't properly secure the subject to the chair. We were fifty percent into power up when the bindings started loosening. The dummy fell forward disrupting the field. Within the blink of an eye, the dummy disintegrated. What was left wouldn't fill an ash tray. Any other questions?" There were none.

"Muki, remain calm and breathe normally. I trust everything will be alright. Are you ready?"

Muki digested the information and nodded in the affirmative. "Wait, I do have one question—the emergency button. If I get in trouble, all I have to do is press the red button, and that will send a signal back here alerting you I'm in danger and need to be extracted immediately, correct?"

"Correct." His words were sound and reassuring, yet he knew no such system was in place. If there were a failure, he could easily explain why the system failed, and no one would know otherwise.

"Muki, John Kennedy was shot at 12:30pm CST. I believe for a first run, we will send you back to Dallas at 9:30am. That should provide you plenty of time to examine the square, and all of the activities before the motorcade arrives. Are you ready?"

"Yes. One other question. When will I return?"

Skorzenzy thought about this for a moment. If she actually figures out who shot Kennedy, the repercussions could have a dire effect on his career. The chances of her unraveling the clues were a long shot at best. "Muki, you will return here at 12:32pm. Hopefully, you won't be noticed, and your extraction will be undetected. Any other questions?"

"No, I'm ready."

"Good. Climb down the ladder and place your feet in the middle of the "X." Larry, Abdul – I watched you two initiate the last start-up. Are you ready to try it again?"

Without a word, Abdul took his station."Aye Captain. Abdul reporting for duty."

"Larry?"

"Professor, I have my doubts about this venture. I really believe—" The professor wasn't interested in another debate.

"Judith, you read through the instructions with no problems. Do you think you can operate the second half of the panel? Muki's life depends on a timely sequence." Judith stared at Muki, jealous she wasn't going first and hurt that she would have to wait to correct the evils of the past.

"Judith?"

Before she could answer, Larry stepped up.

"I'll do it, Professor. Under protest, but I'll do it. I don't think Judith's mind is in proper sync to accomplish the procedure."

"Good. Then let's begin."

Skorzenzy leaned over and spoke into the microphone. "Muki, just relax. You are in good hands. Boys, are you ready?

In unison they responded. "Yes."

"Then let's begin."

Skorzenzy started calling out the orders one by one. The boys flawlessly executed the task with no problems.

The final command was issued, and Larry depressed the *slip initiate* button. Muki disappeared.

* * *

The bright sun shone beautifully in Dealey Plaza. Throngs of people were waiting to catch a glimpse of the promising young 35th President of the United States—John Fitzgerald Kennedy, and his lovely wife Jacqueline Kennedy. JFK had refused to listen to his advisers about skipping Dallas completely. There were numerous articles in the paper warning Kennedy to stay home. He wasn't welcome in Dallas. He brushed the concerns aside and continued with his nationwide tour.

It was just as she remembered from the history books. From her perch in the bell tower of the Records Building, she could easily make out the Grassy Knoll and the Book Depository Building. She had the perfect advantage point to view everything. Her thoughts were filled with elation. She was going to witness history firsthand.

As she adjusted to get comfortable, her ears detected a voice over a two-way radio.

"Eagle One, this is Firefox. Are you in position?"

She couldn't detect where the radio was located. She assumed it was the Secret Service doing a perimeter sweep.

"Eagle Two, this is Firefox. Are you in position?"

Why couldn't she detect the source of the message? They were close, yet she couldn't see anyone.

"Eagle Three, this is Firefox. Are you in position?"

Dammit, where are they? They have to be close. She leaned over the rail of the bell tower and scanned the plaza. It was filled with hundreds of well-wishers waiting to welcome the couple from Camelot. *Nothing unusual.* She heard the voice again.

"Eagle Four, this is Firefox. Are you prepared?"

"Roger. In position and awaiting orders."

"Roger, Eagle Four. Remain in place. Code word *Knight* will initiate plan. Repeat, code word *Knight*.

"Roger. Out."

Code word *Knight*, thought Muki. What and who are talking to each other? It must be the Secret Service. Who else would be communicating with each other? The history books never made mention of a code word *Knight*. She shrugged off the cryptic message and settled in to enjoy the view. Like many others that bright sunny autumn day, a new chapter was going to fill the history books for decades.

12:15PM

Her daydreaming was broken by the static of the two-way radio.

"This is Firefox. Initiate plan. Code word *KNIGHT*, repeat, code word *KNIGHT* is a go."

This time the voice was much closer. She leaned out to view the square. There was no unusual activity at first glance. Everything appeared normal. She could hear the throngs of people on Main Street yelling and cheering as the motorcade slowly made its way towards the plaza. She removed the small Nikon hand-held camera and started filming. She started with the Grassy Knoll and moved to the Book Depository. Nothing out of the ordinary. Wait, what was glinting in the sunlight on the roof? She pushed the zoom button. On the roof were two men in painter's coveralls. *Why would painters be on the roof?* She kept filming. "Oh no," she gasped to herself. One of the painters removed a rifle with a scope on it. The second painter was scanning the plaza with a pair of binoculars. His main focus was on the intersection of Main and Houston. She could see him pick up a two-way walkie-talkie.

"Firefox. Eagle Two in position. *Operation Knight* is in motion." He placed the device back in its belt holster. *If that's*

Eagle Two, where are the other three? She panned to the Grassy Knoll and zoomed in.

12:20PM

The camera settled on two policemen behind the wall. They appeared to be making sure there were no unwanted persons behind the fence. Again, she saw one of the men remove a walkie-talkie. "Firefox. Eagle Three in position. *Operation Knight* is in motion."

"Roger" came the words from the radio close to her, yet still unseen. *Where are they?*

12:25PM

She could hear the motorcade getting closer. The thunderous applause and cheers were intensifying. Any minute the caravan would turn onto Houston Street. What could she do to warn the president of the impending doom?

12:26PM

The motorcade turned onto Houston Street. Her throat choked up. She could see John and Jackie waving to the crowd. They were such a handsome couple. John was using the smile that launched his political career. Women swooned over John and his good looks. They also admired Jackie as a true mother, a first lady, and fashion trendsetter. Jackie always kept up appearances in public even though she was aware of her husband's extracurricular activities. Despite John's infidelities, she very much loved him, or so it appeared.

The crowd waved back and cheered with a welcome reserved only for Southerners. Even though he was a hated "Northerner," he was the President of the United States and by the greeting he was receiving from the crowd, one would have thought he was a native son. But not everyone.

"Firefox, Eagle Four. *Knight* is now in view."

"Roger Eagle Four. Proceed with plan. Out."
"Roger."

12:28PM

Where are they? They have to be close. She panned the camera back to the Depository. The painters were still on the roof. One of them was aiming his rifle at Kennedy's car. Another glint caught her attention. There was another rifle pointing out of the sixth floor, two windows from the east end of the building. She panned to the Grassy Knoll. One of the officers was also holding a rifle. He wasn't panning the crowd though. She could tell his gaze was centered on Kennedy's car. *It is a conspiracy. The theories were right. Oswald could never have fired six shots that rapidly with an Italian bolt-action rifle. But who are they and why Kennedy? Why did he deserve to die?* She needed to know. But how?

She leaned a little farther over the banister looking for a clue. The sound of a window being opened all the way was discernible over the roar of the crowd. Directly below her, she could see two men with binoculars watching the motorcade move by.

"Firefox. Eagle Four. Target is approaching kill zone. All units stand by."

"Roger Eagle Four."

"Eagle One. Any activity in your sector?"

"Negative. Eagle One is clear. *Knight* is a go."

"Roger."

Where is Eagle One? One area she hadn't examined was the grass plaza to the south of Main Street. She backed the zoom angle out and peered hard into the viewfinder. *Nothing, Nothing, Noth...wait. What are they doing?* The camera settled on two men who were deliberately standing behind the crowd on the high bank. They looked like Secret Service but weren't acting like it. One of the men was training his set of binoculars on Kennedy's car. The picture Muki developed in her mind was frightening. It literally was a killing zone Kennedy was moving into. The word *hurry* was caught in her throat. She started sweating profusely as the motorcade approached Commerce.

12:29:30PM

The black limousine inched onto Commerce Street. She felt as if everything were going in slow motion. *Why are they slowing down? Why? Someone has to warn them.* Her suit was plastered to her from the sweat pouring out of her pores. Her respiration and heartbeat were reaching new highs, as she tried to warn the president and will the driver to speed up.

12:29:45PM

She slowed her heartbeat enough so she could form the words and scream as the camera kept filming. "Mr. President! Mr. President!"

John Kennedy turned his head to his right and looked up. Muki couldn't believe what she was seeing. She felt as if he were looking straight at her. His smile was one of reassurance and goodwill. She screamed again as he moved his head back to the left.

12:30:00PM

The sound of rifle shots echoed back and forth across the plaza as the deadly lead bore into Kennedy. His body rocked back and forth as each new bullet entered the frail human body, shattering bone and sending deadly fragments into his vital organs. It was the last shot from the Depository that sealed his fate. She watched as the back of his skull exploded. Pieces of brain and blood splattered all over Jackie.

Muki screamed without hearing herself. "They've shot the president! They've shot the president!" None of the bystanders could hear her screams. They were all cowering on the ground trying to understand what had just happened. She kept screaming and pointing in all directions trying to get the attention of the Dallas police officers who stood in shock. She pointed wildly at the Depository rooftop, the Grassy Knoll and the Grassy Plaza.

"Firefox. We have a problem. Eagle Four. Target directly

above you. Take her out."

Muki looked down at Houston Street in disbelief. She could feel four pairs of eyes boring in on her. Two pair came from the Grassy Plaza; the other pair came from the men directly below her.

"Eagle One, Firefox. Do you have a shot? Over."

"Negative. Eagle Four is moving in."

"Roger."

Muki didn't realize at first what was happening until one of the men disappeared from the window. She panned the camera back to the Depository. The two men were still there. One with binoculars, the other with the rifle—pointing straight at her.

"Firefox, Eagle Two, We have a shot."

"Negative Eagle Two. Pack up and observe. Eagle Four is dealing with the problem."

Muki now knew she was the target! She carried the evidence that would prove Oswald didn't act on his own. In fact, she didn't remember seeing a rifle pointing out of the room Oswald was supposedly in. Hopefully, she had captured enough evidence to prove her theory. But now was not the time for reflection. She was trapped in the bell tower of the Records Building with no escape route.

12:31:15PM

The door burst open. Before her stood a man over six feet tall and at least two-hundred and fifty pounds. He wore white painter's clothing, identical to the men on the Depository roof. She couldn't see the evil in his eyes behind his reflective sunglasses.

"Give me the camera and you won't be harmed." His tone was threatening.

Muki remembered the stories her father had told her of the North Vietnamese police and their tactics. Do what they ask, and they will let you go. She thought about it for a few seconds looking at her watch. "And if I don't?"

The man said not a word and removed a pistol with a silencer on it. "Any more questions?"

12:31:50PM

Muki slowly handed the camera over to the imposing man. "This is Eagle Four, tell Skorzenzy we have..."

His words were followed by a bloodcurdling scream as she disappeared.

12:32:00PM

The control panel came to life as the automatic sequential timer marked 12:32pm. Abdul and Larry only monitored the panel to ensure everything was working perfectly.

Muki reappeared in the middle of the floor. According to the monitor, she was entirely intact and alive. Everyone breathed a sigh of relief except Judith. "My God, what's all over her suit?"

Judith waited for the machine to power down and then bounded down the stairs. Muki crumpled to the floor.

"My God, it's blood. She's covered in blood."

Judith quickly started examining Muki for any injuries.

Even though the left side of the suit and her face was covered in blood, she couldn't find an injury. What she did find made her jump back. The remains of an index finger were wrapped around the camera she held with a death grip.

"Muki? Muki? Are you alright?" pleaded Judith.

Abdul and Larry were now down the ladder and stood over their comrade. "Muki," called Abdul. "Muki, wake up. Are you okay?"

Slowly, she opened her eyes. They were filled with terror. "No, No. Get away. You murdered the president! Get away!"

"Muki, it's Aby. Aby. You're safe. You came back." His tone wasn't overlooked by Larry and Judith.

"Aby?"

"Muki, it's okay. You came back. You're safe now," he reassured her.

She fixed her eyes on Abdul, and realizing she was safe, put her arms around his neck and kissed his cheek. She whispered into Abdul's ear as she regained her senses. "It was horrible, just horrible. I saw the whole thing. They killed Kennedy in cold blood, and a man was going to kill me. I was handing over the camera when I was pulled back. But, there's more." Tears were streaming down her face. "But there's more. Skorz—"

The loudspeaker interrupted her thoughts. "I'm glad you are safe, my dear. Please come and tell us what you've learned."

Muki waved at the professor indicating she was okay. As she steadied her feet with the help of Abdul, she whispered a warning. "Skorzenzy was somehow connected."

Again the loudspeaker crackled. "Muki, please come and share your experience." She nodded again.

Skorzenzy had been against traveling to this portal. If what he thought was true, then Muki and her friends would never be allowed to leave the premises alive, but not until he gained his revenge. After all, he had nothing but time on his hands.

* * *

"Firefox, Eagle Four. We have a problem. Tell Skorzenzy the subject escaped. Eagle Four needs a doctor. Right hand is obliterated. Request a doctor."

The voice on the other end was cold and calculating. "Negative. Eliminate him. Out."

"Roger. Out."

CHAPTER 13

AFTERMATH

Skorzenzy directed Muki back to the suit room and allowed her to change out of the bloodstained clothing and into her street clothes. He was (as were the others), very interested in viewing the film she'd returned with.

Muki emerged from the room looking a little more composed and gathered.

"Graduates, I believe it's time to visit the viewing room and see what treasures our traveler returned with." The group agreed.

Skorzenzy led them back through the control room and into the waiting area they first came to. He turned left and approached two metal doors. He fished out the key chain, identified the correct one, and opened the door.

Florescent lights immediately revealed a large theater capable of seating at least fifty people. "Graduates, please take a seat. I need to load the camera."

The kids each found a seat. Judith chose to sit by herself in the middle of the second row. Abdul, Larry, and Muki took the last row and moved to the middle.

"Captain, I believe our young ensign is going to give us a show."

"Abdul, shut up. This is serious," replied Larry.

"Muki, what was it like? Did you really see who shot Kennedy?" Larry's curiosity was getting the better of him. Muki didn't respond. She stared straight at the blank screen. Larry and Abdul could tell she was still mentally back in Dallas.

The lights dimmed, and the first clips of the film appeared. The quality was spectacular, much better than the 8mm films of the day.

The camera panned back and forth showing all of Dealey Plaza. Skorzenzy decided to fast-forward to within two minutes of the shooting. He didn't want the others to see if she had captured all the participants that day.

When he slowed back to real time, the camera was pointed directly at the roof of the Book Depository. "Dammit," he swore under his breath. "She's seen too much."

"Abdul, Larry – look. Look at those men." They couldn't deny one of them was holding a gun and wasn't scanning the crowd. Something was in the shooter's cross-hairs.

"Muki, did he shoot Kennedy?" queried Larry.

Her eyes were glued to the screen. "They all shot him, all of them." Skorzenzy heard her comments through the floor microphones. "They all shot him." Her gaze never left the screen.

The next noise was crackly, but audible.

"Firefox. Eagle Four. Target is approaching kill zone. All units stand by."

"Roger Eagle Four."

"Eagle One. Any activity in your sector?"

"Negative. Eagle Four is clear. *Knight* is a go."

"Stop it," yelled Muki. "Stop it."

As much as Skorzenzy wanted to oblige her, he too needed to see how much she actually witnessed. Muki lowered her head and started crying. "They killed him. They all killed him."

All eyes were transfixed to the screen as the past from fifty-two years ago flashed before their eyes. Even Skorzenzy saw details his father failed to mention.

Kennedy's car very slowly made the left turn onto Commerce Street. His face turned and smiled at the camera. The sound of the crowd and cheering was drowned out as Muki was hysterically yelling at the motorcade.

"Mr. President! Mr. President!"

The next sounds were unmistakably gunshots. The camera was zoomed in on Kennedy, and you could count over five shots entering his body, the last one being the head shot. It was like watching a Wes Craven horror movie as his head exploded, showering brain matter on Jackie and the car.

There were screams from the crowd, but again Muki's words drowned out the background noise. "They've shot the president! They've shot the president!"

Abdul put his arm around Muki in an effort to calm and reassure her it was alright. He could feel her small body tremble as tears flooded her eyes. Larry stared on in amazement. Judith, sitting by herself, was thinking of only one thing. She would be next. She would have no trouble pulling the trigger and killing her great-grandfather. Maybe, with luck, she could also do what the Allies and saboteurs failed at miserably—killing Hitler.

Skorzenzy was shocked to see five bullets were fired at Kennedy. All of the stories he'd heard said there were only three shots fired by the Firefox conspirators. Obviously, someone didn't know how to count. *Five—interesting. I wonder who didn't fill out a proper report. I'll have to retrieve my notes when time allows and revisit the question.*

"Graduates, I believe we've seen enough for one day," came Skorzenzy's voice over the intercom.

"No," cried Muki. "There's more."

All eyes stayed on the screen as the dead president was being whisked away to Parkland Hospital. The same crackling voices came through the audio.

"Firefox. We have a problem. Eagle Four. Target directly above you. Take her out."

"My God Muki. They saw you?" asked Abdul.

She raised her head and stared at the screen. In a small whisper choked with tears, "Yes."

"Eagle One, Firefox. Do you have a shot? Over."

"Negative. Eagle Four is moving in."

"Roger."

My God, thought Skorzenzy. *I always wondered why so many people who witnessed the events that day wound up missing, dead or no longer accountable. They were searching for a person who wasn't even from their time. Fascinating. Absolutely fascinating.*

"Firefox, Eagle Two, We have a shot."

"Negative Eagle Two. Pack up and observe. Eagle Four is dealing with the problem.

"Turn it off, please turn it off," cried Muki. Her pleas went unheeded, and the film continued.

They could hear the banging on a door over Muki's sobs. The sound of wood splintering was very clear. The camera moved up, and revealed an extremely large man wearing painter's coveralls, a cap and sunglasses.

"Give me the camera and you won't be harmed."

They could see Muki raising the camera towards the man's large hands. The next sound sent shivers up their spines. There was a bloodcurdling scream, and the camera went black.

The film ended. The only sound was Muki still sniffling.

The house lights came back on. The sound of footsteps echoed from the back wall as Skorzenzy returned to the theater. He took a seat between the group and waited.

Judith broke the silence. She turned around, looked, and glared at Skorzenzy. He could feel the hate radiating out of her eyes. "Professor, it is very apparent the machine is in excellent working condition. I insist I should be the next one. I have a score to settle—the sooner the better."

"Patience, my dear, let's digest the first trip before we decide on the next one." He turned around, looking at the other three. "Muki, how did it feel to revisit real history in the making? Did it excite you? Were your nerves tingling as the motorcade pulled onto Houston Street? How did you react when you saw the gunmen on the rooftop? Did your gut tighten as the car turned onto Commerce? What was it—"

"Enough," demanded Abdul. "Can you not see how distraught and traumatized she is over the events she witnessed? Have you no compassion, man?" Abdul's tone wasn't of resentment, but more of a knight coming to the rescue of a maiden in distress.

"I apologize for being so direct, Abdul, but it's best we discuss it while the memory is fresh and vivid."

His tone became more fatherly and soft. "Muki, tell us. What was it like?"

She wiped the tears from her eyes and regained herself. "I was excited and frightened all at the same time. It was the most exhilarating experience I've ever encountered." She flashed a small smile at Abdul. "At first, I thought the gunmen I identified were Secret Service. Obviously, I was wrong. A terrible pang pulled at my stomach as I knew there was nothing I could do except to yell out a frantic warning. Seeing Kennedy turn and smile at me almost put my fears to rest, but I knew better. The men I saw were there for one reason—killing Kennedy. It was horrible watching his head explode, and seeing the look of disbelief and terror in Jackie's eyes as her husband died in her arms."

She took a breath. "The real horror was when I realized the voices on the walkie-talkies found me, and I was the new prey. I'm very thankful we agreed to my return at 12:32pm. I doubt the man who came to take the camera would have allowed me to live. I was terrified."

Skorzenzy let her descriptions sink in for a few moments.

"Would you do it again?" he asked.

"Honestly Professor, at this time, I would have to decline. History is best left in the past and debated amongst scholars. The truth could be too much for the general public to digest. How would one go about retelling Kennedy's assassination and making it believable?"

One question, the most obvious one, had not been addressed, at least not yet.

"Muki," questioned Larry. "Did you see Oswald?"

She wasted no time with the response.

"No." She took a breath. "I saw the window he supposedly fired from. No one was in that window, but two windows down, there was another team of men."

"So Oswald didn't shoot Kennedy?"

"If he did, I didn't see him or catch it on film, so I would have to conclude he didn't shoot Kennedy." Muki was regaining her wits and confidence with each response. "Was he part of the conspiracy? The film is inconclusive based on what I witnessed. Would I do it again? Possibly, but I would choose a much less controversial date."

Skorzenzy couldn't pass up his earlier wisdom or warning.

"Muki, I believe I tried to dissuade you from this time in history. Maybe next time, you'll heed the words of an old man, eh?"

"Maybe," she replied back. "Maybe."

"I believe it's time for a break and some reflection. Is anyone hungry?"

"No," yelled Judith. "This is not a time to eat. This is a time to return to the past and correct the mistakes. I'm sorry Muki couldn't save Kennedy. I won't make the same mistake. I will avenge my family name and rid it of its dark past. I'm ready. I'm ready to go now." Judith's hatred laced her words.

"NO!" declared Skorzenzy. "You have neither the correct temperament nor attitude to go back objectively and seek your revenge. Do you think I built this machine so we could send assassins back in time to kill only those we, (the US government) didn't like? No! I built this machine in the hopes of furthering mankind's knowledge of the past, and building on the mistakes to improve the future. That, my dear, was the thinking behind the project. What if Muki could have warned Kennedy and someone actually believed her? How would the future or our past look now? What ramifications would befall history if our actions changed the past?" The professor became so wrapped up in his oratory and lashing of Judith, he failed to properly choose his words. He was unknowingly justifying all of Larry's prior comments about dabbling with the past.

Larry listened intently as each point he presented was shot down by the same man who was echoing his own words.

"Professor, then why proceed with any more experiments? You have validated every point I was arguing earlier. You implied I was being childish and unreasonable, yet now you have turned 180 degrees by supporting my very position. Why?"

He was in no mood to argue his points or theories. He was tired and hungry. He rose up from the chair and moved towards the entrance. "If anyone is hungry, join me. This has been a very trying morning." They could hear his footsteps move down the corridor.

Muki looked back and forth at Larry and Abdul. "Judith, come here, there's something you need to hear."

Judith sprang from her seat and quickly moved towards the trio. "The only thing I want to know is when is that old man going to send me back. I need to do this. I need to avenge my past."

Muki wasn't listening.

"Judith, shut up. There's something else I learned that the camera didn't detect. Just before I was brought back, I know I heard one of the men mention Skorzenzy's name. I can't be absolutely sure, but if I am, it could explain why he didn't want me going back to that date."

"Agreed," said Larry. "Despite my reservations with this whole project, I'll acquiesce to his wants and demands. I promise not to antagonize him anymore. I'll be vocal while not appearing argumentative, and Judith, you'd better reel in your attitude. Skorzenzy is correct in not letting you settle an old score. In your current state, that would be the same as adding gasoline to a fire in hopes of extinguishing it. It would be a disaster."

Judith slumped her shoulders in resignation. Larry was right. She needed to put her hate on hold if she wanted to convince the professor she was worthy of visiting the past. "Okay," was all she said.

"Hey, I don't know about the rest of you, but I believe the professor is correct. Captain, I suggest we join the old man and see what type of food synthesizer he has hidden in the compound. Hell, he might have a normal transporter we could use." Abdul's comments broke the tension in the air. The four rose up and ventured out to find the professor and hopefully, a bite to eat.

CHAPTER 14

MISSION TWO : PLANNING

The group easily found the professor and the cafeteria. The professor was sitting on a stainless steel bench and table. He was apparently in deep thought as he munched on a ham and cheese on rye.

Skorzenzy turned and greeted the graduates as he finished a bite of his sandwich and washed it down with a cold glass of tea. "Good of you to join me. Help yourself. Go to the selector on the microwave and scroll through the vast menu. I'm sure you'll find something of interest." Abdul couldn't believe it. He was only joking when he referred to a synthesizer.

The kids approached the oversized microwave. Abdul decided he was more knowledgeable than his mates and quickly took front and center. He pushed the menu button, and a holographic picture appeared on the face of the door. The menu easily rivaled the most exotic and elaborate eateries in the world. The choices ranged anywhere from Filet Mignon, Steamed Clams and Baked Alaska, to a simple burger and fries. He chose a ten-inch rib eye with mashed potatoes, green beans, tossed salad with French dressing and apple pie. Within two minutes, the chosen meal appeared behind the viewing screen. "Wow, Captain," he exclaimed. "It really works."

Larry was still being cautious, "Yeah, but what does it taste like?"

As Abdul opened the door, his senses were met with the true aroma of a perfectly cooked steak. "We are about to find out." Without examining the plate, he asked the professor where the cutlery was.

"Look on the plate, son."

Sure enough, all of the cutlery was on the plate. Even the salad fork. He gingerly grabbed the fork thinking it would still be releasing heat from the cooking operation.

Skorzenzy didn't look back. "It's perfectly safe," was all he said.

The professor was right. The fork was perfectly chilled. He looked at his friends with confusion. He then picked up the spoon and sampled the mashed potatoes. "My mother never made them this good. Larry, this is great. Professor, what about drinks?"

Skorzenzy raised his left hand and pointed to the opposite counter. On it rested another machine resembling a large refrigerator. He hastened over to it and identified the menu button. The display filled with every beverage known to man. From fine wines to a can of coke.

"For the meal you chose, may I suggest an appropriate selection?" asked Skorzenzy.

"Yes Professor. What would go well with the meal?"

"I would choose either the Chàteau Paillas or perhaps the Chàteau de Chambert depending of course on your sensitive palate, and for the dessert, a robust cognac. I'm sure you will find those choices much more satisfying than the standard soft drinks you would normally waste on such extravagance."

Abdul accepted the offer and made the selections. Within seconds, the door to the refrigerator opened, revealing both glasses of wine and the cognac. He chose the first glass he could reach. Before he could manhandle it, Skorzenzy rose from his chair and approached.

"This is fine wine, not a beer keg festival. You must check the color, savor the aroma, and let the liquid breathe." Skorzenzy removed the glass from Abdul. He held it up and examined the color as he gently swished the liquid from side to side. "Very good," he commented. He lowered the glass to his nose, took his left hand and wafted the scent towards his nose. "Ah, very nice. Maybe a little more aging would be in order, but still, a fine choice." He then took a small taste and rolled the warm liquid around on his tongue. "Yes, very robust indeed. An excellent selection, Abdul. Enjoy your meal."

Abdul stood in amazement at the process required to check for quality. He gathered his senses and took his meal to the table, sitting directly across from Skorzenzy.

Muki marveled at the technology and the quality it produced. She moved back to the microwave and chose one of her favorite dishes—Roast Duck with Water Chestnuts and Brown Rice. Larry and Judith were next. The pangs of hunger were overtaking any mental reservations they held concerning the quality and texture of the food, plus, the smell of Abdul's steak and Muki's roast duck had them salivating. Judith chose a simple Vegetarian's Lasagna Delight with a side salad covered with a light vinaigrette dressing. Larry chose a childhood favorite and staple of his family—Chipped Beef covered with brown gravy on white toasted bread, better known as shit on a shingle, buttered corn on the cob, sweet peas and Cherry Cobbler.

The kids were devouring yet savoring the meal at the same time. The occasional comment on the quality of the food was heard between bites. "Oh man." "This is great." "Wish my mom cooked as good as this."

Skorzenzy finished his sandwich and took another drink of his tea. "I believe I need something a little more exciting today. Excuse me." He rose up and walked over to the refrigerator.

"Hey, Scotty. Think he's getting his daily dose of Geritol?" Larry cracked a smile. Something he'd refrained from doing over the last few hours.

"Yeah, too bad he doesn't have a pocket tricorder." Abdul enjoyed the missed humor. Even Muki and Judith had a laugh with the exchange.

Skorzenzy returned to the table with a large bottle and five glasses. "Unlike my new esteemed colleagues, my hearing is fine. I felt the occasion required something more eloquent to celebrate Muki's travels." He placed a perfectly chilled bottle of Dom Perignon Vintage 2000. He carefully filled each champagne flute and placed them before his guests. "To many more successful voyages and discoveries." He raised his glass and waited for the others to follow suit. One by one the glasses lightly clinked with his. "Cheers," said the professor.

"Cheers," replied the four. Each took long sips of the nectar fit for the kings.

Skorzenzy replaced his flute on the table and looked up at Abdul. "I've been thinking about who should be next." Judith was hoping it would be her, but she feared her temper of late would go against her cause. "I believe the next subject, if he's willing..."

"Dammit," Judith muttered.

"...should be our intrepid brown Star Trek fan. Judith, you must temper your emotions, and Larry, I don't think you've fully signed on with the adventure as of yet." He looked directly into Abdul's dark brown eyes. "Are you up for the challenge, Scotty?" Yes, the Star Trek references had not escaped his notice. He would use Abdul's imagination for his acceptance.

Abdul studied the offer as he bit into his last piece of apple pie. He took a small drink of the superb cognac and sat back. Inside, he was bursting to say yes, but instead, he chose to maintain restraint.

"Professor, I would be honored to take the voyage and travel to where no man or beast has been for over two thousand years."

"The Pyramids, my friend? But we've already been there and seen the wonders of the Egyptian culture."

"No, Professor. I prefer to witness one of the greatest acts in mankind's history."

His response stumped the professor. What could be more vital in man's history than solving the myths of Egypt?

"Then where, Abdul? Where do you wish to travel?"

He took another long drink of the cognac. He found the drink not only soothing and warm; it relaxed his overactive mind and sharpened his senses.

"The Crucifixion of Jesus Christ. To be exact, I wish to follow Judas Iscariot and find out if he accepted the thirty pieces of silver, and proceeded to hang himself in dismay for his actions."

His words were a shock to all. Never had he shown or mentioned any thought of religion for over six years. His world (or so they thought) revolved around one thing, and one thing only—Star Trek.

"Why there?" asked Judith. "I don't understand."

He knew his choice would baffle his friends, but then, they didn't know everything about him. For years, he'd been fascinated with the raging debate among Christians concerning the fate of Judas. One side held strong to the belief that Judas was fulfilling the prophecies of the Old Testament. He was chosen to betray Jesus before being born, thus allowing his soul to ascend to heaven. The other side was staunch in their support that since he allowed Satan to harden his heart and betray the "Son of Man," after which he chose to commit suicide; therefore, his soul was condemned to the fiery pits of hell. And then, there was a minority group, who actually believed he was the first vampire.

"Why, it's elementary, Judith." His tone was reverting back to a poor imitation of James Doohan. "I believe it would benefit mankind immensely to determine exactly what happened to him. According to the discussion I heard, my parents and their scholastic friends debated about his fate with no definitive answer. Perhaps my trip will shed light on the truth, and save those "blowhards" from arguing on issues they could only speculate on. I will admit, despite enjoying watching all those academians turn red and pop neck veins as they vie for position in an attempt to sway each other, which was an exercise in futility, I could walk in wearing my original Star Trek tunic, and enlighten the so-called enlightened ones and triumphantly correct them all, of course, with a gleam in my eye." He started laughing with his dissertation and the thought of embarrassing his parents and their so-called friends.

His oration left his friends speechless. In all their years together, he seldom took a serious note with any issue or shown any desire of real religious interest. But, now they were seeing a different side, one he'd concealed remarkably well from them.

Skorzenzy broke the silence. "My friend, you have chosen and orated well. I agree with your assessment and analysis. However, in order to accomplish your wishes, I must warn you of the dangers. The place you chose is barren with little cover. I will have to scan the computer banks to make sure that when you appear, you aren't noticed. I'll need to fashion a garment and sandals for the time period. We can't have you traipsing around in a strange white suit. You would literally stick out like a sore thumb and create more interest than desired. Still, even with the hazards, I believe it is a worthy mission."

"Wait a minute," interjected Larry. "Are you saying he's going to have to remove the suit and hide it during his trip?"

"Of course he will. He can't very well remain incognito wearing the suit, now can he?"

"He could use the red danger button and be instantly transported back if he detected trouble, couldn't he?"

Dammit Larry, you're making this harder than it needs to be. Maybe I should have chosen you second.

"Of course he could, but if he is detected before making his discovery, or even getting close to the truth, then the venture is wasted. Is it not?" The answer/question was condescending and mocking.

"I agree with the professor," replied Abdul. "What is the point of traveling back if I'm instantly brought back with no new information. Professor, I have no problem with the proposal."

"Before you agree Abdul, I'm sure this trip is going to require a few days of investigation. I have a special pouch for the trip which will be strapped on to your chest inside the suit, but the rations will be very limited. Water will obviously be of the highest priority. You will have to use it sparingly. Also, the rations will consist mainly of jerky and dried goods. Are you still willing to go?" Skorzenzy sat back as Abdul digested the information.

"Yes, I am."

"Good. As soon as the meal is finished, we shall adjourn to the dressing room and begin the preparations."

"Wait a minute," said Larry. "If I'm remembering correctly, Abdul will be in real time, correct?"

"Correct."

"What are we supposed to do for two days while he's gone?"

Skorzenzy furrowed his brow and sarcastically replied, "What else, Mr. Kowalski? We wait." *Why can't his inquisitive mind accept my achievements? He showed so much promise during the landing. I hope his attitude changes or there will be few options available.* He rose up and made his way into the corridor.

"Abdul, are you nuts or plain insane?" Larry's words were hard and precise.

"Negative Captain. I'm going where no man—"

"Knock off the shit, Abdul, This is serious. This isn't some video game or comic book adventure. This is real life. What you're proposing is highly dangerous, and I'm still not convinced the professor doesn't have ulterior motives. You heard what Muki said, or did you choose to block it out? Skorzenzy, or his family, were somehow..." He stopped himself from finishing his damning statement concerning the possibility that the professor's family was potentially involved with the Kennedy shooting.

"Larry, that may be true, but I'm sure Skorzenzy's family wasn't involved with Pontius Pilate or King Herod's plan. Muki came back in one piece. Shaken, but in one piece." He placed his left hand on her shoulder with a reassuring grip. "Muki, what do you think?"

She could see the want in his eyes and understood from the short time they'd spent together, trying to talk him out of the journey was pointless. "I have every confidence Abdul knows what he's doing. He's right. I did come back whole. A bit shaken, but whole."

"See Larry, it's settled. I'll be fine." Abdul looked at Judith. "What do you think, Barbie? Should I go or should I stay?"

If there were one thing you didn't call Judith, it was Barbie. The last person to refer to her as "Barbie" found a crowbar flying at his head.

"Look, you psychotic little shit. Call me that one more time and I'll personally send you back in time and impale your skinny ass to the cross!" She almost fell over as she vaulted up from the bench as she berated Abdul. "I should be going back, not you. Who in this room gives two shits about what happened to his soul? No one. No one, you hear me! We should be going back and killing all of those murderous bastards of the Third Reich and my fucking great-grandfather. But no, we're going back to see what someone named Judas may or may not have done. This is BULLSHIT!" Her friends had feared she was boiling under the surface, they just didn't realize how much. She'd been silent for way too long.

"Look, you cheerleader wannabe."

Judith struck out and slapped Abdul hard across the face.

"Wannabe cheerleader? I'm gonna kick your ass right here, right now, and there's nothing your wimpy ass can do to stop me."

Abdul rubbed the spot on his face, which was instantly starting to turn red.

"You bitch. Bring it!"

Muki couldn't take it anymore and proceeded to defend Abdul with her words.

"Did you learn nothing back at the diner? If I were Skorzenzy, I too wouldn't send you back in your current state. You are an uncontrollable ball of hate. You're probably right about him not being able to defend himself. But, as long as I'm standing here, you won't touch him again in anger. Do you understand?" Muki's black eyes were filled with rage as she stared Judith down.

"Tell him not to call me Barbie again, okay? Tell him, or I'll take on both of you!"

Muki looked deep into Abdul's eyes. "Abdul, promise."

"I promise. I just wanted to see if her high beams would turn on if I pissed her off. Mission accomplished, eh Captain?" It took a few moments for the others to catch on. They instantly looked at Judith's heaving chest. Mission accomplished. She was on full beams. Larry couldn't help but let out a small laugh.

"Perverts," was all she could say.

"Okay, now that's settled, Captain, would you escort me to the transporter room? It is time Judas and I had a talk."

Larry slapped Abdul on the back. "Aye Scotty, it is, despite my reservations, it is." The four left the cafeteria.

CHAPTER 15

AD 33

"Are you ready, Abdul?" asked Skorzenzy.

Abdul was standing on the "X" on the floor. "Aye Admiral. Ready and willing," came his reply.

"Okay, give us a few minutes. I need to go over a few instructions with Judith."

"Aye Admiral. Don't want to spread my molecules all over the universe. Even I acknowledge one of me is enough. I don't think the universe is ready for me to repopulate every planet or celestial body." Muki couldn't help but laugh with his comment.

"Judith, are we clear on how the control panel works?"

She nodded in agreement. After all, she was the one who directed the instructions to Larry and Abdul when they sent the chair back. "Yes, I remember the exact procedures and also to pay close attention to the sequential counters."

"Very well then. Show me that you can follow instructions, and you, my dear, will be our next traveler, if that is alright with you?" He knew the answer she would provide, but needed to hear the words.

"Yes Professor. I won't fail."

"Good." He leaned into the microphone. "Abdul, prepare for departure."

"Aye Admiral."

"Larry, Judith – enter the coordinates. Commence start-up!"

They dialed in the correct latitude and longitude. Skorzenzy had convinced Abdul that being placed ten kilometers north of what was known as Potter's Field would be safer. For him to appear in the middle of the quarry could result in dire consequences. Abdul agreed.

"Initiate!" Judith and Larry were completely focused on the sequential timers. Skorzenzy stood by their sides with the manual close at hand. It had been many years since he'd personally given the orders and didn't want to forget a step. He admired watching Judith as she performed the commands with a fluid motion. She was crisp and in control. He needed her to regain that composure for the travel she would surely embark on. His life could depend on it.

Skorzenzy called out the final command and Abdul disappeared.

* * *

He found himself in a barren, sandy land. The sun was baking down on him. *Good. No one's in sight. I need to find a small grove and strip down.* If he was reading the sun correctly, it was around 1:00pm, give or take an hour. He hoped the date they decided on was correct. By their calculations and recollections of the Bible, Judas betrayed Jesus the day before the Feast of the Passover. By all estimates and the calendars they consulted (with the exception of the Greek Orthodox calendar) the date should be March 24, 33 AD, the day Judas betrayed Jesus in the garden of Gethsemane. What no one was sure of, was when Judas returned the thirty pieces of silver to the priests and then traveled to Akeldama and hung himself. They hoped that he performed the act, if not that night, the next day.

What intrigued him the most about the story was why Judas took his life. His master Jesus told of things to come. He told Judas and the other disciples at The Last Supper that one would betray him—one who would kiss him on the cheek as a sign to the authorities of the man they sought. Jesus spoke openly about his execution for the sins of man. He would die so man could live. Maybe Judas didn't understand the parables as described by the Apostle John. Jesus spoke these words before he broke the bread and poured the wine. "Greater love has no one than this, that he lay down his life for his friends." John 16:2.

It was right there. Jesus was acknowledging his passing, wasn't he? Now I see the confusion. If I were Judas, I too would have been puzzled and confused. But would I have turned in my Master? Would my parents have turned in the Dalai Lama if they felt his words were disparaging and sinful? Interesting.

He looked around, collected his bearings, and headed south. He could barely make out a small grove of trees to the southwest.

Within an hour, he'd changed into his proper attire and hidden the suit within some of the fallen branches. He decided to rest in the grove and conserve his meager allotment of water and jerky. He would eat and drink later. He lay back and dozed off, thinking of possibilities he would witness or hoped to witness.

Abdul woke in a panic. Something warm and soft was brushing against his skin. At first, he couldn't make out what was touching him until it bleated. It was a sheep. No, it wasn't one. He was surrounded by a flock of the white animals. They were milling about bleating and scratching at the hard ground for grass. He could make out a few voices as the herders moved the flock towards Jerusalem. *That would make sense. They're preparing for the Feast of the Passover, and sacrifices would be required.* Abdul rose to his feet and brushed off the dirt. He was about to dig into his chest harness and fish out some jerky and water until one of the sheep herders started moving towards him. *Hmm, this might be a little tricky.*

The shepherd approached waving his wooden staff in a motion which could be construed as threatening or friendly. It was difficult to tell. By the dust on his white robe, it was evident he'd traveled a good distance to attend the festival. Dust clung to his clothes like a cloak. His black beard and hair glistened with the specks of soil coating his hair.

The shepherd called out waving his staff. "Come here, come here."

The words were foreign yet familiar. He called again, this time waving his staff in a friendly manner.

The shepherd called out waving his staff. "تعال هنا تعالتعالتعال هناهنا" (come here, come here).

The words were foreign yet familiar. He called again, this time waving his staff in a friendly manner.

"تعال هنا تعال هناتعال" (Come here. Come here). He flashed a smile at Abdul as he waved, showing a mouth with few teeth. Abdul studied the dialect and realized it was a northern version of Arabic. For once, he was thankful his parents had forced him to learn as many languages as possible—Arabic being one of them. He rolled the strange syllables in his mind and came up with the proper reply. "مرحبا صديق. هل أنت ذاهب إلى لسلامعليكم المه المهرجان ؟" (Hello friend. Are you going to the festival?).

The man smiled and agreed. "I am taking my finest sheep to sacrifice at the Temple of David. I'm also going to see the man Jesus. They say he performs great wonders. He has traveled across the region telling great tales of healing and miracles. Some say he's the Messiah, others say he's a Heretic. Personally, I'm impartial. If he is the Messiah, what a blessing he will be to our plight. If he is a Heretic, the Sadducees will find him out through the laws of Moses and levy the appropriate punishment. Either way, I wish to see this man everyone is talking about. Would you join us for the remainder of the journey? The sheep can be stubborn as you've seen."

The man's attitude was extremely upbeat and exciting. Unfortunately, Abdul hadn't signed up for any agriculture classes at Stanford. He doubted they even offered such a course. Most of the students weren't interested in taking classes where they would actually get their hands dirty. That type of work was for the middle-lower class, not the cream-of-the-crop. "Yes, friend, I would be very willing to help you with the flock."

"Friend, what is your name?"

"Abdul."

"Where do you hail from, Abdul?"

Where indeed. He couldn't say he was an American. He pondered for a moment. One topic he wasn't keen on and avoided like the plague was geography. He figured if he wanted a geography lesson, he would make enough money and travel the world self-teaching himself, and learning more than just facts and places. He would experience them, and maybe someday write his own more interesting version than the dry ones thrust on him through the primary school years.

"Athens, I hail from Athens."

"Athens? Then you are Greek, no?"

"Yes, I'm Greek."

"Your dialect doesn't sound Greek but then what would I know. I've never met a Greek before." His new friend then studied the perfectly clean robe and unworn sandals he was wearing.

"My friend, how is it your garments are so clean? For such a long journey, I would expect the sands would have worn your clothing well. But yours are clean and unfrayed as if recently purchased at the market."

Abdul wasn't sure he was being questioned or interrogated. Next time he would pay more attention to his choice of words and descriptions. The saying 'where no man has traveled' filled his head.

He needed to deflect and confuse the man for a moment so he could fabricate a good story.

"Friend, friend?" asked Abdul. The ploy worked. The shepherd displayed a look of embarrassment.

"Excuse me for poor hospitality. My name is Akhmad. A shepherd from the north."

"Akhmad, I am employed by clothing merchants. I sailed across the Mediterranean in the hope of offering our goods and opening up a new trade route. We spin only the finest fabrics and silk for nobles and clergy. My employer is hoping to open a few shops in the near future.

Akhmad reached out and felt Abdul's robe. "Yes, very nice, very nice indeed. Of course, a shepherd such as I would never be able to afford such fineries. Times have been difficult enough paying the Roman tax collectors and feeding my family. Perhaps someday I too shall own such fine garments." He pondered the idea for a moment. "It's getting late. We should continue to Jerusalem before the festivities are fully under way, and all of the prime accommodation has been taken."

Abdul nodded in agreement. Akhmad looked up at the setting sun, thankful the heat of the day was starting to dissipate. He wiped the sweat from his weathered, worn brow. "Friend Abdul, would you have any water for a parched tongue?"

Without thinking, he reached into his tunic and removed two of the plastic vials of cool water. He tore one open and handed it to Akhmad. Akhmad stared in amazement at the clear wineskin. His face contorted in confusion. Seeing his reaction to the plastic product, he needed to think fast. "Another product we may be selling. A wineskin that doesn't burst."

The words eased any doubts Akhmad harbored. Abdul drank his water first showing Akhmad the product was safe. Akhmad smiled and quickly downed the cool, clear water. "To Jerusalem, my friend."

The town was full of people milling about with excitement and joy. Passover was the greatest event of current times for the Jewish faith. Moses tried to warn Pharaoh to let his people go. If not, Moses' God would come like a thief in the night and kill all of the firstborn children. Moses warned all the Jews and followers to paint sheep's blood on the outside of their homes. If they did, the angel of death would pass by, and so it came to pass. After much anguish, Pharaoh finally agreed to let Moses and his people go.

"Abdul, I have business with the priests. Would you mind tending to the flock?"

"Friend, I would be honored, but the hour gets late, and I have a merchant to seek out." He wasn't seeking out a merchant; he needed to get to the garden of Gethsemane, in hopes of witnessing the abduction of Jesus.

"I understand friend. Shalom."

"And to you Akhmad. Shalom."

Abdul moved out of the crowded, bustling market, making his way east of town. He found a small alley and removed his watch from the chest pack. 10:00pm. He needed to hurry to the garden. There were no records concerning what time the Roman guards would arrive and abduct Jesus. The only clues available concerning the time were speculative. The accounts of the Apostles only detailed that Jesus went to pray to his father for such a long time, that none of the disciples were able to stay awake. Hopefully, it was closer to midnight or the earlier hours of the morning. The high priests were hoping to take Jesus with the least witnesses possible. Jesus had been greeted earlier in the week by throngs of people hailing him as "the Son of God, The Messiah, the prophet, their savior." A public arrest could trigger a much unwanted revolt which could cause Pontius Pilate and the Roman Empire to enforce stricter, more rigid policies of conduct for the people and the high priests. Jesus was a direct threat to their power and self-indulgence.

He removed the rough sketch he'd prepared to show where the garden was located, and ventured off in the moonlit streets.

He could see torches in the trees and detect heavy snoring from the bushes. *This is it. I'm in time. Now—to get close enough, yet not be seen.* He chose a small group of thick bushes and settled in. He removed the camera, making sure it wasn't damaged during the trip. The small, green, power light turned on. He pushed the *record* button and was greeted with the red light. *Good, everything is working.* He pointed the viewfinder in the direction of the eleven men laying on the ground and resting against trees.

Even in their sleep, one could feel the urgency of the situation. These men, the followers of Jesus, all carried haggard, worried looks etched on their faces. Jesus told them that he would be betrayed and he was. The Roman guards must be on their way to arrest Jesus. *How would I have reacted if betrayed by one of my closest friends? Would I have lashed out or sent him on his way? But that would only be a friend, not the "Son of God."* He pulled out a piece of beef jerky to quell the groans arising in his stomach. Being detected by a growling stomach could cause him to be placed in an extremely awkward position.

He was lost in his thoughts trying to decide how he would have reacted if he'd been a disciple. His thoughts were interrupted by a stern, hard voice. "My friends, is it not enough you cannot stay awake in my hour of need?" Abdul saw a man in his thirties, dressed in a white robe, talking to the men. His hair was shoulder-length.

One of the men stirred and looked up at the man. "Master," *It's Jesus.* Abdul started recording. "We have not the strength you possess. We all tried to stand vigilant, but our bodies cried for sleep. Can you forgive us?" The man was pleading with tears in his eyes.

"Yes, I can forgive you." The other men stirred and listened to the words of Jesus. "I only hoped you could have willed the power to fight off sleep. This is the last earthly night we shall spend together. Judas has done his mission. The guards will be arriving soon."

One of the men stood up with anger in his words. "Master. We will not let them take you. We will lay down our lives for you." Abdul was trying to remember what man said what as chronicled by the Apostles, but his memory wasn't answering. He was locked in with the unfolding events.

"My friends, you will not take up arms or inflict injury. Have you not heard my words? Have you not learned the messages I spoke?" The men stared in confusion. "Judas did what was required of him. He is performing the will of my father. □ One of the men spoke. "Does your father wish for you to be imprisoned and tortured at the hands of the Romans? Is it your father's will that you die, yet no crime has been committed?"

Jesus addressed them all. "Yes. It is my father's will, for if I live, then man will die. If I die and people believe, then man will be saved." Abdul was shocked by the words. Even he was having a hard time understanding the words Jesus spoke. *No wonder priests, clerics, and theologians, have argued about the meanings of the Bible and the parables Jesus spoke. I'm listening to them firsthand, and even though I know the end of the story, I too am having a difficult time understanding his words. However, his words are true and reassuring. Love pours forth as he calms his disciples' fears and oddly, mine also.*

"Soon, I will be taken before the priests to answer to the false charges they have contrived. The truths I have spoken and shared with you and those who believe, threaten the foundations of man-made rules and laws. Instead of listening and understanding the scriptures as documented by Moses, David, and Job, they would rather hide behind their own laws and distort the words of the prophets to maintain their positions of power and authority. They love their own words and have hardened their hearts to the true words and meanings I have spoken."

Another man spoke up. "Master, if what you say is true, then let us flee to another land where we can find safety and refuge."

"No!" he replied. His word was sharp and commanding. "Have you heard nothing of what I said?" The disciples' eyes filled with tears at their Master's rebuke. "My father has spoken, and it is the path I must take. But fear not, for we shall see each other again when my body is made whole for those who believe."

As his voice trailed off, the sound of soldiers approaching could be heard in the distance.

"My friends, it is time." All the disciples stood. The torches became brighter and brighter. In a few minutes, the court was surrounded.

A Roman officer stepped forward with his servant, separating himself from the others. "I come for the one they call Jesus." He looked at Judas. "Where is the one we seek?"

A man no more than five foot six and maybe 150 lbs stepped forward. "It is the one I kiss." Judas moved towards Jesus with tear-laden eyes. "Rabbi, Rabbi," and kissed him on the cheek.

"I am instructed to obtain your arrest and escort you back to Pontius Pilate." The soldier, along with his servant, approached Jesus. "Will you come in peace, or be forced?"

"Yes. I shall go with you in peace." No sooner had the words left his lips, than one of the disciples grabbed a sword, severing the ear of the Roman soldier's servant. The officer and his men unsheathed their swords and prepared for battle. The air was filled with tension. Jesus moved towards the servant saying the words, "Love your enemies." He then placed his hand on the wounded ear and healed it. After performing his last miracle, he turned and addressed all the men.

"No, my friends, there is no need for bloodshed. What I do, I do for you."

Abdul couldn't take his eyes off Jesus. He could feel the power and serenity which surrounded him. He was trying to understand how this man, no, this "Son of God", was so willing to fulfill the wishes of his father. He felt a force enter his body like nothing else he'd ever experienced. His body filled with a warm peace he'd never felt before. A word formed in the back of his throat and quietly escaped his lips with a pleading tone, "Father."

Jesus stopped and turned back. Abdul thought he was going to say goodbye to his disciples. Instead, he looked straight at him. His faced filled with a calm and peaceful serenity. "Go in peace my son." He turned away and joined the soldiers.

As Jesus was led out of the garden, Abdul found himself exhausted—mentally and physically. Without giving it a second thought, he laid down in the brush preparing for the most wonderful, deep sleep of his life, contemplating the events he'd witnessed while pondering a heavy thought, *I am witnessing the birth of Christianity.*

* * *

He was woken by the cool wind blowing in the garden. He opened his eyes and stretched. Everyone was gone. He pulled his watch out of the chest pack—10:00am. He'd been asleep for only six hours, yet never felt more refreshed. He was used to playing games with Larry late into the night and then crashing for ten to twelve hours, and when he awoke, he felt like a hammer was banging in his head. Not the case this time. He felt rejuvenated, relaxed and reborn. He removed a packet of water and beef jerky. He was surprised he wasn't famished and dying for a Big Mac and fries. Ah, the breakfast of champions washed down with thirty-six ounces of red coke.

He rose, removed a piece of jerky and water pouch and started towards Akeldama and history.

As he walked, he couldn't release the image of Jesus staring at him before going into captivity. *Did it really happen? Did I truly witness the "Son of God" preaching and teaching to his disciples? He would know soon enough when he returned, and they viewed the film.* The camera Skorzenzy provided would only record. There was no pop-out, side viewer for playback mode. The camera was built with that specific feature so the camera operator couldn't alter any of the events they were watching, or possibly tamper with the evidence.

He arrived at Potter's Field at 10:30am. Not another soul was in sight. *Of course not. They would all be in town preparing for the Passover Celebration.* He found a tree and sat down, resting his back against it, recounting the events of the prior evening.

At 11:15am a man slowly and painfully came into view. By his actions, he was terribly distraught and distressed. He was frantically looking to and fro for something, but what? He slowly moved towards the largest tree in the quarry. He removed a rope from inside his tunic. *Judas!* Abdul removed the lens protector and started filming.

Judas took care climbing the tree. He went onto the first branch, attaching one end of the rope to the branch and the other around his neck. He was kneeling as if asking for forgiveness for the terrible act he had willingly accomplished. Abdul zoomed in on his face. Tears covered his face. His lips trembled as words, too soft to hear, left his mouth. He stood up, bowed his head, and prepared to leap.

A voice with the ferocity of thunder filled the quarry. "Stop! What are you doing?"

Judas looked about, confused and scared. Abdul moved a little closer.

"Who is there? Why are you troubling me?" His words were unsure and shaky.

"It is I. The Alpha and Omega. I, who created all. I, the Father of Jesus of Nazareth."

Judas fell to his knees. "Oh God, I have forsaken you. Please forgive me for I am only a man."

"How can you forsake the one who wrote in the book of life the act you were destined to commit since your inception in the womb?"

"Lord, forgive me. Forgive me for being weak."

"Come off the tree. Your place has been reserved. It was written my son would be betrayed, and so he was. Only my son and I can forgive the sins of man when he sins. Come down and reap your reward. You will be the instrument of truth and knowledge. You will teach others that to believe in all other gods will lead to damnation." The sound of the voice was frightening. Abdul was hearing the words in his mind, not through his ears. He looked at the audio level detector in the viewfinder. It was off the scale.

Another voice boomed over the quarry. "He is mine!"

Abdul panned the landscape looking for the source. *There. Something to the left is moving. MY GOD!* Abdul lowered the camera and stared at the mammoth creature approaching Judas. It was over eight feet tall. Its face resembled a man and a creature at the same time. The facial features were heavily scarred and creased. Its feet and arms were more animal than man. Long talons and claws protruded from its hands and feet. Behind its body was a pair of battle-scarred wings. They were the color of dried blood. They hung four feet above and aside from its body. The dry dirt moved in great clouds as the creature walked closer to Judas.

"He is mine! It was I, the Angel of Darkness, the fallen one, who chose this man to kill your son. Therefore, I shall claim his soul, and he will sit on my right hand and rule the Earth with me." Without thought, he let the camera slowly lower to his side, subconsciously hoping it was pointing at the scene unfolding before him. He didn't want to watch this through the viewfinder. He needed to document the events with the naked eye.

"No! He is mine, Lucifer. You shall touch no hair on his head. I have written—"

Lucifer tired of the argument.

"Oh Mighty and All-Knowing," his tone was of mockery. "I, the fallen angel, am claiming this man for my doing. If you wanted him so badly, why then did you have him kill your son? Another test like Cain and Abel? No, this one is mine," he declared.

He came within three feet of Judas.

"Judas, my son. I, and I alone, placed the thought in your heart and mind to betray the Son of God. Because you followed the directions well, I have a place for you in my own kingdom, much more suited for your likes, than what *he* proposes. I shall shower you with unimaginable gifts and riches. You will enjoy all of the physical pleasures and pains of the flesh. You will rule this world by my side."

Judas cowered on the ground. He was caught between two titanic forces vying for his very soul.

"Please leave me," cried Judas. "Please let me die in peace."

Lucifer was disgusted with the display of human emotion.

"Judas Iscariot, I offer you powers beyond your comprehension, and yet you cower at my feet and sob? What type of man are you? If you will not join me willingly, then you shall forever burn in the fires I've stoked for weak souls." Judas said nothing.

His last words were followed by the sound of a thousand

horns crashing through the air. The ground shook with the volume. Abdul almost fell from the massive vibration. The horns sounded again, shaking the earth and knocking leaves and limbs off the trees. Rocks slid down the side of the quarry walls. Abdul frantically looked around. *What is coming?*

Two large white orbs appeared in the middle of the field. Abdul shielded his eyes. The orbs were brighter than the sun, yet they produced no heat.

"I see," called out Lucifer. "Again, you send your archangels to do your bidding. Welcome, Michael and Gabriel. It has been too long since we last fought. I look forward to our rematch."

The orbs slowly transformed into human angelic forms. Their bodies were adorned in gleaming bronze armor. Each carried a brilliant gold sword and shield. They appeared to be twins at first glance. They wore no head armor, allowing their long blond manes to swirl around their perfectly unblemished, chiseled faces. Attached to their backs were wings much larger than Lucifer's, and unlike Lucifer's battle-worn pair, theirs radiated with a brilliant golden aura. They appeared to be made of pure gold as the sun glinted off the colors, but they moved with the gracefulness of goose down. One of them stepped forward.

"Lucifer, you are right; it has been too long, but the wounds are still open." His voice resembled the sound of a baritone trombone—deep, throaty, and rich. "Leave this place. Judas is ours."

"Gabriel, I still have a place for you on my right hand. Together, we could rule Heaven and Earth."

Judas looked up quizzically. "Wait, you said—"

"Silence human!" bellowed Lucifer. "Gabriel, I shall not ask again. Join me or pay the price."

"Lucifer, I will die for my God before I join forces with your legions." The air was filled with the smell of burnt brimstone. Thunder erupted from the cloudy sky. The ground shook with the force of a devastating earthquake. Abdul fell to the ground with the rumbling and shaking. Within seconds, the field was filled with thousands of grotesque, horned creatures. They reminded him of the monsters from Tolkien's *Lord of the Rings* movies. The sight filled him with terror. *Was he going to become a casualty of war? Should he have chosen a different time period?*

As Lucifer prepared to wage battle with his legions against Michael and Gabriel, the clouds erupted with an indescribable sound. Words couldn't begin to describe it. The sound was like a tsunami crashing over the landscape. Lucifer and his legions were thrust hard against the dry land. They gasped and grappled to stand but their attempts were futile. Michael and Gabriel were unfazed. They stood like statues towering over the creatures before them.

"ENOUGH! There will be no battle today, Lucifer," commanded the voice. "Instead of shedding useless blood on the soil, we shall share Judas. He will be a message to the world. He will walk the earth until the end of time. He will carry a mark for the ages to remind man what happens when they turn their back on God. He will honor neither Heaven nor Hell. He will walk the ages of time as a reborn undead. He will be forced to live off the blood of man as he sacrificed the blood of my son for man. So it is spoken, so it is written, so it is done!"

Michael and Gabriel stood watching over Lucifer's legions. "I believe our Father has offered an excellent compromise," said Michael "I would rather have battled, but the Father has decreed no fight today. I trust you will honor the agreement. If not, you shall not live to fight another day."

Lucifer knew he was temporarily beaten. He offered no resistance. He regained his footing and turned towards his army. "Legions. We have again been victorious." The army cheered with the declaration. "We have lived to fight another day. On that day, we will be mightier and stronger. We will storm the gates of Saint Peter and banish God and all his weakling angels to the depths of the bottomless fiery pit!" The army broke out in a cacophony of cheers and chants. Pleased with his performance, Lucifer turned back to Gabriel. "Our next encounter will be your last." He turned his back on Gabriel, raised his hands in the air and clapped them together. Sparks and lightning bolts spewed forth. In an instant, he and his army disappeared.

Gabriel and Michael approached Judas. He rose to his feet, visibly shaken with the events. "What did God mean I will walk with the undead for all the ages?"

Michael approached him, drawing his massive golden sword. Before Judas could say a word, Michael plunged the sword into Judas' heart. "My God, they're killing him," murmured Abdul. He zoomed the camera as close as he could, and noticed there was no blood seeping out of the massive wound. Instead, there was a strange glow surrounding the sword. *What's happening?* Michael removed his sword and held it towards the heavens. "In the name of our Lord and God, I submit your soul to its rightful place."

Abdul watched as an apparition formed over the archangel taking a temporary human form. *It's Judas?* The specter looked at Abdul and then disappeared in a flash.

Michael took his place by Gabriel. They waited for the soulless body of Judas to regain consciousness under the shade of the tree. Judas' skin was no longer olive-colored. It was a pasty, ill-looking, white. He stirred and slowly came to his senses. "What have you done to me? Why is God doing this to me?"

Gabrielle's words were deep and menacing. "It is His will, and His will has been done." He and Michael turned away and vanished. The clouds, which had shaded the battlefield, surrendered to a cloudless blue sky.

Judas lay under the tree trying to understand what had just transpired. Abdul rose to his feet and started walking towards him. He wanted to render assistance if he could. Judas noticed Abdul approaching. He rose to his feet, stared at him, and instead of having words come forth, the only sound was an evil high-pitched hiss. Abdul stopped. He was still a good fifty feet from the tree. Judas moved towards Abdul with a purpose, one he wasn't sure he cared to be enlightened with. Judas was twenty feet from Abdul when the first rays of light hit his skin. Judas screamed in horror as his flesh burst into flames.

"No!" shouted Abdul.

CHAPTER 16

VIEWING

Abdul removed the watch from the chest pack as he picked up the pace and ran to the west. It was difficult to concentrate on the digital read-out, but he could make out he had two hours before the machine activated. If he weren't in the suit, he could be permanently stuck in time. As he gasped for each breath, he declared to himself that he would start a real exercise regime when he returned.

He was still trying to decipher what he'd witnessed. His mind struggled to connect the dots. The garden, the betrayal, the battle of Judas' soul. There would be plenty of time to digest and analyze the information once he returned, and they sat in the comforts of the viewing room. For the moment, he needed to hurry and get ready.

* * *

"Any minute, our Indian explorer should be returning," professed Skorzenzy. Since Abdul's absence, the group and the professor kept their distance. They would converse during meals, but that was about it. The revelation that Skorzenzy's family was somehow responsible for the death of the 35th president was unnerving. Only Judith would truly engage him during the meals. She was giving the best sales pitch of her life to convince Leonoid she was calm enough to make the trip back. She hoped Skorzenzy was buying her story of reform. Time would tell.

The room filled with the electrical hum as the generators sprung the machine to life. The console panel lit up, illuminating the anxious faces of Larry, Judith and Muki. Static electricity filled the air as the magnetic field increased, announcing Abdul's return.

The sequential timers were on automatic for the return voyage. Judith and Larry were only monitoring the board to make sure there were no glitches. A white light erupted from the center of the floor. They could detect Abdul's body as it started coming into vision. The look on his face was of confusion and disgust. The loud whine of the generators dissipated as he took full shape. He fell to the floor. Muki raced down the ladder to help him up.

"Abdul, are you alright?" Her words were more loving than reassuring.

"Yeah, I think so. Man, that was close! I put the suit on with only five minutes to spare. Next time I'm taking a GPS or breadcrumbs. The landscape all looked the same. If it weren't for the flock of sheep—"

All of Muki's senses came alive knowing he wasn't harmed. She noticed the suit wasn't white anymore. It was covered in a brown substance. It permeated her nostrils. "What the hell, Abdul? You smell like rotten fish or worse."

He stood up and tried to brush himself off. He proudly sniffed the air and proclaimed, "History, dear Muki, history."

"Smells more like a dung heap if you ask me." She took a few steps back in search of cleaner air. Abdul made his way to the stairs and climbed up to regale his adventures. The other three also stepped back as he ascended. They agreed with Muki— Abdul smelled putrid.

"Scotty, get into a bit of shit on the voyage?" queried Larry. "Did the Romulans have a secret weapon you weren't aware of?"

Abdul actually ignored Larry's levity.

"Sheep shit. Okay. It's sheep shit! I had to leave my suit in a grove of trees, and somehow I left a little jerky in it. I can honestly say, Slim Jims would be a big hit in ancient times." He laughed at his comment.

Skorzenzy and Judith were more interested in how the trip went. "Do you have the camera?" asked Skorzenzy?"

"Of course." Abdul pulled it out of the chest pack and handed it to Skorzenzy.

"Graduates, I shall commence the viewing in thirty minutes. That should be enough time for him to change clothes, clean up, and perhaps get something to eat." He exited the control room.

The group left the operations room and headed to the changing room, keeping a good three feet behind Abdul. The smell was a bit oppressive. All three wanted to pummel him with questions, but were unable to form the correct words. Abdul had a strange look of peace on his face and a faint aura surrounding him.

Muki couldn't take the silence anymore. Since her near-death experience, she was convinced, by Abdul's movements, he'd witnessed something phenomenal. She couldn't stand the suspense. "Abdul, what did you see?"

His words were smooth and clear, an oddity for him. "You'll see." He moved into the changing room and closed the door.

The three stood and stared in silence.

* * *

"Are we all settled and ready for our next history lesson?" Skorzenzy's voice crackled over the speakers.

Only Larry responded. "Ready, Professor. We even brought our popcorn and sodas for the show."

His levity fell flat as Abdul responded. "Shut up, Larry."

Skorzenzy turned on the projector, and the times of old appeared before their eyes. Nothing remarkable at first. The scenery was unexcitingly sparse. The rays of the brilliant Middle Eastern sun magnified the scarcity of life and vegetation. The next picture was of Abdul grinning from ear to ear. "This is your captain speaking. Red Alert, Red Alert. Scotty, give me everything you've got. The Klingons and Romulans have laid a trap. Spock, I need to know how many and from what direction. Uhara, notify Star Fleet Command we're under attack. Mr. Sulu, plot a new course. Scotty, I'm going to need warp eight in fifteen seconds. Mr. Chekov, full shields forward. Load photon torpedo tubes—one through four. Phasers on stand-by. Only kidding, guys." The group, even Skorzenzy, laughed with the bad impersonation of Captain Kirk.

"Only kidding, guys. I know if I tried this shit at home, Judith would pummel me into tomorrow. Okay, I'm going to pan around so you can see everything in the area. Professor, we chose a perfect spot. There is no sign of life in the vicinity. By my bearings, I'm northwest of Jerusalem. I believe there's a small grove of trees to the southeast." The camera zoomed in and showed the appearance of an oasis. "I'm going to make my way there and change into something more casual. And viewers, let me tell you something of the climate—it's hot as hell. Kirk – out."

The screen went black for a few seconds. The room was deathly quiet. The next picture blinded their eyes. The camera was pointed directly at the sun. They could hear Abdul laughing in the audio. "Yeah, I planned that. Hey Judith, can you see me, can you see me now?"

She was rubbing her eyes from the blinding shot.

"Abdul, you're an asshole," she quipped. Larry and Muki snickered with the continuing duel between them.

Muki turned to him and pinched his arm. "Still the prankster I see." He said nothing. His eyes were glued to the screen. Disappointed he didn't respond, she turned her attention back to the narration. *What did he see? What happened to him?*

"I'm going to take full advantage of this most interesting situation. I can do and say what I want and not be reprimanded. I'm in heaven with the exception of the disturbing wake-up call." They could see he was surrounded by sheep. "Look at this, a whole herd of Michael Jordan Fruit of the Looms just itching to be sheared. I wonder if they've been modified to guarantee not to pinch and be relaxed fitting?" He broke out laughing. The auditorium filled with laughter.

Even Skorzenzy couldn't escape the moment. His voice was filled with humor." Abdul, you have a gift for the obscene, don't you?" His eyes remained on the screen.

"Wait, before they become lamb chops, let me show you my new attire." He panned the camera from his chest to his feet. The white robe and sandals were a perfect fit. "Judith, you might be the July centerfold for Playboy, but I'm the poster child for "Indian Man of The Month." More laughter. It was obvious Abdul was in his element and wasn't about to let it go to waste.

"Hey, looks like I've got company." He panned the camera across the herd which was raising a thick cloud of dust. The camera stopped, revealing a sheep herder. He was holding a large staff and waving it at Abdul. "Appears I need to stop filming. I believe this man wants to talk to me. Maybe he'll show me the way to a house of virgins. Oh, the possibilities are too much to comprehend. Kirk – out."

The screen went blank. The group shielded their eyes in anticipation of another prank. Even though there was no picture, something was being picked up with the audio. It was the sound of deep breathing.

Judith was preparing for the worst. "Abdul, if you're about to turn this into a porn film, I'm gonna kick the shit out of you."

Larry agreed with Abdul. "Yeah, I doubt the zoom would help him at all."

Abdul was now sitting on the edge of his seat. Muki had never seen him so intense or disconnected. His quietly mouthed the words. "Watch—just watch."

The sounds continued as the camera moved forward. The group could hear leaves and small branches breaking and being shuffled about as the picture moved forward in the darkness.

In a barely audible voice, they could hear Abdul. "I'm in Gethsemane. If we guessed right, I should find the disciples in the garden." The camera moved forward and stopped. In a very hushed tone. "Yes, yes. They're all here." He moved the camera over the eleven men. A few were talking; the others were resting. "This is amazing. Jesus must be in the Solitary Garden praying. This is amazing." The group looked on in disbelief. They were becoming a part of religious history. They were on the threshold of what would become Christianity.

The screen went blank. The sound stopped.

"What the hell?' roared Judith as she sprung from her chair turning on Abdul. "Is this film full of your childish antics? Could you not resist the temptation of being a fool for once in your miserable lifetime?" Her anger was growing with each word. "This is real history. Are you deliberately trying to mind-fu—"

Abdul only stared at the screen with his answer. "Judith, be patient. I accidentally pushed the power button off. I swear. I recorded everything I saw. Please, sit and watch." His words trailed off. "Sit down and watch."

Larry and Muki were both now looking at Abdul in confusion. They both carried the same thought, *What happened, and why is he acting so strange?*

It took some time for their eyes to adjust as the picture returned. The moonlight was partially blocked by the limbs of the tree, making it difficult to see all the men in the grove, but the man standing in the middle of the group was illuminated with something other than the moonlight. There was a hazy aura wrapped around him, allowing him to be clearly seen.

For the next few minutes, Abdul and his colleagues watched in fascination with the exchanges between Jesus and his disciples until the scene appeared to be coming to life.

"No!" he replied. His words were sharp and commanding. "Have you heard nothing of what I said? My father has spoken, and it is the path I must take, but fear not, for we shall see each other again when my body is made whole for those who believe."

The theater filled with sounds of clanking armor as the men Abdul was recording stared and milled about in confusion.

"My friends, it is time." All the disciples stood. A Roman officer stepped forward with his servant, separating himself from the others. "I come for the one they call Jesus." He looked at Judas. "Where is the one we seek?"

A strange aura was starting to envelop the theater as the film progressed, causing all but Abdul to feel a bit of uneasiness. None could identify what was happening, so they chose not to make mention of their feelings.

The next recorded word was a pleading Abdul. "Father."

They watched in fascination as Jesus stopped, turned, looked at the camera and spoke directly to Abdul. "Go in peace, my son." The screen went blank. The house lights went up. None of the graduates said a word. They were lost in their own mortality and experiences. Even the room carried an unusual warm electric feeling. Skorzenzy came in and sat down with the others. For what seemed like an eternity, no one spoke.

Skorzenzy had always doubted the beliefs of mankind when it came to religion. If science couldn't prove a belief or theory, then it was tossed out as pure speculation, or in the case of religion, pure humanistic foolishness. How many wars were spawned by religious beliefs and to what gain? Too many to count, with both sides claiming Pyrrhic victories, at best. The one tangible result was the thousands of lives sacrificed for an unsubstantiated belief. Pure and utter nonsense. But now? Now he was introduced to the undeniable truth—this man did live. He still doubted all the miracles, but he couldn't deny that the film captured more than a man. It was the look in Jesus' eyes when he looked at Abdul and spoke. He felt the man was looking deep into his soul as if announcing a warning. Muki broke the silence.

"Abdul, how did it feel to have Jesus look straight into the camera?"

"I was very humbled. No one else could see me. I don't know how, because by this time, I was standing in plain view. I pleaded with him internally to escape, as I knew what was to come. His look assured me everything was as it was to be."

As it was to be? Muki questioned herself.

In a subdued tone, Judith asked, "Is there any more?" The fury she exhibited earlier was gone.

Still staring at the screen and mostly oblivious to those gathered around him, he replied with a quivering tone. "Yes."

Skorzenzy wasn't so sure he should play the rest of the video. He felt as shaken as did the others. The image of Jesus going into captivity was playing again and again in their minds.

"Are you sure, Abdul?" inquired the professor. "I think we've seen enough to convince us of the validity of the Bible. I know you chose to see what happened to Judas, but is it necessary for the rest of us to visit what is to come?"

Abdul moved his head to the right. "Professor, I implore upon you to show the rest of the film."

Muki looked at Abdul in stunned silence, as did Larry. *I implore you? What the hell?*

Larry couldn't stay silent any longer. "Abdul, are you okay? Seriously. You're giving me the creeps. If I weren't convinced you were sitting here, I'd think Shakespeare was speaking through you."

"Larry, I assure you that I'm of full mind and body. I realize the path I traveled was one of my own choosing, and not the path I should have been traveling."

Larry couldn't take it anymore. The Abdul he knew, the one who played video games into the night, pulled pranks at every opportunity, and used every bad pick-up line in the world—was gone.

"Path, my ass. If this is some type of sick stunt or act, I've seen and heard enough."

Abdul remained staunch. "Larry, apparently I have changed somewhat, yet I assure you it is a change for the better." He looked back at the professor. "Please Professor, resume the viewing."

Skorzenzy was skeptical, yet he could tell by Abdul's words that there was more, much more, to learn from his travels. He hesitantly retired to the projector booth.

The lights went black. The screen revealed a vast quarry of clay. The sun was beating down on the dry, parched ground. Swirls of dust rose and settled on the ground as the wind blew across the   parched landscape. Abdul's voice broke the solitude. "I was there. I witnessed Jesus Christ calming his disciples as he prepared for his inevitable end. How can one describe these events and be believed? To my friends, I hope upon my return the film I carry will provide the information and knowledge we seek, for I fear my thoughts and recollections would never explain the true essence of the events I'm witnessing."

The scene changed. Abdul was zooming in on a bedraggled man approaching the largest tree in the grove. As Abdul zoomed in, they could see the man's garments were torn, and his face was filled with grief. He removed a rope, climbed the tree and tied it around the limb, then secured it around his neck.

As the viewers prepared for the man to fling himself off and die, the auditorium thundered as an undecipherable voice boomed over the speakers. "STOP!" A light fixture broke. Paint peeled from the walls, chairs shook with the sound, and sweat beaded on the foreheads of the group as the temperature in the theater started rising. Skorzenzy frantically tried to adjust the volume setting to low. It wasn't responding. He shouted into the microphone. His words were drowned out as the voice continued.

"WHAT ARE YOU DOING?" He tried to switch off the projector with no luck. He attempted to unplug the power feed and was met with a strong electrical shock. He feared for himself and the others what the rest of the film would reveal. He rushed down the stairs. Everyone but Abdul was covering their ears. Skorzenzy yelled for them to leave the auditorium immediately for their own safety. Larry and Judith jumped up as he grabbed their arms and pointed at the doors. Abdul calmly stood as if nothing were happening.

"Abdul, we must leave immediately," pleaded Muki. Larry and Judith were pushing on the bar release. The door refused to budge. "Abdul, Abdul, please come with us!" She looked back at her friends. They were banging and kicking at the door. Nothing. "Abdul, stop it. Please stop it." Muki begged.

He looked at his friends—his brother, his sisters. His words broke through the thunderous noise from the speaker. "Relax my friends. Calm your fears and sit. We are safe. Please sit down and watch." Reluctantly, they moved back into the theater and sat down.

The dialogue continued between Judas and the unseen force as they slowly retook their seats.

Another voice erupted over the quarry. "He is mine!"

The group gasped at the sight appearing before their eyes.

"Abdul, what the hell is going on?" screamed Judith.

"A battle between Heaven and Hell," was all he could say.

"He is mine! It is I, the Angel of Darkness, the fallen one, who chose this man to kill your son. Therefore, I shall claim his soul, and he will sit on my right hand and rule the Earth with me." They could see the camera being lowered.

They sat in fear and anticipation as the powers of Heaven and Hell were preparing to do battle.

Muki cowered in her seat now, tightly gripping Abdul's right arm. "My God, Abdul!"

"He is mine, Lucifer. You shall touch no hair on his head. I have written—"

The room was more than uncomfortable. The temperature was at least a stifling 90 degrees and climbing. They could almost feel the desert winds whirling around the theater.

The sound of a thousand horns filled the room, cracking glass and knocking off more paint. The screen flashed with a magnificent white light revealing two glowing orbs. It was brighter than the sunset, yet it didn't scorch their eyes. The temperature in the room spiked another fifteen degrees.

"What the hell is going on?" cried each one with panicked voices.

Abdul remained poised in an attempt to calm his friends. "It is the power of the Almighty."

Skorzenzy rose up, still nursing his shocked hand, "We need to leave now, graduates! I've seen enough!"

A voice banged into his brain, "NO!" None of the others heard the words as he was flung back into his seat.

They watched as two orbs emitting a whitish, yellow hue, turned into two massive archangels preparing for battle. They were not watching events of the past; they all now knew that somehow the occurrences had traveled back. They stared on in fascination as Lucifer and God argued over the soul of Judas. They were shocked back into reality as the word. "ENOUGH!" boomed through the speakers. Four of the speakers exploded in a cascade of fire, showering the room with yet more debris. The viewers were visibly shaken and scared. They didn't want to continue watching, but they knew a force had barred the escape route, and the projector was running on its own. They could only sit and hope their fragile lives weren't going to become a part of history.

"I believe our Father has offered an excellent compromise. I would rather have battled, but the Father has decreed no fight today. I trust you will honor the agreement. If not, you shall not live to fight another day."

"Legions. We have again been victorious." The army cheered with the declaration. "We have lived to fight another day. On that day, we will be mightier and stronger. We will storm the gates of Saint Peter and banish God and all his weak angels to the depths of the bottomless fiery pit!" The army broke out in a cacophony of cheers and chants. Pleased with his performance, Lucifer turned back to Gabriel.

"Our next encounter will be your last."

The screen filled with terrifying flashes of lightning and flames. The sound of the thunder exploded the last four speakers.

The viewers attempted to shield themselves from the flying debris as they moved their arms over their heads and tried to curl up in the seats.

When the debris stopped raining down on the shaken audience, they looked up to see Gabriel and Michael approaching Judas. "What did God mean I would walk with the undead for all the ages?"

They watched as the one called Michael approached Judas and unsheathed his sword.

Muki had sat long enough in silence. She begged to know what was going on. "Are they going to kill him?"

He only stared at the screen and whispered, "Watch."

The students and Skorzenzy sat in awed silence as the soul of Judas slid out of the sword, hovered over Michael's head, and ascended.

The screen went blank.

CHAPTER 17

DECOMPRESS

No one said a word. Each of them, except Abdul, had chosen the strongest alcoholic beverage the synthesizer could produce. Skorzenzy's choice was scotch. Judith—Jack Black. Muki—gin and tonic. Larry—rum. Abdul was sipping a glass of plain water. They didn't know what to say as the beads of sweat dried from their damp clothes. Muki's experience had been educational and enlightening. But this, this was completely different. Not only had Abdul filmed the abduction of Jesus and the battle for Judas, the past had somehow traveled back with him through the camera.

Skorzenzy wasn't totally convinced of God and the afterlife, but he couldn't deny that a force of extraordinary power was ever-present during the viewing. Maybe he would re-read the Bible in a different context. Maybe he would try to be objective instead of testing each chapter with litmus paper. Maybe? But only after he corrected the mistakes of his superiors.

"My friends," Abdul broke the silence after taking another sip of water. "We were in the presence of God, the creator, and his son Jesus Christ. I could never have fathomed the internal peace which came over me when Jesus stared into the camera. He was talking directly at me. Not his disciples or the Romans—me. It was amazing. The warmth and the peace that rose in my body is indescribable. I believe—"

"Abdul," snapped Larry. "Snap out of it, boy. You're back. You're back on planet Earth. You do remember Earth, right?" Abdul shot a look of disgust at Larry.

"I'm sorry you so easily brush off my comments and experiences. It would do you well to heed my words and listen. You would benefit immensely if you opened your heart and your mind." His disgust was rising with each word. "I realized that for years, He's been trying to talk to me. But, I chose poorly not to hear his words. I—"

Larry rose from the table and slammed his fist on the stainless steel top. "Enough," he yelled. "Enough of this shit and going back in time. I knew from the start this was a bad idea. Muki almost gets killed by an organized band of assassins, and now Abdul comes back as a monk." He directed his rant directly at Skorzenzy. "Professor, I hold you personally responsible."

Skorzenzy took none too kindly to the accusations leveled against him. *Your time will come, Larry. Your time will come.* Skorzenzy did his best to remain calm and even-tempered as he addressed the charges.

"Larry, I'm sorry you fail to grasp the amount of knowledge we are revealing from the past. Muki's experiences will change the current thinking of how, and possibly why, John Kennedy was shot; and Abdul brings us proof that Judas did betray Jesus, thus revealing the hidden truths of history. And isn't that what historians crave for? The truth?"

Larry could not care less.

"I don't give a shit or a rat's ass about the past, and how we can rewrite it and put all the scholars at ease, so they can write a thousand more books, which, in the end, will be no closer to the truth than they are today. It's time for us to be leaving. We've seen enough."

"Speak for yourself, Larry." Judith stood up and walked within a foot of him. *Good, she's almost ready. She, in the end, will be my staunchest supporter and ally.* Her voice was loud, but she kept her normal demeanor in check. "Larry, it's too fucking bad you refuse to see the big picture, and who are you to tell the rest of us what to do?" She stood looking up at him, her eyes piercing into his. "I, for one, have no problem with the risks of traveling back in time. Life is a risk, and I would rather die doing something important than sitting on my ass making babies and saying everything will be alright. That might be good enough for you, but not for me." She turned and looked at Muki and Abdul. "Muki, do you regret going back?"

"No."

"Abdul, do you wish you'd stayed here in the safe confines

of our world?"

"No, Judith. For if I'd stayed, I'd have never learned the truth. My soul would still be wandering around—"

Judith wasn't letting him steal her show with another long oration detailing his newfound faith.

"See, Larry. They went back and survived. Granted, Muki's was a bit hair-raising as we saw, and Abdul, well maybe given his spiritual experience, he might actually become tolerable. Nonetheless, the gleaned knowledge outweighs the risks." Muki and Abdul nodded in agreement. Skorzenzy sat back and finished his scotch.

Larry wasn't convinced and wasn't going to let Judith push him into an uncomfortable corner. "Fine, do what you want, but I'll have nothing to do with this. I'm done."

"Good," she replied. "We don't need your help." Actually, she did. If the professor allowed her to make her trip, she would need Larry's help. Skorzenzy was too old to run the console, and Muki's short stature wouldn't allow her to operate the controls properly. She carefully chose her next words and softened her delivery to a pleading level. The hard sharpness in her words softened. "Larry, I must go back, and I *will* need your help. Please help me go back and at least have the opportunity to try and cleanse my family's name."

He could see the pleading look in her green eyes. He was cautiously touched with her rebuttal.

"Judith, it's not safe, no matter what the price. It's not safe. Muki and Abdul were lucky. They had escape routes. You want to go back to Nazi Germany and possibly redirect your great-grandfather's path, or maybe try to kill him. You will be in the heart of the Third Reich and its barbarity. How can I possibly be a part of that?"

"Because I must try. I must! I've carried this burden my whole life and now have an opportunity to try to do something about it. Maybe I can convince him of the evil and destruction Hitler and Himmler have planned for all of Europe. Perhaps he will succeed where Rudolf Hess failed. Hess tried to broker a deal with the British and was imprisoned for life. Granted, his trip was ill-advised and poorly planned, but maybe with some luck, I can persuade him to kill Hitler before it's too late." Larry couldn't ignore her last comment—*persuade him to kill Hitler before it's too late*. What if Judith could convince Bormann to eliminate Hitler. He knew from The History Channel that there were over forty failed attempts on his life. The one with the most promise was the July 20th bomb plot. He found himself questioning his own reservations.

"Judith. How would you convince him, and how would you get into Germany undetected?"

She hadn't thought that far ahead. She looked at Skorzenzy for direction. "Professor?"

"You raise an excellent question. How indeed? Getting you there won't be a problem. I've been thinking, and decided that if you go, you'll be sent to the Reichstag. Hitler never used it after the fire in 1933. You will, however, need proper identification and documents. If the scanners and copiers still work, I believe we can produce passable papers, but I will require assistance."

"Professor, that won't be a problem. My friends and I are very adept with all the new technology and photoshopping programs. Get us a good internet connection and we'll do the rest." She looked back at her friends, hoping for their participation. Muki and Abdul nodded yes. Larry's face held reservations.

"I'll help, even though I'm against this. However, before we go any farther, how long will she need to be gone. It's not as if she can walk in and tell her great-grandfather to kill Hitler and then leave. She'll surely be arrested. This is going to take some time and solid planning. If we work out feasible realistic details, then I'm in. If not—"

"Don't worry, Larry, I won't go until I'm convinced I can carry out the mission and return safely."

"Then it's settled," smiled Skorzenzy. "Let's see if we can't prepare Judith for her voyage."

* * *

Two days later, the group was pleased with the forged documents and the tentative plan. Judith would be given five days, and only five days, to accomplish the mission. It was agreed to send her back to February 1938 right after the Anschluss of Austria. Morale would be high in Germany. Hitler wouldn't be paranoid or consumed with plans of conquering all of Europe. The seeds were in place, but the planning and preparations were months away. Security would be lax as Himmler's Leibstandarte was still in the formative stages.

The Gestapo was another problem, but they too were still learning their craft. Judith would pose as a typist/stenographer from Potsdam who'd moved to Berlin after her father died. Being an only child, she'd come to Berlin for work in the hopes of being employed by the party.

CHAPTER 18

GERMANY

Larry and Abdul took their familiar stations at the console. They knew exactly how to work the machine. They didn't need any instructions; still, Skorzenzy stood by their sides just in case.

Judith climbed down the stairs and made her way to the "X" on the floor. She was bursting with anticipation of meeting her great-grandfather, and hopefully convincing him to eliminate the man who was about to bring more death and destruction than Europe or the world had ever known. If she couldn't talk him out of supporting Hitler, then she might be forced to end his life. She knew if he died, she would never exist. But wasn't it a small price to pay in order to save the lives of millions? She stopped on the "X." "Ready."

Skorzenzy leaned in to the microphone. "A few minutes, my dear. We're having a little difficulty with the coordinates."

She looked up and could see the three men apparently arguing over an issue.

"No." Larry said to Skorzenzy. "I've double-checked the numbers. It is 52.5186°N and 13.3760°E."

"Larry, I believe I'm more knowledgeable in such matters. After all, I did design the machine, and was responsible for making sure all the planetary geometric measurements were properly loaded."

"Professor, I don't give a rat's ass about the past. I've checked the numbers three times. Those are the correct coordinates. If we use yours, she could easily appear on Scheidemannstraße in plain view of everyone. Is that what you want?"

Skorzenzy couldn't disagree with Larry's logic. He looked at Abdul and Muki for assistance.

"Muki, Abdul. Do you agree with Larry's deductions on the

coordinates?"

Abdul agreed. Muki agreed, but needed to convince Leonoid. "Yes, I too have checked Larry's numbers. The coordinates are correct. If we use yours, she'll appear outside to the west of the building."

Skorzenzy wasn't entirely convinced, but he relinquished being outnumbered three to one. "Very well." He dejectedly turned towards the microphone. "Judith, are you ready?"

"Yes."

"Very well. Larry, Abdul – initiate start-up." They moved with robotic precision with the assigned tasks.

"In three...two...one."

Judith disappeared.

* * *

The smell of burned, charred wood singed her nostrils as she took in her first breath of Nazi Germany.

Judith cautiously looked about the meeting hall. The floor was covered with fallen timbers and debris from the fire. It was obvious Hitler had no desire or intention of rebuilding the structure. It was a tomb for the failed Weimar Republic and supposed Communist uprising. It was a warning to other dueling parties or peoples what would happen if they attempted to stand in Hitler's way. They, like the building, would be destroyed.

"Okay, I need to change and hide the suit." She exited the old meeting room and walked down the corridor, carefully making her way through the rubble and debris. She found a small anteroom the fire hadn't damaged. She shed the suit and stuffed it in a closet. The chances anyone would actually investigate the building were remote. Who would be looking for a traveler or her belongings from the future, and if they did find the suit, how would they explain it? God forbid they should find it. Confident she'd properly stowed the suit, she examined her new wardrobe. She wore a decidedly conservative brown skirt and white blouse. The clothes fit much too loosely for her liking, but she wasn't there to be noticed; she was on a mission and the less attention she drew, the better chance she'd have of accomplishing it.

Satisfied she was presentable, it was time to venture out into prewar Germany and her destiny.

* * *

According to Skorzenzy and Muki, it would be best to exit the building on the west side. If anyone saw her coming straight out of the building, she could become an instant martyr for the Communist Party. She found a small door and walked into the sun of Nazi Germany.

Judith could smell the cool spring breeze blowing through the trees. It invigorated her soul. To her left, she could hear the sounds of a vibrant city, so she confidently made her way towards the noises, and was greeted with a street full of activity. People were scurrying about with a brisk step in their walk. *Yes. They're still basking about the Anschluss of Austria. They've reunited with more of their lost Aryan brothers and sisters.* Every store and building proudly waved the most infamous flag history would malign—the swastika. *If these people only knew what their beautiful city was going to look like in six years, they wouldn't be so happy.* With luck, maybe she could save them the coming horrors and atrocities.

The smell of fresh pastries wafting through the air reminded her that she was a bit on the hungry side. Unlike Abdul, she couldn't carry the supplemental food pack as it would be extremely difficult to conceal. She confidently walked towards the store emitting the aroma of baking bread. She felt herself being swept up with euphoric atmosphere until she noticed an abandoned storefront. The white bold letters were sloppily painted on the windows which hadn't been broken out. "Nein. Juden!" ("No Jews!") The words ignited her memory with scenes of Dachau, Buchenwald, and the notorious Auschwitz. Images of the piles of dead, discarded bodies and those who survived the brutality of the camps flooded her mind, raising a tear of anger to her eyes. A voice full of happiness brought her back to reality.

"Guten Morgen, Fräulein. Would you care for a cake or pastry this fine morning?" A short, rotund man was unrolling the canopy as she strode up. He appeared to be in his mid-fifties and full of life.

She quickly dabbed the telltale tear away.

"Ja, ein Backwaren wäre wunderbar zusammen mit einer tassee kaffee." *("Yes, a bakery would be wonderful with a cup of coffee.")*

Who would have thought the two years of German she took in high school would pay off? She'd questioned her choice back then, but Latin and French just didn't suit her. Too girly for her tastes. She handed over a freshly minted Deutschmark to the shop owner. He eyed it with suspicion as she bit into the pastry and took a drink of the rich, thick coffee.

"Why is everyone in such a good mood this morning?" she quizzically asked.

"Have you not heard the good news, Fräulein?"

She wiped the cream from her face. "Nein. What news?"

"Where have you been, my dear? Hitler has reunited Austria with Germany. We are again one land, undivided by barriers or borders. Hitler's Third Reich is rapidly expanding as he promised. We will once again take our place in the world with the other great nations. And he's doing it without military force. He is rebuilding our nation and providing our people with national pride once again. He is accomplishing all of this without firing a shot. Hitler will lead us back to prominence without instigating a war." The storekeeper seemed quite impressed with his knowledge and oration. Judith knew better.

Inadvertently, between her last bite and sip of thick coffee, she blurted out, "Die Zeit wird es sagen, die Geschichte wird urteilen." *("The time it will say history will judge.□)*

"What was that, liebchen?"

"Nichts, nichts. I was thinking of something else." The storekeeper wasn't so sure. This young woman was acting a little odd. He might need to notify his brother-in-law, Hans Schmidt, of this strange woman's behavior. He'd already been rewarded with a small taste of the favors of The Third Reich when he turned in his friends, the Hanovers, who had been harboring a Jewish family. His efforts were rewarded by a small stipend from the government, with promises of more money in the future. His thoughts of potential riches were interrupted.

"Excuse me, Herr."

"Yes, Fräulein?"

"Where can I find the Kroll Opera House?"

He studied the question for a minute.

"My dear, it's down the street about six blocks. You aren't from around here, are you?" His questioning look put Judith off for a minute.

"No Herr, I hail from Potsdam. My papa recently died, so I decided to come to Berlin and look for a job."

"They don't have jobs in Potsdam?" His voice took on an interrogating tone.

She started to feel uncomfortable with the inquisition. "Of course they do, but with my papa gone, I decided it was time to move on and be at the center of the new government." She hoped he bought her sincerity.

"Yes, yes of course. My apologies for sounding so untrusting. Six blocks down and to your left.

"Danke, Mein Herr. Auf Wiedersehen."

"Auf Wiedersehen, Fräulein." He rubbed the crisp new mark between his fingers admiring her as she strolled away. *Hans will be back in two days. I can wait.*

* * *

Judith was amazed with the electrically charged atmosphere as she moved to the north. The streets were filled with people going about a normal morning. They were singing and glad slapping each other. Women were throwing flowers as trucks filled with soldiers passed by honking their horns while the soldiers replied with boisterous shouts and song. She uneasily felt herself getting caught up in the excitement. Several jubilant citizens bumped into her with tears of joy in their eyes. It was an unofficial parade atmosphere.

She shook her head in an attempt to regain her senses. She was developing a small understanding of the German people. They reminded her of the crowds which gathered for the races she competed in, or more recently, the campus protests. With racing, she understood the draw of being around powerful machines, but seriously, why would a person sit outside for four hours drinking beer with no idea what was going on. She felt the behavior infantile and futile, but now she was witnessing it firsthand. *If they only knew.*

She trudged on until she came to the Kroll Opera House. It was a majestic three-storied building with two more stories on the back side. *Probably the main theater.* The building was a flurry of activity as men and women dressed in German uniforms were coming and going. They carried a different persona than the rest of the citizens she'd passed. They were stiff and machinelike. They didn't carry the same smiles the throngs she passed through were displaying. These men and women were serious, and moving with a purpose. She took a deep breath and entered the building.

The massive hallway was filled with reporters and men dressed in black SS uniforms. She saw one of the cuff links and could make out, Leibstandarte. *Hitler's personal bodyguard.* She gawked in amazement as the crowd slowly parted. Hitler, Himmler, Goebbels, Goering and Bormann were revealed. The leaders of the Third Reich stood no more than fifteen meters from her. If she had a weapon, she could easily have ended the reign that minute. She smiled at the thought of watching them bleed out as she was handcuffed and hauled to jail. Her jailers would never be able to comprehend or understand how her actions were saving them all and the Fatherland from complete and total destruction. Her smile widened at the thought of those men dying. What she didn't realize was her dream was clouding her vision, for she didn't notice the large man in a brown military uniform approaching her.

"Entschuldigung Fräulein. Entschuldigung. Kann ich Ihnen helfen?" ("*Excuse me Miss, can I help you?*")

The words were a rougher dialect than high school, but she understood the man was asking if she needed assistance.

"Danke Herr, I'm looking for the receptionist. I want to apply for a position." She turned to look at the man who was being so helpful. His face was round and pudgy. He reminded her of the Pillsbury dough boy. His black hair was well-receded and slicked down. His eyes were dark and soulless. *It can't be!*

"Perhaps I can help with your search. My name is Martin Bormann, Adolf Hitler's secretary." She froze in her feet, mouth gaping wide open. Bormann was entranced with her beauty, yet he detected something vaguely familiar in her eyes.

"Miss, about the job." Bormann's words awoke her from the shock.

"Yes, yes, the job," she stammered.

"What is your specialty, Miss? Miss...I don't believe we've been properly introduced?" Judith thought for a moment, trying vainly to remember the name Skorzenzy settled on. *Ruth, Anna, Claudia? No? Yes, Ruth, Ruth von Reichman. That's it.*

"Herr Bormann, my name is Ruth von Reichman."

"Pleasure to meet you, Ruth. Now, what skills do you have to serve the Third Reich?"

"Typist, Mein Herr. I am a very fluid and expert typist. I studied at Stanf....*NO. Not Stanford you idiot. Think. Think.* Stadardman Gymnasium." She knew that he could easily check the facts which would result in the lie being exposed. "It was a small private school my father ran when he wasn't performing his normal duties at the butcher shop. Papa died a short time ago. I came to Berlin to start a new life, and hopefully be an asset for the new government and our Fuhrer."

"Ah, so you come from good stock. It is a shame your father passed before witnessing the complete Renaissance and rebuilding."

"Yes, it's a pity."

"I'm in need of a typist at this moment. Especially one as young and pretty as you. Take the lift to the third floor and find Gertrude. She will provide all the necessary forms for you to fill out. You may start tomorrow if that's not too soon." He took out a small notepad, wrote a note and handed it to her. "Make sure you give this to Gertrude."

Judith was in a whirlwind. Things were happening much too fast. Thinking straight was becoming an impossibility, yet if she were to succeed, it was a necessity to pull herself together.

"Danke, mein Herr." The light in her green eyes sparkled with the answer, again giving Bormann a sense of déjà vu.

"Please, in private call me Martin." He peered into her eyes looking for a sign of recognition. Judith turned and started for the lift.

"Excuse me Ruth. One other question." For the second time in as many moments, she froze.

"Have we ever met before? I have this strange sense of familiarity."

She turned her head slowly to the left, only revealing half her face. She flashed her best Marlene Dietrich smile and replied. "Not in this lifetime." She winked and proceeded forward.

CHAPTER 19

INTRODUCTIONS

She was immediately hired. Gertrude was a bit suspicious with Ruth's bold attitude, but when she handed her the written note, her face went flush, and she quickly obtained the proper forms with an apologetic smile.

Judith spent the remainder of the day obtaining a flat. Gertrude was more than helpful in directing her to a building close to the Opera House. Most of the women who worked in the building were living there. The party had confiscated the structure from its former Jewish owners, and saw to it that their staff were close in case they needed to burn the midnight oil.

She tried to pay for the room in advance, but the clerk dismissed her gracious offer. He informed her the "Party" would take care of the expenses. She settled in and made her way back into the nightlife of Berlin. She was amazed how similar it was to any major city in the United States. People were bustling about, taking in shows, strolling down the boulevards and window shopping. It was hard for her to imagine the horrors which awaited these people. She shuddered with the thought. In six short years, the streets would be filled with burnt-out city blocks, debris clogged boulevards, and rotting corpses. There would be no gaiety, no smiling faces. Instead, their gay attitudes would be replaced with grim looks and sights of fear, desperation, and death.

She purchased a small coffee and returned to her room. It was time to get some rest and prepare for her mission.

* * *

The office she was stationed in was an open-air room. Unlike the offices in the U.S., there were no partitions, dividers or individual cubicles. The ceiling was twenty feet high and blanketed with fans every fifty feet to provide continuous circulation and ventilation. All the windows were partially opened allowing a crisp breeze to waft through the massive room. Women of all ages were busily drinking coffee, smoking cigarettes, and hammering away on typewriters. A steady stream of officials was coming in and out of the oversized cherry oak door at the rear. She could hear the crisp sound of heels clicking with the words "Heil Hitler" following directly after. She was overcome with the frenzied activity and was somewhat enthralled with the expert efficiency surrounding her. What disturbed her the most, was the admiration she found herself contemplating with the men in the black SS uniforms. They were everything the history books described – young, handsome, blond-haired, blue-eyed, and imposing. One of the officers walked by her and flashed a boyish, dangerous smile, "Guten Morgen, Fräulein." She felt her knees buckle, and her stomach flip-flop. *How could a man so handsome and polite be part of such an evil regime?*

"Ruth, over here," called Gertrude. Judith snapped out of the haze and found her voice.

"Morgen, Gertrude. Is it always this busy and hectic?" Gertrude rolled her eyes with dismay.

"Child, it is only going to get busier as Hitler expands our borders. He is the man who will lead us out of this downward spiral, and remove the yoke the Jews and allies have placed upon us. He is going to bring us back to glory and power. German efficiency will again rule the continent of Europe."

Judith thought back to the words of the baker. They were almost identical. Hitler truly had a grip on these people. The mass rallies at Munich, Hamburg and Berlin, along with the constant propaganda being issued by Joseph Goebbels, was having its desired effect.

"Ruth? Ruth?" Gertrude was becoming impatient with her. "Ruth, if daydreaming and soldier carousing is what you are good at, I trust you will not work out. We are an integral part of the Third Reich, and our duties are taken very seriously. If you aren't able to provide one-hudnred percent attention to the job at hand, I suggest you seek employment elsewhere. I have no time for babysitting." Gertrude's words were harsh and condescending, but she erred with the tone. Was it not Bormann who suggested she be employed here? The fire she'd placed on idle was brewing again.

"Gertrude, I trust you will have no problem informing Herr Bormann why I'm not working here?" Her tone was threatening. She narrowed her eyes and moved within a foot of Gertrude's face. "Well? What have you to say?"

Gertrude wasn't used to being challenged by any of her charges, but this woman was different. She possessed a quality not found in many German women. She was articulate, confident and demanding. The idea of having to explain to Herr Bormann why this girl shouldn't be allowed to work in the office could result in dire consequences. Judith's outburst garnered the attention of a few of the girls. They'd stopped working and were decidedly taking in the stand-off. Gertrude could feel the eyes boring in on her. She knew several of them would die to have her replaced. Her lower lip quivered along with a single bead of sweat which formed on her brow.

"Gertrude," the voice boomed across the room. The man started walking towards them. He didn't carry the same swagger as the soldier, but his darting eyes warned the women to get back to work. "I see our new maiden found her way to the correct office." Gertrude was well relieved at the interruption.

"Yes, Herr Bormann. I was just going over her duties. I believe she will be an excellent addition to the staff." She displayed a motherly smile with pleading eyes. Judith let her stew for a few moments before answering.

"Yes, Herr Bormann. Gertrude was preparing to show me around and discuss my assigned duties." Judith could see relief sweep through Gertrude's eyes.

"Excellent," he boasted. "Gertrude is a bit rough on the girls, but I assure you that she is an efficient cog in our government. Without her, who else could keep these girls focused on their important tasks and functions for the Third Reich?" Another sigh of relief overcame Gertrude.

"Herr Bormann, I have no doubts about her efficient methods. I look forward to working with her and the other girls who are providing the Third Reich and our Fuehrer with such important tasks." What did she just say? *Our Fuehrer? Get a grip Judith. Get a grip.*

"Quite so, Fräulein. Quite so. So Gertrude, what task will our newcomer be assigned?" Gertrude was going to assign her to the stenography and transcript pool. She needed at least four more women to keep up with the mass edicts coming from his office and was strapped to stay ahead. She knew failure would not be well rewarded. She'd heard stories of those who failed to live up to current standards.

"Herr Bormann, I was thinking of putting her with the other girls in order to maintain a smooth flow of information out of the office." He studied the idea for a moment, then looked at Judith. The sense of familiarity stirred him again. He intently studied her eyes looking for something to trigger his memory. Something in the eyes was most curious.

"Nonsense. I can't have her working with the common women. I believe her talents would best be served as my personal assistant. Have her take the desk next to my door. She answers only to me. Understood?"

Gertrude realized arguing with her boss would not only be counterproductive, but it could also result in severe consequences. She dropped the topic and apologetically agreed.

"Jawohl, Herr Bormann."

He looked at Judith. "Of course, if that's all right with you, Fräulein?" His words were more searching than sincere.

"Yes, Herr Bormann. I would enjoy that very much."

"Excellent. Then it's settled. Gertrude, make sure she fills out all the forms and is issued proper I.D. You have until noon to finish the task. I'm taking Ruth to lunch." He turned away and disappeared behind the doors.

Gertrude spent the next four hours tending to all the required paperwork and photographs. It reminded Ruth of Freshmen orientation at Stanford – filing out form after form, getting an I.D. Badge, reviewing office and party policies. Judith could tell Gertrude was not a woman to trifle with. The first stop was getting the I.D. Badge. The photographer at first ignored her request. He was busy drinking his morning coffee and reading the current issues of *Der Zeitung*. She moved closer and repeated the request a little more sternly. He nonchalantly took his eyes off the paper and was met with her glaring stare. He jumped up and apologized for his transgression. When she told him that it must be finished by day's end, a look of distress covered his face.

"Gertrude, you know it takes two days to perform a proper I.D."

She moved a little closer to the man and informed him, "It is by the order of Martin Bormann!"

He asked no more questions and went to work. Judith was amazed at the clockwork efficiency the staff demonstrated. Yes, she lived in a democracy, but reflected back to the endless hours she stood in line at the CDOT waiting to get her California Driver's License. *Those folks in Washington and Sacramento could learn something from the Germans.* She shrugged off the thought and followed Gertrude.

They arrived back at her office at 11:45am. Gertrude was visibly nervous. "What's wrong, Gertrude?"

They were the first words she'd spoken to her since the morning outburst.

"Child, being late is not acceptable or tolerated. Herr Bormann might appear to be a nice man, but trust me; he cares not for fools, and will dismiss anyone who ignores punctuality. It is the one fallacy of the new government I don't care for, but it is for the best."

Gertrude showed Judith her desk and went back to work.

It was a common wood table, four feet long and three feet wide. It had a typewriter, an ink well, canister of pencils, and a few reams of paper and carbon paper. *Carbon paper. This is going to be fun.* She then looked at the keys and froze. She could speak German, but reading it and typing it was a different matter. She sat down and opened the first drawer on the left and let out an unheard sigh of relief. There were two books in the drawer— Mein Kampf and a German dictionary.

"My dear, are you ready?" She hadn't heard Herr Bormann open the door. He was standing behind her right side. She turned and looked into the lifeless eyes of her great-grandfather. His look was unnerving her. It wasn't a look of lust or leering, more of an interrogating gaze.

"Why yes. I was just getting my desk organized."

"Excellent. You can finish that when we return. I have reserved seating at Helga's Hofbrau. It is the finest in Berlin. I hope it meets your satisfaction?" It was more a statement of her accepting the proposed eatery, than a question.

"I'm sure it will be fine, Herr Bormann."

"Excellent. We leave now."

* * *

They were hustled through the waiting patrons and seated in the VIP section. She couldn't help but notice there was a full wine glass and a cigarette butt in the ash tray. Maybe the wait staff hadn't properly cleared the table in their haste to seat the dignitary and his guest. Any other time she would have demanded the table be cleaned, and no questions asked; however, she knew that attitude would prove dangerous.

"Herr Bormann," she quietly asked. "Shouldn't the wait staff be summoned? It appears there was a customer before us."

Bormann surveyed the table and chuckled. "Calm yourself, liebchen. I have a matter to discuss with one of our brightest young officers. Fräulein, while we wait for him to return, I have a question. When I look in your eyes I feel we have met somewhere, yet I'm not able to recall where or when."

"Herr Bormann, you flatter me with praise. I'm sure you have me mistaken for some other young woman."

"No, my dear, I never forget a face. There's something very familiar in your eyes." Judith was becoming nervous. She could detect beads of sweat forming under her dress.

"Herr Bormann."

"Please, call me Martin."

"Martin, I'm sure—" An unfamiliar voice interrupted the conversation.

"Herr Bormann, I apologize for my absence. There was a minor issue to be resolved." Judith looked up. The young man wore a strapping uniform. He stood over six feet tall, extremely fit and very charming.

"I hope it wasn't a major problem."

"No, not all," He removed his cap and sat down beside Judith. "It appears the procurement department misplaced a request for the concrete today. With a few calls and jostling, the material will be received on time."

"Excellent news," replied Bormann.

The gentleman lit a cigarette, took a drink of his warm wine, then turned his attention to Judith. His voice was calm and soothing. "And who might you be, Fräulein?"

The words Judith wished to speak were stuck in her throat.

"Excuse me for my poor manners. This is my new assistant, Ruth von Reichman. She hails from Potsdam. This is her first day on the job. She's come to our fair city in search of assisting the party."

The man returned his gaze towards Judith. He took her left hand and lightly kissed it. Judith blushed with the warmth of his lips. "My name is Otto Skorzenzy." Her blood went cold, and she fainted.

* * *

Judith awoke in a haze. Her mind wasn't focusing. She was still in a fog from the earlier meeting. Her mind attempted to organize the events. She opened her eyes and looked around. Her pupils moved in and out focusing on the ceiling fan dangling over her head.

"Ah, you're waking up. You gave us quite a fright." She was sure the voice was Martin's, but the surroundings were different.

"Where am I?"

"My dear, it appears our young lieutenant took your breath away." She could hear another man laughing.

"Herr Bormann, I know I'm a ladies' man, but never have I witnessed such a response with a simple kiss of the hand. I'm wondering what would happen if it were her lips?" Both men laughed as Judith regained her composure. She sat up, clearing the cobwebs and finding her bearings.

"What happened? The last thing I remember is being introduced to our dinner guest."

"My dear, you fainted." Otto replied.

Fainted? I never faint. What the fuck? Wait! What did he say his name was? Her eyes were dancing in their sockets as she pulled up the memory from lunch. Otto and Martin took a careful interest in Ruth. They were preparing to jump in again if she blacked out. *My God! That's it. It's not just his name but his features. This is Leonoid's father. OH SHIT!*

Otto moved closer to her. "Fräulein, are you feeling okay? Should we summon a doctor or take you to the dispensary?" She didn't decipher all of his words; what she recognized was the concern in his face. His eyes were probing about her like her pediatrician did years ago as he asked all the questions on how she felt, and if she hurt.

"No, I'm fine. I somehow lost my breath—that's all. I'll be fine. Please, I'll be fine."

Otto looked at Martin, not quite convinced. "Well, Herr Bormann? Should we take a fair maiden's words or should we call the doctor?"

Martin intently studied Judith's face. A strange pang welled up in his stomach. Her facial features were more than familiar. He knew he'd seen this woman before, but where, where? *A rally? An admirer? A picture? A picture!*

"No, I believe she's fine. I believe with the current loss of her father, the long travel she made, and all the excitement and activities she's been exposed to, have taken their toll. Ruth, I believe you should return to your flat and get some rest. Tomorrow we shall start anew. Go home."

She was shocked she was being dismissed. She wanted to protest, but noticed something strange in Bormann's eyes. He wasn't dismissing her based on current medical conditions. His inquisitive eyes revealed something more important.

"Danke, Herr Bormann. I believe rest is exactly what I require. Herr Skorzenzy," she almost choked on the word, "it was a pleasure making your acquaintance. I hope to see you again." She stood up, unconsciously bowed, and left the room.

Gertrude asked no questions as Ruth walked by, yet she sternly warned, "Be on time tomorrow."

* * *

Bormann rose from the table. "Otto, I believe we will have to finish our business another day. I have an appointment I almost overlooked. I apologize for today. We shall meet again next week. In the meantime, if you need me, please call."

Skorzenzy stood, saluted, and left the room. Martin waited five minutes then called Gertrude on the intercom informing her he was leaving for the day, and wasn't to be disturbed unless it was Der Fuehrer himself. All others could wait."

Her voice crackled over the desk intercom. "Jawohl, Herr Bormann." He rose up and exited through the back door. He must be sure of his hunch.

* * *

Judith didn't talk to anyone as she walked briskly back to her flat. Not only was she in the presence of her great-grandfather, she'd met Leonoid's father. The resemblance was too much to shake off. She removed the key, opened her door, closed it and fell on the bed. She needed to regroup. This was all too much. Her feelings of hatred for her great-grandfather were diminishing. This, she couldn't let happen. She must stay focused. If she couldn't kill him, at least she could warn him of things to come. And what of Herr Otto Skorzenzy? He has to be the father of Leonoid. The resemblance is more than coincidence. Killing him could trap her in Germany permanently. Is it worth the risk if she gets a second chance? The thoughts swirled in her head as the spring breeze lulled her to sleep. *Three more daysss.....*

* * *

He burst into his house yelling. "Gerda, Gerda. Where are the family photos?"

His wife was busy tending to their daughter Eva. "Martin, what is it? What's wrong?"

"I need to find the family photos. Where are they?" The gruffness in his tone did not endear a pleasing response.

"Martin, what's this about and why are you so frantic?"

Realizing he was out of character, he calmed down and turned his charm back on.

"My dear wife, I'm sorry if I frightened you. I'm doing some research for Goebbels. You know how insistent he can be."

Gerda curled her lip in disgust. "What does that wretched little man want this time?"

Martin was in no mood to banter with his wife on this topic. "Please Gerda, where is the old family photo album."

She humphed and told him where to find it in his study. He thanked her and hurried off. "Gerda, please do not disturb me. This could take some time. I don't want Goebbels being displeased."

He could see her shaking her head as the words came from her mouth. "Wretched little man." A small smile crept on his face.

"Where is it? Where is it? Where...ah, there it is." He removed the photo album and gently placed it on his desk. He remembered detesting the nightlong parties his parents held, which required all the children to be in attendance. He cared not for having to look at the volumes and volumes of photos his parents were so fond of showing their friends. Most times it was an insufferable exercise. But now, he was thankful his father took the time to document the entire family with meticulous energy. He gingerly opened the fragile cover and slowly examined each and every page.

His eyes carefully scanned every photo with a keen eye. He rushed through none, whether it contained a female or not, in fear he would lose a clue. Three-quarters of the way through he stopped and stared. He gently picked up a photo and placed it under the desk lamp. *Louise.*

CHAPTER 20

DAY 3

Judith awoke in a cold sweat. The room was shrouded in a bluish hue from the full moon. She crawled out of bed and stood in front of the window breathing in the refreshing, damp Baltic air. The streets were void of any passersby or troops. The sound of trees moving to and fro added serenity to the quiet scene. She glanced at the clock face illuminated by the moonlight; 3:00am. *3:00am? How long have I been asleep?*

She sat back down on the bed wishing she'd brought some cigarettes. The professor wasn't opposed to the idea, but correctly pointed out they could easily unravel her plans. How would she explain a Marlboro in Germany? Plus, he reminded her, it was detrimental to her health.

She lay down and reviewed the day's events through her head. She wasn't used to losing her composure in any situation, whether it was driving in a race, cramming for three finals in one day, or rejecting the slew of suitors at Stanford. But this, this was something altogether different. The professor tried in vain (as he did with Muki) for her to choose a different era of time. He feared she wasn't prepared for such a difficult venture. He alluded several times that her psyche must be on full alert at all times. The period she was thrusting herself into would test her resolve. He was right. She felt herself being swept up in the euphoria and precision of the people; something she'd never been exposed to before. In two days, she'd been in the presence of Hitler, Himmler, Goering, Goebbels, her great-grandfather, and Leonoid's father. How was she going to kill Martin, or at least convince him of the path Hitler was taking the country down? *How? How?* She wasn't able to bring any books or photos of the destruction coming to Germany. Who would believe it?

She could write a letter to Martin detailing how the war

would progress starting in 1939 – Poland, Denmark, Holland, Norway, France and finally Russia. She quickly erased the thought. The wrong person might think she was a spy, and she would become a guest of the Gestapo. Not a pleasant thought at all. Then what? What could she show or tell him that might spare the Fatherland from becoming a wasteland? *Think Judith, think.*

She thought back to Muki's vast library on the topic. She remembered Muki raving over a book about a woman who was forced to accept the advances of an officer in the SS. The name of the book was...*Those, those who...Those Who Saved Us.* The officer was in charge of....Buchenwald. That's it. That's her angle. If she can convince him that Buchenwald is only the beginning of the tragedy and shame Germany will be yoked with for decades to come, Germany might still have hope.

Pleased with her analysis, she set the alarm for 7:00am and fell back asleep. A smile lay on her lips.

* * *

Martin awoke from the tapping at the door. "Martin, Martin. Come to bed. It's late, and you know you need your sleep. Please Martin, open the door and come to bed."

He wiped the sleep from his face." Just a moment, Gerda." His eyes focused on the grandfather clock across from him. It chimed 2:00am. He rubbed his eyes and looked down at the photo clutched in his right hand. "It's her."

"What was that, Martin? Please come to bed."

"Nothing, Gerda. Please go to bed, I'll join you in a moment." He could hear her shuffling away from the door. He stood up, placing the photo in his left breast pocket, closed the album and placed it back on the shelf. He was filled with anxiety and anxiousness over the discovery. The last time these feelings flowed through him was when Adolf Hitler became Chancellor and dictator of Germany. He tried to believe it was coincidence, but his conscience told him otherwise. There was more to Ruth von Reichman than met the eye.

He removed his tunic, hung it on the coat hanger, turned off the lamp and joined Gerda in bed. His sleep would be fitful at best.

* * *

"Guten Morgen, Fredrick. How is business of late?"

Fredrick was finishing up placing the pastries on the counter. He wiped his hands and stuck out his hand. "Hans, good to see you. I gather by your looks, the pastries in Austria aren't nearly as delectable as mine?"

"Ja Fredrick, they are good, but nothing compares to yours."

"Is all well in Austria? Was there any trouble from the opposition?"

"Nothing we can't deal with. Those opposed were convinced it was the best for all if you know what I mean?" Both men laughed warmly.

"So, anything new since I left Berlin?"

Fredrick went to his register, pushed the sale button, removed the wooden money box, and lifted the fresh mark underneath it. He felt it best he put it in a safe place, so none of his employees mistakenly used it as change. He turned and held the bill up to Hans. "As a matter of fact, yes. A few days ago, a rather attractive young woman bought a strudel and coffee with this bill. I don't remember the last time I saw one so new. I wanted you to see it before I passed it on."

Hans moved the bill between his fingers. "Fredrick, it does feel a bit odd." Hans removed a mark from his pocket and held them together. "Why would you be concerned with this mark? It appears to be in order, and the Gestapo has many more important duties to tend with."

"She was acting rather queer, and I feel it my duty to report anything out of the ordinary, am I not?"

Hans studied the mark a little more closely, knowing if Fredrick's suspicions proved out, the Reich would more than double their orders for the army; plus, it could help his rise in the ranks.

"Fredrick, I'm sure it's nothing, but I will turn it over to the Reichsbank for authentication. If our query pans out, maybe we will both benefit, no?" Each man laughed as Fredrick poured them both a good cup of coffee. They touched their mugs together. "To the Third Reich and Adolf Hitler."

* * *

Judith awoke right on time. She was anxious to get to work and talk with Bormann. She was convinced she could turn the tables of history. She would insist he go to Buchenwald and tour the facility. With luck, he would also travel to Dachau. With his newfound knowledge, he might be able to persuade Hitler and Himmler that these people—these Jews—although listed as parasites and those responsible for the WWI defeat, would be better used in the factories or farms.

She looked in the mirror, quite displeased with her appearance. Her hair was tousled, and her clothes were crumpled. The first night she'd been careful to place her clothes under the mattress, and wrapped her hair in a pony tail. She was too exhausted last night to take care of those issues. The same clothes would surely throw suspicion on her from the other girls, and possibly Martin. She could claim that settling her father's affairs and the travel to Berlin reduced her funds, but surely a woman of her looks possessed more than one change of clothing? It was the only story she could use.

She did her best to spruce herself up and walked back into the air of the Third Reich.

* * *

"Guten Morgen, Gertrude."

"Morgen." Gertrude raised her eyes as Ruth walked by. "Excuse me, Ruth. This is a professional office and your appearance is not satisfactory for your station." Judith froze in her tracks. Despite the dressing-down she handed Gertrude yesterday, she knew it wouldn't work twice. She turned and explained her current dilemma. Gertrude listened with a wary eye. Not totally convinced of the tale, she suggested that if she could not afford new clothes, she should meet with the quartermaster and see if proper clothing could be obtained until she received her first payment. Judith thanked her and moved towards her desk, relieved the ruse was working. She sat down and reviewed the documents she needed to transcribe. She picked up three pieces of paper along with two pieces of carbon paper, stacked them neatly and fed them into the typewriter.

The intercom on her desk erupted to life. "Ruth, are you in?" It was Martin's voice—forceful and hard.

"Jawohl, Herr Bormann."

"Good. Come in here immediately." His tone forced a small bead of sweat to form under her armpits.

"Jawohl." She stood up and walked towards the door. She turned the handle and entered his office.

Gertrude removed her finger from the monitoring button. She picked up the phone and dialed the number to the local Gestapo headquarters. "Captain Hans Mueller, please."

* * *

Judith entered the room. Bormann was sitting behind his desk looking straight at her.

"Yes Martin." Her familiarity was not well received.

"You will address me as Herr Bormann in my presence." His tone carried none of the kindness from the last two days. He knew something of considerable importance.

She felt faint and weak but now was not the time for a loss of composure. Time for the real Judith to resurface. Without balking, "Jawohl, Herr Bormann." She proceeded to a chair and seated herself.

"Fräulein von Reichman. I need you to explain a matter of great importance."

"Of course, Herr Bormann."

He slipped his right hand into to his left breast pocket, removed what appeared to be a worn photo, thoroughly examined it, stood up and placed it in front of Judith. His black eyes bored into hers with incredible force. "Who are you?"

* * *

"This is Captain Mueller. How may I help you?"

"This is Gertrude Manstein, assistant to Herr Martin Bormann."

"Yes, Frau Manstein. How may I help you." His tone was firm and impatient.

"Herr Captain, we hired a new girl on Monday, a Fräulein Ruth von Reichman. I am finishing her documents and was verifying her background history." She could hear him sigh with disgust.

"Frau Manstein, I'm a very busy man. You should talk to one of my assistants for such affairs."

"Herr Captain, I apologize for the intrusion. I felt it a matter of grave importance since she is serving as Herr Bormann's personal assistant." Her tone was stern and questioning. "I believe it best if you personally saw to the matter."

Mueller studied the request for a moment.

"Yes Frau. I will personally look into the matter. I will have an answer later this afternoon. Will that please Herr Bormann?"

"Yes. I will relay your message and efficiency to Herr Bormann."

A smile crept across his face. With his flawless execution of stifling the opposition in Austria, a possible counterfeit ring, and now a background investigation of Bormann's personal secretary, making colonel by the end of the year was within his grasp.

"One question Frau, could you please describe this woman?"

He jotted down her description, removed the notepad from his tunic pocket and studied the information.

* * *

A lump formed in her throat as she stared at the picture. It was old and worn, but the resemblance was striking. She felt as though she was looking at herself a hundred years ago—hair, smile, and figure – identical.

He retook his seat and peered at her with no emotion. "Fräulein, I repeat my question. Who are you and why are you here?" There was no place to run. No one to call. For the first time, she wished Larry would have accompanied her on the mission. There was no alternative, but to confess why she came and what she hoped to accomplish.

"Herr Bormann, I am your great-granddaughter, Judith Anderson. I was born in 1995 in Charlotte, North Carolina. I've traveled back from the future in hopes of changing the past." Bormann's face was blank with emotion. Did he believe her or would he pick up the phone and call the Gestapo? If he did, she would kill him before the words left his mouth.

He leaned forward, clasped his hands together, rested his chin on them and looked up. "Is there more?"

This was the door she needed. He hadn't written her off yet. His eyes were studying hers for truth and information.

"Herr Bormann, Adolf Hitler is moving the country to war. In 1939 Germany allied with Russia will invade and conquer Poland. In the next three years, the swastika will stretch from the Atlantic, Mediterranean, Baltic and Black Sea. In 1943, the tide will turn with the loss of the 6th army at Stalingrad, the defeat of Erwin Rommel at El Alamein, and the allied naval introduction of sonar. America will enter the war in 1941 after Japan bombs Pearl Harbor. America's entry will seal the fate of Germany. Berlin, Dresden, Hamburg, Cologne and Frankfurt will all become pyres of death from the British and American bomber formations. In 1945, the war will end with the total destruction of *our* country."

Bormann never flinched as Judith took a pause.

"Continue."

She took a breath, hoping she was getting through.

"The worst is what the allies will uncover. The greatest mechanical, efficient, elimination of human life. We call it the Holocaust. Himmler, with the assistance of Adolf Eichmann, will build dozens of extermination camps with one purpose—the elimination of all Jews. Over six million people will perish at camps such as Dachau, Buchenwald, Treblinka and Auschwitz."

Bormann sat back in his chair and studied her face. She wasn't lying; her words were well-chosen. He did question one point. "You say that we are going to enter into an alliance with Russia. Why?"

Now she needed Muki for the finer points of history

concerning the who's and why's. "Herr Bormann, I can only guess. If Germany enters into a non-aggression pact with Russia, maybe Stalin will believe Hitler's eyes will never look east." He studied her response.

"Interesting. Now, why should I believe such talk? Most would think one insane and should be properly locked up. Granted, you are the striking twin to my half-sister Louise, whom I've seldom seen or heard from, but I pose the question again. I should consider these issues, why?"

"Herr Bormann, have you been to Buchenwald? Have you visited the camp and seen how the current prisoners are treated?"

"No, my dear, those are matters for Himmler and his police force. I have more important issues to deal with than nursemaid Himmler and his staff." His lackadaisical answer inflamed her. She jumped up out of her chair, placed both hands on his desk, and responded with a firm and challenging tone.

"Martin, if you don't listen to me, in six years this majestic building, along with thousands of others, will look like the Reichstag, only worse. The Allies will fill the skies with thousands of heavy bombers and destroy everything in their path. Millions of innocent lives will be snuffed out because no one questioned Hitler. How will you feel when Russia and the allies split Germany into two separate states, along with Berlin. Yes, Russia will own half of Berlin and half of Germany." That got his attention.

Despite his attempts to dismiss many of her "stated facts," the thought of Russians infesting his country was most disturbing. He knew from discussions that as soon as Hitler calmed Chamberlain and Great Britain, Poland would be forcibly annexed if not invaded. He smiled at the idea of the lands which would be controlled by the Third Reich, but if she were right, and if she were from the future, it wasn't a pleasant idea.

He looked into her eyes, feeling the rage and hatred building in them. "Calm yourself, my dear. What would you have me do? Kill our leader? Start another Civil War, or perhaps tell the people your fascinating stories of the future? What would you have me do?"

His words didn't provide a feeling of confidence. At least he hadn't dismissed everything she'd spoken of, at least not yet. She knew what she'd do; she'd kill that son-of-a-bitch Hitler in a heartbeat. She bit her tongue, tasting the salty blood, fighting back the words that she knew wouldn't hasten her mission, but would result in the reverse.

"Herr Bormann, have you visited Buchenwald or Dachau?"

"I already told you I'm much too busy to deal with police matters." His rebuke stoked her fire.

"Too busy?" Her tone was borderline threatening. "Are you too busy to save our country from complete and utter destruction? Are you willing to sit behind your ornate desk while thousands perish each day?" She was back in her form. Her eyes gleamed with fire and intensity. Bormann stood up, glaring at her.

"How dare you accuse me of not caring for this country! How dare you address me in such a manner! Do you know what I can do to you?" He was used to people cowering away when they were threatened with the power of the state. Not Judith.

Her voice became louder and sounder. "How dare you refuse to believe the fate of a nation for personal glory and position! I came here to kill you so my family would avoid the shame and disgrace you weighed upon our name." Her words stopped him from pacing the floor as he attempted to digest and understand her warnings of the future.

"You, a simple woman, came back to kill me? Me, the personal secretary to Adolf Hitler." His voice was wavering, and his prior confidence was slipping. "You are no more than a spoiled schoolgirl who I should personally bend over my knee and provide a thorough spanking."

"Touch me and I'll gouge your eyes out, you pompous fool!"

Her raised voice and conviction kept him at bay. He'd never been in the presence of such a strong-willed woman who obviously disregarded authority figures. She moved within a foot of him as she continued her tongue-lashing.

"I risked everything coming back here. If I kill you, I will never be born, you idiot. I don't care if you don't believe everything I've said—it's irrelevant. What is relevant is visiting Buchenwald. You will see with your own eyes what Himmler and Hitler have planned on a mass scale. I understand the ridiculous lies being spread about how the Jews are the enemy. How they're responsible for the past failures and economic woes. The hatred and current policies in place will do more to hasten the demise of Germany than the numerical superiority America will bring into the conflict."

Sweat was now covering her face as she worked herself into a froth. "Those people could be an asset to this country instead of draining the country of its limited resources. The policy is utter stupidity, and any man with half a brain should recognize this foolish folly."

Her last statement angered him. He'd listened up to that point, but her direct accusation of him being a simpleton was too much.

"Sit down, Judith!" He commanded. "Sit down and be silent." She obediently took her seat.

"I have been with the party since the beginning. I'm very aware of our racial policies and their intent, for I took the notes at the meetings and passed the orders and legislation to the proper channels. As far as building camps with the sole intent of exterminating people, I'm sorry. I find the notion utter nonsense. We are only imprisoning those who are a threat to the new government. There are no policies enacted which call for the mass execution of these people."

Judith interjected. "If we could travel to Buchenwald—"

He quickly cut her off. "Silence. I'll let you know when and if you may speak again." He paused a moment before formulating his next move.

"For debate purpose only, if what you say is true, do I survive the war and if so, what role am I bestowed?" He was baiting her, and she knew it. Her answer was direct.

"You disappear in May of 1945. Your body is never found or identified. Your wife survives and escapes to Italy with the children. Unfortunately, she falls ill and dies in 1946. The children are taken in and cared for."

He studied her words looking for a weakness. "Interesting." He walked towards one of the windows, taking in the vibrancy of the citizens and traffic below. He breathed in the fresh air, paused, and turned around.

Like most of the hierarchy and officials of history, they always worry about how historians will remember them. "How will history remember me. Favorable or not?" His tone of interrogation lifted. It was one of true interest.

She rose from the chair and took two steps towards him. This was the opening she'd hoped for. "History will brand you as an accomplice to Hitler. You will be tried in abstention, found guilty, and sentenced to hang."

"Hanged? What an unpleasant way to die. But what crimes am I convicted of? I am only a personal secretary carrying out orders." His look was probing. She didn't hesitate.

"It won't matter. Many of the men put on trial will make the same claim that they were only following orders. The court will reject the defense and render the guilty verdicts."

"And what of the Fuhrer, what happens to him?"

"He takes the coward's way out. He commits suicide along with Himmler, Goering and Goebbels. There are others, but I don't remember their names." If she were lying, it would have shown by now, but that wasn't the case. Her voice never wavered, and her body language was true. He found her story quite fascinating, but her mention of the invasion of Poland was shocking. He knew Hitler planned on the invasion no matter what the French and British threatened. Hitler confided in him many times how Poland was an obscene partition of land turned over to a race of people who couldn't tie their own shoe-strings. They would become part of the Third Reich either willingly or by force. He cared not which course would be required to obtain their lands.

"Very well." He moved back to his desk and looked at his calendar, then depressed the intercom button.

"Gertrude, do I have any appointments this morning I've failed to write down?"

"Nein, Herr Bormann. No appointments until four o'clock this afternoon."

"Thank you." He picked up the phone and called for his car to be ready in ten minutes. Judith breathed a sigh of relief. There was hope for the family legacy.

He rose from the chair. "Judith, shall we?"

* * *

"Captain Mueller, please."

"Who may I say is calling?"

"Max Shubert of the Reichsbank."

"Danke. Einen Moment bitte."

"Guten Abend, Herr Shubert. Do you have pertinent information for me?"

"Jawohl, Captain. The mark is a definite fake." Hans raised an eyebrow with interest.

"You're positive, Herr Shubert? There is no mistake?"

"Jawohl. The paper and ink are not the products we use. If our economy is flooded with this currency, the entire economic structure could collapse."

"Danke, Herr Shubert. Your name will be in my report."

"Danke, Herr Mueller."

Hans sat back analyzing the new development. He picked up the phone and dialed in the extension.

"This is Sergeant Graffen."

"Sergeant, this is Captain Mueller. Is the background check on Ruth von Reichman completed yet?"

"Nein, Captain. We are still checking her."

"When will you be finished, Sergeant?"

"Herr Captain. I don't see the application being fully processed until late this evening or early next morning." Hans was not pleased with the news. He needed to know now.

"Sergeant, listen closely. The application will be completed by 3:00pm this afternoon. Am I understood?"

"Jawohl, Herr Captain."

Mueller hung up. He knew the sergeant wouldn't fail him, for failure brought severe consequences. He, SS Captain Hans Mueller, was the consequence. He drummed his left hand as he hung up the phone and stared at the wall clock – 10:00am.

* * *

Judith and Martin exchanged no words on the two-and-a-half hour drive. She knew if Bormann weren't convinced of the future, hers could easily be cut extremely short. She kept trying to get a read on his face. Did he believe her? Would he try to stop the escalating events? Or would he simply turn her over to the Gestapo and purge any records of her existence. The thoughts weren't terribly comforting.

Martin was transfixed with his own dilemmas. His eyes never wavered far from her. She was much too self-confident for a woman of this time. She carried an aura of defiance he was unaccustomed to. He stared at her eyes looking for a slip, a mistake or fear, but it never surfaced. Her expression was one of confidence, sincerity and pleading. He studied her recent rendition of events to come.

The resemblance is not coincidence. The features of Louise cannot be overlooked, and her knowledge of this era appears to be uncanny. Hitler wouldn't be pleased the plan for Poland was somehow leaked. How would she know? Perhaps Brauchitsch or Beck had informed the British. They have never cared for Hitler and would take any measures necessary to embarrass the party and have Hitler removed from power. Or perhaps it was that pompous Goering, who speaks too much when indulging in the fine wines and ample amounts of heroin he easily obtains. Regardless, I'm bound to inform Adolf and the Gestapo of an apparent leak. And what of these camps? Surely, Hitler's hatred of the Jews wouldn't be as maniacal as she described. If it came to that, would it not be counterproductive having an entire industry devouring resources which would be better allocated for the war effort.

As he mulled over her description, the one obvious question he never asked needed to be addressed.

"Judith."

"Yes, Herr Bormann."

"How did you get here?"

She never considered having to answer the questions, but then being found out wasn't part of the plan either. She turned to her right watching the landscape fly by. "I wish I had a cigarette."

Bormann snapped his fingers and demanded one from the driver, which he quickly surrendered and handed to him. He passed it to her then lit a match. She coolly inhaled the smoke.

Her lungs stung with the strong tobacco, forcing a succession of coughs.

"Smoke much, my dear?"

"Not really, but where I'm from we have filters, which supposedly remove all the harsh chemicals and tar from the tobacco. I'm not used to a nuclear cigarette." She took another drag with more desirable results. She exhaled, then turned to Martin.

"There's a machine in Pioche, Nevada designed for time travel." Martin looked up and noticed the driver's attention was directed to the conversation instead of the road. He cranked up the privacy window to keep the discussion private. He resigned his eyes and dejectedly went back to the task at hand—driving.

"A man by the name of Professor Leonoid Skorzenzy was contracted by the United States government to build a machine capable of perfecting time travel. As you can see—it works." She took another drag; her lungs were enjoying this strange new tobacco as the rush of nicotine started calming her nerves.

He was cautious with his reply as he contemplated the name of the professor. "Yes, quite so. But why come back here?"

"I've already explained that. Imagine if your forefathers were related to Genghis Khan or 'Ivan the Terrible,' wouldn't you want to correct the mistakes of the past and cleanse your name?" He contemplated the situation.

"Yes, I can see your point. Not many would be rejoicing with their deeds unless, of course, they were bent on the same missions."

"Exactly. And that is the burden you will thrust on *our* family name. I came back to remedy the problem." She exhaled and stamped out the butt.

"I see." They spoke not another word for the next hour.

12:30PM – BUCHENWALD

The guard at the gate approached the car and requested their identification. He snapped a quick salute, discovering who the main passenger was. "Wait one minute please." He went into the small guard shack and placed a call. He returned and waved the car in.

Commandant Koch greeted the car with a hastily assembled honor guard as it approached his office.

"Herr Bormann, it is a great pleasure to see you. To what do we owe the honor?"

"Herr Koch, I came to see how the enemies of the Reich are being treated."

"Very good, Herr Bormann, let me show you and your guest around." Bormann looked at Judith. She shook her head no.

"Herr Koch, it appears my secretary has not the stomach for such matters. Let her wait by the car while you introduce me to German efficiency against those who oppose the 'New Order'."

1:00PM – BERLIN

"Herr Captain, you have a call from Sergeant Kruger," came the voice over the intercom.

"Send it through, Anna."

"Kruger, I hope you have good news," came his probing tone.

1:00PM – BUCHENWALD

Bormann was glad he'd turned down the opportunity of dining with Commandant Koch before touring the facility. He knew the treatment of prisoners would be brutal and harsh. After all, they were standing in the way of progress and a new Reich. But never did he believe the depravity the state would lower itself to. These were no longer human beings, but shells filled with a lifeless soul. Their bodies were emaciated and thin. What were once eyes filled with promise and dreams, were dark pools of gel emitting no light. They reminded him of lifeless gnomes as they toiled in the quarries and worked on expanding the camp. He visited one of the barracks and couldn't help but throw-up. He didn't appreciate Koch's ill-timed comment of him not having the stomach for such important work. The smell was worse than any latrine he'd visited. Yes, these people were enemies of the state; but was it necessary for such barbaric treatment?

What unnerved him the most was the total plan for the camp when it was completed. They were to receive experimental ovens to dispose of the dead. It would be cheaper, require less land, and be more efficient with body disposal. He'd dismissed Judith's comments concerning the mass extermination of prisoners and Jews with ovens—until now. He would consult with Hitler and Himmler upon his return. If her knowledge of body disposal were genuine, how much else was true?

Koch escorted him back to the car. Bormann thanked the Commandant for his informative visit and promised him that he would supply a favorable report to his superiors. Commandant Koch thanked him for the compliment, clicked his heels and hailed a crisp "Heil Hitler."

He entered the car and motioned the driver to leave, and not soon enough. She looked at him. He was visibly shaken.

Her eyes attempted to penetrate his stiff exterior for an assurance in what she'd told him."Do you believe me now?"

He rolled down the window partition. "Driver, I need a cigarette."

4:00PM – OPERA HOUSE

They spoke not a word on the return trip; instead they both chain-smoked the entire way back. He was extremely disturbed with his findings. He cared not for the criminal element—Jews, Gypsies or others deemed unsuitable for the new government—but this, this was abominable. If Hitler did start another war as Judith described and Germany lost, those in power would be forced to flee or take their own lives.

The car pulled up in front of the Opera House. His driver opened the door for him and Judith. All eyes were staring at them as they made their way to the lift. Judith wasn't sure, but she thought one of the women whispered the word *Gestapo*. Her blood turned cold.

The lift stopped at the third floor. They both exited and walked into the main office area. Gertrude was standing by her desk wearing a most unsettling smile. "Herr Bormann, you have a guest waiting in your office."

He wasn't pleased she'd let someone in his office without his presence. He waved her off as they passed. He showed little concern, but Judith detected something else. The evil smile of vindication coming from Gertrude was silently informing her that the person waiting for them was in regard to herself.

Bormann opened the door. Behind his desk holding a small picture was Captain Mueller.

"Good afternoon, Herr Bormann, I trust you've enjoyed your drive through the country?" His eyes moved from the picture to Judith.

"Herr Captain, what business do you have with me? I'm late for an appointment." Mueller stood, laid the picture back on the table.

"I'm here for Fräulein Ruth von Reichman. She has some questions to answer."

CHAPTER 21

INTERROGATION: DAY 4

He wanted to keep her close and out of the clutches of the Gestapo, but for the moment, Captain Mueller held all the cards. He could have maneuvered a story detailing her genealogy, but he couldn't disclaim the counterfeit money. He reluctantly watched her marched into captivity. The arrest would temper his stance with Hitler and Himmler on the proceedings of Buchenwald. The captain thought it wise he held onto the photo until the situation was cleared up. Mueller's parting words were cryptic and threatening. "No one is above the party. Heil Hitler."

* * *

Instead of being able to convince Bormann on the coming peril to the Third Reich and its citizens, she was tied to a chair in Captain Mueller's office.

SS Captain Hans Mueller was an imposing man—physically and mentally. His facial features reminded her of Brad Pitt or Val Kilmer. These were the only two men she felt close to as a child. Growing up as a teenager, she'd purchased, framed, and hung posters of both men on her walls; dreaming of the day she might meet one or both of them. But, unlike her adolescent heroes, Hans Mueller's eyes were filled with a terrifying cold emptiness. Not since the incident at the truck stop in Jean, Nevada did she feel her life threatened. She knew the methods of the Gestapo always produced results, and those unfortunate enough to have the pleasure of being a guest, were seldom seen or heard from again.

"Now, Miss von Reichman, if that is your name." His words were cold and heartless. "A woman as pretty as you, and wishes to remain so, would be wise to answer my questions truthfully. You see, I would hate for such a fine specimen to go to waste. A woman of your looks and build could quite easily produce many children for the Third Reich. Of course, you could do it willingly or not."

The thought of being raped by this man turned her stomach, but she might not have any alternative. She remembered the words the instructor of the 'Personal Defense Course' told them, "If you're going to be raped, remember, your attacker needs to feel he is in control at all times. If you submit to his desires and come on to him, it could distract him enough for you to escape." She hoped she would have an opportunity to test the theory.

He removed the mark she'd used to purchase the pastry and coffee three days ago. The thought of being caught with false currency crossed her mind and the professor's, but they hoped the copy would raise no alarms. They were wrong.

"Tell me, where did you obtain the currency, Fräulein? Are you part of the Communist underground who would enjoy toppling our government? Or perhaps you're a British spy attempting to gather information on our activities?" The questions were cold and calculating as his steel-blue eyes bored into her. She couldn't help but notice the small device the fingers of his right hand were stroking. It resembled an undersized vice.

"Fräulein Reichman, while you attempt to summon a lie for the first question, please tell me your correct name. There is no record anywhere in Potsdam of a Ruth von Reichman, or your father." Fear registered across her face as Mueller stood up and walked towards her. Tears of fright began running down her face. They were masked by the beads of sweat appearing out of every pore as he came closer.

"You wish not to answer my simple questions, then perhaps a little proper motivation is in order." He chuckled at his small joke as his placed her thumb in the device. "Please Fräulein," he stroked his left hand against her quivering chin wiping away some of the tears, "they are simple questions. Provide me the answers I seek, or I shall be required to find a more sensitive area." She could feel the metal head of the vice squeezing her thumb. "Fräulein?"

* * *

Judith awoke in a daze. The last thing she remembered was telling Captain Mueller her full name – Judith Anne Anderson of Charlotte, North Carolina.

Her throat was dry and scorched. She could feel her right thumb throbbing from the small vice he'd used on her. She'd wondered at times how such a little device could be so effective. She now knew the answer to the question—very effective. Her right cheek still stung from the heavy slap he'd inflicted on her with his black leather glove. As her senses returned, she noticed all her clothing, except her panties, had been removed. She tried to adjust her arms, but was met with a fierce pain firing through her shoulder blades. The pain indicated her arms were bound behind her body so tightly that any movement created its own pain.

"Ah, I see our Fräulein is awakening from her sleep." She could see the outline of the captain behind the lamp he turned on, forcing her to squint her eyes.

"What a most unusual and fascinating story you weaved in my office. I felt such a tale should be properly investigated and analyzed in my play room. Do you approve?" He let out a small laugh. "Now, let's start with the truth. Who are you and what are you doing in Berlin?"

Despite her recent injuries and pain, she repeated her previous answer. The restraints caused her response to be forced, "I.....told.....you,....My...name....is...Judith....Anne...Anderson. I'm....from.....Charlotte......North......Carolina. She was exhausted just getting the words out.

Mueller slowly moved into the light, rubbing the vice in his ungloved right hand. "Yes, yes Fräulein. So you've said. However, maybe I wasn't persuasive enough." He moved his gloved left hand under her left breast and lifted it, slowly moving his index finger over the nipple. No matter how much she willed it not to rise, the touch of leather was triggering the neurons, making it erect. He moved the vice over it. "Now Fräulein, it pains me watching you writhe in pain, but I must know the truth. Now, one more time. What is your name and why are you in Berlin?"

She knew her temper would literally be the death of her, but if she were going to be tortured, she would fight with the only weapon she could—her voice. "Look, you Nazi son-of-a-bitch. I told you who I was and where I'm from." Small droplets of blood and spittle sprayed out of her mouth. "I'm sorry you're too fucking stupid to understand such a simple answer."

Mueller turned the vice until it made contact with her nipple. He saw her wince as he increased the pressure. The pain was wracking her, yet she still remained defiant. It was people such as this she'd come back to kill and eradicate. He applied more pressure.

"Fräulein, you're trying my patience. Again. What is your name and where are you from?" His tone was getting more threatening and impatient.

"I told you, you dimwitted.........fuck!'

He applied more pressure causing tears to well up and pour from her eyes. She saw white flashes each time she closed her eyes from the welling pain. She gathered all of her strength, opened her eyes, and stared straight into Mueller's. Her body trembled as she lashed out at him.

"I'm..sorry.....I.....won't....be..able.....to...watch......the..... likes.....of..you.....die.....when.....your," she gasped for air, "world......comes.........crashing.....down......between........the Russian......British......and.....American......armies. I hope......you die.........screaming!" She passed out.

* * *

Mueller was used to interrogating people and getting the required answers in a timely manner. But this woman—she was different. She carried a resolve and confidence not yet encountered. He picked up his phone looking for answers.

"Herr Bormann. Captain Mueller here. What can you tell me of this woman Judith Anderson or Ruth von Reichman."

Bormann's knuckles turned white as his anger rose up against the question. It was wiser, for the moment, to vent his frustration on the metal handle than the voice on the other end.

"Why do you ask, Herr Captain?"

"She's sticking by her story with great resolve. So far, my normal methods aren't producing acceptable results."

"Herr Captain. Am I to understand the Gestapo is having a problem interrogating a prisoner?"

Mueller cared not for the slight. He hoped Bormann would help solve the puzzle.

"Not at all, Herr Bormann. I was only hoping you could help supply some information to validate her claims. Is there anything I should know?" The stand-off was now in place. Both men detected the other knew more than they were willing to reveal—at least over the phone.

"Herr Captain, I suggest we meet in private to discuss the matter in a more appropriate setting."

"Agreed. Name the time and place."

"The Hofbrau on Linderstrauss, say 7:00pm."

"Jawohl, Herr Bormann, I'll see you there. Guten abend."

"Guten abend, Herr Mueller." He heard the line click as Mueller hung up, and then another click before he rested the receiver in the cradle. He rose from the desk, walked to his door, and slowly opened it. He looked down the long hall. All the women were working but one—Gertrude. She felt her boss glaring at her. She was in the process of notifying her cousin who worked for Himmler of the meeting between Bormann and Mueller. She slowly replaced the phone in its cradle. Small beads of sweat were permeating from her brow as Bormann approached. His voice was quiet and rough. "Gertrude, follow me."

* * *

Each man nervously took his seat as the waiter handed them menus. "What may I get our prominent guests of the Third Reich?" the young waiter asked. In unison, they requested a beer.

This wasn't a meeting for politics or positioning. It was one of discoveries and a current oddity—truth.

"Herr Captain, by the tone of your voice this afternoon, I feel it safe to believe you've uncovered, how would I say, some interesting information."

"Herr Bormann, you would be correct. She is a remarkable

woman. Never in my years of police work have I met such a—"

"Gentlemen, your beers."

"Danke. Don't interrupt us again. Understood?" The waiter retreated back to the kitchen.

Bormann picked up his stein and took a long drink. "Yes, she is a very remarkable woman. What has she divulged so far?"

Mueller set his mug down, wiped a few droplets of beer from his face, looked for sincerity in Bormann's eyes, and decided he also knew her strange story.

He leaned over as he addressed Bormann, testing the waters. "Charlotte, North Carolina." He studied the captain's look. "Yes."

"Judith Anderson?"

"Yes." Mueller sat back planning his next line of attack. Before he could complete develop his next move Bormann leaned forward.

"Did she mention the future?"

Mueller took a long drink, set the stein down, lit up a cigarette and mulled over the question.

"Berlin surrounded by Russian, British and American troops?"

Without acknowledging the facts, each man nodded in agreement. Mueller leaned forward. "What shall we do?"

Martin knew the answer no matter how much it pained him. "Exactly, what shall we do with her? Have you already filed an initial report to Himmler?"

"Yes."

"That is most unfortunate. How much information did you supply?"

"Only that I have a young woman in custody who was working in your office. No more."

"Excellent. Himmler will eventually require a full report on the woman. I suggest you've already deduced the knowledge she possesses would be counterproductive to our Fuhrer's future aims and policies?"

"Yes. What course of action do you recommend?"

"A swap."

Bormann laid out his plan for making Judith disappear.

CHAPTER 22

DAY 5

The last four days had been spent in silence. Professor Skorzenzy spent most of his time locked up in his office. The kids explored the remainder of the complex, or at least those rooms they were allowed to enter or found. The hours were filled with monotony and boredom. Several times, Abdul and Larry talked about the oversight of the military not installing, or at least leaving behind, a Play Station 2 or 360 X-Box. It would have broken up the endless hours which were running together. The only indicator of time and date was the military clock in the cafeteria. But even if they had left one, would Abdul been fully engaged with the game? Larry wondered, because he was still distant and aloof since his return. His trip had left a lasting impression on his heart and soul. Larry tired of the preachings Abdul was bestowing upon him and Muki. It was becoming quite maddening.

Muki, on the other hand, tried to keep everyone's spirits upbeat with her recollections of history in Dallas. She was still trying to understand why the man used Skorzenzy's name as she was being pulled back to the future. Several times she tried to engage the boys with helping her figure out the puzzle, but after a few hours of debating her recounts, the boys lost interest and resumed their aimless milling about. Upset they weren't as interested as she, she proposed they go back and watch the video Abdul returned with. The boys would always answer with an affirmative, "NO!" No one had re-entered the theater since the showing. They (including the professor) weren't going to tempt fate again, or at least until Judith returned. Yet even then, it wouldn't be necessary as she wasn't allowed to take a camera with her.

The kids were milling about in the control room when

Skorzenzy emerged from his office. "Prepare. The machine should be activating in five minutes. Please take your places." Obediently, they went to their assigned positions and waited for their colleague's return.

On cue, the console lights started lighting up one by one. The hum of the generator supplying the power broke the silence of the room. Abdul watched the sequential timer as it counted down to zero. Static electricity filled the room as the centrifugal force of time filled the platform. Their eyes were fixed on the monitor for the first signs of Judith's triumphant return.

"There it is," said Larry. "Something's wrong. Professor, something is seriously wrong." The four pairs of eyes were glued to the monitor. They could see the suit, but it was behaving strangely. It wasn't maintaining its shape. It was dancing about erratically in the power field. The same question and look of concern flowed over their faces as the machine shut down. "Where is she?"

* * *

The group descended the ladder to the platform floor. The suit was in perfect condition with the exception of some soot and the smell of burnt wood.

"Where is she, Professor?" cried Larry. "Why wasn't she in the suit?" Skorzenzy could offer no answers. Larry's gaze turned on Abdul and Muki. His eyes filled with water. "Where is she?" They shrugged their shoulders with the same confused look.

"Let's retire to the cafeteria and sort this out," suggested Skorzenzy. Each one retrieved a sandwich and drink from the synthesizers and collected at a common table.

Skorzenzy started the session, "Any thoughts?"

"It's obvious something is amiss. Judith is too smart not to be in the suit at the correct time. I fear she is the guest of an evil force," offered Abdul.

"What the hell, Abdul? You fear *she* is the guest of an evil force?" Larry felt he was being much too analytical, and any more of this changed persona needed to stop.

"No shit. She went back to Nazi Germany, you dumb shit. Of

course there's an evil force. The whole fucking country is evil, and she thrust herself into the heart of hate central!" Larry looked at Muki.

"Well, Miss History Encyclopedia, do you have any thoughts, or are you going to sit there and remain silent?"

Muki cared not for his accusing tone or suggestion she was doing nothing. "What would you have me do, Larry? It was her choice to go back and try to kill Bormann, or at least show him the future to befall Germany. We all tried to talk her out of it. If anyone could have persuaded her, it was you. But no, you curled up in a ball and chose to ignore the gravity of her choice. So, before you go chastising anyone in this room, take a good, long hard look in the mirror. You also bear the burden of the blame, you self-righteous shit!"

Muki, of course, was correct. Larry had halfheartedly attempted to dissuade her, but his effort was to say the least, lackluster. His anger with Skorzenzy had clouded his judgment when he required it the most. The fault lay with him. He sat back down placing his head in his hands. "It's my fault. It's all my fault."

Skorzenzy was touched by the affection Larry was displaying.

"I believe I have an answer. Abdul is correct in his analysis; she has fallen into the wrong hands. Despite her impetuous, and at times, irrational behavior, she would not have missed being in the suit at the determined time, even if she weren't able to perform her mission. There is only one option available—someone has to go back and try to find her." The three kids stared at him.

"You can't be serious?" stated Muki. "Whoever goes back could share the same fate. It's a bad idea." A few minutes of silence passed as the proposition filled their minds.

The thought of Judith being in the hands of the Gestapo or worse was more than Larry could tolerate.

Skorzenzy looked deep into his glass of scotch. "My dear, I didn't say there wouldn't be risks."

"Risks?" replied Muki. "Of course you didn't say there were risks. You never do. Instead, you toss about subtle hints knowing full damned well we wouldn't consider them." Larry and Abdul looked on in amazement. Even at the restaurant when she took on the two rednecks, she maintained her composure; but not this time. Fire flew out of her black eyes as she berated him.

"If you wanted to warn us, or at least stop us, you would have been more insistent. Instead, you would back up and let us argue with each other to decide the issue. What bullshit." He took another drink. Before she collected herself, she spouted off something she should have kept quiet. "And why did the man who lost his hand mention the name Skorzenzy? What has your family to do with JFK's assassination?"

The boys were stunned. Yes, they'd talked of the incident with no enthusiasm. But Muki was now accusing the professor of complicity in the act. Why?

He took another drink. "My child, I know nothing of such a plot as you would have us believe. I'm sure it's merely a coincidence." Regaining his senses and hoping to divert attention, he steered the conversation back to Judith.

"As I was saying, of course there are risks. There are always risks, and while we sit here attempting to place blame on conditions which can't be altered, *our* precious Judith is in peril. Someone will have to go back and free her."

"How?" asked Abdul. "If she's incarcerated, how will we get close to her?"

Skorzenzy pondered the thought. It would be exceptionally difficult to free her from the clutches of the Gestapo if that's who was holding her. He remembered the stories his father told him of their methods and cruelty. Even though his father was a member of the SS, it was the Schutzstaffel and not the Waffen-SS which was responsible for bringing dishonor to those men who died fighting for their country, and not the lackeys who hid behind dark doors heaping disgraces on his country. His father always told him it was Himmler who was responsible for the atrocities. His father's men fought bravely and with honor on all fronts.

"We know who she wanted to see and why. We'll start with Bormann first."

"So," said Muki, "Are you just going to walk in and ask Hitler's secretary where they stashed Judith, and then demand they turn her over to you?"

"Brilliant, my dear Asian. Your idea is brilliant. In a sense, that's exactly what Larry's going to do." For once, he sounded sincere. Larry was taken aback by the comment, even though he was contemplating the required mission.

"Larry," asked Skorzenzy. "How is your German?" Like Judith, he was forced to decide which foreign language to study in high school. The choices were so vast—Spanish or German? He believed he'd travel to Europe long before he chose Mexico, so German it was.

"Passable at best, Professor."

"Passable is unacceptable!" he fired back. "You must be fluent and believable, or you may suffer the same fate as Judith. It is time for a crash course. I have a voice recognition program you will use to hone the language."

Larry didn't care for being told what he was going to do, but based on the current circumstances, this wasn't the time to start a debate. "Very good, Professor. The sooner we start the better." No one objected.

Larry spent the next four hours being reschooled and grilled in the German language. Each time he spoke incorrectly with pronunciations or verb tenses, the computer would point out his blatant mistake by releasing a shrill siren into the headphones he was wearing. It was worse than having a teacher stand over you and demand perfection. If a verb tense were wrong, the speaker would respond with "Dumpkopf!" Or if he changed the personal from the proper he would hear, "Stupid!" Yet he endured the insults knowing Judith's life depended on him.

While he boned up on his German, Leonoid and Muki spent the time planning Larry's mission. It was proving daunting. They agreed he would need to return as an officer of high rank in the SS. Based on a quick search of the Nazi Party in 1938, it was decided he would return as a major. Posing as a general or colonel could easily be verified and sniffed out, whereas being a major would add some credence to his post without triggering an in-depth investigation. He was going to masquerade as a personal assistant assigned to Bormann by Himmler. The only way the ploy would work was if Larry made contact with him and convinced him of the true gravity of the situation and the consequences of history. Judith wasn't as versed in history as Muki, but she did know enough to divulge the mistakes Hitler was going to make; thus possibly causing a dynamic change to modern history. It was a gamble, but the risks outweighed the alternative—Judith being a prisoner of the Gestapo.

"Larry, are you ready? Is your German good enough for the plan to be enacted?"

"Ja Professor. Bin ich in der Lage, Narr Hitler selbst" (*Yes Professor. I will be able to fool Hitler himself*).

"Excellent. Your uniform is ready along with your papers. Now, let's get your suit fitted."

* * *

Four hours later, Larry was prepared for his trip to the past.

"Remember Larry, you will only have forty-eight hours to find her and bring her back"

"I understand."

Skorzenzy looked at Muki and Abdul and gave the command. "Send him back."

CHAPTER 23

BARGAINING

Like Judith, Larry found himself in the ruins of the Reichstag. The smell of an accelerant was still detectable in the air. He moved about with considerable care. He didn't want to damage the suit or his immaculate uniform. He was surprised at his reaction when he put the uniform on. He knew what it stood for, and the evil associated behind the skull and crossbones. Despite those thoughts, it was empowering him with a hidden force. Even Muki, Abdul and the professor commented how he was carrying the uniform—like a true Aryan.

First things first—he needed to hide the suit. He made his way out of the room and noticed small, fresh footprints in the dust and debris. He traced them to a small room off the main hallway. He followed the footprints to a closet. When he opened the closet door, he detected the dust had been recently disturbed. *This must be where Judith put her suit.* He placed both of their suits on the shelf and closed the door. It was time to get to work.

With very little time to complete his mission, he made his way to the Kroll Opera House, confidently throwing himself into the thick of Nazi Germany as SS Major Rudolph Weimar.

He was amazed at the respect the residents paid him as he walked down Scheidemannstraße proud and sure of himself. He lost count of all the salutes being heaped upon him. He responded with a flick of his hand and kept moving. Even the citizens were making a path as he strode along the sidewalk. They would smile and nod in silence as he passed by. As in Judith's case, he was awestruck with all the party flags flying at every storefront and fluttering from every open window in the brisk spring breeze. It was an exhilarating, yet eerie feeling all at once.

"Guten Morgen, Herr Major. Perhaps a cup of coffee or

maybe a fine pastry for the morning start?" Larry checked out the short stubby shopkeeper. His face matched the rest of his body—round and disgusting. Obviously, the owner sampled one too many of his own products, but it was his eyes. Despite the smile the man flashed, his brown eyes were prying and sinister.

"Danke, sir. I would enjoy a cup of coffee, but I seem to have no money on me. I was running a bit late this morning and forgot to grab my money clip."

"No problem. It is my pleasure to help the state any way I can, plus I'm sure you'll put in a good word to Captain Mueller if you see him."

Larry knew this man was more interested in his own welfare than the states; it was written all over his plump face.

"Danke and yes, I will make sure I put a good word in." He accepted the pastry and the piping hot coffee. He wasn't a big coffee drinker, but after tasting these wares, he could be persuaded to consider it. He thanked the shopkeeper and moved down the street.

He was charged with the energy surrounding him until he noticed the abandoned building. The majority of the glass was broken out. There was one half-pane of glass perilously hanging in the frame. The white skull and crossbones glared off the glass with the words "Nein Juden, (No Jews)" underneath it. He felt his blood boil as he stared at the sign knowing the fate of the past owners. His step became more urgent as he resumed his search for Judith.

* * *

Bormann and Mueller were sitting across the desk in silence. Each thinking the same thing—now what?

The plan they devised would work, but it would be better if there were a third party to assist with the problem of corroborating the story. Judith knew too much for her own good. After his meeting with Bormann, Mueller had returned to the basement and questioned Judith further. She told him (under much duress) the fate of Nazi Germany and its leaders. At first, he found it laughable until she told him of Rommel's failure in

North Africa, the thousand plane bomber raids the Americans and English would start amassing in 1943, and the utter destruction of Germany's finest men in Russia. The thought of Russians on German soil was most unpleasant.

When he felt Judith could supply him no other useful information, he decided that if he were not going to survive the war, then he should make an attempt for his name to continue on in the future if she returned. Much to the dismay and strong protest from Judith, he planted his seed in her, all the while telling her what an honor it was for her to carry his potential heir.

Bormann detected the small smile on the captain as he relived his victory of the night before. The smile unsettled him. "Mueller, I trust my great-granddaughter is in good health?"

"Yes, she is. Why do you ask?"

"Why? She is my flesh and blood, that's why, and I will be most displeased if any harm has come to her."

Mueller cared not for the unspoken threat.

"Herr Bormann, must I remind you of the position you are currently in? It's not an enviable one, to say the least. You hired a spy and a counterfeiter. How do you think Hitler will react to the news?" Mueller hoped his ploy would put him on the defensive.

"You would be correct, Mueller, yet how do you think the Fuhrer would feel if he knew you'd wounded or killed a captive who holds the destiny of Germany in her mind? I'm sure he would shower you with medals or even better, a ward at Buchenwald."

Mueller was trumped. Neither man could win this argument, but it was worth the futile attempt.

"Yes, you would be correct. Now, how are we going to execute our plan? We need a good reason to have Gertrude arrested without raising suspicion. What if Skorzenzy accompanied us?"

"No, no. He's not high enough in rank. We need someone of higher rank and importance, but I don't want them to be a local."

Mueller agreed with the deduction. The majority of officers in Berlin were all connected in one way or the other.

"Then who?"

The intercom on Bormann's desk sprung into life. "Herr

Bormann, there is a Major Rudolf Weimar to see you. I told him that you were busy, but he's being quite persistent."

"Gertrude," His monotone voice was plain and hard. "I told you not to disturb me until my meeting with Captain Mueller was finished. Did I not make myself clear?"

She took a deep breath. The lashing Bormann heaped on her was still stinging in her gut. He knew she'd been eavesdropping on his conversations. If her treasonous acts continued, she would be digging in the quarries of Buchenwald. "No sir, your instructions were quite clear. The major says it's a matter of utmost importance."

"What business does he have with me?"

Leaning closer to the speaker box, she quietly replied. "Ruth von Reichman."

Both men sat in stunned silence for a moment as her words sunk in. He suspiciously glanced at Mueller and replied, "Send him in." He focused his eyes on Mueller with suspicion. "Who did you tell and who is this Major Weimar?"

A look of confusion filled Mueller's face. "I've told no one, and I have no knowledge of a Major Weimar." Both men were fearful of this man and curious at the same time.

Bormann rose and opened the door to receive his guest. Mueller followed close behind. Both of them were startled with this young major. He walked down the aisle of desks kindly nodding at the women as he passed.

"Who is he?" asked Mueller.

"I've never seen him before." He turned towards Mueller with quizzical eyes. "He isn't one of yours?"

He sheepishly replied. "No."

The young major stopped within a meter of Mueller and Bormann, clicked his heels together and yelled out with a deep boisterous voice. "Heil Hitler!" All the typewriters went silent as the women took in the scene. Bormann and Mueller returned the salute with much less enthusiasm.

"Major?"

"Major Rudolph Weimar, Herr Bormann and Captain..."

"Mueller. Captain Mueller. Officer-in-charge of the local Gestapo." Mueller was regaining his composure to a degree, but was still intimidated by this man; not just because he was of a higher rank, but he was also much more confident than any soldier he'd been involved with.

"What may we do for you, Major?" asked Bormann.

"I have come to discuss an urgent security matter of the Third Reich; however, I believe it best we discuss the matter in private." Larry nodded his head in the direction of the quiet typists.

Bormann glared at them. The room erupted with the hammering of keys. "Of course. Please come in."

Mueller and Bormann took their respective seats while he remained standing at attention.

"Please Major, take a seat and rest. We are all friends here?" The question Mueller posed wasn't convincing.

"Thank you, gentlemen." Larry removed his hat and seated himself next to Mueller.

He wasted no time with small talk. Skorzenzy warned him to be precise and forceful. Any sign of weakness or uncertainty would be immediately sniffed out with dire consequences.

"Gentlemen, I'm here to resolve a matter of state security. I have information that a woman recently arrived in Berlin with fantastic stories of our beloved Fatherland and the fate the future holds. If you know of this woman or her whereabouts, it would benefit all of us if she were disposed of with great secrecy."

The other two men listened and arrived at the same question. "Who sent you and what affair is it of yours?"

Larry knew this crossroad would arrive. The professor was right about being blunt and forceful. "That gentlemen, is irrelevant. What is relevant, is the health of the state and our continued support of the Fuhrer and his vision for a united Europe, or would you disagree?" He should have finished his statement with Europe instead of stopping with a question. Of course they weren't going to disagree.

Mueller took the reins—this was his forte. "Major, I don't disagree, but I would like to see your papers and know who sent you if it would not be an inconvenience?"

Larry feared Mueller would push too hard. He looked at Bormann for a sign of guidance or perhaps a deflection with the captain's concern. Instead of playing out the politics, Bormann cut to the chase.

"Yes Herr Major, we know of this woman. In fact, our good captain has her in custody as we speak, and yes, the information she has recently divulged is unsettling on many levels." Mueller didn't care for being interrupted, yet he was willing to remain idle for the moment.

"What plans do have for our young Fräulein, if I may be so bold as to ask?"

"Of course you may. I have been instructed to return with her."

"And just where would that be, Herr Major?"

Larry didn't skip a beat. It was obvious from the earlier comments that they were able to extract vital information from Judith.

"The future, Herr Bormann." He let the words sink in.

"Why should we let you take her?" asked Mueller. "Based on what we've learned so far, she could provide a glimpse of our future, and possibly correct the upcoming mistakes she speaks of. It would do us more damage to turn her over instead of gleaning all the information that she possesses."

Larry took the comments in context. Mueller was right, but were the risks worth it?

"Herr Captain, you are correct." Mueller was disappointed with the response. He was trying to lay a trap and failed.

"Not knowing everything Ruth has revealed, let me provide some more insight. By the end of 1941, Germany will be at its zenith of power. All of Europe and most of Eastern Europe will be under the swastika, along with North Africa. However, on December 7, 1941, Japan will bomb Pearl Harbor in the Hawaiian Islands. America will be thrust into the conflict. Why is that important you might ask?" He gave neither man a chance to respond.

"It is vital because Hitler, in a fit of rage and solidarity to his Japanese ally, will declare war on the United States; thus, the mistakes of the past will be fulfilled. Germany will again have a two-front war on its hands. If you think Germany suffered from the Versailles Treaty, think again. All of Germany will be laid to waste. This majestic building will be nothing more than a decimated pile of rubble."

Mueller was still thinking how they could benefit from the knowledge. Before he could ask a question, Larry turned towards him.

"Captain, I'm sure you're trying to figure out how to use this knowledge for the advancement of not only the party, but for your benefit. Who will believe your story of gloom and doom? Hitler, Himmler, Goering, or perhaps Goebbels? How will you describe the horrors of the future and the failures to come? I believe even Herr Bormann understands the consequences of defeatist talk." It was true. Who will believe that Hitler's thriving Germany will fall to such defeat and destruction?

"Let's say we hand her over, then what?" demanded Mueller. "You may not understand how the Gestapo works. Reports have been filed, and questions will be raised."

Bormann already had this problem resolved. He pointed to the intercom on the desk.

"I have a solution for the problem. Herr Major, I believe it is in our best interests that this issue disappears as rapidly as it arrived." The men nodded in mute agreement.

Bormann pushed the intercom button down."Gertrude, come in here now!"

* * *

None of the women dared question why Gertrude Mannerheim was being escorted out by the two SS officers and Bormann. They were relieved the overbearing cow was being carted off. She never appreciated or complimented any of their work; rather she would always take credit for their labors. One could hear the whispers—*good riddance.*

* * *

Larry waited patiently in Mueller's office with Bormann as the captain went to retrieve Judith. Larry sat poised and motionless.

Bormann was relieved his great-granddaughter was leaving, yet displeased at the same time. "Tell me, Major Weimar—"

"Sir, you may call me Larry."

"Ah, Larry. What is she like? I gather from the short time we spent together, she is a woman of great drive and enthusiasm. I also detect her drive could outweigh sound judgment at times."

Larry allowed himself to relax for the first time since his arrival. He chuckled with the comments.

"And how! Judith is one of the smartest women I've ever known. She's as quick as a whip, and yes, her fire and drive have gotten her in trouble more than once."

"Does she have a man in the future?"

"Not at this time, sir. She's very distant when it comes to men. I believe her rebuff of males stems from her past. I'm sure she told you, in no uncertain terms, how she feels about you and the Third Reich?"

It was now Bormann's turn to laugh. "Yes, she was very vocal about her heritage. But, I'm still curious, is there a way to avoid this dark future each of you speak of?"

Larry pondered the thought for a moment.

"Sir, the obvious answer to your question is yes. In seven years, Berlin, along with many other cities, will lie in ruins. The only advice I can give is to attempt to lessen the pain on future generations."

The door to the office opened with Mueller and Judith. Larry gasped as he saw the wounds on her face. Her left cheek and eye were puffy from repeated hits, and her lip was scarred. Her hair was hastily combed in an attempt to clean her up. What concerned Larry the most was the look in her eyes—distant.

"Judith, Judith. It's Larry. Do you recognize me?"

She moved her head in the direction of the familiar voice. Unbelieving, she whispered, "Larry? Larry?"

"Yes Judith, it's Larry."

She rushed to him and fell in his arms crying. "Larry. Oh my God! It's really you." She hugged him as close as she could get. He felt like she was trying to press herself into his body. "Larry, oh Larry." She looked up, placed her hands on his cheeks, pulled his head down and kissed him as tears of joy flowed down her face. As she released him, he could see the fire in her eyes building.

"No Judith, not now. Now is not the time. Promise me, now is not the time." She ignored his plea.

Her pent-up anger now had an ally, she hoped. "Do you know what the motherfucker did to me? Do you? If I had a gun.."

He had to stop this and stop it now. She left him no recourse. He raised his gloved hand and slapped her hard across her already bruised cheek. "Judith, shut up!" He commanded.

Mueller approvingly smiled with Larry's disciplinary technique.

"Gentlemen, I believe our business here is concluded. It's time we returned home."

Their silence was their approval. Larry and Judith walked out.

"Herr Mueller, I have one question, does anyone else know of Judith and her presence?"

"Yes, but it's nothing to worry over. He is my brother-in-law, and once I tell him how many more pastries the Third Reich is going to purchase and fatten his pockets, he'll agree with anything I tell him."

"Excellent."

CHAPTER 24

DEBRIEFING

Judith proved to be back in form as she fought Larry the entire time he was helping her put on her suit. She wanted to go back and kill them all for the terror and pain they'd inflicted on her. Larry used every verbal trick he could think of to no avail. But when Judith slapped him repeatedly, he was left with no other option. He cold-cocked her. He saw the anger and unbelieving look beaming from her eyes as his left fist met her face. He knew when she awoke he would be looking for cover, but at least they'd be back in the complex.

* * *

The machine was still throttling down when Judith began her tirade. "You son-of-a-bitch! How dare you hit me! I'm going to kick your ass and then castrate you, you mother—" Her rant was harshly intruded upon by the speaker system surrounding the platform.

"ENOUGH!!!" yelled Skorzenzy as Judith squared off against Larry. "It appears history did nothing to tame your vile tongue and attitude. Both of you settle down and report to the console, NOW!"

She looked at Larry, letting him know she was far from finished with him. He nodded and wisely let her go first.

Muki was aghast at the physical damage radiating from Judith's face. "What happened? Are you all right?"

She stared at Muki as her body shivered with the thought of being all right. "Do I look all right? Do I sound all right?" She glared in Larry's direction. "And that son-of-a-bitch was in on it!"

Skorzenzy stepped forward sensing the situation was again turning grave. "Judith! Enough! I'm sure Larry had good reason to do whatever he did to you." He looked at Larry for help.

"She wouldn't shut up. She left me no choice."

Skorzenzy flashed a smile of moderate approval. He took in her superficial wounds, deciding she wasn't in dire need of medical attention. "Muki, take Judith to the bathroom and clean her up." Muki accepted. She moved to grab Judith's arm, but was quickly rebuked.

"Don't fucking touch me. Any of you!" With that outburst, she turned and walked in the direction of the bathroom.

"I think it best Muki if you accompanied her. Appears her trip was much more traumatic than yours or Abdul's." She agreed and followed her. Skorzenzy turned back to Larry.

"What the hell happened back there?" Larry decided now was not the time to discuss the happenings. He was tired, hungry, and needed to cleanse himself of the past.

"Professor, all in good time. I need to get out of these disgusting clothes and clean up. I'll meet you in the cafeteria in four hours. I need some rest."

Skorzenzy wasn't pleased Larry was giving orders, but he decided it best to give him some space. After all, time was not a precious commodity, for the moment.

* * *

Four hours later, the group met in the cafeteria to recount Judith's harrowing adventure. She made it a point not to sit with the group. She took a table across from the others and nursed a Seven and Seven. It was evident that whatever happened to her wasn't going to disappear any time soon.

Larry was finishing up his meal of grilled salmon on rice, mixed vegetables and a tossed salad, potatoes and green beans, when the professor started the discussion.

"Tell me, Larry," his tone was more composed and even than when they'd returned. "What was it like?"

He took a long drink, wiped his mouth with a napkin, and began. "Professor, it was the most impressive and loathsome time

I can remember. I could taste the evil lurking in the air despite the pomp and circumstance being displayed by the populace. It amazed me how these intelligent, efficient people could ignore the warnings of the pending disaster. I lost count of how many buildings were shut down because the owners were Jewish. No one cared or appeared to give it a second thought."

"Interesting. What other impressions were noticeable?"

"I hate to admit this, but I felt ten-feet-tall in the uniform. I believed I carried super powers. One merchant gladly offered me a complimentary cup of coffee and a pastry free of charge. He convinced me that it was for the good of the state and his welfare." The description awoke Judith from her daze.

"Was he a short, fat, disgusting fuck?"

"Yes, that would describe him relatively w—"

"That fat fucker turned me in!" she screamed as she jumped off the bench seat. "He's the one who turned me in!" Her fury was reignited, and without thinking, she let loose what was boiling in her. "'His brother-in-law is the motherfucker who interrogated and raped me. It's a damned good thing I wasn't ovulating, or I'd be carrying the bastard's child! I swear, I'll go back and kill them all. They all deserve to burn in hell and die horrible deaths." She took a breath before continuing. None of them were able to calm her down as she continued with the diatribe. "And you, you cowering pig, you sat and rubbed shoulders with them. I knew you were a coward, but I didn't believe you could be a gutless wonder at the same time." She collapsed on the bench with tears showering down her face.

Larry was the most stunned. He knew Mueller had roughed her up, but rape?

It was Abdul who made the first move, maybe not the wisest action he'd ever taken, but he felt compelled to offer solace. He sat down beside her and unwisely placed his hand in a loving manner on her right shoulder. He could feel her body tremble. He thought it was from her tears. "Judith, it's okay. God forgives yo—" He didn't finish the sentence as she landed a left cross on the bridge of his nose.

"Don't touch me! Don't anyone touch me! Do you understand?"

Larry rushed over to Abdul's aid. He could tell Judith's punch was more than Abdul's nose could handle. Blood was pouring between his fingers.

He looked up at Larry and in a garbled voice declared. "Captain, the bitch hit me! She hit me! I'm pressing charges. Call security! Send her to the brig and have Bones come fix my damned nose. The bitch broke my nose."

Instead of showing compassion, Larry started laughing. It appeared his friend was back. "Aye, Scotty, I'll tend to those issues immediately. Good to have you back, my friend." Larry helped him onto the bench seat.

Muki appeared with a wad of paper towels. Her eyes showed more than concern; they also revealed a touch of longing. She stuffed as many paper towel strips as she could up his nose in an effort to slow the bleeding. She leaned back admiring her work as Abdul turned towards Judith.

In a guttural nasal tone "Judith, are you happy?"

She looked to her right, the anger and hostility leaving her eyes. Even she couldn't help but laugh at the sight. "Serves you right, you geek. I've been wanting to do that for years. I don't know about you, but I feel better." She laughed with her comment.

Abdul unsteadily stood up and demanded, "Captain, arrest this alien! She is nothing but trouble! I fear she will infiltrate engineering and sabotage the warp drive unit. Arrest her!" It was hard to take him seriously with six inches of paper strands growing out of his nose. Instead of Larry agreeing with him, he did what was natural. He laughed, as did Muki, Skorzenzy, and even Judith. The tension of her trip was starting to wane.

After Skorzenzy set Abdul's nose, Judith recounted her harrowing experience with her great-grandfather and Captain Mueller. The group sat in silence as she told them of her impressions and pleadings with Bormann.

"Do you think he believed you?" queried Muki.

"I don't know if he believed everything, but the trip to Buchenwald left a lasting impression he won't soon forget."

"And Captain Mueller. What of him? Will he use the information for personal gain or remain silent?"

"I believe he'll say nothing." Judith looked at Larry for reassurance. "The impression which was prominent, was the fear of Hitler. Even at this point of his career, no one wished to speak any ills of the policy, or the direction, he was taking the country."

Larry agreed.

"She's right. They won't say a word if they wish to retain their power and positions. They might make small suggestions, but to reveal the destruction Hitler was bringing down upon Germany? No, they'll remain silent."

"I'm curious about one issue," queried Skorzenzy. "How will they explain your disappearance?"

Larry offered the answer. "Upon my arrival, Captain Mueller and Herr Bormann were already devising a plan to arrest Gertrude Mannerheim. She worked for Bormann and didn't appear to be a very likeable woman. I was able to hasten the discussion and provide a perfect antidote for the problem."

"I'll agree with that," replied Judith. "She's a horrid woman."

"I see," commented the professor. "One other question. Did you meet anyone else of importance we should know about?"

Judith knew exactly what he was asking, but she dared not let him know. She would tell Larry and the others about that later. "No. No one else of importance." Her words were convincing, but the tone wavered enough to peek his curiosity. He would deal with that issue later.

"Well, Larry. Muki, Abdul, and Judith, have ventured into the unknown. What about you, Larry? Are you up for the challenge, or did the trip to Germany satisfy your curiosity?"

"Going to Germany wasn't a mission of choice—it was necessary. To answer your question. Yes, I want to make my own venture, it would seem only fair." Skorzenzy was pleased with his decision. It would give him some time with Judith, and in her current state of mind, she might be easier to solicit for his plan.

"Excellent. Well, I believe we've all endured a very long day. I suggest we get a good night's sleep before sending Larry on his way." He got up and left the cafeteria.

The others got up to leave until Judith quietly called them over. "I met his father, Otto Skorzenzy."

* * *

Skorzenzy returned to his quarters and opened a worn envelope. He removed the picture and looked at the date—Berlin, 1938. He turned the picture over and examined the three people in the photo. He put it back in the envelope and placed it in his diary. He lay down in his bunk, turned off the light and let his thin smile quiver – *I know Judith. I know.*

CHAPTER 25

HOUSTON

JULY 19, 1969

"Houston, this is Apollo Eleven."

"Go ahead Eleven."

"We have a problem." The controller's face filled with concern. He wanted to verify the problem before disturbing the Project Manager.

"Roger Eleven, what's the problem?"

"Houston, we've lost power to the thrusters."

In a cool, trained voice as sweat filled his pores, he replied, "Roger Eleven." He picked up the phone and buzzed the quarters of the Project Manager. A groggy voice answered the phone. "Is there a problem?"

"Yes sir. Eleven just reported the thrusters aren't working."

The PM stayed calm and collected despite knowing the ramifications of the landing not being successful. It wasn't just the American people watching the events; it was also the Russians. They would love to see the mission fail, and perhaps give them a leg-up in the Cold War. The president was gambling on the success of the mission. He hoped the landing of men on the moon would give him a bargaining chip with the Russians and Chinese, who were illegally assisting North Vietnam. Failure could have dire consequences—funding of NASA and diplomatic relations in the Far East.

"Very good, son. Inform Professor Skorzenzy to assemble his team. We might need them.

"Yes, sir."

* * *

Of all the missions to date, Skorzenzy feared this one the most. So far, none of his past had surfaced, or at least he hoped that was the case. "Larry, are you absolutely sure about this choice?"

"Yes. Unlike Muki, Judith and Abdul, I've chosen an event where the chance of dying or being imprisoned is minimal. I'm not throwing myself into harm's way. I'm traveling back to view one of the greatest milestones in history. I don't see how anything could go wrong."

"I'm not worried about anything going wrong, Larry. I believe there is more information available at local libraries and the internet to satisfy your curiosity."

Larry detected something off in Skorzenzy's query. "Professor, what are you afraid of? You questioned Muki and Judith on their choices, and now mine. Are you afraid I might unravel a family secret?"

Skorzenzy knew he could press no more, at least while Larry was still in the compound, and with Judith still recovering from her trip; he realized pushing the issue could only complicate matters.

"No Larry, nothing   like that at all Take your place while we get in position."

Larry descended the stairs and stood on the "X".

Skorzenzy leaned into the microphone, "Are you ready?"

"Ready, Professor."

"Very good."

He looked at Judith and Abdul. "Send him back."

* * *

Larry was met with a brilliant sun peeking over the eastern horizon as he appeared two-thousand feet northwest of Houston Command Center. Even though the sun was just rising, he could taste and feel the heat and humidity of July in Houston; it was oppressive, reminding him why he chose Stanford over Texas A&M. He was relieved to see he and the professor guessed correctly on his point on placement. The only available maps they found, showed a track/football stadium in the vicinity. That was still the case.

He removed his suit, rolled it up, then placed the I.D. Badge on his jacket and walked towards Saturn Lane. The badge would get him access to the complex, but he wasn't so sure about getting into Mission Control where the action was. He wanted to experience the joy and excitement of those men guiding a spaceship 238,000 miles to the moon with less technology than his current Samson Galaxy. *Amazing!*

He started walking down the asphalt road when a 1969 Dark Blue GTO roared up and stopped, throwing dust and gravel in the air. He froze with a touch of fear as he developed a cover story. If it were security, how would he explain why he was out on a Sunday stroll with no houses close in sight?

He looked to his left as an exceedingly frantic man in his late twenties or early thirties manually rolled down the window.

"What the hell are you doing out here?" Obviously, he wasn't security.

"Ah, I decided to take a walk before coming in. This is my first day, and I was taking in the sights."

"Well, you picked a helluva a day to go strolling. Get in. We have a crisis and need all hands on deck. What division were you assigned to?" Before Larry could answer, the man told him. "You work for me now. I'll handle the paperwork. Now get your ass in!"

He felt as if he were listening to a male version of Judith. Larry didn't question him, since he was no longer worried about a cover story for admission to the show.

He got in the car as instructed.

"My name is Sam Welsh. I'm in command of the back-up scenario. The guy who was in charge of the video link has a raging case of the flu. Dumb shit. He picked the wrong time to get ill. What's your specialty...what's your name?"

"Larry. Larry Kowalski."

"What's your specialty, Larry?"

"Computers/Civil Engineering."

"Interesting combination. Where'd you go to school?"

Without thinking, Larry told the truth. "Stanford."

"Stanford? When did they open a curriculum for computers?" Larry needed to think fast.

"It's a pilot program and hasn't been placed on the main curriculum yet." He hoped Sam bought the story.

"Great. I hope you're a quick learner. You'll have thirty minutes to review the material and take your station. We've got to make sure the video feed from Arizona is in perfect working order."

"Yes sir."

Sam appreciated Larry's quick and concise answers, and the respect he was displaying for his new boss. He glanced at the white package Larry was gripping in his lap. "What's with the white coverall? Planning on becoming a painter if this mission fails?"

Larry didn't skip a beat. "No. It's a developmental suit designed to assist joggers in getting from point A to point B in record time."

"Well, when this is all over, I might be borrowing one. Hell, we might all be needing to get to point B if the mission fails. For the moment, leave it in the car. No one's jumping ship till this is over."

Larry agreed and tossed it on to the back seat.

* * *

After propelling Larry back to 1969, Skorzenzy decided it was time to start the real interrogation. He suggested the "graduates" go to the cafeteria and get something to drink. He would join them shortly.

"What do you think is on his mind?" asked Muki.

"I'm not sure, but for some reason, I don't feel as safe with my accomplice in crime gone," added Abdul.

Muki looked at Judith as she sat a few feet away. It was apparent her nerves were still shaky; coffee was sloshing over the rim of her cup and splashing on the table. "Judith, what is it?"

She slowly looked over and whispered, "I met his father."

Muki didn't understand. "What? Whose father?"

"Skorzenzy. He was there when I met Bormann."

"You met his father? Are you sure?" Muki couldn't believe what she was hearing.

"The resemblance was striking. He has to be his father." She paused before continuing. Something else was pulling on the back of her mind—something Muki said.

"Muki, do you remember what you said when you returned? Didn't you hear a name in Dallas?"

"Yes, I did. The last words I remember were—"

"Skorzenzy." The professor moved into the cafeteria, his right hand concealed in his pocket.

"You foolish, foolish children. I warned you to choose different time periods, but no—you insisted, and now Larry has traveled to another time and another family secret. I'm sorry you ignored the words I spoke and the suggestions I presented. Instead, my "graduates," your future is not as bright as you might once have imagined."

He removed his hand from the pocket.

* * *

"Larry," instructed Sam, "Here's the manual. You have thirty minutes to catch up." Larry took his seat at the small console table. It reminded him of the scenes from Ron Howard's film *Apollo 13* and the vintage clips he'd seen on the History Channel.

Within fifteen minutes, he'd read the manual, familiarized himself with all the controls, adjusted his headset and called for Sam. "I'm ready. What's next?" There was a moment of silence.

Sam couldn't contain the amazement in his voice. It took a new controller at least a full day to digest the five-hundred-page operations manual, and another half-day to understand all the controls; and that was with a trainer guiding them. "Are you sure?"

"Roger Sam."

"Okay, Switch on monitors three and four. Put three on the main screen and pipe four to my station."

It took Larry only ten seconds to perform the task. For him, it was child's play. He inwardly congratulated himself on his quick execution and then started looking at the monitors. *What the fuck?*

Sam looked at his monitor, checked the main monitor, and shook his head. He depressed his headset mike, "Good work, Larry. I now need you to bring up monitors one and two. I need one on the main screen, and two on my monitor." Sam was met with silence.

"Is that a copy, Larry?" Larry couldn't take his eyes off the image from monitor four. It was a perfect replica of the moon—complete with the lunar landing module. There were two men dressed in full astronaut uniforms. Several technicians were moving objects about. They were spraying the floor with a material resembling dust and were setting light stands around the lunar lander. He identified a man with a clipboard going through a checklist and issuing orders. The man turned to face the camera as he continued orchestrating the set. *It can't be.*

"Larry. Is that a copy?" He returned to his senses.

"Negative. Please repeat."

"Turn on monitors one and two. Place one on the main screen and pipe two to my monitor. Also, get your headset checked. We can't afford any technical problems. Understood?"

"Roger Sam." Larry quickly performed the tasks. *It would be so much easier if I could use a split screen app, but the technology hasn't been developed. No photo sharing or side screen modules, or the software to use them. How do these people function?*

The rest of the day was spent checking and rechecking systems and connections. It was redundant and boring, but from the documentaries he'd seen, it's why NASA was so successful. They had no desire to repeat the mistakes of the failed Gemini Missions that took the lives of Gus Grissom, Ed White and Roger Chaffee. The memory of those three astronauts dying in 1967 was still very fresh in their minds. They took nothing for granted. And now, it appeared there was trouble with Apollo Eleven. What, he didn't know yet.

Larry spent the rest of the day trying to figure out how he could maximize the pictures, and increase the efficiency of the control console. The repetitiveness of the back-ups was creating a host of its own problems. He was so engrossed in drawing diagrams and notes, he didn't notice Sam standing behind him.

"What is our rookie trying to do? Rewrite the entire manual?" Larry turned around to see Sam smiling down at him.

"Not the whole thing, just a few minor adjustments. If we combine the back-up systems to a central controller, you could eliminate four stations and reduce errors by at least eighty percent. The problem is—"

Sam had to interrupt him. "Hang on, rookie. I understand you're a quick learner, but the changes you're proposing will take time. Look, it's been a long day, and we need to get some sleep because everyone has to be one-hundred percent tomorrow if anything goes wrong."

"Wrong?" asked Larry.

The smile on Sam's face disappeared. "There's a problem with Eleven" He looked up at the monitor on the wall. "One way or the other, we are landing on the moon tomorrow."

CHAPTER 26

LANDING

JULY 20, 1969

"Apollo Eleven, this is Houston."

"Go ahead Houston."

"Are the thrusters working yet?"

"Negative."

"Roger Eleven, We'll keep working on it. We are T-minus two hours and counting from separation."

"Roger Houston. We'll keep working on the problem on our end."

"Roger Eleven."

* * *

"Wake up sunshine. Time to earn our pay."

Larry rubbed the sleep from his eyes as Sam handed him a cup of coffee.

"What time is it?"

"Time to go to work. We've enough time for you to take a quick shower and put on fresh clothes. My brother left some of his clothes when he visited in May. You two are about the same size. Now get moving."

Larry could feel the tenseness in his boss's words. Sam wasn't screwing around. This was going to be a day of epic proportions for NASA and the world if there were no glitches.

"Right." He got up and headed to the shower.

* * *

"So, what is your plan for us?" asked a nervous Muki.

"My plan? Isn't it obvious, my dear? You and your friends

are going to help me accomplish the mission this facility was built to achieve. We, excuse me, I, am going to correct the mistakes of the past and ensure a future for the world of law and order."

"And what of us?" asked Judith. She was restraining the anger welling up inside.

"That is entirely up to you kids. If you cooperate, we shall become excellent colleagues."

"And if we refuse?" inquired Abdul.

Skorzenzy patted the handle of his 9mm Luger.

"Let's hope it doesn't come to that, shall we? It would be such a waste of promising young minds."

They all understood his connotation.

If Judith learned anything from her harrowing experience, it was to hold her tongue in an attempt to gain the confidence of her interrogator.

"Professor, since it appears we're going to be your guests for a while, tell me one thing. Why did you try to dissuade Muki, me, and now Larry, not to travel back to those time periods?"

"An excellent question I will fully answer. Let's start with your voyage. The chance of meeting my father was slim at best, but I knew you'd meet him."

"How?"

Skorzenzy moved his right hand into his breast pocket and removed an old photo. He studied the picture then laid it on the table. It was a well-worn black-and-white photo of his father, Bormann and Judith at the restaurant.

"Where did you get this?" she asked as her fingers etched over the photo.

"Isn't it obvious? Bormann used a party photographer on most of his trips, except of course the one to Buchenwald. Any photos of the camp could have resulted in another power play with the Communists. This wouldn't do. But a photo of Bormann with an up-and-coming officer and a pretty girl? Good propaganda, my dear."

It took her a moment to decide a new line of questioning.

* * *

"Let's roll, Larry. We need to be at our stations in thirty minutes. Professor Skorzenzy wants to do a full dress rehearsal to ensure there are no bugs, and if I get a chance, I'll go over some of your suggestions about consolidating the back-up systems."

Larry grabbed a doughnut as they left Sam's house.

"That would be great, boss." Larry was pleased his new boss was impressed with his work, but he didn't know how he'd react around the professor.

* * *

The voice crackled over the headset communications system. "Start the landing. Roll camera."

Larry watched his monitor with great enthusiasm and concern. The real Apollo Eleven was circling the moon with booster problems, while back on Earth, everything seemed normal. He watched the lunar lander descend from the black sky; the booster rocket throwing up vast clouds of dust. One thing he noticed was the lack of flame. Of course, no one back home would notice this small detail as there are no cameras on the moon to record the actual landing. He deduced they were using high-powered fans to create the illusion. His headset crackled. "Camera five, on." Larry tapped the appropriate button.

The camera was inside the ship. He could see the surface of the moon rising fast in the viewfinder. It looked just like the original landing. The small window showed the barren landscape flickering in and out through the dust field.

Sam's voice reminded him where he was. "Larry, go to full audio feed." He acknowledged the command. The voice of the acting astronaut echoed through the room.

His head set crackled, "The Eagle has landed." The voice was greeted with a throng of cheers and clapping as they switched to camera six. It was a loop from Mission Control when the Saturn Five launched. Who would know the difference?

"Roger Eleven. Good job."

"Houston, I will be leaving the craft in ten minutes."

"Roger Eleven, good luck."

More applause and clapping resonated in the room.

"Let's look sharp people," came Sam's voice. "Are all systems go?"

He could hear each station checking in. All stations were, "go!"

"Control Center one to Firefox, we are a go."

The unmistakable voice replied. "Roger, we are a go. Repeat, we are a go for extraction."

The door to the craft cracked open allowing the artificial light to creep out of the small capsule.

"Video feed, switch to camera six." Larry acknowledged the command. He flipped the switch and could see the astronaut descending the ladder.

"Video feed, can you sharpen up the image?" Larry made a few adjustments with the filters. The picture was now crystal clear. The modifications he'd made were helping the feed immensely. It wasn't HD, but it was pretty good.

"Video feed. What the hell is that?" The voice wasn't pleased with his modifications. "They are 238,000 miles away. No one is going to believe we're on the moon with such clarity. Drop the filter, now!"

With no emotion, Larry followed the instruction. "Roger Control. Must be a glitch. I'll check it out immediately."

"You do that!" He turned off the filter bypass he'd modified and turned on the original ones. The picture went from crystal clear clarity to a fuzzy, grainy picture.

"Much better video feed."

"Roger. Appears to be a crossed circuit."

"Roger. Check it out when we're done."

"Roger Control."

The astronaut clumsily made his way down the ladder. The actor stopped on the bottom rung. The words he spoke were eerie. "One small step for man, one giant leap for mankind." He jumped off the ladder and the camera picture being transmitted resembled a plane in a tailspin, instead of an astronaut landing gently on the lunar landscape

"What the hell just happened, video feed?" Sam's voice was anxious and irritated.

"Nothing – all systems are working one-hundred percent."

The voice of an irate Skorzenzy pierced the calm. "Where's Wilson? I want him fired right now. The man is incompetent. He crossed the lowering wires when he attached them to the suit."

Larry turned on camera one. It was mounted with a wide lens recording the fiasco. The astronaut was spun several times and landed face-down on the fake landscape. He could see the small silver strands wrapped around the actor.

Skorzenzy removed the man's helmet. "Steve, are you okay?"

"Yeah, but that idiot needs to be fired. I could have broken my neck with the fall."

"Agreed. I just fired Wilson. Adams will take his place."

"Good." The man stood up and brushed the dust from his suit as best he could. The dust clung to him as if the suit were magnetized. Another man came to the rescue with a small hand-held vacuum cleaner, removing the particles that refused to fall.

"Okay, people," commanded Skorzenzy. "We'll resume in fifteen minutes." He noticed the red light blinking on camera one. "Why is camera one still recording, Control? Turn it off immediately."

Sam hadn't noticed the mishap. He, like the others, were focused on the failed moon walk. "Roger Firefox. Video Control, disengage now."

"Roger."

* * *

"Okay," replied Judith. "I understand the chance meeting in Berlin, but why so much concern for Muki?"

Muki substantiated Judith's question, "Yes, why the concern with Dallas?"

He mulled over the question for a few moments. Since these "graduates" would never see the light of day again and divulge the secret, he saw no harm in telling them the truth.

"It's simple. Since the end of WWII, my father and his organization have effectively infiltrated the US Government. It started with the hiring of Wernher von Braun. Without him, the

US space program would still be bumbling around with the gyroscope systems, and their rockets would still be nothing more than scrap metal on launch pads and carrier decks."

Abdul jumped in as he connected the dots. He remembered Jason talking about the V1's and V2's Germany designed as they were studying rocket launch systems.

"Von Braun. He developed the vengeance weapons launched against England?"

"Correct, Abdul. He was a brilliant man. His placement was the first of many patriots to join the US military and government posts. You see, despite America out-producing us during the war, their organizational abilities could not match our efficiency. If we'd possessed half the resources of the United States, we would easily have won the war. However, that is old history. We realized trying to build a Fourth Reich in the ruins of Germany would take decades, so instead of trying to start anew; we looked for a government that would accept our knowledge with open arms."

It made sense to Judith. She was seeing the big picture. "The U.S."

Muki knew the history well, and along with Judith, saw the logic. "Hitler was hoping the Allies would unite with them, combine forces, and keep the Russians from invading Germany."

"Correct, my dear."

"But did you really think they would join arms with a country that built an industry designed to destroy humans? Surely Hitler and the government knew this would never happen."

"An unfortunate miscalculation on our part. In time, we hoped history could overlook this slight misjudgment and recognize the real threat—Communism."

"Slight misunderstanding? Surely you jest, Professor," said Abdul.

"Seriously, they employed over five-hundred thousand men and women to run the extermination camps. What if those people had been used for the war effort and not the antithesis?" added Muki.

Leonoid was losing his patience. "I don't expect you children to understand the threats that surrounded Germany.

Enemies were everywhere, and we were dealing with them in the correct light. The organization was perfect. No other country could have dealt with such a threat as quickly and efficiently as us."

"That's for sure," said Abdul. "Nor would they have been as insane or as paranoid to implement such a ridiculous plan."

"Ridiculous? Ridiculous? We perfected the art, and if the Allies hadn't been blinded by the necessary rights of survival, they would have joined us and stopped the Russians at the Elbe; and perhaps within a year, pushed the mongrel hordes back to the original borders east of the Vistula where they belonged."

None of the kids were willing to push him any further. He was nervously gripping the butt of the pistol as his rage at the failures of the past poured forth.

"Okay," replied Judith. "Why Kennedy?"

* * *

"Adams, if you fail, you'll be joining Wilson. Understood?"

"Yes, Professor. It wasn't all Wilson's fault. The overhead rigging made it difficult to determine the correct setup of the wires. I've added a spreader bar to avoid a repeated performance."

"Excellent. Control, this is Firefox. We are ready to proceed in T-minus one minute and counting."

"Roger Firefox. T-minus one minute and counting."

"Camera six ready?"

"Ready."

"Are the correct filters activated?"

"Roger."

"Firefox, all systems are go."

"Roger. In three, two, one."

Camera one flicked on depicting the grainy black-and-white picture. Larry would have preferred a clearer picture, but Sam was right. Too much clarity for this time era could raise unwanted questions and investigations. The last thing the country needed was more controversy. The country needed good news since the reports coming out of Vietnam were anything but uplifting. The war was slowly pitting the old guard of WWII/Korean veterans against the young crowd who were starting to give outright support to Ho Chi Minh and the Communist Government of North Vietnam.

The astronaut made his way to the last rung and repeated the words. "One small step for man, one giant leap for mankind." He pushed off the rung and fell to the dusty landscape as if he were a feather. A small cloud of dust puffed up under his oversized boots.

"Good," came Skorzenzy's voice. "Proceed to placing the flag."

Camera one showed a technician running up and handing the prefabricated American flag to the actor. His helmet never turned to reveal from where the flag was obtained. The illusion was that he was reaching into his backpack for the item. The actor moved to a specific place twenty feet from the craft. He looked up, as though suggesting he was taking in the breathtaking astronomical sight over his head. He was actually looking for the pencil light directing him to the peg in the floor for the flag pole. He found the mark, and with a little more effort than desired, (but then he was in an almost zero gravity atmosphere), he placed the flag and moved back; illuminating the flag with the lander in the background.

Larry felt as if he was on the moon as the astronaut addressed the world. "I place this flag, not for the people of the United States, but for the people of the world. Let this flag be not a sign of achievement for the United States only, but for all peoples of planet Earth. It should stand as a testament of the human spirit, and the accomplishments a united world can achieve when politics are pushed aside. To the people of Earth, I salute you."

Cheers and applause erupted across the room. Cameras flicked across the world from the Vatican to D.C. To Moscow and Berlin. The images were creating an extraordinary depth of euphoria and joy across a united planet.

Larry knew they were only prerecordings to complete the spectacle.

"Control. Firefox. Good job."

"Roger Firefox."

"We will reset and prepare for the lift-off sequence in thirty minutes."

"Roger, out."

* * *

"Kennedy's policies were detrimental to the cause. His speech of "Ask not what your country can do for you, but ask what you can do for your country," was against everything we'd agreed to."

"What do you mean agreed to?" asked Muki.

"My child, what I know will never be in the history books. My father struck a deal with JFK's dad, Joe. It was us, not the mob, who took care of the voting scandal in Chicago."

"Why not support Nixon?"

"Because he was a loose cannon. He knew, to an extent, how many posts we held, and was planning on replacing the *chosen ones* and starting over. That was an unacceptable position. Joe agreed to go along with our plan. Everything was moving like clockwork until Joe suffered his stroke. Without him to keep the apparatus moving in the correct direction, John decided to revitalize America and institute free thinking without governmental interference. Obviously, this isn't the path we'd agreed to with his father. So, instead of trying unsuccessfully to convince John of the in-place agreement, there was only one option."

"Assassination," said Judith.

"Correct."

"And Bobby Kennedy?"

"Same reason. We had LBJ in our hip pocket. He was perfect. We feared the country would attempt to ease the pain of JFK's death by electing Bobby to office. We couldn't take the chance."

"You bastard," retorted Muki in a harsh tone. "You killed the Kennedys to further your own goals?"

"Quite to the contrary. To further a government of strength and power. There is a difference. Imagine a country of global influence. No country, including Russia, would dare stand up to its economic and military power. We would be the rulers of the world in a perfect society."

Abdul saw the logic in the plan, but then, so did the Romans. "So the U.S. would be the Rome of modern times?"

"Yes. Exactly."

Abdul couldn't help but laugh with the superior attitude Leonoid used to deliver his words. "Well, we know how that turned out. You'd have better luck doing an episode for Star Trek such as "Patterns of Force, Episode #50 from 1968."

Skorzenzy didn't take kindly to Abdul's jibe. He rose up and struck him hard across the face with the barrel of the pistol.

He stood above him, pointing the gun at his bruised face. "It is thinking like yours we shall eventually abolish."

The attack on Abdul stirred a level of anger Muki had never experienced, yet she restrained from lashing out, at least for the moment. She retrieved a paper towel from the counter and applied it to his face to stop the bleeding.

"Okay, let's say I agree with your thinking. How does Larry's trip equate in the grand plan?" asked Judith.

"Ah yes, Larry."

* * *

"Apollo Eleven, this is Mission Control."

"Go ahead Houston."

"Are the thrusters operating?"

"Roger Houston. We have cross-linked two circuits, bypassing the faulty bus. We are a go for lunar landing."

"Roger Eleven, good luck.

* * *

"To all controllers, stand down. The original mission is a go." Sam removed his headset, wiping the sweat from his brow. He knew the simulation was going to be a true test of his abilities and those of his co-workers, but nothing like what he'd just experienced. He now fully understood the consequences of failure. The entire country would never again trust NASA or the government for that matter. Funding would come to an abrupt stop and they would all be looking for jobs. After a few minutes, he regrouped and placed his headset back on.

"Hey rookie, let's get a cup of coffee and a doughnut. I also want to talk about your modifications." He set the headset down and proceeded to the cafeteria. His thoughts now centered on how the "rookie" modified the imaging feed.

"Roger boss. On my way."

Larry met Sam at the coffee bar in the cafeteria. They grabbed a pot of coffee that must have been at least five hours old.

"Doesn't anyone ever make a fresh pot around here?" asked Larry.

"Sure, when they're not working. The older, the stronger, the better, so we say." Each one laughed. Larry really wished he had some of Judith's beans. This stuff he was drinking was a close resemblance to caustic crude oil.

"Now tell me – how did you modify the optics and picture clarity? I've been on the cutting edge of video/camera development for the last five years and have never seen anything that clear."

Larry described how he sharpened the picture without going into minute detail. Sam was amazed, and decided that when this mission was completed, he would be calling Stanford for more information on Larry Kowalski and the courses he took. Larry's knowledge surpassed anything MIT had been working on, and for him, if MIT wasn't doing it, it wasn't important.

The break was interrupted by the overhead intercom box. "All technicians to their posts. Simulated lift-off in fifteen minutes. Repeat, simulated lift-off in fifteen minutes."

"Time to get back to work." Sam rose up and poured another cup of crude.

"Sam, are we really going to fake the landing and take-off?"

He looked at Larry and pushed his black horn-rimmed glasses up his nose. "I hope not Larry. I hope not."

T-minus fifteen minutes and counting.

* * *

"I recognized Larry when you four first entered the barracks. I knew his persona and how difficult he could prove to be with my plans. So far, he hasn't disappointed me."

"How so?" inquired Judith.

"Is it not obvious? He's fought me every step of the way. When has he shown any enthusiasm for the missions? Did he not vehemently attempt to dissuade each of you not to travel back? Did he not mention numerous times, we were tampering with history and should let it lie?" The three nodded in agreement.

"And now, he's going back to unravel one of the greatest hoaxes ever played on the American people."

"Are you saying we didn't land on the moon?"

* * *

"Houston, this is Eleven. We are in position and ready to begin the descent."

"Roger Eleven, all boards are green. You are good for landing."

"Roger."

The landing craft entered the grip of the moon's gravity. Both astronauts kept a close eye on the relay switches tied to the thrusters. They had a narrow window to abort the mission and hoped the relay held.

"Mission Control to Firefox, we are T-minus two minutes and counting. Engage the feed."

"Roger Mission Control, video feed engaging."

"Video Control, engage signal lapse."

"Roger Control, lapse engaged." Larry pushed the video lapse button. He knew what it was for. If anything went wrong, the live feed would be stored and examined before being released for public consumption. NASA was prepared in case the mission was compromised. They could relay to the press the cameras failed, and they were working on it. Who would be the wiser? No one.

"Houston, we are T-minus one minute to landing. Boards are

green."

"Roger Eleven, we see the same. Maintain course and speed."

"Thirty seconds to landing. Landing site in view."

Larry could see the flat barren area chosen. It was perfect, and the model in Arizona was its sister.

"Twenty seconds and—" Alarm buzzers rang through the headphones. Something was wrong.

"Thrusters are unresponsive," The voices of the astronauts were calm as they worked on the problem.

"Repeat, thrusters are unresponsive. Attempting to resolve."

"Roger Eleven, we are seeing the same. Keep advised. Mission Control to Firefox, prepare for execution on my order."

"Roger Control. Awaiting instructions."

* * *

"The question posed deserves an answer, Professor," continued Judith. "Did they land on the moon or completely abort the mission?"

"Yes, the crew did land, and they planted the flag, but all the pictures you see of them leaving the spacecraft were staged, and Larry is a witness to the scam."

"But if we landed, what's the harm in telling the public and letting the truth out?"

"I expected more from you, Judith. Imagine NASA admitting the landing was a hoax. That it was staged. Would the American people ever believe in the space program again? Would Congress continue to fund millions into a farce? I think not. It wasn't worth the scandal, and in the end, no one was hurt. The landing was flawless, and historians are satisfied it was a successful mission."

"Okay, but what harm could it pose today?"

"Judith, you don't get it, do you? The American people are the most fickle in the world. How many stories and movies are still being written and made calling the whole mission a scam? Every year or two, another individual looking for fame and a vast fortune releases newly uncovered evidence to discredit the program. No, my dear, some secrets are best kept a secret, don't you agree?"

* * *

Mission Control erupted in applause and congratulations with the successful staged landing. Everything went without a hitch.

"Good job everyone, good job," commented Skorzenzy as he congratulated all the technicians and actors. "Job well done, Sam"

"Yes, Doctor."

"Bring the rookie to the camera room, so I can meet him and thank him personally."

"Roger."

"Larry, come over to my station. The professor would like to be introduced to you."

"Roger that." He removed his headset and walked over to Sam's station. He was beaming with pride as he drank his cold dark mud. The relief on his face was very satisfying.

"Good job, rookie. Now look straight ahead into the camera and say cheese." Larry chuckled with the comment. He was sure the last words he wanted to say to Skorzenzy were "cheese."

"Mr. Kowalski, I want to thank you personally for a job well done." It was difficult at first to recognize him, but the eyes and the mouth were a dead giveaway. "Thank you Professor, it was my pleasure."

"When I return to Houston, I look forward to discussing your future with NASA. From what Sam has told me, you have some special skills we can use in the future."

"Thank you, Professor. I look forward to working with you and Sam in the near future on magnetic resonating fields."

Sam stared at Larry in confusion, as did the professor.

"Yes, yes. I too look forward to future endeavors. Sam, you can put the crew on stand-down. Mission Control says the problem is fixed, and the craft will land in ten minutes. Shut down your facility and send the people home. Make sure they have all signed the disclosure statements and understand the consequences if they speak of what happened today."

"Yes, sir. I'll see to it personally." The screen went blank.

"Magnetic resonating fields? Man, sounds like I need to go back to school, or I might be looking for a job."

* * *

Neither said much as Sam drove them back to his house. They were both exhausted from the day's events, and sleep was calling their name.

Larry checked his watch several times on the drive back. "What's up, rookie? Got a date or something?"

"Something would be the correct answer."

"Man, you guys from the coast sure talk cryptically. Maybe you spent too much time on the beach, and like your hair, your brain got bleached."

"Maybe. You should try it someday."

"I think I will when this gig is up. I love the work and the people around the program, but I can't sit still for more than three years or so. Hey, if you like it here, you could take me out west and show me the sights." He winked at him with the comment.

"Sam, I'm afraid those west coast girls are more than you could handle." Before Sam could answer, Larry added."I'm beat. Let's get back to the house. We'll talk about it more in the morning."

"Okay rookie."

Larry said goodnight to Sam, closed the bedroom door, and slipped into his suit with an hour to spare. He collapsed on the bed and fell into a deep, well deserved sleep.

CHAPTER 27

TRUTH

"Yes Professor, this is Sam Welsh from the Apollo program. I was calling about one of your students, a Larry Kowalski."

"Who?"

"Larry Kowalski."

"I'm sorry Mr. Welsh, we never registered a student with that name."

Sam dropped the phone and went to Larry's room. The door was locked. He pried it open, only to find an empty bed.

* * *

There was no place in the manual where it stated the subject needed to be standing when traveling through the confines of time. He would make a mental note of that minor detail. Standing up allowed the magnetic field to provide a vertical force that kept the subject in a state of animation. Going through time horizontally was identical to being on a ship in rough waters, or a plane encountering heavy turbulence. None were easy on the stomach, and he paid the price as he reappeared on the platform floor and promptly threw up.

"Welcome back, Larry. We've been waiting for you." The voice was Skorzenzy's.

"What, no brass band or paper banners to welcome me back? I'm disappointed."

"Maybe next time, Mr. Kowalski. Now, if you would be so kind as to join the rest of us. We are very anxious to hear of your travels."

"Thanks for asking if I'm all right." He noticed that none of the others were with the professor.

"Hey, where are the others? I was expecting a big celebration on my return."

Skorzenzy's tone was cold and monotone. "They have prepared a surprise in the cafeteria."

"Okay, can I at least clean up before they spring it on me?"

"I'm afraid that will have to wait. They are most anxious to see you."

"Okay, okay. I'm on my way up." He knew something was wrong; he just couldn't read the signs. Skorzenzy was much more aloof and distant than before. His tone was robotic and cold.

They made their way to the cafeteria, speaking not a word. The tension and the truth they uncomfortably shared was appalling. Larry was a bit surprised to find the doors to the cafeteria locked.

"Are we expecting burglars, Herr Doctor?"

"Something like that Mr. Kowalski, something like that."

He unlocked the door, replaced the keys in his right pocket, and removed the pistol from his left. "Welcome home, Mr. Kowalski" and shoved him into the room.

Larry was startled as he was pushed into the room, but the sensation lasted only a few seconds as he saw his friends, except Judith, held in restraints. He turned around defiantly and demanded an explanation.

"What the hell is going on and why are they tied up?" His anger hadn't allowed him to notice the Luger in the left hand.

"How shall I put this in terms you'll understand?" His thin lips pursed together as he forced his evil smile. "Ah yes. Tying up loose ends. Yes, I think that sums it up." He chuckled with his response, never letting his cold eyes waver from Larry's.

"What loose ends? What are you implying?"

"I believe it best if you took a seat while I explained." He motioned to Judith.

"Larry, a lot has happened since you left. Please, let the professor explain his actions, and maybe you'll see things in a different light."

"Different light my ass! I know all about the faked landing, and the ploy played on the American people."

"Yes Larry, I'm sure you have many things to tell us, but please, let the professor explain." Her eyes were pleading with him to take a seat and listen.

"Yes, Larry, why don't you be a good boy and sit down before I'm forced to assist you."

He was shocked at the brashness of the old man. How was he going to make him sit down? By force? That's when he noticed the pistol being raised a little higher, pointed straight at his chest.

"Larry, please come sit with me." Judith walked towards him, placed a hand on his right arm and guided him down to the table. Again, he noticed the strange look in her eyes. "What's going on?" he whispered.

"Patience, Larry, patience. Please hear him out." He unwillingly sat down.

"Okay Professor, I'll be a good boy; now tell me what the fuck is going on?"

"I could ask you to address me with a little more respect, but then again, what does it matter? As I was explaining to your compatriots, none of you will ever leave the complex to tell your tales of time travel. Wait, let me rephrase—you won't leave here alive." He let the words sink in to ensure Larry understood the seriousness of the situation.

"You see, you foolish children decided, against my better wishes, to choose a different period in time. Sadly, none of you were smart enough to take a hint. Because of your undying curiosity, you forced my hand to take extreme measures. Maybe if you had gone back to the Lincoln assassination, none of this would be necessary. Instead, you decided on the last piece of my family's heritage, and with a little effort, you would connect the dots and place the organization I work for in jeopardy. That, I can't allow."

Larry turned to her for guidance. "Judith, what's he talking about?"

Instead of being understanding, she stood up and lashed at him. "Larry, pull the fucking cotton out of your ears and put it in your mouth. A two-year-old would understand what he's saying." She walked away and stood side by side with Skorzenzy.

"He and his organization are building a new order. One that will bring law and order to the entire planet. I wasn't able to see it when I met my great-grandfather, but since I've returned and the professor explained the master plan, I now see the wisdom and logic in one central country ruling the world."

He was stunned at the words she spoke. He looked at Abdul and Muki for a sign in their eyes that this was all a sick stunt. The returned looks assured him it wasn't a joke.

"Judith, surely you jest after what happened to you in Germany. Seriously, you were tortured and raped by that scumbag captain. You can't really—"

"Shut the fuck up Larry! Shut the fuck up!" The rage he'd seen one too many times was sincere and being directed at him. He now knew how it felt to be a caged animal.

"If I hadn't been so pigheaded and hell-bent for revenge, I would have seen the beauty of the Third Reich and its ultimate goals. My great-grandfather should be hailed as a hero, and not some loathsome toad that silently went along with Hitler. They were laying the foundation for all of mankind."

"Judith, you're not serious. What about Buchenwald, Dachau, Treblinka, Belsen-Bergen and Auschwitz?"

"What about them? They were the necessary instruments to deal with criminal elements infecting Europe. It's a shame the United States doesn't adopt such a plan. Imagine how many millions of dollars would be saved in the courts if we implemented the same system."

"Judith, what the hell are you talking about? What you're saying is utter hypocrisy and insanity. Surely, you don't believe any of this shit?"

She grabbed the gun from the professor's hand, and moved towards Larry, pointing it at his head. "Hypocrisy? Insanity? "Her voice was louder and more violent than ever. "Do I look as if I believe this shit, Larry? Well, do I?" Beads of sweat flowed down her cheeks.

"Okay, okay. I believe you." She returned his answer with a wink. *What the fuck?*

Skorzenzy approached Judith and calmly removed the pistol from her hand. "Well done, my dear, well done. Even I couldn't have convinced him so eloquently. I believe you have gained his attention and confidence. I guarantee a prime position for you in our organization. A woman of your talents is a rare find indeed."

She turned and placed a kiss on his wrinkled face. "Thank you. I look forward to serving the greater good."

"What is the next step?" she asked.

"I must make a trip of my own, and I will need you to travel back to ensure its success. There are a few people I need to visit and convince that removing the funding will have dire consequences for them and their families."

"And if they can't be persuaded?"

"Simple—they'll die."

CHAPTER 28

FINAL MISSION

Larry was not the least bit convinced of this final mission – sending the professor back to convince the general and senator that funding the work he was performing was vital, not just for the interests of the United States, but also of the world. But he was left with little choice. If he didn't help run the console controls, Skorzenzy made it clear that one of the "graduates" would take a bullet to the head for his insolence. He relinquished and agreed.

It had been many years since Skorzenzy had donned one of the suits. Judith eagerly helped him into the suit and checked to make sure it was working properly. "Okay Professor, let's go back and kick some democratic ass."

"With you on my side, child, I don't see how they'll be able to resist us." Each one let out a small sinister laugh. Larry still couldn't believe how accommodating Judith was with this madman's plan. Yet, he knew not to challenge her. His words could have dire repercussions for his friends.

"Shall we?" He motioned towards the ladder. She took the lead and flashed a smile at Larry as she started climbing down. *What the fuck is she doing?*

"Larry, I trust you've entered the correct coordinates and won't have me landing in the middle of the CIA or FBI buildings?"

"The correct coordinates have been entered. You'll appear in General McCulloch's office. I'm sure he'll be pleased to see you."

"Yes, I'm sure he will." He descended the stairs and took his place by Judith.

"Well, my dear, are you ready to go back and make an impact this time?"

"Yes, Professor. I'm ready to erase the mistakes of the past."

"Don't you mean *we* my dear?"

"Of course, I'm just excited about the mission is all."

"Good. When this is over, you will have the satisfaction of knowing you helped set a new course for the United States and the planet." She nodded in agreement.

"Larry," shouted the professor, "we are ready. Initiate the sequencer."

Larry acknowledged the order. He motioned at Abdul and started the operation.

The low hum from the generators filled the room with its soothing sound. Larry and Abdul watched the sequential timers and flawlessly executed the correct commands.

While they were running the console, Muki watched the monitor to ensure everything was working properly. She couldn't help but notice the smile on Judith's face. *What is she up to?*

"We are at fifty percent, Captain. Keep a close eye on the power surge read-out. It jumped on your last mission."

"Roger, Mr. Scott."

"Power is sixty percent. All systems go," called Abdul.

"Something's not right, guys. Look at the monitor." Muki detected that Skorzenzy's facial skin was distorting, almost as if it were being reshaped.

"We can't. We're busy. What's the problem?" asked Larry.

"It's the professor. His skin looks as if it's turning into rubber."

"What's going on?" yelled Skorzenzy over the humming sound. "Is there something wrong? Is the machine malfunctioning?"

"Negative," called out Abdul. "All systems read nominal. We are a go for launch. Approaching seventy-five percent power."

"Guys, he's looking really weird right now. I think you should shut it down. His suit is compressing against his skin."

"Something's wrong," yelled Skorzenzy. His words were warped. He couldn't get his vocal cords and mouth to respond to his commands. He was also feeling the suit press against his skin as if the fiber optics weren't working.

Judith looked at the professor and held her hand out. There

was no distortion with her suit. It was working perfectly. "Did you really think I would join forces with an asshole like you? If you did, then you are the dumbest motherfucker I've ever met. Your father..."

"Eighty-five percent."

"...and his henchmen all deserve to die. When this is over, we're going to tell the truth about everything, and your organization's plan of infiltrating the United States government."

He couldn't get the words out of his mouth. The suit was wrapping around him like a cocoon. He tried to pull the pistol from his pocket, but his arms were glued to his body as the magnetic field increased. *What have you done*, his eyes pleaded with her.

She opened her hand and let the fiber optic battery fall to the ground. The magnetic field picked it up and smashed it into the wall. Fear gripped his eyes. His mind shouted for the system to power down. His heart rate and respiration were climbing to dangerous levels.

"Ninety percent."

She could read in his eyes the hatred and loathing he felt for her, but was helpless to fight back.

"Goodbye motherfucker." His body could no longer take the massive pressure. In a split second, his body imploded on itself and was slammed into a wall, or at least, what was left.

"One hundred percent!" called out Abdul, and Judith was gone.

* * *

"Hilda, has Senator Hodges called yet?"

"No, General. His assistant said he wouldn't be available until later this afternoon. He's in a meeting with the Appropriations Committee."

"Very good, I'll try back later." He clicked off the interoffice microphone.

As he lifted his finger, he noticed a field of static electricity dancing on the walls as a white glow filled the office.

He reached for his phone as the body of a female appeared

before him. *Is she wearing one of the suits?*

The body's eyes noticed the look of fear and dread in his as he appeared to be summoning help. "Don't do it, General, I'm a friend. I bring a warning."

He was having a difficult time being convinced to listen to her, in that he noticed what appeared to be body fragments clinging to the "Top Secret" suit. He placed the receiver back in its cradle and did his best to retain his composure.

"Who are you?"

"My name is Judith Anderson. I was transported here from the complex in Pioche. As soon as my friends realize what I've accomplished, they will start the process to take me back. General, are you listening to me?" His eyes were still gazing at the bloodstained suit. She took a moment to follow his eyes. She saw what had the general's full attention—fragments of bone, tissue and blood. Without missing a beat, she continued with the warning.

"Those are the remains of Professor Leonoid Skorzenzy. He was to accompany me on this trip to convince you and the senator that defunding the complex would result in extreme measures."

McCulloch was regaining his lost confidence. "And what would those measures be, if I may ask?" His finger was twitching on the interoffice button.

"General, as I said, I don't have a lot of time and don't wish to enter a useless debate. My actions have saved your life. The machine that you funded works. I'm proof of that. In two weeks, you and the senator are going to pull the plug and shut down the complex. Why? Because it works. Skorzenzy will be furious and will attempt to come back and change your mind."

"And if he doesn't?"

"Then he'll kill you." The words shocked the general.

"But more importantly, it's the overall plan he represents and supports." She removed a small piece of paper and tossed it on his desk. She could feel a field of static electricity building around her.

"On that paper is a list of names. Those men are earnestly trying to rebuild a Fourth Reich in the United States government. I trust you'll take the correct measures and stop them?"

"How do I know what you're saying is true?" Her image started to shimmer.

"General, you can sit on the list or take action. The choice is yours."

He studied the list in awe – Secretary of State, Secretary of the Navy, Federal Reserve Chairman..."

* * *

"Scotty, let's bring her back."

"Aye, Captain. Warp thrusters on full."

* * *

"Goodbye General."

He sat in stunned silence as she disappeared.

"Hilda."

"Yes, General."

"Get me the Directors of the CIA and FBI—we have a problem."

"Yes, sir."

CHAPTER 29

ANALYSIS

Muki was correct; Judith did have a plan. She couldn't hear what was being said as the machine was reaching critical mass, but she could tell the professor was in dire straits. It was when she saw the battery fly out of Judith's hand, she knew what the result was going to be—he would be crushed by the magnetic g-forces.

"Larry, she's killing him!" she screamed.

He glanced at the monitor for a second. A smile crossed his face as he went back to manning the console. "Couldn't have happened to a better asshole," he muttered.

"You have to stop the process now!"

"We can't. We passed eighty percent and must complete the transfer, or we may jeopardize her life as well. We'll let the transfer complete, set the timer to two minutes, and bring her back."

"Okay."

"But what of the professor?"

It was Abdul's turn, "He will meet his Maker. That's a meeting I'd love to see as he's banished to the Halls of Hell. Good riddance!"

She knew the boys were right; she just didn't know how to deal with being an accessory to murder.

* * *

The kids went to the rim of the platform and examined the remains of the *good professor*. "Okay," said Larry, "who's on janitorial detail?"

"Sorry Captain, it's not in my pay grade."

"Muki?"

"Nope. Maybe when we bring her back, the machine he

created will finish the job." All three enjoyed a good relaxed laugh.

"Let's get back to the console. She should be returning shortly."

* * *

She appeared with a look of defiance and confidence.

"Good to have you home, madame." She couldn't quite make out the voice, but she knew it was one of the boys.

"The next one of you morons to refer to me as a madame, is going to get their ass kicked." Her answer filled the room with uproarious laughter. "Assholes."

As she made her way to the ladder, she noticed something missing. "So, where's our protégé?"

"Dust to dust, ashes to ashes, and molecules to oblivion!" answered Abdul. "Fifty percent of his body was crushed to the size of a basketball when you took the first trip. What was left disintegrated in the magnetic field upon your arrival. Proof we need to work the bugs out of the transporter mechanism. Such a shame."

She started climbing up the ladder. "Couldn't have happened to a better fucker. I still can't believe he thought I was going to assist in his plan. Foolish old man."

She reached the top of the ladder and found her friends beaming with pride. Muki was the first to rush over and give her a hug. "It's good to have you back."

Judith didn't know how to handle the display of emotion. Her hard interior melted with the embrace. She earnestly returned the hug. "So am I Muki, but don't think I'm letting you drink my coffee."

She gave the only reply she could, "Judith, you're such a bitch, but a good bitch," and hugged her again. Larry and Abdul were next.

"Good to have you back, Ensign. I'll make sure I file a proper report to Star Fleet on your mission. The only critique I have will be your handling of—"

"Shut the fuck up, Abdul."

He started laughing, "I'll also make note of your disrespect for a superior officer."

Larry was next. He wasn't sure how to approach her. He was still smarting from when she struck his face. Judith walked up to him and could detect the hurt in his eyes. "Larry, I'm sorry for hitting you. I had to make it believable, and as we've seen, it worked."

"Yeah I know, but damn, it sure hurt, and I'm still not sure…"

She looked deep into his eyes. "Hey you dumb shit, quit feeling sorry for yourself and kiss me." Her friends were stunned with the request. Instead of waiting for him to make the first move, she stood on her tiptoes, threw her arms around his neck, pulled his face forward and planted a passionate kiss on him.

"Okay, now that's out of the way, I need a shower and something to eat. Who's with me?" She headed to the changing room before anyone could answer.

"Way to go, stud, how's it feel to join the crowd?" asked Abdul.

"Huh, what do you mean?" Abdul took Muki in his arms, and they kissed long and hard. "It's a great club to be in, Captain." He took Muki's hand and headed to the cafeteria.

* * *

"Now what?" asked Larry. "How are we going to explain where we've been for the last week? It's been a week, hasn't it?" They backtracked to determine how long they'd been in the complex.

"Let's see, Captain. We arrived on Friday. Muki went to Dallas for one day; I spent two days in the Middle East; Judith was in Germany for five long, harrowing days, and you spent two days in Houston. That would be…where's an HP when you need it? That would be thirteen days."

"Thirteen?" quipped Judith. "How did you ever graduate, you idiot? It's only been ten days by my count."

"Au contraire, Miss, you forgot to add the first night we spent dodging the devils of Vegas, and the two days we spent planning our trip. I stand behind my algorithm. Thirteen is the correct number."

"Are you sure, Scotty? I thought the correct number was three, no more, no less. The correct count is three."

"And then we throw the Holy Hand Grenade?"

"Exactly Judith, we throw the Holy Hand Grenade and blast that damned rabbit into eternity." They all laughed over the Monty Python reference.

"Seriously, what and where do we go from here?"

"Good question," said Judith.

"We could always go get the films in the theater and use them," added Muki.

"No fucking way. I'm not going back in that room after the events we encountered with Abdul's recording. I'm willing to let a sleeping dog lie. That was one experience I don't want to repeat again—ever." They all agreed. Best to let whatever Abdul brought back remain in the room.

Larry continued, "Okay. We can't bring back any live footage. Is there anything we can at least take as a souvenir?"

"We could take one of the suits?"

"And do what with it?"

No one had an answer.

"While you're thinking about our scavenger hunt, Judith, why did you kill him? What happened while I was in Houston?" *Yes, why did she kill him*? The other two wanted to address the question, but didn't know how.

She took a long drink of her oversized margarita, licked her lips and explained.

"Skorzenzy was the tip of an organization designed to take over the United States government and build a Fourth Reich from within. Unknown to General McCulloch and Senator Hodges, this machine was designed to achieve that very purpose."

Larry was taking in what she was saying, but there was an apparent gap. "But what about his diary we found, and everything he wrote about correcting the mistakes of the past?"

"Subterfuge. It was merely, for the most part, a mask covering the main goals."

"And what were the main goals?" asked Muki.

Judith took a long sip of her drink and continued "At first, I didn't understand how our trips were connected, except Abdul's, and why he was trying to persuade us to pick different time periods we visited. My trip to Germany proved his lineage. His father was one of the top men in Germany when the war ended. He was picked up by the Allies, and enlisted by Donovan and the OSS to provide any and all information on the inner workings of the German military and the capabilities of Russia. Larry's trip exposed the farce that was fed to the American people concerning the first moon landing, in which our deceased friend played an integral part; and Muki's knowledge of who killed Kennedy was icing on the cake per se."

Muki was still not convinced. "Judith, it still doesn't make sense."

"It does when you look at the political platform of the Third Reich. Of all people, Muki, it should be crystal clear. Here's a hint—Kennedy wanted Americans to think for themselves."

Muki disseminated the comment, and like a light bulb turning on, her eyes lit up.

"Of course, with Kennedy as the president, people would stand as individuals and think for themselves."

"Exactly."

"The space landing proved the American people would believe anything the government proposed. With Kennedy out of the way, Skorzenzy's team was in place to propose the "Great Society Package" to Congress, and convince Americans they were eradicating the poor; which, in essence, they were only attempting to build a solid political base like Russia did with their five-year plans. Give the people government housing and a small stipend and they'll be happy."

"Larry, give her a cookie. Correct, Muki. The only problem they couldn't see was the escalation of the war in Vietnam and the explosion of drug use. Those two events turned the country away from politics for both rich and poor. Everyone wanted to go to work and support their families. Political manifestations were no longer a major topic, thus upsetting the timetable Skorzenzy and his group envisioned."

"Now it makes sense, Ensign," added Abdul. "With the

machine, they could go back and correct the mistakes that had cost them taking over our government."

"You would be correct, Mr. Scott. And we were pegged to help. Larry, I apologize for my actions and ill-treatment towards you. You knew something was wrong with the entire scenario, but I was too focused on making amends for my ancestor's mistakes. Can you forgive me?"

He thought about her apology for a minute, leaned over and kissed her. "This time I will, you crazy bitch, but only this time." She threw her arms around him and shed a few tears of joy.

Larry stood up from the table after wiping some of her tears away. "Boys and girls, there are two items on our agenda. One, it's time to resume our vacation; and two, I propose we destroy this complex so those in power or wish to have power, do not possess the ability to travel back and correct the mistakes as they see them."

The other three stood up and wholeheartedly agreed.

"Captain, it's time to blow this joint sky-high!"

CHAPTER 30

VACATION

Larry looked in the rearview mirror as the four sped away from the complex. He watched as the complex imploded upon itself. He remembered reading that the magnetic power of the machine when unchecked, would feed upon itself after fifteen minutes. It was a built-in safety feature for destruction if something happened to go wrong. Skorzenzy calculated that all critical personnel could be safely evacuated in fifteen minutes. Appears he was right as the small outbuilding slowly caved in. What Larry found interesting, was that there was no smoke or flame to alert a passing plane or motorist from the highway of an emergency. No one would ever know the complex existed.

He looked over at Judith and passed a smile as he punched in one of her favorite songs by AC/DC. "Highway to Hell."

He pulled up to the crossroads and asked, "Which way shall we go?"

"Muki lifted herself from Abdul's shoulder," North, Larry. Let's go north."

"Aye, Captain, based on the state of the engines, and after consulting with Mr. Chekov, lay in a course for Wendover. I think we all need a bit of R&R before trekking into the unknown."

Instead of chastising him for his usual comments, the other three chimed in as Larry pulled onto US 93, "and boldly go where..." The words were drowned out as AC/DC took over.

* * *

None of the kids took notice of the late model Cadillac as it passed by heading to Vegas.

"Boss, isn't that the Camaro we were chasing a week or so

ago?"

Nathan smiled, revealing his golden teeth as he removed the cigar from his mouth.

"Yes."

I hope you enjoyed the story. If so, please do not hesitate to post a review on Amazon, Goodreads are any other site of preference.

Other works include:
Destination D.C. Book two of the Gateway series
Occupation
Terror at the Sterling
Love's True Second Chance
Why Did Everything Happen?
The Baseball Coaching Manual: Little League to High School. Volumes I & II
Final Delivery
Goober and Bill

You can follow me on twitter: @Jeff Dawson59
Facebook: www.facebook.com/pages/Occupation/231877123504847
Website: http://jeff-dawson.blogspot.com/
Email: LDDJEnterprises@gmail.com or
        Jdawson41@netzero.net

Upcoming releases

Target Berlin: Third book in Gateway series May/June
Sabotage: 2nd book in Occupation series May/June release
Redemption: 3rd book in Occupation series November
Irving Titans: May release

Ghost Writing
Cracking Up by, J.J. Reinhard March/April release